SPIRITCHILD

DANIELLE LAUREN

OACHOA PUBLISHING

SPIRITCHILD

DANIELLE LAUREN

OACHOA

First published in Great Britain in 2022 by Oachoa Publishing

Copyright © Danielle Lauren, 2022

Danielle Lauren asserts the moral right to be identified as the author of this work in accordance with the Copyright, Designs and Patents Act 1988.

This is entirely a work of fiction. The names, characters, places, and events portrayed in this novel are either products of the author's imagination or are used fictitiously. Any resemblance to actual persons, living or dead, events, or localities is purely coincidental.

A CIP catalogue record for this book is available from the British Library.

Jacket, map, and internal illustrations by Lena Yang.

Hardback ISBN: 978-1-7397410-0-6

eBook ISBN: 978-1-7397410-1-3

Printed and bound in Great Britain by Clays Ltd, Elcograf S.p.A.

For anyone who ever doubted themselves.
The power is in you.
It was there all along.

PREFACE

A WORD ABOUT CONTENT

While this is entirely a work of fiction, there are some scenes that some readers might find upsetting, including violence, references to sexual assault, and child death. If you find this kind of content to be triggering, please proceed with caution.

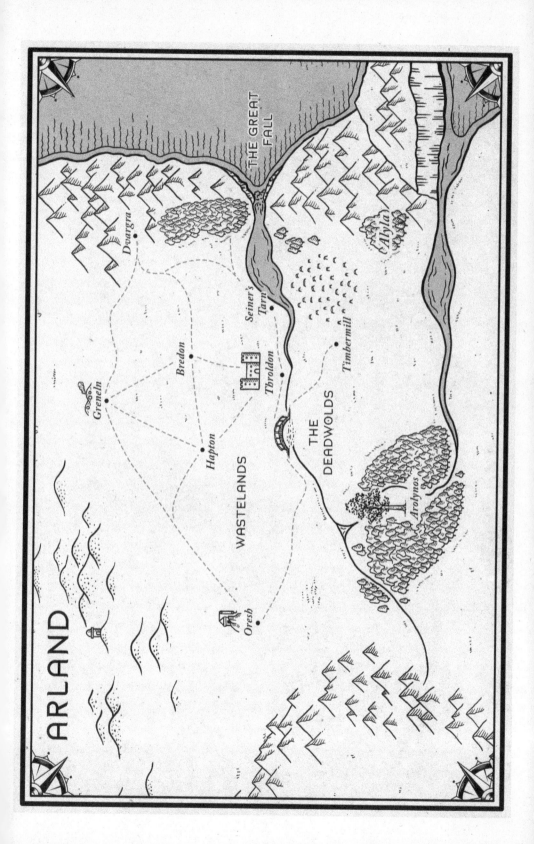

ONCE UPON A TIME, A FAMILY
LIVED IN HIDING...

The wild peal of the gathering bell dragged Andrew from the depths of sleep.

He jerked awake in the pitch dark, limbs tangled in the covers, and dropped over the edge of the bed with a loud *thud*. Lissa rolled over, her eyes still cloudy with sleep.

'What's wrong?" she mumbled blearily.

"I don't know," Andrew said, finding his boots and shoving his feet into them. "I'll go and see." Gathering the covers to her, Lissa sat up to watch as he threw a coat on over his long-johns, and opened the door to look outside.

The orange, flickering glow that lit the air could only mean one thing.

"Fire!" he yelled, dashing from the house. In a village built of wood and straw, a single errant spark could be devastating. He ran straight to the well in the village centre, where all the yelling seemed to be coming from.

When he reached the square, he halted his headlong flight so abruptly he all but fell over his feet. It took a minute for him to register what he was seeing.

Fire was *everywhere*, and spreading fast. There was no way they'd be able to put it out before it consumed the village. Villagers ran screaming across the scene, eyes wide, hair wild and dusted with ash. Soot smeared more than a few faces. Blood on others. And walking calmly through the fray, unfamiliar figures stalked after them.

A man ran towards him, but Andrew didn't recognise him. He wore a cruel smile, and carried a fencing mallet wrapped in barbed wire.

Andrew frowned. How had he gotten wire caught around his mallet? Then he saw the way the man held the mallet aloft. How he gripped it, ready to swing.

Andrew threw himself to the side just as the mallet smashed into the corner of the Millers' house beside him. He tumbled into the wall, just missing the rain of broken plasterwork and timbers beneath. Clouds of dust and debris blew over him, and he threw an arm up over his face to shield his eyes.

The cause of the fire was clear now — the Unity raiders had found them.

Suddenly, everything hit Andrew in an assault on his senses: the heat from the fire, the screams of friends and neighbours running for their lives, the choking smell of smoke and burning.

Stumbling back, he edged along the wall, away from the advancing raider. The man swung his mallet again in a great, overhead arc that smashed through the timbers supporting the low eaves of the house. Andrew avoided the blow, but wood and roof-shingles rained down on him from above. As he lurched backwards, his fingers curled around a fallen rafter, broken off halfway along — not a mallet, but good enough. The raider hauled uselessly against his weapon, now tangled in the splintered wreckage of the roof. Andrew lifted his meagre length of timber and swung it with enough force that when it hit his opponent's head, the wood cracked into two.

The raider staggered to the side, releasing his grip on the mallet. Andrew dropped the now-useless rafter, scrambled to his feet, and ran back towards the home he'd built with his own hands.

He burst through the door and ran straight for his axe, tucked away out of everyday reach.

"Lissa! It's the Unity!" he yelled. She appeared at the door to their daughter's bedroom, boots already on her feet. In her arms, the tiny shape of his little girl clung to her mother, bundled in blankets.

"Papa?" her voice quavered as she peered at him from behind her mother's hair with wide, green eyes.

"It's going to be alright, Sweet Pea." He tried to inject some calm into his voice, forced a smile onto his face. He turned to Lissa. "Go to the cabin." The small hut, over the river and outside the village limits, was where he stored his forestry equipment — the tools that were too sharp or heavy to have lying around with a little one running amok. It was also on the route to the lumberyards of Timbermill; they could seek aid from there if the worst should happen. "I'll meet you there," he said, lifting the axe over his shoulder. The village was still full of others who might need his help this night.

Lissa's face crumpled as her eyes took in the axe and the determinedness in his gaze, but she just lifted a hand to his cheek. The maple-wood wedding band he'd carved for her himself gleamed dully in the glow of the nearby fires.

"Be careful," she begged, tears shining in his eyes.

"Always," he promised, planting a kiss into her palm. "Now go. They haven't started working through the village yet, but they will." Lissa nodded. The Unity raiders always made sure to hit every household wherever they attacked. No one missed out on their cruelty.

"Papa?" Their daughter's cries cut him to the core.

He planted a quick kiss on her head. "Go with Mama now," he said. "I'll meet you later." He exchanged a look with his wife. She nodded, and her eyes, hardened by years of running, of hiding, still teared with emotion. He leaned forward to snatch another kiss from her, lingering a second longer this time, then dashed back out into the chaos.

He heard the raiders working through the houses now, getting closer with every second. The flames jumped higher and hotter, the heat telling Andrew how near they were to his family. He glanced back to see Lissa duck behind the house, away from the raiders. Clutching their daughter close, one hand pressing her little face into her shoulder so she wouldn't see, Lissa cast one last look at him. *Go,* he urged her silently, with a nod that he hoped was reassuring.

Lissa's jaw clenched, but she nodded in return. Her lips formed three words. Three words that had completed his life. He smiled.

I love you too, he mouthed back. A ghost of a smile flickered across her face, and then she turned and ran, carrying his whole world within the circle of her arms.

A knot inside him loosened. They would be safe. Now he could turn his mind to the rest.

We need to get everybody out, was his first thought. And then a spark jumped to the house beside his, the thatch catching the blaze in an instant.

Without hesitating, Andrew broke down the door and barrelled into the kitchen.

"Xander!" he yelled. "Lilly!" They'd been neighbours since he'd built his house next to theirs; their children played together in the meadows in summer.

Smoke began to pour down the chimney like black water, before rising again to cling to the ceiling.

"Xander! Lilly!" Andrew pulled his coat collar over his nose to hold back the worst of the smoke, and headed to the stairs. He heard a shout, and the family of four appeared at the top, stumbling down from the upper floor, the babe in Lilly's arms, while Xander hurried Harry stumblingly along in front of him. Andrew lifted little Harry into his arms, and together they rushed from the house into the hellscape of the night.

He put Harry down and turned to Xander. "Run," he urged. "Get out of the village. Head towards Timbermill. Keep your family safe." Behind his neighbours, he spotted the shapes of raiders calmly picking through the wreckage of the still-burning village, as if they had all the time in the world. "Go!" he said, pushing the family on towards the outskirts of the village.

They ducked between two wood-stores, and Andrew skirted back around the edge of their house, keeping to the shadows. He listened out for the sounds of the raiders, the screams of villagers punctuated by their cold laughter. As he rounded a corner, he found a gang of four of them, tormenting the baker's daughter, Mary, and holding her son Charlie hostage as they beat on her.

Without even a moment's pause, Andrew raised his axe up over his head and charged, bellowing his rage as he went.

The group looked up as he ran at them, and the one holding Charlie tossed him aside to face the new threat.

Andrew aimed his axe at the man who'd been beating Mary, and was rewarded with a howl of pain as the blade bit flesh. Yanking the axe free made a horrible wet sound, and he swallowed his revulsion at how it felt to cut bodies instead of wood. He spun to take on whichever of the remaining three wished to try him next. This was his home, these were his people, and he was damned if he was going to give them the satisfaction of seeing him run scared.

The next raider he faced had a long metal bar of some sort with a reach surpassing that of Andrew's axe. Then there was one behind him as well. And the third.

The man whose arm he'd cut spat curses and profanities, egging his men on as they closed in around Andrew.

The one with the bar struck first, and Andrew lifted his axe to block the blow. While he was occupied with that, the other two struck hard at his exposed side. Andrew kicked back to give himself more space, but there were too many of them. And he was a woodsman, not a fighter.

Mary screamed at them to stop, for someone to help.

"Run away Mary!" he yelled at her. "Take Charlie and run!" And then he was too busy holding off attacks from all sides to make sure that she did.

Andrew swung his axe at the first one to come at him — the man was in his forties, and had a thin, greying beard — just a normal man, but turned to violence and greed and hate.

The man dodged Andrew's swing. As the axe followed through, throwing his balance left, a starburst of pain exploded up Andrew's right side. Turning, he saw the third man — young, less than twenty-five — dancing away, his fist still raised as if he meant to strike him again. And then the world tipped, and the ground came crashing up to meet him.

The pain followed after, but it was so overwhelming that Andrew could do nothing but lie on the cold ground and endure it. His limbs were made of lead, his axe lying useless under lax fingers, while his head rang deafeningly with the impact of a metal bar struck unseen from behind.

The pain, when it came, was blinding and white-hot. Andrew squeezed his eyes shut against it, gritted his teeth, and endured.

Through the ringing that filled his ears, he heard a boot crunch against the dirt by his head. He cracked one eye open, and despite the stars that danced across his vision, saw the leering face that bent over his.

"Every man for himself," the man said.

And then the beating began.

A boot connected with Andrew's side. Another forced the wind out of him with the strength of a bull, leaving him gasping. The bar cracked again across his back, and pain radiated outwards, paralysing him with agony. And he knew he wasn't walking away from this.

Through the pain, the only thought Andrew could muster was his desperate wish that Lissa would get out, and that his daughter would get to live in a better world than this.

Then something hard struck him across the face.

And he was slammed into cold oblivion.

Cowering in the shadow of the Thatchers' home, Lissa stood frozen with fear as her husband launched himself at those monsters.

They'd blocked the bridge, likely to stop villagers doing exactly what she'd been planning to do. And so she'd had to retrace her steps, to think of another route out of this fresh hell.

And now she was paralysed, helpless to do anything but watch as Andrew hit the ground like a stone. She watched as he struggled to regain his feet. Bit her lip until she tasted blood when that metal bar fell on him again. Felt hot tears cut runnels through the soot already caking her face when he stopped moving altogether.

The only thing that stopped Lissa from leaping at those raiders like a wildcat was the tiny figure still clutched in her arms.

"Mama?" her daughter's voice pierced the veil of white noise that filled Lissa's ears. She held her head close so that her sweet girl couldn't look around. Couldn't see. "Mama!"

The change in tone got through to Lissa — because her daughter wasn't looking at her father as Unity raiders made a punching bag of his body. She was looking at the house behind her.

Lissa heard the groan of timbers shearing as she turned to look, just in time for the whole building to collapse in on itself.

She launched herself away with a cry, but she'd been standing in the shadows of the eaves, and couldn't twist away fast enough to avoid the roof battens as they hurtled to the ground under the weight of the thatch. Something hard collided with her head, and in a heartbeat, she was buried under a mountain of straw.

Spitting and coughing, she clawed her way out of the wreckage, hauling her daughter with her.

"Are you alright, Sweet Pea?" she asked, brushing straw and dust from her. And then she saw the lump under her baby girl's soot-covered hair. The trickle of blood from her ear.

"No," Lissa murmured. "No no no, please, no." She thrust her ear to her daughter's chest, and nearly sobbed with relief at the steady beating inside. Gently brushing the hair away from her little face, Lissa lifted her daughter and staggered from the pile of debris that used to be someone's home. The world tipped on its axis, and it took all of her focus not to drop her precious cargo, or collapse to the ground.

As the village swam before her, her vision doubling over itself, the one thing that remained in sharp relief was the sight of Andrew, still lying broken in the street.

She wanted to go to him. But she needed to get her sweet girl to safety. Quickly.

The two opposing needs tore her heart into two.

A ragged sob escaped her, and it shocked her, how inhuman it sounded. Like a dying animal, the cries tore out of her with claws and teeth. Her grief-wracked screams went unnoticed in the general horror of the night, just one more victim at the Unity's cruel hands.

She didn't know when she sank to her knees, or how she managed to crawl into the small shelter of a burnt-out husk nearby, but it was there that the tears finally ran dry. She was empty. Hollow.

Lissa looked down at her daughter, and felt the tears well again.

She *had* to survive.

She'd never prayed before in her life. Not properly.

Andrew had once told her about the spirits of the world. The ones the elves believed in — part of a bigger story about one of his marvellous travelling adventures, from long before he'd met her.

And for some reason, some... *instinct* buried inside her, she prayed to them.

Not the gods she'd been taught as a child, but the spirits of a race she'd never met.

Desperate words spilled from her without thought.

But when they were done, a glow surrounded her.

The light outshone the flames.

And she smiled as it engulfed her.

PART I

1

A LITTLE BIT DIFFERENT

It was well known that the forest spoke to those who knew how to Listen.

There was a strained silence in the air today.

It wasn't an audible kind of silence — the peaceful sounds of the forest filtered through the trees: leaves rustled in the morning breeze, birds trilled happily in the distance, the river played its burbling symphony far below. The soft glow of sunlight painted dappled brushstrokes across the branches of the Great Tree.

But the very spirits held their breath.

Fae's heart drummed in time with her bare feet as they pounded against the smooth wood of wide branches, the forest canopy whipping past her in a yellow-green blur, the strange silence going unnoticed in her haste.

Not that she would notice anyway.

It was still early, the walkways of Arolynos empty but for a keen few as she flew like a ghost across the limbs of the elven tree-city, her ash-blonde hair whipping out behind her like a banner.

This was normally the time of day Fae carved out for her dance practice, but the call for assistance had come even before she'd had a chance to lift her swords from the shelf.

And when she'd heard that a group of first-year students had fallen from the Spars, she'd dropped everything, running with the sure-footedness of someone who'd grown up in the trees.

Bek was a first-year.

She swallowed her panic, the thought pushing her into a sprint, and she burst into the physica heaving for breath, her ocean-green eyes darting around the clinic for any sign of him.

Shaped like two overlapping flowers, the clinic's treatment bays protruded out from an elliptical platform like petals. In at least eight of these bays were children sporting an array of injuries. The throngs filling the rest of the clinic appeared to comprise mostly of their families.

Fae spotted Zora tending to a patient, and ducked through the waiting parents to appear at the healer's side.

"Ah! Fae!" Zora looked up as she approached. "Thank Eah you're here! I could use your help." She shot an exhausted glance at the unprecedented numbers filling her clinic, tucking an errant strand of dark, sun-kissed hair behind one pointed ear, the normally smooth strands sticking out at odd angles.

"Of course." Fae's eyes continued to scan the bays, looking for a face she knew almost as well as her own. "Is Bek...?"

"He's over there." The boy sitting on the bed piped up, pointing across the room as he straightened to get a better view.

"Dashel, sit still!" The boy's mother hovered nearby while Zora tended to the gash on his head.

Zora abandoned the stitch she was trying to place. "He's fine. Had the sense to stand well back while these jungle cats tried to prove who could leap the furthest." The colour draining from the face of Dashel's mother told Fae just how close that game had come to ending in disaster.

Dashel, oblivious, beamed up at her with sparkling grey eyes. "Penny said I couldn't do it," he said, his voice bubbling with the excitement of someone who was used to having his adventures end up in the physica. "But I proved her wrong! I jumped even further than they did!" He pointed an accusing finger across at the other bays.

Fae sighed, but a wry smile tugged at her lips. Dashel was young enough not to have developed the pointed tips to his ears that marked the transition to adolescence in elves, and yet he was more fearless than many of the adults she knew, even the scouts.

"Hush, Dashel, keep still," his mother said again. Turning her own, paler grey eyes on Fae, she smiled wearily. "They decided to settle this debate by jumping between the Spars, of all places." She shook her head and shot a glance at her son, who looked not at all sheepish. With nothing below, and the nearest neighbouring platforms a good twenty feet away, the long, straight-and-narrow Spars stretched over a yawning opening in the forest canopy, and were a tempting challenge for daredevils like Dashel. "He's lucky it's just the skin that needs stitching."

"Eight stitches and counting," Zora said as she measured out another length of suture. "Although, of course, it would go a lot faster if this jungle cat could *sit still*." Dashel did look sheepish then, the tone in Zora's voice unmistakable. Fae shot the boy a wink, and he grinned back without moving.

"There's Bek!" he declared suddenly, careful not to jostle as he pointed.

Fae whipped around, and spotted a familiar blue-eyed face in a sea of elven greys. She turned to tell Zora she'd only be a minute, but the healer waved her off before she could speak, her eyes intent on her work.

"Go. See for yourself that he's fine, and then dive in."

With a quick smile to Dashel and his mother, Fae ducked from the bay and found Bek sitting to one side, keeping out of the way of the chaos. A wave of relief washed over her, and her heart finally calmed.

Her brother in all but name, Bek was a fellow orphan of Arolynos, and the only one who truly understood what it was to be a little bit different. She recalled when he'd first arrived, small and silent. When he'd first trusted her enough to speak, in his quiet way. He still rarely spoke, and only to a very select few, but he'd been her little shadow ever since.

Nudging her way through the throng of waiting parents, Fae crouched down before him, her eyes scanning for injuries despite Zora's reassurances.

Bek's eyes lit up upon seeing her, and she smiled.

"Are you alright?"

He nodded, his hands coming up to make shapes in the air. *I stayed back. I wasn't on the Spar when it broke.*

Fae started. "Broke?" She repeated the word with the corresponding hand-sign to make sure she'd understood correctly.

Bek nodded again. *It splintered in the middle when Dash was jumping. He only just made it.*

Fae's blood ran cold at the thought. Dashel's slight weight should not have been enough to snap one of the Spars. Even if it had been, she'd never heard of *any* part of the Great Tree breaking. Some Aethyrial magic kept it vibrant with life. The vast *oachoa* — a veritable giant of the forest, towering hundreds of feet over its neighbours — had been home to the elves for centuries.

At least, that's how it always used to be.

Over the last year or so, there had been a spate of stories like this, getting worse with every telling. Branches breaking; leaves withering for no reason, leaving gaps in the canopy; and whispers that the forest floor was no longer safe to wander alone.

As if the eternal sanctuary of Arolynos was... fading, dying.

A prickling awareness, strange and familiar, tickled the nape of her neck, and she turned.

But there was nothing there, as always. Just the clinic bursting with patients and their families. The air was thick with a creeping sense of unease, worried glances and hushed words exchanged about the signs of degradation in the forest of Il'arys. About the change in the Aethyr...

She swallowed the instinctive fear that hazed her vision at the thought of Arolynos withering around them. At the idea that even the spirits were affected. The spirits that all elves could sense to some extent.

Except Fae.

Burying that old sense of having lost something she'd never even had, she placed a hand on Bek's shoulder. "Why don't you head to school? Fera will be wondering where you all are. I'll meet you after."

Bek's fingers danced around each other. *Ty said he'd take me on his way to Circle.*

Fae tried looking over the heads of elves all significantly taller than she was, and failed. "Ty's here?"

And Sheha. Bek nodded through the throng, where Fae just managed to catch a glimpse of the twins, their yellow-gold heads bowed over their work. One was setting a broken arm in a splint, the other bandaging what looked like a nasty gash. Both highly skilled healers, they also made up two of the seven governing Eldra of Arolynos.

"Alright." She turned back to Bek, absently brushing a lock of dark brown hair from his eyes. "I need to start helping. Are you alright waiting here?" Bek nodded, and she planted a quick kiss on his head before rising.

Fae scanned the clinic. Most of the children looked to be taken care of, but that still left the backlogged waiting area that she'd noted as she hurried through. She wove her long hair into a quick braid, taming the waves into a silvery rope that ran down the length of her spine, and making sure to keep her still-round ears tucked in. She located Zora, finally finishing up with Dashel.

"Where do you need me?"

Zora straightened, blowing an errant strand of hair from her face. Her startlingly pale eyes, a shade of softest cloud, stood out in stark contrast to the richness of her coffee-brown skin as they inventoried the patients in the bays. Small for an elf, Zora still stood an inch above Fae, but her height did nothing to diminish the authority she wielded over the physica.

"Well it seems our intrepid young felines are all being seen to." She poked Dashel in the ribs, eliciting a giggle. "Could you check on Loren, over there?" She indicated an elderly man sitting to one side with his life partner, both men wearing matching smile-lines. Fae could see without asking why Loren was in the clinic.

"Lungs again?" she asked, as the man dragged in a breath, his chest heaving.

Zora nodded. "He's well into his fifth century, you'd think he'd stop overdoing it!" She rolled her eyes, and bent to look Dashel in the eye. "What is it with all of my patients testing my limits today?" The boy had the sense to look at least a little sheepish, even if his eyes still twinkled. She straightened again. "Just make sure he hasn't done anything serious—"

"Check his heart, circulation, and get him some *polabreh* to clear his chest," Fae finished. "Got it." She'd been working shifts at the physica since it became clear that, far from needing supervision, she was already operating above the level of most of the other healers. She had a sixth sense for it.

And while she loved what she did — she was damned good at it — she often felt like she could be, *should* be doing... more.

Zora smiled gratefully. "Thank you."

"No problem." Fae waved to Dashel, rolling her sleeves up past her wrists as she left him to Zora's ministrations. "See you soon, Dash!"

"Not too soon please!" his mother replied for him.

Fae laughed, and turned to her first patient.

· · · ·

She was just checking in with Bek after sending Loren away with a stern reminder of his age, when a tall, rangy figure strode easily through the slowly clearing clinic.

"Fae! Bek! Eh!" Ty hailed them. At over six feet tall, and lean with it, the healer was of typical elven build, with the traditional grey eyes of his people, and a smile for everyone he met.

"How's our newest recruit doing this morning?" Ty grinned down at Bek, who beamed proudly in return. "I hope we've had plenty enough mischief for our first week?" he added with a conspiratorial wink, his choppy, golden-yellow hair just brushing his forehead. Bek nodded emphatically. Fae grinned at the exchange, knowing full well that Ty and Sheha themselves had played their own daredevil games on the Spars when they were younger.

Bek's hands played quick shapes in the air. *Are you teaching class today?* As a highly respected healer, Ty taught his fair share of classes at the school. But as an Eldra, he was often busy with his other duties.

He didn't miss a beat however, signing straight back in the hand-speak Bek preferred while saying aloud, "I am later. I have a Circle meeting this morning." He grimaced. "The Whisperers want to discuss the situation with the Aethyr urgently." He ran a frustrated hand through his hair. "And this morning's excitement will only make them more worried." Casting a quick glance down at Bek, he rearranged his face into a wide smile. "Shall I stop by your class later?"

No, thank you, Bek signed. *I'm just glad I will have friends nearby.* He smiled shyly. Fae felt a pang of guilt. He'd been so worried about starting school, and she hadn't been there for him much as she would have liked, what with her own classes and shifts at the physica.

Ty ruffled the boy's hair and crouched down to his level. "From what I've heard, you've been making plenty of new friends on your own without help." His eyes flicked pointedly to the youngsters being tended to around the clinic. "Just make sure your good choices rub off on them, not the other way around." He winked, and Bek beamed with pride.

"Are you on your way out?" Fae asked, noting that Ty's patients had all left.

He straightened, smiling down at her with storm-grey eyes to drown in. "I am indeed, if Bek's ready?" Bek jumped to his feet in answer, eager to be off.

"Let me walk you out." Together they walked across the clinic to the waiting area, a small platform directly off Primary Brachear.

Ty turned with one foot braced on the huge tree limb that made up one of the main thoroughfares across the city. "I meant to ask you, I could use a hand with my Junior Echa class this afternoon if you're free?"

Fae beamed, the worrying events of the morning replaced by a glimmer of pride.

"I should be free after noon," she said, delighted to be asked. "I'm only with Zora this morning. Covering for you two!" It was a great honour to be asked to step in for two of the most skilled healers in the city. She relished the opportunity to demonstrate how capable she was, especially when not everyone believed it as much as Ty. He and Sheha had never doubted her abilities. "I can come by when Sheha gets back from the Circle."

"Perfect!" He grinned, his eyes lingering on hers just a moment longer than necessary.

Fae's smile turned shy, and she turned to say goodbye to Bek before the heat rising into her cheeks thoroughly embarrassed her. He'd moved off a short distance and was watching two small birds that appeared deep in conversation in the branches just beyond the platform. Her joy soured, and she swallowed a familiar twinge of jealousy at Bek's ability to do something that was as simple as breathing for the rest of her kind, and yet had forever alluded her.

Bek's perception of the Aethyr had always been particularly strong. The ease with which he Listened to the inane chatter of the birds, unconsciously using his sense of the spirits within the creatures to understand them, still took Fae's breath away, even after all these years.

Sheha emerged from the clinic then, her yellow-gold hair, an exact match for Ty's, scraped back into a neat tail. The birds hopped away to continue their musical discussion elsewhere.

"Come on, we're already late!" Sheha strode across the platform, and hopped nimbly onto the Primary walkway that would take them into the centre of Arolynos. "See you later Fae!"

Bek scrambled to follow, and Ty fell in behind, his long strides easily keeping up with his sister. With a quick wave over his shoulder, he threw Fae a farewell wink, and then they were gone.

Fae watched the space where they'd disappeared through the trailing branches. She wished she could go with them. Hear about the problems with the Aethyr. Sit by Ty's side...

She shook her head abruptly to dislodge her errant thoughts, then drew in a breath, and turned back to the clinic. She tried not to notice the patches in the canopy that should be full of spring newness. The spots of brown decay that should be budding with life.

Instead, she threw herself into her work.

As she helped Zora and the other healers work through the remaining patients, Fae felt the same prickling sensation again — the familiar yet strange feeling that she was being watched. The silent eyes that had watched her her entire life.

She sighed at the tickle up the back of her neck, and continued her work, knowing without looking that if she turned, she would see nothing but patients and healers doing *their* work.

Sheha returned from the Circle just past noon.

"Eh, *Niha*!" Sheha greeted Fae warmly as she entered the clinic, her wide smile a mirror of her brother's.

"Eh, Shae," Fae replied. "How was Circle?" Sheha levelled a look at her that told her all she needed to know. "That bad?"

Sheha blew out a frustrated sigh, running her fingers through hair the same sunlit yellow as the golden leaves above. "It's not that," she said. "It's just maddening dealing in riddles and unknowns. Hardly conducive to solving problems."

"What's the problem?" Fae asked.

"The Aethyr," Sheha said, lowering her voice. "The Whisperers think that all the unbalance in the forest is connected to them, that there's something wrong in the Spirit Realm, with Eah'lara itself." Fae's blood chilled instantly. That couldn't be good. And of anyone, the Whisperers would know. As the most sensitive to the dialogue of the Aethyr, they dedicated their lives to interpreting the murmured messages of spiritkind. That the degeneration in the forest could be as deeply rooted as the Aethyr themselves... a shiver ran down Fae's spine.

Sheha chewed her lip pensively. "But I'm not sure I believe it. It doesn't sound right."

"You didn't say that, did you?" Fae asked, pushing the implications of Sheha's news to the back of her mind.

Sheha snorted inelegantly. "Of course I did!"

Fae rolled her eyes with a smile. Of course Sheha questioned the Whisperers on their sacred wisdom. She'd never been one to blindly accept the opinions of others. "What did they say?"

"That if I wanted to join the debate, my brother and I should embrace our 'true calling' and Listen for ourselves." She made air-quotes with her fingers, and let out a bark of laughter. "As if I have time for that! Anyway —" she straightened, and looked around the physica "—what have I missed?"

"Plenty!" Zora said, appearing from a side bay. "But it's mostly under control now."

"Good," Sheha said with a smile. "Oh." She stopped abruptly, her ears twitching subtly where the points protruded from beneath her hair. "Seems like Ty's feeling the pressure." She winked at Fae. "You'd better get going. He told me he recruited you into helping with his class today."

Fae nodded. "He did. Zora, if you have no further need of me...?" Although teaching class seemed so trivial if the very forest around them was falling apart. Weren't there more important things to do?

Zora waved her off. "Go on, off you go. We can handle it from here." She tucked another flyaway strand behind her ear. "Thank you for today."

"Anytime," Fae said. Then, turning to Sheha, "Dinner at yours?" She needed to know more. What exactly had the Whisperers said? Something about this connection to the Aethyr had her insides twisting into knots.

Sheha nodded. "Bring my insufferable brother with you," she said, with a quirk to her lips. "I haven't seen him outside the Circle in weeks!"

"I'll bring him!" Fae promised quickly. She paused. With all the signs of failing in the forest lately, she felt the need to gather the little family she had and hold them close. To reassure herself that they were safe. "Do you mind if I bring Bek? It's... been a strange day." She looked at Zora who, along with her partner Fera, was Bek's guardian when he wasn't acting as Fae's shadow. "If it's alright with you, Zora?"

"Yes, yes," the healer answered with a smile. "He'll love it. Anything to spend another minute with you, Fae. The boy adores you."

Fae smiled. She adored him too. If anything happened to him... she couldn't bear thinking about it.

"Bring him," Sheha said. "The more the merrier. It's not like he dominates the conversation anyway." Even with his hand-speak, Bek generally preferred to sit and listen.

"Great!" she said. "I'll see you later then!" Fae's grin felt paper-thin on her face as she raised her hand to wave, and left them to the rest of the patients.

As she stepped out of the physica, she stopped to watch a mass of dead leaves drop from the canopy above, the myna birds nearby taking flight in protest.

2

ALL CRYPTIC, NO CLUES

The classroom Ty had chosen was up high in the crown of Arolynos, where the canopy cover was more sparse. Unfettered sunlight streamed in easily between the leaves, making it an ideal location for cultivating herbs that preferred the bright, open skies to the dim shade of the forest floor. Living branches were woven together to create a solid floor underfoot; some had even been trained vertically to form walls around two thirds of the space. The final third — as well as the ceiling — was left open to the elements.

Up here, it was harder to hide the strange withering in leaves that should have been fresh with spring greenness. The gaps in the canopy where foliage had simply given up and fallen from the branches. Fae spared the trees a worried glance, and then turned her attention to the class.

"... you each have a plant to identify," Ty was saying as Fae slotted herself in at the back of the room, his eyes barely flickering at her arrival. "There are texts available at the front here to help you. I want you to identify your plant, and create your own fact sheet about its identifying features and properties from your findings. Senior Echa Fae will be on hand to assist." He sent her a wink as the students turned, having missed her entry entirely. "Begin."

As the Junior Echa scrambled to sift through the books at the front, Ty slipped past them to stand with Fae.

"Sheha said you were struggling," Fae said, cocking one eyebrow at him. "But you seem to have everything in hand."

Ty folded his arms, watching his students like a hawk. Fae's skin tingled as he brushed against her arm. "You weren't here at the start," he said, without taking his eyes off them. "I had to put on my Eldra face."

Fae grimaced. "Ouch."

Ty's mouth twitched at the corner. "Indeed," he said.

They watched the Junior Echa as they flipped through the texts and scribbled their findings on their own sheets.

"How do you do that?" she asked.

Ty turned to her. "What?" he asked. "Cow a class of overexcited youths?"

Fae fought a giggle. "No," she said. "I mean how do you feel what Sheha's feeling? And vice versa." They'd been doing it as long as she could remember.

Ty shrugged. "It's a twin thing," he said. Twins were rare enough among elven offspring. What Ty and Sheha did though, that was inexplicable.

"Useful," Fae said appreciatively.

"Hm." He watched as the Echa began flicking eagerly through their chosen texts. "I was in the middle of my Ebon exam when Sheha fell from the Spars, did you know that?"

"No," Fae replied. "You never mentioned that part before." Although she'd heard the story enough times.

Ty nodded. "When I screamed out that I was falling, Jax thought I was trying to get out of the test. I was in so much trouble." His hand rubbed absently at the back of his neck. "It wasn't until later that we found out Sheha had fallen." His twin still wore the scar across her collar bone from a nasty break as a result of it. "Larah still insists the Aethyr reached out to me when Sheha was hurt. But it's just..." He shrugged again. "Just a twin thing." He smiled ruefully at the inadequacy of his explanation. Fae could well imagine how Larah — a crotchety old Whisperer and a true ancient among elves — would react to Ty's explanation. To her, the Aethyr had a part to play in everything, even the most mundane.

"You have to admit though," Fae said, "it does sound awfully similar to how the Aethyr communicate." From how she'd once heard it described, the dialogue of spiritkind was an abstract thing; images and emotions. Feelings and senses alone.

Ty uncrossed his arms to shove his hands into his pockets, arching an eyebrow down at her. "You're starting to sound like them now." Whisperers.

"Pfft, what? Me?" Fae said, pressing a palm to her chest. "You and I both know that's not possible." And she couldn't quite keep the note of longing from her voice, despite years of practice. She'd pestered the Eldra Whisperer about it endlessly as a child, begged her, convinced that she could *learn* to Listen, if she only tried hard enough. If only someone would show her how.

And then there were the times when she felt like she was being watched, as though someone stood behind a curtain beside her, just waiting for her to pull it back and *see*... But try as she might, she'd never heard the Aethyr's harmony. And its lack left an aching hollow inside of her.

"Listening is something you're supposed to be born with," she continued, ignoring the rock in her gut, and the familiar glance of pity Ty shot her. "And I wasn't." Swallowing the lump in her throat, she waggled a finger at Ty, forcing her tone to lighten. "You and Shae, on the other hand..." Ty's gaze lingered on her a second longer, the emotion behind his eyes something she couldn't bear to see from him. "Maybe Larah's right you know," she pushed on, willing him to stop looking at her like that. "You two *do* have a strong sense for it, for all that you like to ignore it. I think you'd make *great* Whisperers..."

Ty narrowed his eyes, and chose that moment to glance abruptly behind her. "Oh look, someone needs help." Turning her by the shoulders, he strode over to a student who was doing just fine on their own.

Fae laugh was strained. At least he was no longer looking at her with that same old pity in his eyes.

It was a conversation the twins always avoided. They likely did have a strong enough sense of the Aethyr to be Whisperers, but they were born healers, and just didn't find the call to spiritkind as alluring as she did.

But for Fae, it drew her, called to her, in spite of the silence in her head.

It pulled at her, beckoned her heart to leave her body and soar with the wind and the birds. It filled the space left behind with an ache she feared she would never be rid of.

To commune with the spirits of the world... she thought wistfully, painfully, and not for the first time. If she had that, maybe she wouldn't feel so... misplaced. Like a songbird without a voice. She rubbed absently at her chest, as if her heart had already answered the call within her and left her with just the empty ache instead.

It was strange though; in those moments when she felt as if she *could* Listen, when those whisperings tugged at her from behind the curtain in her mind... she was sure she need only focus to hear them clearly...

Another student raised a tentative hand, and Fae was quickly swept up in the task of answering questions on medicinal plants and their functions — too busy to be occupied with the philosophy of Listening to the Aethyr.

And the nagging sense that she was missing something.

After the Echa class, Ty taught another with the Ebon — the most senior students in the school. Fae stayed, even though she wasn't supposed to be advanced enough to study at their level. These students were at least a decade older than her, often more. Even so, Ty didn't ask her to leave. She'd always been a keen learner, but his acceptance of her place among the most skilled of them stoked a warm feeling inside her. Pride, perhaps, and something else.

Yet, sitting in this class, it was all too easy to see how she didn't quite fit with the elven norm. Elves her age were still emotionally quite young — some not even graduating to Junior Echa yet — whereas her intellectual peers were decades older. As a result, she often went unseen by either group. There was a strange sort of discomfort in not having somewhere to fit, in not having a group to gravitate towards, but she'd eventually grown accustomed to it, like the ache of an old injury, and learned how to go her own way.

She was just... different.

Fae looked around the class with a sigh.

Elves were a race of many colours, but all shared the appearance of having been touched by sunlight. Hair glinted with shades of gold whether palest blond or deepest black. And the sun-kissed glow to each varied skin tone was as much a trademark feature as the elves' tapered, upswept ears.

Fae's skin was so pale it bordered on pallid, her eyes a conspicuous ocean-green in a sea of typical elven greys and blues. Her hair was so pale it was almost silver — a cool shimmer of moonlight, a pale reflection on a pool of gilded gold, set apart from the glittering fish beneath the surface.

She wore her unusual hair tied back to cover her even more unusual ears, which were agonisingly late in developing their classical elvish tips. A younger Fae had tried eating more, thinking her ears would come in if she gained some weight, but neither her height nor her ears had responded to her attempts.

Despite her best efforts, she remained dwarfed by her tall brethren, even some of the children.

But, she spread her fingers out before her. She had small, nimble hands; healer's hands. A noble occupation.

It was a point of pride for her, and the skill that had earned her a place as a Senior Echa, only one rank below the Ebons that shared her class now.

It was a complex class — exactly the challenge Fae needed. She earned herself a headache wrapping her brain around the neurological pathways and physiology Ty outlined, but she was buzzing by the end of it.

As the rest of his students trickled away with dazed expressions, Ty looked up at her with a smile that made Fae's heart skip a beat. "What did you think?"

Fae beamed. "That was fascinating!" Her eyes flicked to where the last Ebon trailed out of the room, massaging both temples. "Although, I think you might have given some of your students second thoughts about becoming healers."

"That's partly the idea." He flashed a grin.

"You're impossible!" Fae laughed. "When's your next class?"

"Are you serious?" Ty replied incredulously. Seeing the earnest sincerity in Fae's eyes, he sighed. "I'm teaching the Ebons again next week. You're welcome to sneak in again then if you wish." He shot her a wink.

"Thanks!" she effused. She already couldn't wait. "Oh! Sheha said to bring you to dinner. She misses you."

"She didn't say that."

"No," Fae admitted. Neither twin showed their emotions easily. Elves tended not to. She knew Sheha loved her, and Bek too, but it was a gentle kind of love, a quiet kind. The kind only seen in the details: the smaller actions, the little moments. "But she does. I don't need your twin-thing-sixth-sense to know that." She put on her best pleading eyes. "Please, come." She didn't need to pretend that she wanted him there too.

"I suppose I can do my lesson-planning afterwards…" he said, rubbing his chin thoughtfully, making a show of considering it. But Fae caught the twinkle in his eye.

"Good," she said. "I'll see you there?"

Ty dropped his hand and waved her away. "Yes, yes, I'll be there. You go ahead, I have a few things to wrap up here."

Fae grinned her triumph and left him to it, making her way down to where ranks of new students were dispersing after classes.

The walkways were a mass of young elves filing from their classrooms, chattering and laughing as they went. Flying above the commotion, a pair of nightingales spiralled through the air. Almost everywhere else in Arolynos, the trailing branches of the oachoa tree formed an inverted forest through the city. But here, the canopy soared thirty feet high, leafy vines hanging in curtains high above, catching the sunlight and casting a softly dappled, golden glow over the living walkways that wound through the leaves.

Flashes of colour winked above as iridescent myna birds swooped through the vaulted tree-canopy, joining the nightingales in their aerial dance. Fae tried to ignore the sinking feeling in her stomach when she noticed how few there were for the time of year.

She turned her attention back to the milling students, and spotted Bek's dark hair over the heads of the other Knots.

"Bek!" she called, waving when he turned her way. His face split into a grin, and he ducked through his peers to reach her.

"How was school today?" She signed as she spoke aloud. He didn't need her to do both, but it helped her practice.

Bek's fingers were a flurry as he replied. *Brilliant!* His hands formed the words, but his face told her all she needed to know. *Some of the other students hand-speak too! And Fera said that we're going to start a scrapbook next week, and that we should look out for things we want to put in it!* Fae couldn't help but grin along with him. She was glad to hear there were other children familiar with the scouts' hand-speak. It was a weight off her mind to know Bek could converse comfortably with at least some of his peers.

"Sheha has invited us to dinner." she said, her hands making the corresponding shapes. "Would you like to come?"

Bek nodded vigorously. *I didn't see Ty today,* he signed. *Was he very busy?*

Fae laughed as she ushered Bek away from the school. "Let's just say he had his hands full with his first classes too."

They walked along twisting boughs, swept aside draping branches, passing students and parents as they went, finally emerging onto the wide thoroughfare of Primary Solar. One of the seven main limbs branching from the centre of the Great Tree like spokes of a wheel, it was around fifteen feet wide, and one of the busiest routes through the city. Smaller walkways speared off into the canopy as they passed, diving into the yellow-green backdrop, but Fae and Bek remained on the Primary — the most direct path between the school and the Circle at the heart of Arolynos. The Circle where the Eldra both met, and made their homes.

It was quiet as late afternoon turned towards early evening. Most people would be home, preparing for the evening meal.

Fae smiled to herself. *Although Ty will still be late.*

She was setting the table an hour later when Ty finally did arrive.

"Sorry!" he said as he walked into the kitchen, looking as if he'd jogged across Arolynos to get there. "I know, I'm late."

"By your standards, you're early," Sheha said, carrying steaming dishes of roasted vegetables, and a rich stew of spiced pulses and wild garlic to the table. Bek followed behind with a platter of fresh flatbread, the warming scent curling up from the plate in wafting tendrils. Tearing a corner from one, he popped a piece into his mouth, his lips curving up in quiet appreciation as he was put to work carrying things to the table. Ty ignored his sister's jibe and dropped into a chair.

"Uh uh," Sheha said, wagging a finger at him. "Hands." She pointed towards the washroom. Ty frowned and stuck out his tongue childishly. Sheha rolled her eyes at his back as he disappeared to wash up. "Fae," she said, "can you grab the rice for me please?"

"Of course," Fae replied, scooping up the bowl heaped high with fragrant rice that made her mouth water. Family dinners hadn't been as frequent in the years since Ty and Sheha were elevated to Eldra — they were both so busy with their work. Once, Fae had spent every night at Sheha's table, most nights Ty had been there too. And then Fae had coaxed Bek along to join them. The first night, he'd been silent as a moth in the corner. That had been when Ty suggested learning hand-speak; he knew a scout who'd be happy to teach him, if he liked.

Fae placed the rice on the table. Straightened the dish of vegetables beside it. She spotted Bek's fingers sneaking towards another piece of flatbread and clicked her tongue in warning, smiling as he retracted his hand with a pout. There were lots of happy memories around this table. No matter how different she felt among the rest of her people, she'd always had somewhere to belong here.

"Smells good, *Niha*," Ty said, drawing a deep breath through his nose as he returned to his seat. He grabbed a flatbread from the top of the pile and dropped it onto his plate. "Mmm, *dahka*!" he murmured appreciatively. Serving himself a mammoth portion of everything, he tucked in without pause.

"Long day, *Tiho*?" Sheha asked, one eyebrow raised as she, Bek, and Fae finally took their places at the table. Bek reached out to snag the flatbread he'd already sampled, and set about ladling improbable quantities of *dahka* and rice onto his own plate.

"Vegetables too," Fae reminded him quietly. Bek shot her an unconvincing glare but spooned a respectable portion of the vegetables onto his plate as well.

"Mm," Ty mumbled around a mouthful of food, "I always forget how busy a new term is. And meeting the Whisperers this morning just made it busier."

"Oh yes," Fae said, ears pricking up. "How was that?"

Ty waved his fork dismissively, but his brows knitted together. "It's just more of the same. They've been talking about a sense of foreboding in the Aethyr for... well it feels like forever, but we've never been able to identify a cause."

"And now, with the fading in the forest..." Sheha added uneasily. Indeed, the reluctance of nature to flourish come spring was just like that... like it was fading away. And if the Great Tree itself was dying... Sheha shrugged, but the gesture was weary. "They seem to think there's a link. And they're convinced the cause is somewhere in the human lands."

"But they haven't been able to give us a reason *why* they think that," Ty pointed out, gesticulating with his fork again.

"Isn't Listening a bit like that though?" Fae asked. "All cryptic, no clues?"

"Well indeed," Sheha said, with a guilty glance at Fae. She knew more than anyone how much Fae's inability pained her. "Which only makes it all the more difficult for us to decide on an appropriate course of action. The Whisperers — and anyone else with a strong enough sense of the Aethyr — are becoming more and more agitated. This foreboding they feel is only getting stronger. The forest is getting worse, and we're still none the wiser as to why." Her shoulders drooped, then she voiced the question that was so terrifying, most elves chose not to confront the bone-chilling possibility they might yet have to face. "If the Great Tree dies," she whispered, "where would we go?"

Fae reached over to grasp her hand. "It won't come to that," she said, although she didn't feel the reassurance of her own words. It felt as though that was exactly what was happening. The Great Tree was withering where it stood. And they were helpless to stop it until they understood *why*. Even if it was linked to the Aethyr, who knew how to heal the spirits? Her stomach turned itself over, wringing itself out against her ribs, but she squeezed Sheha's hand and forced a small smile. "It isn't natural though," she agreed. "Any of it. Did you hear about the Spars snapping today? Dashel Willow nearly cracked his head open falling from them."

Sheha nodded, blanching, and Fae remembered Ty's story about her own fall from the Spars. And that was without a healthy limb of the Great Tree breaking at random. Sheha ran a hand over her face, deep fatigue lining her features. "What I wouldn't give to have the libraries of Alyla just a *little* bit closer! We could research properly — there could be records of something similar happening before. A botanical sickness we could treat, maybe. Or just an idea of where to even start." But the forests of Alyla were far away to the east, nestled against the Hearthstone mountains, home of the dragons.

"Can't you ask Artimus?" Fae asked. Artimus was another Eldra, an academic, and probably the most learned elf in all of Arolynos.

Sheha made a scornful sound in the back of her throat. "Artimus and Fabre don't bother with Aethyrial studies. Eah'lara is the realm of the Whisperers' expertise, not the scholars'. In truth, I just don't think he likes getting into debates with Adara, or Larah." She shook her head in frustration. "The libraries though..." She sighed wistfully. "You know, they say that before the dragons became so reclusive, they shared their knowledge with the library custodians in Alyla? There could be knowledge buried in those stacks that predate the Rains!"

Ty dropped his head into his hands with a groan. "But Alyla is weeks of travel away. And there's no guarantee that they'd have any more information on this than we do, either botanical or Aethyrial. Honestly, just thinking about it all again gives me a headache." He rubbed at his temples.

"Couldn't you just send somebody to look into the human lands?" Fae asked. "See if the Whisperers are right?"

"We talked about it," Sheha said. "But the human lands aren't safe. We won't send anyone there without a good reason."

"Why aren't the human lands safe?" Fae asked, confused. "Surely they're just people, like us?"

"Yes," Sheha answered slowly, "they are. But over the last few decades, the plains have filled with raiders and bandits. It's not safe to travel; it's not safe anywhere. Even their capital is an anarchistic mess, ever since their monarchy was overthrown. No—" she shook her head with a finality that said she'd made this decision already "—we won't send anyone unless we have no choice."

But it felt as though they were running out of time to make that choice. Through the window behind her, Fae glimpsed a curtain of leaves floating free of their branches, edges curled and brown. If the Aethyr *were* the problem, wouldn't it affect the whole world? They inhabited *all* forms of life. Could the danger in the human lands be related to the fading in the forest?

"What do we do then?" she whispered. She couldn't ignore it any longer, no matter that the rest of her people seemed content to feign ignorance and carry on with their daily lives. *Something* was happening to Arolynos. Something that would affect all of them if they couldn't stop it.

"I don't know," Sheha replied, and her voice was also lowered to a whisper, as if admitting a guilty secret. Fae's heart sank. If even the Eldra didn't know what to do, what hope was there for Arolynos? She glanced around the table. What would become of them?

Bek watched the exchange with wide eyes. His fork was paused halfway on its journey to his mouth, the flatbread long since consumed.

Ty cleared his throat into the tense pause.

"Fae snuck into my Ebon class this afternoon," he said, changing the topic with no attempt at subtlety.

Fae straightened in her seat. "I did not sneak!" she protested.

Bek giggled at her vehement denial.

Sheha grinned faintly, grateful for the distraction. "Did he do his lecture on neurological pathways? He loves to torture new Ebons with that one."

Fae nodded. "It was fascinating!" she said. "I can't wait for the next one."

Sheha shook her head, smiling. "You should have made Ebon years ago, *Niha*," she said. "Your talents are wasted stagnating at Echa-level."

Fae shrugged. "Ebon are at least ten years older than me," she said. "I don't yet have the 'requisite experience' to join them, *Niha*, or so Fabre keeps telling me. It's alright." She smiled wryly. "I'll be the best Ebon the school has seen in centuries when I finally do make it!"

"That you will." Ty said. A thought seemed to occur to him. He cocked his head. "Why do you still call Shae 'sister', but you never call me 'brother'?"

Fae laughed. "I grew up in Shae's house," she said. "Of course she's my sister."

"But," Ty argued, "we're twins."

Fae paused to think about it. She looked between the two of them. "I don't know," she said honestly. "Shae tucked me in at night, braided my hair, you know, all that sort of stuff. You were always..." She hesitated, searching for the right words. She couldn't explain it, but she had had never considered Ty as fraternal. What they had had always been different. "I don't know, the funny family friend." Heat rushed to her cheeks.

He wasn't *just* a friend either.

"Ha!" Sheha barked a laugh, and Bek giggled as Ty sat back in his chair, a hand slapped over his heart.

"You wound me!" he declared with mock gravity, but he shot her wink as well. "Just as well. One sister is enough trouble to deal with."

Sheha swatted his arm. "Remember who cooked your dinner, ingrate!"

Ty feigned injury, and Fae laughed at their easy banter, Bek grinning quietly as he watched them from his seat.

Fae allowed herself a contented sigh. Whatever they were to each other, these cherished few were her family.

But, as another flurry of leaves curled up and dropped from the branches outside, she couldn't fight the cold knot of dread in her gut at whatever unknown blight was threatening that family, and their home.

3

WHISPER-THIN, SPIDER-SILK

The next day, Fae gave Bek a squeeze before releasing him to join his new friends, clustered together before the school. He held onto her a moment longer before stepping away, turning briefly to sign, *Love you, Niha.*

Fae's heart warmed. *Love you too, Tihito,* she replied, adding the extra inflection used for younger family.

Bek grinned and skipped off to join his new friends. She smiled when she saw him hand-speak to a young boy with curly red hair. The boy replied with faltering hands, his movements crude and stuttering next to Bek's fluency.

And he was worried about making friends, she thought, turning to make her way back along the Primary. She wasn't due at the physica for another half-hour, so she took her time, strolling along the wide thoroughfare through the canopy, breathing slow, deep breaths, and relishing the relative peace of the morning.

A sound in the trees drew her eyes into the canopy.

The wind whispered through the leaves, but the feeling of being watched — the same prickling awareness that had plagued her most of her life — raised the tiny hairs at the nape of her neck. She turned instinctively, as if she had a hope of catching whoever it was — or *whatever it was.

But there was no one there, as always.

As a child, she'd imagined — had hoped — the feeling was the watchful eyes of the Aethyr, if the Aethyr *had* eyes. But any Whisperer she'd asked had gently, but firmly rebuked the idea. She'd quickly learned to keep her thoughts on the matter to herself.

But it still niggled at her. And that feeling, like she was missing something, plagued her daily. Like she'd forgotten something important. Something that mattered. Over years of fruitless wondering, she'd eventually pushed the feeling to the back of her mind. It did her no good to obsess over something she just couldn't fathom.

Normally, the tingling awareness would creep up on her when she least expected it, and then disappear again just as quickly — always fleeting. She could go weeks, sometimes months without feeling it, forgetting all about her bone-deep yearning for that connection to spiritkind, and then a single brief touch would bring back all her childish notions, and leave her spiralling with renewed longing. And hope.

But this time, the touch didn't dissipate; it stayed with her, like a bird gliding overhead, its shadow grazing hers as she walked. She stopped to look behind her again.

The whisper of leaves was a quiet susurration around her. It brushed against her senses in a way that made her want to close her eyes...

But there was no wind to rustle the leaves. The air was utterly still.

She blinked.

Primary Solar was empty. And yet the air felt... full.

Nearby leaves fluttered gently on a non-existent breeze. The branches tilted, as if gravity had tipped its head, conceded to some greater force. The leaves began to pull towards her, floating on an invisible current, tugging their vines inward like tiny sails pulling their ships into harbour. As if the trees themselves reached for her.

Fae squinted her eyes, half expecting to see something different if she changed her point of view.

A handful of leaves fell from their tethers and gathered in the air. Then more followed. And more. They pivoted, turning like a flock of birds until they formed an uninterrupted sheet of foliage that rushed at her. Before she knew it, she was surrounded, the leaves a vortex spinning dizzyingly around her. Leaves the fresh green of spring, but also the yellows and coppers of autumn. And the dark, rotting brown of death.

Fae's eyes widened. Up and down the Primary, draping branches were drawing in towards her, as if pulled by invisible strings.

And yet more leaves drifted towards her.

And then she heard it again.

Whispers in the trees.

Her heart pounded so hard it felt like it might leap from her throat. Hope spiralled up inside her, winding tighter and tighter until she thought she might burst with it. Was it the Aethyr?

She chastised herself instantly. She'd been told over and over that it wasn't possible. She'd been born without the natural sense for spiritkind. A rare defect — a word that always made her feel dirty — but one with which she'd been burdened.

Then what was happening with the leaves?

Strange eddies in the air currents often swirled through the Village. They sometimes made the leaves behave erratically; almost ethereally.

This must be the same. Easily explained.

But the hope inside her was like a bubble that would not burst.

Then the whispers turned to screams.

Fae clamped her hands over her ears, ducking her head against the sound.

It was shrill and keening. It was ear-piercing and sad. It was...

She looked up, hands pressed against either side of her head. The drooping, willow-like branches of the Great Tree reached for her, the delicate, pale-green leaves trembling at the end of their tethers as if...

They're in pain.

Fae gasped.

The trees. The spirits within them. She *could* hear them. They were *calling to her.*

They were screaming in pain. Pleading for help.

The Whisperers were right.

The Aethyr were in trouble.

Her eyes widened impossibly further. She was rooted to the spot, stunned. Only half believing. This couldn't be real. Her mind couldn't decide if she was imagining it or not. And yet...

This must be what madness feels like.

The screams were everywhere.

They were all around her.

Inside her head.
Calling her.
Leaves whirled without wind.
The trees reached for her.
And then, all at once, the screams rushed in.
And hit Fae like a crashing wave.
Her surroundings blurred dizzyingly.
She blinked.

When she opened her eyes, she was... somewhere else.

She stood in the centre of a human village, surrounded by open, rolling countryside. She blinked again as the dazzling sunshine of a midsummer's day blinded her, unshaded by the forest canopy. Unlike the familiar, gently dappled sunlight shining through the trees of Arolynos, it was bright, and harsh, and too warm. The scent of fresh baked bread wafted over the breeze and the sounds of distant farming carried through the air.

Ahead, a gathering bell hung proudly in the square, shining in the sun. The village hall sat squat and strong off to one side, built of solid stone and thatched with neat, packed straw. The public house stood tall nearby, built of stone and slate. Neat, wood-framed houses hung back to either side, giving way to the hub of the community. The distant sails of a mill flapped softly in the wind, turning lazily on this summer's day. A waterwheel splashed somewhere nearby.

At the sound of laughter she turned to see a human girl running from the village hall chased by a tall, dark-haired man. He caught her gently, scooping her up and tossing her into the air. Behind them, a woman followed, a small smile on her lips. She kissed the child lightly on her head, and ushered her back inside. His arms freed, the man gathered the woman up in his arms. As they shared a kiss, Fae noticed the matching bands of carved wood on their fingers, polished and dark against their skin.

Something about them was achingly familiar... like Fae knew them from somewhere before...

A water trough nearby caught a glimmer of sunlight and reflected it back towards her.

She turned away from the glare.

And the vision changed.

Around her, fire raged.

Buildings collapsed, their silhouettes crumbling shadows against a glowing orange backdrop. The outline of the village was visible in snatches between curtains of smoke and ash. Only now, it was rubble.

In the middle of it all, the gathering bell swayed sadly in place in the central square. The dulled bronze surface shimmered in the heat of the blaze, flames licking across their own reflection.

Panic hung thick in the air. People — humans — ran from ruins, fear-stricken, searching frantically for lost family, or shelter. Most simply fled.

The sound of coarse laughter cut across the crackle of hungry flames.

Fae stood in the middle of it all, shocked by the carnage, mesmerised by flames. Waves of heat buffeted against her. It seeped through her clothes, drawing sweat from her skin, the sting of it hot against her cheeks. Clouds of acrid smoke caught in her throat and brought tears to her eyes, the smell of burning so strong it made her gag: burning wood, burning stone, burning flesh.

A shout went up, breaking the spell. And the sound of cold laughter grew nearer.

Fae cast about for somewhere to hide. Instinct told her she didn't want to be found. But everything was burning. There was nowhere to hide. And in the seconds she wasted not running, a group of human men rounded one of the few buildings still standing. They wore cruel smiles and violence like a mantle. They looked... hungry.

The men caught sight of her instantly, and fear broke over her in a wave, rooting her to the ground. The malice in their eyes gleamed in the light of the flames as they stalked towards her.

One carried a spade over his shoulder, repurposed to cause pain. He swung it, and everything slowed, the vision forcing her to see every detail. To watch the motion of his arms as the muscles bunched then straightened, highlighted by the flickering firelight as he brought the spade to bear.

The make-shift weapon glinted in the half-light as it arced towards her.

She could do nothing but blink and stare as it drew nearer, inevitably nearer.

The spade collided with the side of her head with a low, dull crack, *and she was knocked to the ground in a blinding crash of pain.*

She felt every part of her body jar against the earth: elbow, hip, shoulder, skull.

A booted foot connected with her belly, another with her back.

She curled around herself but the motions felt sluggish, her body slow to respond.

Blows rained on her, the weight of heavy heels and hard toecaps reverberating through her body as they struck.

When she thought she would surely black out, a cry went up from the other side of the village. The men turned towards the sound, distracted by the prospect of new prey. They moved away, leaving Fae in a bloodied heap on the ground.

Easing to her feet, she retreated as far as her battered body would carry her from the carnage.

She sank down behind a burnt-out building. Her head pulsed painfully, and she lifted a hand to it gingerly. A warm, sticky wetness matted in her hair. She was bruised all over. When she breathed, her entire body hurt, a wash of nauseous pain punctuating every movement.

In the distance, screaming.

But the vision pulled her attention elsewhere, and she was moving away from her shelter, through the village once again. The crackle of fire and the ring of voices faded to a muffled background burble.

A voice murmured softly nearby. It whispered fervently. And it tugged at her, like a memory buried deep...

Fae rounded a crumbling wall. A woman crouched in the corner between two walls of a husk that had once been a house. Her hair was grey with dust and debris, her forehead marked by an angry swelling. Curled up in her lap was a small child. Only the slightest rise and fall of her tiny chest indicated that the girl was alive. She was covered in soot, and unconscious, her head tucked against her mother's arm.

The vision drew Fae to them. And something about them echoed in her mind...

As Fae approached, the mother's whispered words became clear. A plea. A prayer.

"... Hold her safe until she can step into the world, unafraid. She is more than the best of us." She paused. "She has the Spirit within her."

At the final utterance of those words, a soft, golden glow enveloped the woman and child, and finally Fae.

The village disappeared behind the light.

The glow grew, engulfing everything around them.

The light burned brighter, brighter.

Fae shielded her eyes.

And blinked.

And found herself elsewhere again.

This time, she saw endless expanses of land.

The might of the Hearthstone mountains slumbered to the east, the age of the dragons who lived there grating through her bones.

The sounds of dwarven picks rang out from the mines north of Dvargra, the eternity of the mountains anchoring her.

The serenity of the great forest that housed Arolynos in the south sang through her blood, lifting her.

And within all living things, the Aethyr bobbed benignly, unseen by most, but visible to her now.

The webs that wove between the people and the races of the world played across her fingers.

Whisper-thin, the threads tied them all together. Fine as spider-silk, strong as steel, every living thing in the land was connected by an immense, intricate web. Every living thing, part of the whole.

And across the web, a blackness marred the weave.

It was corrupt and broken and poisonous.

It torched and tore and maimed.

And she could not look away.

The threads of the humans were blackest of all. And as she traced the threads, they grew blacker still.

The Aethyr shrank from the encroaching darkness, leaving a gaping hole in the web.

They wept at the sight of it, as they clung to their anchors in the Spiritual Realm, swept up in an unrelenting tide of death.

Their cries of anguish were terrible to hear — spiritual beings, ripped from their moorings.

Hot tears streamed down Fae's cheeks. Cold sweat slid icily down her
spine. Her heart raced, pounding in her ears, shaking her to her core.
But still, she could not look away.
This wasn't normal. Wasn't right.
She felt a rough push from the side.
Her brow wrinkled.
She heard a distant voice, familiar.
Fae!
She opened her eyes.
And the world rushed back.

Two almost identical faces peered down at her as she blinked her eyes open.

Sheha and Ty watched her anxiously as she regained her bearings.

"Fae?" It was Sheha. "Are you alright? What happened to your head?"

Fae blinked again, her thoughts a muddied haze. Behind the fuzzy outlines of Sheha and Ty, the leaves of the great *oachoa* tree stirred, floating at the end of their branches.

And a sudden rain of healthy leaves dropped from the canopy, swirling past in thick drifts, unnoticed by the two healers with their focus entirely on Fae.

No wind disturbed the dead still of the air.

She pulled herself up until she sat hunched over between Ty and Sheha. Something hurt, but she couldn't focus enough to work out what. Her thoughts were a mess of fragments tossed about in a storm. And underlying it all, an unrelenting urgency pulsed at her — a need to *go*.

"I'm okay. I think. I..." She clutched at the wisps of the vision as they swirled around her head, neither dissipating, nor slowing enough for her to grasp. But a part of her felt like she'd... *recognised* pieces of it.

Whispers. Calling. Pleading.

"Can you hear that?" she asked the twins. They exchanged a concerned glance.

"Are you sure you're okay?" Sheha asked again. "Do you feel dizzy? You must've hit your head on something..." Her brow furrowed, distorting her face. Sheha never frowned. She was always laughing, her eyes constantly crinkled and smiling. Ty was the one prone to fits of seriousness. And his face gave nothing away as he watched her.

Fae shook her head, ignoring how sluggish it felt, how the world slid drunkenly to the side. She had to get up. Her heart still pounded a war drum in her chest, but the hope she'd felt before was replaced with a sense of urgency that wasn't hers. A knowing that time was running out.

"I need to get to the Circle," she decided, standing with a little help from Ty. The council of Eldra had been discussing the Aethyr just yesterday. They would know what to do.

Ty's hand gripped her arm as he pulled her up, and she swallowed a hiss of pain. Nodding her thanks, she gently disengaged his helping hand.

Her arm felt bruised under her clothes. Her sides ached. Every movement sent bolts of pain though her body. Her thoughts eddied again. What had happened?

Was it... real?

"It can wait," Ty said, his arms hovering towards her as she swayed on her feet. "What happened to you?"

"I'm fine," Fae insisted, fighting to stay upright. If the pain had been limited to one part of her, she might have favoured a side. As it was, her body ached all over, her limbs weak and sore. It hurt to breathe. It hurt not to.

Ty's eyes narrowed.

"At least let us have a look at you—" He went to help her again, but she waved his hands away.

She drew in a shaky breath, and stood as straight as she could. They needed to *listen* to her. She felt twitchy, like time was running out. They didn't have the time to fuss over her. "Please," she said, meeting his eyes, "I need to speak to the Eldra."

She felt both gazes on her, weighing her. They kept staring at her head, and she lifted a hand to it. Winced as her fingers met broken skin.

Behind her, Fae felt the wind stir in her hair, heard it twirling the leaves of the Great Tree. Heard the vague whispers...

Whispers she'd never heard before today.

Was this what it was like to hear the Aethyr?

She looked up at the twins — they showed no signs that they heard the whispers too, nothing in their eyes but concern.

They didn't know the half of it.

Fae held her ground, the whispers at her back filling her ears.

Eventually, Ty let out a reluctant sigh. "Alright." He glanced across at his sister. "We're going there anyway."

Fae blew out a breath of relief. And winced at the pain.

"Thank you," she said quickly, avoiding the piercing look she sensed from him. But she couldn't hide the way her body shook when she went to put one foot in front of the other.

Violent tremors wracked her, and she stumbled.

"Eah!" Sheha swore, ducking to help her. "Okay, physica first," she said, looping her arm under Fae's. "The Circle can wait. What *happened* to you?" Deep grey eyes, a mirror of her brother's, studied her. But Fae still didn't know what to tell them, how to describe it. Was it a dream? A vision? A hallucination?

The scenes were still vivid in her mind's eye. And they had been so powerful. She could still feel the blackness crawling across the fabric of the world. Spreading.

Her head pounded.

The way the Aethyr shrank away from it, leaving a gaping hole in their wake... The Aethyr were the life in everything. If they couldn't enter the blackness, what was happening within it? Within Arland?

If the Aethyr couldn't exist, it spelled the end of all living things.

Including Arolynos.

Fae's breath caught in her chest, her gut twisted with a soul-wrenching fear.

As if in response, more leaves showered down over them from the canopy above. Sheha swore softly. A muscle clenched in Ty's jaw.

Fae suppressed a shudder.

"You've got it wrong," she said, breath coming in short gasps. Her eyes pleaded with them. "I can wait. This can't."

4

THE SPIRIT WITHIN

The twins stared at her.

"Enough of this," Ty said, his voice made of stone even as he wrapped his arm gently around her. His eyes blazed darkly. "Let's hear whatever it is that's so important, and then we're going to the physica." His tunic smelled of fresh herbs and sunlight, his body strong and solid beside her while the world still insisted on dipping and swaying. She squeezed her eyes shut against the disorientating way her vision swam, and pressed her temple against his side. His heart beat gently in her ear, and the sound of it set her feet back on solid ground.

Not quite trusting herself to speak, Fae nodded and allowed herself to be led to the Circle.

As they walked along the wide walkway of Primary Brachear, Fae concentrated on putting one foot in front of the other, her eyes fixed on the smooth wood beneath her feet, until finally, the path sloped up to bring them to the Circle proper.

Where the huge Primaries of the Great Tree radiated out from the main trunk, a cavernous fissure dived down into the heart of the forest giant, as if it had torn itself down the middle to provide the elves with their tree-top haven. The crevasse easily stretched fifty feet across, and at least as deep, and was filled with the tree's own resin, polished to such a high shine that it was as clear as the waters of a mountain spring.

Standing in the Circle was to float over the heart of Arolynos itself.

And this was where the Eldra discussed matters of the greatest importance.

She leaned heavily on Ty, her hand fisted in the fabric of his tunic as they traversed the polished floor. The stiffness in his spine told her just how much he misliked her choice to hold off on seeing a healer.

The murmured conversation of the Eldra stumbled to a halt as he helped her into a carved, high-back wooden chair.

"What is this?" Hara Lyn spoke first. As the Leader of the People, she sat at the head of the vast, oval slab of solid wood at the centre of the Circle. "Ty? Sheha?" She drew herself up, and looked to each of them in turn. Her long braided hair looped around at the nape of her neck, and the tips of her tapered ears curved gracefully upward toward the crown of her head.

"We *tried* to take her to the physica," Sheha said with a helpless shrug, "but she insisted on coming here first."

"Well aren't you healers?" Jax remonstrated from his seat to Hara's right, his voice strong and sure. He was old even by elvish standards, the deep creases at the corners of his eyes perhaps the only sign of his age. Outside of the Circle, he was both renowned healer and teacher, able to deliver a stern lecture with barely more than a glance.

"I assure you she wanted nothing more than to come here," Ty said, his tone informing them exactly what he thought of it. "Let her say her piece and we'll be on our way."

Jax's thick, white-grey eyebrows raised just enough to warrant notice, but he remained silent. The twins had been his best students since even before rising to Eldra themselves; it was rare for either to address him with anything but deference.

"Alright," Hara said with a nod. She turned her gaze towards Fae. "Fae?"

Expectant silence fell around the assembled Eldra.

Artimus and Fabre sat opposite Jax. As scholars, both preferred dealing in collated data and verifiable facts; histories and records and written words — the direct opposite of how Whisperers operated. The two professions didn't cross paths very often.

With Ty and Sheha standing sentry to either side of her, the only Eldra absent, Fae noted with a sinking heart, was Adara, the Eldra Whisperer, so immersed in the spirit dialogue that she was hardly there even when she *was* present.

Listening and divining the messages of the Aethyr required years of dedication. Only the Whisperers could claim such skill. And Adara was beyond gifted, with decades of experience to draw on. Fae had sorely hoped for her counsel.

Fae concentrated her attention on keeping her hands from shaking before looking up to find Hara's gaze.

"I think..." she glanced out into the canopy, the leaves of the trees now suspiciously still, and she felt a moment of doubt. But the pain radiating through her body was real. The message was real. "I think the Aethyr are trying to tell me something," she said.

Hara stilled, but it was Fabre who spoke.

"You're not a Whisperer," she said brusquely, ignoring the unique fact that Fae had never even *sensed* the Aethyr before, let alone interpreted anything from them. Fae bristled at the reminder. But that had all changed now. "What makes you say that?"

"I... saw something," Fae began, and even though they were true, the words felt woefully inadequate to describe her experience. Instead, she slowly rolled up one sleeve. Beneath, a large, purpling bruise flowered. She blinked at the mark, proof that it hadn't just been in her head. That the force of the vision had somehow ripped through the fabric of Eah'lara to affect her physically — something she'd never heard of before.

"What is this?" Jax asked calmly, his eyes glinting with shrewd intelligence. "You should let someone have a look at that."

"This is what happened in my vision," Fae said, her whole body taut with pain.

There was a pause. "I don't understand," Hara said.

Fae took a breath, steeling herself for what she was sure would be a collective disbelief — she still wasn't sure if *she* fully believed it. "The fading in the forest — it's not just Arolynos. It's affecting everything — all over Arland," she began. "I saw the webs that connect us all together. Elves, forests, dwarves, mountains, humans, the plains." She carefully rolled down her sleeve, recalling the way she had *felt* the age of the mountains, the beauty the forests. "And the Aethyr, I saw them too. They *showed* me what's wrong. There's a... a blight in the web. A blackness..." She clutched her hands in frustration at the futility of words to describe it.

"It's hurting the Aethyr. It's as if the Aethyr cannot go wherever the blackness spreads. As if they're dying in its shadow. They're being ripped from Eah'lara. I felt their pain—" She shuddered. Composed herself. She looked up at the Eldra surrounding her, confusion and concern marring their faces. An involuntary shiver shook her frame, and she winced as it wrenched her bruised ribs. The reminder of what else she'd been shown. "There's fire, and destruction in the human lands. I saw them, hunting their own, torching homes, attacking innocent people... people who were just going about their lives..." Her voice disappeared into a whisper as her mind replayed the horrors of her vision, her bruised body throbbing a cruel reminder.

Ty cast a glance at his sister, and Sheha disappeared momentarily, reappearing with a blanket from her chambers adjacent to the Circle. She draped it around Fae's shoulders, her hands lingering to offer a moment of comfort.

"I'm not a Whisperer," Fae murmured to herself. Relaying it back to the Eldra still hadn't helped her answer the most confusing question: why had the spirits chosen *her* to communicate with, of all people? She'd *never* heard the Aethyr before. Why hadn't they shown this all to the Whisperers, who'd been calling for action for months, maybe even years?

Why her?

"She's right, she isn't a Whisperer," Fabre repeated disparagingly from her end of the table, her auburn hair tied into a knot as severe as her expression. "And the Aethyr do not inflict physical harm."

"The Aethyr do what they must to be heard." A dreamy voice carried into the Circle from the right. Fae looked up to see Adara traversing the elegant bridge that led to her chambers. The Whisperer brushed aside a curtain of trailing vines to walk across the clear polished floor of the Circle, and step up to the table.

Adara had a sort of ethereal quality to her. It was in the way she drifted around, in the vague way she spoke when she deemed it necessary to do so, and in the way her eyes rarely seemed to focus on anything in front of her, gazing instead toward something transcending the mortal world: Eah'lara — the Spirit Realm.

Fae didn't think she'd ever been so glad to see her.

A strained silence descended around the room as Adara glided across to Fae, her white-gold hair floating like a cloud around her head. She lowered herself to look Fae in the eye.

"The Aethyr must feel a great need for our help if they have chosen to reach out directly." She placed a gentle hand on her shoulder in solidarity. "They honour you." She stood and turned an icy glare on the two scholars.

"I warned you of this. As have Larah and the others. There are signs! Your dithering and delays and insistence on *proof* have forced the Aethyr to make their peril known through one wholly unprepared for their truths." She turned to Hara, her head high, and spoke with uncharacteristic directness. "How much longer must we wait? There has been darkness in the human lands for years. It is past time to act. If we do not, I can see only death and destruction, and it will reach out to all of us. It will cover the world." Her eyes blazed angrily, but her voice remained level, wrenched under control by a will of pure steel. "The forest already begins to fade around us — the suffering of the Aethyr has reached so far, it touches even our borders. We can no longer hide in our trees. If we continue as we are, all life will be forfeit. Including the Great Tree itself." The room fell silent as everyone digested her words. Fae openly stared at her. She'd never heard Adara speak more than two sentences in one conversation, and certainly never with such vehemence. But she was glad the Whisperer chose now to speak, while the sense of urgency still thrummed through Fae's veins.

Artimus cleared his throat.

"The humans are not all as bad as that," he chided gently.

Adara turned her icy glare on the scholar. "The darkness that surrounds them affects the very natural order of the land. The spirits themselves weep! This, we told you. Look at Fae! Now they *show* us the wrongs in humanity. In this, Fabre, you are right — have you ever seen the spirits manifest physically before?"

"It would do us no harm to investigate," Jax placated, his voice soothing despite the tension in the room. "And it would do ill to neglect spiritkind." He shrugged. "It has been many years since we liaised with the humans. Perhaps it is time for us to reach out the hand of friendship once more."

Hara waited silently for everyone to finish, her elbows resting on the table, hands steepled before her face.

"We have grown too comfortable in this haven my ancestors built for us." She sighed deeply, and the admission seemed to age her a decade. "Adara is right to say that we have hidden away in these forests, isolating ourselves from the world." Her troubled gaze dropped to the tabletop. "And now the Aethyr themselves suffer for our neglect." She took a moment to collect herself before straightening to meet the eyes of her fellow Eldra. "It is past time for debate and discussion. It is time to act. Send envoys to the humans, and to the dwarves too. Let us see if they have experienced any unsettling signs, as we have. We are long overdue in tending those friendships in any case." The sadness in her eyes pinched at the corners of her face. "We have stayed away too long."

The Eldra fell to discussing specifics immediately, and the focus of the room fell away from Fae. Endless questions churned through her head. Why had the Aethyr chosen *her* to send their message? Why now? And what was the relevance of the human woman? And the child?

She traced the grain of the tabletop with one finger as her head filled with the white noise of her thoughts.

A patient kind of silence fell around her, and the sudden change jolted her from her reverie. She looked up to see all eyes on her.

"Sorry?" she said. Hara smiled sympathetically, but it was Ty who spoke in her defence.

"I think Fae has offered us enough." He stood. "She's clearly exhausted, and owes us a trip to the physica. We can continue this tomorrow?" He phrased it as a question, but no one thought to mistake it as such.

Hara nodded. "It is not by chance that this issue has come to us twice in as many days. We should all take some time to give it our full consideration." She met the eyes of each of them, lingering a moment longer on Fae, before nodding again. "Tomorrow. Then we act," she said softly. She stood, and left the Circle without another word.

Fae, suddenly exhausted, went to push herself up, and felt a hand rest on her shoulder. She looked up to see a small curve to the corner of Sheha's mouth, and a barely perceptible shake of her head.

Fae stayed put.

They waited for the other Eldra to disperse; some back to their chambers, branching away from the Circle like spokes on a wheel; some returning to their other duties elsewhere in Arolynos.

"I'll meet you there?" Sheha said, sending her brother a look, the points of her ears twitching — a rare sign of unease.

Ty gave a curt nod in response, and Sheha narrowed her eyes at him before turning to leave.

When only Fae and Ty remained in the Circle, he knelt down in front of her. Concern, and something darker, harder, warred in his deep, grey eyes.

"How are you?" he asked, his face the flat calm of the ocean before a storm.

"I'm just shaken, that's all," Fae replied, trying to soften the tension in him.

In truth, she felt far worse than she thought she had any right to. She went to stand, to prove to him — and herself — that she really was fine.

Fire lanced over her back and ribs, stealing the breath from her in a ragged gasp. She cried out, doubling over, instinctively curling inwards. But the motion pulled her back muscles taut, shooting pain up her spine instead. Her knees gave out beneath her, a helpless whimper escaping her lips.

Then Ty's arms were around her, and before Fae knew what was happening, he'd scooped her up, lifting her easily. She stubbornly wanted to insist that there was no need, that she could make it on her own, but when she looked up and saw his face, his jaw was clenched tight, and his eyes blazed ahead. She swallowed her words and let him carry her. Besides, her head felt as though it might split in two, and Ty's arms felt safe and warm around her. She squeezed her eyes shut against the world, and leant into his shoulder, willing the pain to ease. Ty, moving with all the grace of his race, didn't jostle her at all, and carried her swiftly from the Circle.

When he finally put her down, he'd only gone as far as his own chambers, a short walk from the Circle. He gestured for her to stay put, and turned to prepare what she recognised as a simple first aid. He put some water on to boil, and gathered some items together: herbs from a basket on the sun-drenched windowsill, bandages from a cupboard, a tea-pot, and a pestle and mortar. Collecting everything onto a tray, he carried it over to Fae's chair, pulling up a stool for himself.

"Where?" he said, his eyes flicking to her head. The look behind his eyes belied his calm exterior, and she silently moved to remove her shawl and belt. The movement pulled at her back and her arms, but she gritted her teeth and eventually slid the shawl from her shoulders, leaving her in the soft linen of her blouse and skirt.

She took a breath, and lifted the blouse to show him the source of her pain.

Even she was surprised at how bad it looked. Deep purple and red bruising bloomed across her entire right side, with more marks and broken skin stretching around to cover her back. She stared at herself, speechless with shock. Ty's initial intake of breath was his only reaction as he studied her bruises with the pragmatic eyes of a healer.

Fae watched him, lost for words.

"There you are," Sheha said as she walked in. "I wondered where you'd got to when you didn't turn up— Eah!" she swore when she caught sight of the discolouration stark against Fae's pale skin.

Ty nodded, although his face betrayed nothing. "Aside from the gash on your head, it looks as though the worst of it is on your back," he said. "And your head has already stopped bleeding. Does it hurt here?" He met her eyes as he pushed gently on her abdomen. She shook her head. He paused, considering. "Would you like Sheha to take over?" Fae shook her head again. She felt just as comfortable with either of them. Ty nodded again. "Turn around and lift up your shirt." Sheha came over then, pulling a blanket from a chest beside the couch. Ty turned his back, and Sheha helped Fae to lift the blouse up over her back, handing her the blanket to cover her front.

"It was only a vision," Fae whispered. "I didn't know they... hurt..." she trailed off, still at a loss as to how to describe it. Ty was silent as he worked, feeling around her ribs for breaks. Sheha watched him for a minute, and then retreated to the kitchen where she began preparing something to eat. Fae smiled. Sheha always cooked when she was worried.

Once he had satisfied himself that there were no serious injuries, Ty sat back and met Fae's eyes with a sigh.

"There are stories, centuries old, that tell of a kind of Whisperer they called 'Seers' — they saw visions. But I've never heard of anything so physical." He shook his head as further words failed him. "Why didn't you say something when we found you?" Instead of keeping her injuries covered until she stood before the collective Eldra.

"I..." How to explain the urgency that had filled her? That her body's suffering was trivial beside the suffering of the Aethyr? Fae dropped her gaze, unable to hold his. "I guess I didn't really believe it was real," she said to her hands. "It was only when I had to describe it that I had to admit what had happened."

Ty reached over and gently lifted her chin. "You should have told us." His sad smile showed the worry beneath his stony calm, and she felt guilty for not confiding in them before reaching the Circle. Sheha continued to potter, but there was a stiffness in her spine that said she was listening. Fae dropped her gaze into her lap again. Ty sighed softly, and stood to tend to her head. As he parted the hair around the wound, Fae's jaw clenched against the stinging reminder of her vision. She let out an involuntary hiss, despite his gentleness.

He carefully washed out the wound, and numbed it with a salve of florestem and willowbark. As he stitched the skin back together, Fae remembered the blow that had created it. Her arms came up around her chest, where they'd kicked her. "They saw me — the humans."

Ty stilled. He tied off his stitch before crouching down by her side.

"The humans — in your vision — *they* did this to you?" he breathed. He stared at her. Sheha dropped a plate in the kitchen, the glazed clay shattering loudly against the wooden floor. She bent to retrieve the pieces with shaking hands and finally turned, her normally smiling face lined and taut. She stared, then voiced the same word Fae had been wondering herself.

"How?"

Fae shook her head. "I don't know. But... I don't think that was the point of what I saw." Her memories of the vision were already fading into fuzzy outlines and vague impressions. All that remained clear was the sense of urgency that continued to nag at her thoughts, the sense that she should be *going*.

Only, one other part had caught in her mind.

She swallowed. "I saw a woman. Her village burned around her but she was... praying. She was holding a child, and praying. To the Aethyr, I think." She paused, making sure she remembered it right. Sheha stilled, waiting. When Fae looked back at Ty, he seemed to be holding his breath.

"What was she saying?"

Without even thinking, Fae repeated the woman's words to him. They were burned into her memory with fire and violence.

"She said something about saving her child. She said, '*She has the Spirit within her.*'"

Ty sat back on his heels and exhaled a long breath. Sheha came over from the kitchen, and sank into a chair. Ty exchanged a glance with his sister, then took a long look at Fae before speaking.

"Have you ever heard about Joa's Last?" he asked slowly. She shook her head no. He blew out a breath, paused, and then took his seat on the stool again, looking into the middle-distance, as if recalling a lost memory.

"Ty," Sheha said from her seat. "You can't think...?"

Ty glanced at his sister. "Why not? It fits."

"It's just a story."

Fae looked from one to the other. "What is? Who's Joa?"

Ty gave her a long look, and stood again. "Let me finish stitching that wound, then we can talk it over," he said.

Fae sat in silence while he finished his work, her mind too full to think straight. She needed answers before she started asking more questions.

Sheha rose, and draped a knitted cardigan around Fae's shoulders before putting the finishing touches to the soup she'd made.

Ty tied off the final stitch, and carried the tray back over to the kitchen. Sheha leaned in to murmur something that Fae couldn't hear, but she caught a snatch of the conversation that followed.

"—she may have lived in my house," Sheha said softly, her words barely audible, "but she's always felt safer with you." Ty's eyes flicked to where Fae sat, still in the chair in which he'd put her, and he muttered something back, his face flat and unrevealing. Sheha's scowling rebuke put an end to the exchange, and Ty disappeared into the bedroom, emerging with extra blankets, placing them neatly folded on the end of the couch.

While Sheha ladled soup into three bowls, Ty replaced his stool with the final chair in the room. He took a moment to order his thoughts, before leaning forward, his arms resting on his knees.

"To understand the story of Joa," he began, "we have to go back a little further..."

5

BATTLES TO WAR

Ty shifted in his seat, and laced his fingers together where they hung between his knees.

Once upon a time, there was one Spirit.

She was the Mother Spirit, Aethyreomma — the first Aethyr. She was the embodiment of the earth. No; more than that. She embodied all that we know. The earth, yes, but also the seas, the sky, and the stars.

Aethyreomma loved the earth. She loved the forests of the southern mountain ranges, teeming with natural life. She loved the cold, northern mountains, rich with veins of gold and gemstones. She loved the vast, open plains in between, and the endless, glittering seas around them all.

For a time, the earth was a peaceful, quiet place. The sun shone warm upon it. The rains nourished the soil. The two moons illuminated the night. And the only creatures to call it home were the mighty dragons, who were the kings and queens of the land and sky.

And, so perfect was it, that other life began to take form. First came the fish, swimming down the rivers, and through the ocean waves. Then birds soared through the skies. Small creatures colonised the land, and then bigger ones. And before long, the earth was covered in all manner of life. And Aethyreomma was overjoyed to see it.

In time, came elves. They came into a world brimming with natural wonder, and they grew to respect it, for they knew no different. They built their homes in the forests, living alongside the myriad creatures that had come before them.

Later, dwarves appeared in the mountains. They lived in harsher climes, and were hardy and resilient folk.

Centuries more passed, the elves living in their forests, and the dwarves in their mountains, each learning and developing new skills and crafts from their environment. The two races crossed paths, although seldom, as their realms were far apart.

And all the while, the Mother Spirit looked on, marvelling at the vitality of the world.

Then one day, a new race emerged, stumbling across the plains. They were not gifted with grace, or resilience. They were neither tall and willowy, like the elves, nor stocky and strong, like the dwarves. They were neither, and they were a little of both. They were humans.

The humans bred quicker than their sibling races, and their numbers swelled. But they sickened and died easily. And they made up for their shortfalls in one thing: resolve.

The humans made their homes on the plains, harvesting trees and grasses to build shelters from the ground up. After a time they began digging the earth itself, farming crops and mining materials. While the elves and the dwarves looked to the nature around them, the humans looked to themselves, and worked hard to improve their race. They built trade, infrastructure, even religion. And the strength of their divine conviction only spurred them on to reach for more.

The humans took over the plains, their paths overlapping with the other races of the world, their borders encroaching on the forests and the mountains. And with their growing population, and the expansion of their territories, tensions rose between the races as each sought to protect its own.

And Aethyreomma looked on, knowing fear for the first time.

Eventually, the inevitable happened: humans took what wasn't theirs to take. They stole from the forests, uprooting trees and hunting the animals that made their homes there. They mined from the mountains, digging out rocks and resources to build their towns and cities. They hunted the mighty dragons, for reasons beyond reason.

They waged a kind of war on the rest of the world, plundering and taking.

The elves and dwarves confronted the humans, asking them to stop. Telling them to halt their destructive actions. But the humans knew no other way to make room for their people but to expand, take, and consume.

And that's when the first skirmishes broke out between the races.

Skirmishes turned to fights, fights turned to battles, battles turned to war.

Those years are penned only in blood and fire, as the War of the Races tore the land apart, killing thousands, spilling violence and death into every corner of the earth.

When Aethyreomma saw what was happening to the world she so loved, her sadness knew no bounds. She knew not what to do, how to stop her children from killing and destroying.

And so the Mother Spirit wept.

She wept for seven years.

For seven years, the Spirit tore herself apart, and each tear carried a piece of herself to the earth.

For seven years, the Rains of her tears washed away the sins of the races, and quenched the fires of war at last.

After those seven years, a million pieces, *millions* of pieces of the Spirit inhabited every living thing on earth. Giving all life spirit. And giving the world new life.

Time passed, and the races of the world rebuilt themselves anew. Elf, dwarf, and human numbers alike had been worse than decimated in the War of the Races. As they slowly picked up what was left of their people, and knitted them back together again, each race steered well clear of the others, keeping rigidly to their own respective territories. The dragons, whose numbers had fared the worst, retreated to their peninsula in the east, and have barely been seen since.

When the time came again for humans to out-populate their resources, they set out to the south and to the west, giving the forests and the mountains a wide berth.

And so it was for hundreds of years. The dwarves kept to their mountain strongholds, the elves their forest utopia, and the humans branched out into the plains, building towns and cities and roads between. All living peaceably enough, but all apart.

Not long after the Rains, the elves became aware of the Aethyr. The spirits had not been there before the Rains, but now the forest teemed with them. And for the most part, even the most skilled of Whisperers felt only the faintest of susurrations from the Aethyr; feelings and whispers for which they were named.

But one elf boy with an unusually strong Aethyrial connection was born, and he was called Joa. He claimed that the Aethyr *showed* him things, something no Whisperer had ever claimed before. He claimed that he did not merely Listen; that he Saw. And he began to predict events that were yet to pass: births, deaths, weather, wars.

His tutors did not know what to make of his claims — they did not understand what he was. And so he, along with his predictions, was dismissed as a strange kind of insanity. And indeed, over time, like many strong Whisperers before him and since, he lost his grip on the physical world.

When he eventually passed on, Joa left behind a journal of his visions, and the predictions that were borne of them. The journal was archived. And spent many long years gathering dust.

Centuries after his death, scholars rediscovered his diaries, and noted the predictions of events that had since transpired. Initially, these were considered nothing more than coincidences. But over time, more and more events were linked back to an entry in Joa's journals, and the connection could no longer be ignored.

Scholars began poring over his works, matching his predictions with centuries of history. Those that had no match, they made note of.

One in particular worried them.

Joa's last entry detailed a growing sickness in the earth. One which would seem distant, but far-reaching. The sickness would spread through the land, and with it would come a child of the Spirit, embodying the Spirit within them; one who could wield the power of Eah'lara to bring a stop to the devastation, and deliver the world's people from their own end.

. . .

Ty paused to stretch his limbs. He noticed Fae's empty bowl and stood to put it to one side. He talked as he pottered.

"Not many believe the old stories any more," he said as he washed and cleared away the dishes. "Scholars argue that, if the Aethyr were all parts of the same entity, they would speak with one voice." He shrugged as if he wasn't convinced. "Even the Whisperers tell us that isn't the way of it, so the stories can't be true. The Aethyr must have always been there, they say. I think it's one of the only things they've ever agreed on." He turned back to her. "I, personally, like the old versions. They make better stories than the histories do at least; there was war, there was rain, the war ended — just doesn't have the same elegance to it." He sat back down, and leant back on in his chair, tipping it onto two legs while he remembered his place in the story.

"A lot of Joa's predictions *have* occurred, but the journal entries that correspond to them have a tendency to be rather cryptic; they leave a lot to interpretation. Many argue that Joe's Last is the same; that there's more room for interpretation in it than first appears. For there to be a sickness in the world, there would have to be a sickness in the Aethyr. And for there to be an individual with the 'original' Spirit in them—" he made air-quotes with his hands "—was inconceivable. So it couldn't possibly as simple — or as dire — as that."

He dropped his chair back onto four legs with a *thunk*. "But—" pointing a finger at Fae, he sat forward and rested his elbows back on his knees "—the words you heard in your vision..." he trailed off, spreading his hands in a way that suggested the impossible might have just become possible.

Fae's head spun. "You think this child I saw is some sort of embodiment of the Mother Spirit?" she said, somewhat incredulously. "That she's going to wield the power of the Aethyr, to save the Aethyr?" Ty exchanged a glance with Sheha. Fae wagged a finger between them. "Hey, I know that look — don't do that twin-thing-secret-glance to shut me out." She looked from one to the other. "What do you believe?"

"Well, it's all starting to take a sort of shape now isn't it?" Ty smiled and helped her to her feet. "Joa's final vision finally has a match. *'She has the Spirit within her'*. But what happens next, I don't know." He walked her from the living room. Stopping at the door to the bedroom, he held it open, waving her through. Fae hovered in the doorway, and turned back to him.

In the space of a morning, she somehow felt as if her whole world had changed, and likewise hadn't changed at all. As if a door had opened, and now stood waiting for her to walk through it.

"What do I do now?" she asked.

"Sleep. Rest." Ty said with a small smile. He reached out and tucked a stray strand of hair behind her ear. "We can theorise more on legends and prophesies tomorrow." He leant forward to press his lips lightly against her forehead, and closed the door between them.

6

FRAYED EDGES

Fae jolted awake to the feeling that she'd forgotten something important. She recognised that tug of urgency, the sense that she had somewhere to be, and it wasn't here.

She heard the murmured rumble of nearby conversation as the world filtered back in past her sleep-addled senses, and blinked her eyes open.

She'd fallen asleep in Ty's bedroom, and she had to smile at how very *Ty* the space was. It was clean and fresh, but had little effort spared to decor. The bed was of simple construction, the blankets plain and unadorned. A hand-woven rug lay upon the floor, but did little to soften the bareness of the room. Any personal effects lying about the place all seemed to be related to his work; books — medical and otherwise — overflowed from shelves carved into the branches that framed the room, and small planters of herbs lined the window sills.

The door to the living area opened a crack, and Ty's face appeared in the gap. Seeing that she was awake, he edged into the room and shut the door silently behind him. "How are you feeling?" he said, keeping his voice lowered.

Fae pushed herself up slowly to a seated position, mentally noting how her body felt as she moved.

"Good, I think," she said. "All things considered." She moved cautiously, expecting something to twinge painfully at any minute, and remind her just how *not* good she was.

She lowered her legs carefully over the edge of the bed. Her entire body was one, steady ache, every limb both tender and stiff at the same time. But she wasn't shaking anymore, and her head no longer throbbed. The rest of her, however, still felt black and blue.

Stretching her arms out in front of her, she winced despite herself. She glanced up at Ty — his face remained neutral, but his eyes darkened.

"Correction," she said with a wry smile, "I feel exactly as I should the day after..." she trailed off. Avoiding his eyes, she stood, testing her footing. Aside from the ache in her legs, she was steady enough. Even Ty relaxed back against the wall.

"The Eldra are here," he said as she padded across the floor to the washroom, "I didn't want to leave you here alone, and Hara didn't want to wait. She wants to speak to you again."

Fae looked into the mirror over the basin and cried out.

If anything, she looked *worse* than yesterday — deeper stains were now showing through the superficial bruising, which was darkened and mottled; the swelling beneath the gash on her head had discoloured, and the resulting mark spread across her temple all the way to her right eye. Black and blue clung to the skin around her eyes, and she had a split in her lip she hadn't even noticed before.

She looked truly awful. She turned to face him again, aware now why his lips pressed together like that.

"Can I clean myself up a bit first?"

Ty's responding smile *almost* reached his eyes.

"Of course," he said, pushing himself upright. "Towels are on the shelf. Take as long as you need."

"Thank you," she mouthed gratefully, and ducked back into the washroom to make the best of her disheveled appearance.

When Fae stepped into the living area a few minutes later, she felt worlds better. The warm water had loosened *most* of the stiffness in her muscles, eased *some* of the residual pain. But the silence that fell at her reappearance reminded her just how bad she still looked.

Sheha's eyes widened at the sight of her.

"Please," Fae said, suddenly very self-conscious, "don't stop on my account."

"Fae." Sheha recovered quickly. "Come and sit down. How are you feeling?" She patted the empty seat next to her, her face an almost perfect mirror of her brother's concern. Fae avoided the gazes of the other Eldra as she made her way to sit among them, but it was impossible not to notice how horrified they were at her appearance.

The sadness on Hara's face deepened to bracket the skin around her mouth. Jax eyed her with gentle concern. Fabre and Artimus wore matching disgust on their faces, although Fae knew it wasn't directed at her — elves were a peaceful people and, while skilled in many ways, they avoided violence at all costs. Adara gazed out into the trees from where she stood by the door, set apart from the group.

Fae sat in the seat Sheha offered, and Ty handed her a cup of hot tea from across the table. She nodded her thanks and wrapped her hands around the warmth of it, bolstered by his care of her more than the concern of the others. It was the little moments, the small gestures, that warmed her heart.

"I'm okay," she said to them. "Just a little bruised." She gestured to herself, "As you can clearly see. But, thankfully nothing serious." She smiled ruefully. Their expressions didn't alter.

She didn't know what to say to them. She had no words of comfort to offer. So she took a sip of her tea, taking the moment to compose her thoughts while their eyes bored into the top of her head. Placing the cup on the table, she looked around at the Eldra — the most respected among the elven community, the ones who had taken her in when she had no family to care for her. And yet they looked to her now as if *she* would provide answers. As if *she* knew what to do next.

She met their eyes one by one, wondering who would break the awkward silence first. Her eyes eventually came to Hara, who appeared to be waiting for her to say something, and finally back to Ty. The wrinkled concern on his face had smoothed, and he gave an almost imperceptible nod. It gave her the spur she needed.

"I guess you're all here to discuss what happened yesterday," she said. It wasn't a question, but the Eldra nodded in agreement, one by one. "Then if you could all put your eyes back into their sockets, let's discuss." Ty's mouth curled up at the corner. Sheha grinned openly. The others shifted uncomfortably in their seats.

"I believe the last point of discussion," Fae volunteered, "was the matter of whether or not to send an envoy to the humans. Surely that goes without saying?" She looked around at the Eldra gathered. Whoever went, and wherever they went, *someone* needed to go. Her hands clenched around her cup, the feeling inside her becoming hard to ignore as it urged her to go. *Go*.

But where? And why? The Aethyr were hurting, yes, but what was she supposed to do about it? She'd been hoping the Eldra would know. That someone here would know, but it seemed as if they were looking to her for answers just as much as she'd been looking to them.

"The question isn't whether or not we send someone," Hara corrected gently, clearing her throat. "That is without question. The question is *where* to send them? To whom?" She clasped her hands tightly and rested them on the table before her. "Throldon is the capital in Arland, but its political state has never been stable. And we are long out of touch with their world." She sighed, and Fae was struck by how tired she looked. "Our knowledge of them is outdated. But what we do know is this: power shifts between a faction known as the Unity, distant royalty, and no one at all. The city has been a chaotic ruin since they first began fighting over it." She made an uncharacteristic sound of exasperation in her throat. "There is a reason we've had so little to do with humans! They become so easily wrapped up in their own petty disputes, that they do not see, nor care about the world. Nor even their own people around them."

"They can't all be like that, surely?" Fae said, thinking of the parts of her vision that had shown her a peaceful existence, unrecognisable from the world Hara was describing.

"No, child." Jax leant forward in his seat to rest his arms in front of him on the table, wrapping his hands around a steaming mug. "They are not all that way. There are some, known as Peacekeepers, who travel the land giving aid and support to those who need it. They provide healing, spiritual solace and even help to rebuild where it is needed." He smiled gently. "For the most part, humans are more like them than the Unity. But people are afraid." His expression darkened, and he regarded her from under heavy brows. "They are afraid for their families, for their livelihood, and for themselves. They bend to the ideals of thugs to protect themselves. It becomes their way of life; how they survive." He passed a hand over his face, and leant back in his chair again. "Humanity has slowly fallen into a kind of gruesome wilderness. The Peacekeepers are there, holding it together by fraying edges, but they are few and far between now, and hard to find."

"What is this 'Unity' that you mentioned?" Fae asked, having never learned any human history.

"The Unity—" Artimus cleared his throat and straightened, his thick-set ears disappearing into wild, greying hair "—started with a man called Russel Stuart. And it has become the predominating force in Arland." He stared into the bottom of his empty cup, his voice darkening. "Stuart appealed to the worst of humanity with his message of 'every man for himself'. No man beholden to anyone. No man to pay taxes to another, nor toil over land not his own. To the poor, it sounded like the freedom they craved. But it tore down any remaining social structure the humans had with one simple phrase. And it turned into what we know humanity to be today — dangerous, primitive, and savage." Artimus paused in his narrative to stand, and walked over to the stove.

"The Unity has the primary political structure in Arland, if you can call it that," he said, helping himself to more tea from the pot. "Last we heard, Russel's son, Malcolm, now carries the torch for his father's mantra. He began by murdering his own father. You could say he's a kind of leader, if they believed in such things." He resumed his seat at the table with a freshly filled cup, taking a sip as he did so.

A measured silence fell around the room.

Artimus glanced around the table, his expression sheepish. "I'm sorry —" he lifted his cup. "Did anyone else want some more?"

Ty exchanged a long-suffering look with Sheha as he got to his feet. "I'll put another pot on," he said.

Fae's frown deepened as she considered everything she'd heard. Humans sounded truly awful. She wondered how the peaceful village she'd seen in her vision had space to exist in a race that seemed so thoroughly rooted in violence.

"Why rely on the humans at all?" Fabre spoke brusquely, always seemingly irate at something. "What of the elves in Alyla?" She glanced about the table, waiting for someone to second her thoughts. "Hearthstone? Perhaps the dragons have something to say on this. What of the dwarves?" When no one was forthcoming, she pushed on, her tone taking on a desperate edge. "There are others with whom we could collaborate." She straightened, and gave an impatient huff. "I propose we send an envoy to each of these cities with the same message. We'll need to collate our findings before we act." She paused, and added a reluctant afterthought. "Do we even know how to locate these Peacekeepers? If they *are* the only force for good left in humanity, we should at least seek them out." She folded her arms. "Even if they are clueless about the spirits that surround them."

"Not all are as ignorant as you might fear." Adara spoke up from her position in the doorway. She turned to face the group, but her gaze focused *elsewhere*. "There is one who hears the voices of spirits as we do." Her eyes found Fae as she spoke. "Find her, and there is hope." A gentle breeze drifted through the open door, sending her ethereal hair wafting about her head in a hypnotic dance. Her eyes followed the wind, and she turned back to her vista.

Fae stared gaping at the Whisperer's back.

Of course.

A familiar, desperate prayer filled her ears.

"The woman in my vision." she whispered. "She's alive?" It had seemed as though everyone in the burning village would surely die. Hope bloomed in her chest. Perhaps, if this woman could be found, they might find some answers. Maybe she could help.

Adara glanced over her shoulder to fix her with an unusual gaze of dove grey flecked with moonlight... and a tinge of sadness.

"The Aethyr showed you this for a reason," was all she said.

Fae's heart kicked at her words: *The Aethyr showed you this.*

The Aethyr had spoken to her. A smile pulled at her lips.

"Yes," Hara said, "Ty mentioned there was more detail to your vision than we discussed yesterday." She waved a hand towards Fae, inviting her to elaborate. "What more did you see?"

Fae steeled herself, and began from the beginning, relating the experience in as much detail as she could remember. When she came to the woman's prayer, there was an unnatural stillness in the room.

"What?" Fae said, looking around the table.

Hara leaned forward, her face gone ashen. "Do you remember arriving here, in Arolynos?" she said, her eyes on her hands, clasped together so tightly her knuckles were white.

Fae hesitated. "No," she said, her forehead creasing in confusion. She was so young when she moved in with Sheha, barely five, and she'd never remembered anything about what happened before that. "I was told I was an orphan, brought here to be cared for. No one knew my parents." She looked between Hara, Artimus, and Jax — all had still been Eldra back then. "Why?"

Jax exchanged a meaningful glance with Artimus. Both looked to Hara, who in turn watched Adara as she stared out into the canopy.

"Fifteen years ago," Hara began, "Adara came to me in my quarters. She was not yet Eldra, but she was already the most gifted Whisperer we'd seen in decades." A small smile caught at Adara's lips, the only sign that she heard the words of her Leader. "She was hysterical," Hara continued. "She'd had a dream, but insisted it was real. I tried to calm her down, but that only upset her more." Hara's eyes flared at the memory. By the door, Adara absently rubbed her hands over her sleeves. Hara turned back to the table. "She told me about this woman, and the child, and the prayer.

"When I finally convinced her to return to her rooms, we walked back through the Circle." Hara looked up, and met Fae's eyes at last. "And there you were. A tiny little thing, covered in soot and smelling of smoke. Your hair was black with it, your hands and feet scraped and torn. You'd come out of nowhere. But Adara recognised you instantly. 'That's her,' she said to me. 'We must keep her safe.'"

Hara drew in a shaky breath. "And now you've seen the same. Although what it means, I do not know."

Fae's thoughts raced, careening through the corridors of her mind.

It wasn't about the woman in the vision. It was about the child.

She was the girl from her vision. Which meant...

The world dropped out from under her.

Fae stared at Hara.

"I'm... human?"

7

HUMAN

Hara's eyes held a tinge of sadness. She nodded.

"Yes, Fae, you are human."

Fae's mouth dropped open, as if words wanted to come out, but none seemed up to the task. She was human.

She was *human*.

That was why she couldn't sense the Aethyr. But then, why the visions now? She felt everyone's gaze on her. The prickling sense of being watched — those familiar silent eyes — tickled at the back of her neck. The feeling that she was missing something important. She barely noticed it, her mind swimming through syrup. And a wisp of memory glimmered from the depths of her mind like a coin, just out of reach.

She glanced over at Sheha, but she looked just as shocked at the revelation. Across the room, Ty's expression mirrored his sister's. They hadn't known.

Finally, Fae said, "I don't understand."

"The ways of the Aethyr are rarely clear, child," Adara said, finally leaving her post by the door to crouch beside Fae. "But they certainly have an interest in you for some reason, to send you to us." Her eyes held Fae's for a long moment, as if contemplating her properly for the first time. "They show you your past." She smiled. "Perhaps they will also show you a glimpse of your future..." Then she rose, and swept from Ty's home without a further word.

"Well she's right about one thing," Artimus said on the heels of her departure. "Messages from Eah'lara rarely make any sense at all."

"But you've got to admit," Ty said, recovering from his shock to bring another pot of tea to the table, "this poses a lot of questions." He brushed a comforting hand over Fae's shoulder, but she was too lost in her own thoughts to notice.

"Yes, but let's not forget the matter at hand," Fabre said. "And that is this darkness spreading across Eah'lara."

"Indeed, but is Fae's presence here relevant to the solution?" Jax asked.

"Even if she is, we can still send envoys to the other races while we work that out," Artimus said. "The first half of Fae's vision could merely have been a place-holder — a way to insert the message they truly wanted to share. It could have no relevance at all."

Sheha collected herself enough to snort inelegantly. "I find that unlikely, don't you? What about the mother's prayer?"

"All mothers believe their children to be special," Fabre scoffed. "There's no way a human could possibly understand the weight of those words. Nor is it possible for a *person* to have 'the Spirit' in them. It was more likely just a desperate prayer from a desperate woman."

I'm human... Fae's mind stuck fast to the one point that shook her foundations to the core, turning it over and over as the others talked.

"And what about her sudden, magical arrival in the middle of Arolynos from a burning village in Arland?" Sheha was arguing.

The peaceful village scene played in Fae's mind. Then the one of fire and death. Which part of humanity did she belong to?

"That's just the point," Artimus said. "We don't know yet. And while we untangle *that* riddle, we can still be sending scouts out into Arland to investigate what's going on in the world."

"We should send envoys to Dvargra and Alyla also," Fabre insisted. "We must seek counsel from all sources."

"Agreed." Hara stood. "Send three groups to counsel with all the races. If the troubles in the human lands are affecting the natural order as far as our forests, if they blacken the Aethyr themselves, then it affects all of us. Perhaps our allies have seen other changes we should know about."

One after the other, the other Eldra stood in agreement.

The action brought Fae snapping back to herself and she stumbled to her feet, pushing her chair back to crash to the floor.

"I'll go." The words flew out of her, yanked by an invisible tether that pulled on something deep inside her.

Hara silenced her with a gesture. "No Fae," she said firmly. "I know you want to find answers, but you are in no state to travel. Physically or emotionally. This is a lot to handle, and we need to decipher your part in it." Her eyes softened, and she took both of Fae's hands in her own. "I'm sorry, but you will stay." She turned to the others. "Inform the scouts. They have a long journey to prepare for. They will know who to send. We will pick this up after preparations are made."

And with that, the meeting was over.

Ty showed his fellow Eldra from his home, and for a moment, Fae was left alone, her mind a whirlwind of information it had no idea how to absorb, trying to untangle the significance of it all.

Within the maelstrom, a common thread shone through.

Her *mother*.

Who was she? *What* was she? How had she — a human — communed with the Aethyr? Where was she now? Was she even still alive? What was the meaning of her prayer?

Fae massaged her fingers against her temples, a sharp ache blooming behind her eyes.

Her vision blurred as the ache worsened, and Ty's kitchen lurched away from her. She squeezed her eyes closed, but even through her eyelids, she saw the light in the room brighten to piercing intensity.

She opened her eyes a crack.

But Ty's home had disappeared.

All around her was blinding white. She shielded her eyes.

"What the...?" she muttered to herself.

Then her pain vanished. All of it. She staggered at the sudden relief.

She felt ten times lighter in an instant. Her muscles were no longer knotted in pain, her skin no longer stung, and the deep ache of bruising faded to a dull reminder. All in the time it took her to draw breath. She straightened, lifting a hand to her head, and felt only a slight tenderness. Like the gash Ty had painstakingly stitched had been only a bruise.

The light around her dimmed to a bearable level, and she was finally able to look around.

Soft white surrounded her. And among the white, shimmering threads glinted, almost invisible against the light.

The familiar sensation of being watched, of someone hiding behind a curtain in her mind returned. The hairs at the nape of her neck prickled.

Fae. *A voice sounded in the infinity around her. No, many voices. Like a choir singing in her ear.*

In her head.

It is time, *the choir continued.* She will carry us into the darkness, and lead the mortal races into the light.

"What?" *she exclaimed aloud. But the multi-voice wasn't finished.*

Born of the Mortal Realm, bound by the Spiritual, she is the one Eah has waited for.

Spiritchild.

Reality seemed tipped on its head. First her forgotten past, now a foretold future? Spiritchild? Human?

What am I?

The voices could only be those of the Aethyr... but the Aethyr didn't communicate with spoken words. They used feelings, and abstract sensations... didn't they?

"This is ridiculous," *she told herself firmly.*

She blinked.

Ty's home reappeared around her. The light was gone. Ty's long strides thumped gently on the walkway outside as he returned from the Circle.

Fae let out a sigh of relief.

Her head swam. She was so tired.

She made her way towards the couch to lie down.

Ty stepped into the room.

Her vision blurred.

And the room disappeared again.

. . .

Arolynos sprawled below her, a spreading network of connected trees, the giant oachoa at the centre. The small lake just south of the Village sparkled in the sun, and the huge forest of Il'arys gleamed a verdant green around the tree-city she called home.

The Edge Mountains reared up across the far eastern horizon; leagues distant, but so insurmountably vast as to be visible even from here. Dry, dusty lands covered the south as far as the eye could see, and to the north, the glimmering trail of the Amedi River snaked its way across the land, from the west, all the way to the Edge.

As Fae admired the glorious landscape before her, the vision moved.

She flew through the air, heading north, her journey tracing the lazy path of I'dyll River through the forest below.

As she flew, the ground below sped past.

The forest gave way to open plains.

Great swathes of grassland extended before her in every direction. Small collections of stones dotted the landscape; forgotten playthings of a giant child.

The ground moved beneath her at an alarming pace, sweeping the view away.

She crossed a river, a road, a desert wasteland.

To the east, towns and cities lit the horizon with their glow.

To the west, open plains stretched for miles, a single cluster of lights marring the flawless flats.

Another road flew past beneath her, the land undulating as she passed.

Hills took over grasslands. The terrain became dry, and windswept; its only inhabitants straw-like blades and bracken.

Her flight came to an abrupt stop.

The barren hills rolled for miles in every direction, and Fae stood atop the king of them.

All around her stretched a vast expanse of empty countryside.

Snatches of sunlight escaped through low-lying clouds to bathe the ground in teasing moments of warmth.

But Fae stood in shadow.

She turned.

Behind her stood a large, stone monument that looked to have been there for centuries.

At first it appeared elvish in design, but it was inscribed with words that *were not. The structure towered above her, the apex of its domed roof held up by seven columns around a circular dais. Carvings covered the stone, intricately woven around the lettering that Fae didn't recognise.*

In the centre, stood a rough-hewn pedestal, somewhat out of keeping with the elegant design of its housing.

Atop the stone, a small, child-like figure sat, its back to her.

She lifted a foot onto the steps set around the great stone base.

And around the dais, others moved to do the same.

Their features were hidden, no more than silhouettes moving towards the centre of the dais from the shadows.

Fae took one last step.

And tripped.

As she fell, she was struck by how out of place the sensation was here.

Her body tensed, preparing for the impact of the ground beneath her.

She felt a hand on her shoulder. And opened her eyes.

She was back in Ty's home. He stood before her, concern etched into his features.

Another path awaits you, Spiritchild. The voices, not belonging in this place, faded as she regained her bearings.

Eah waits for you.

"Fae?" Ty's voice anchored her, and she refocused on the world around her.

"I'm okay," she said, arranging her face into a smile. "You just startled me is all." She didn't know what to tell him. It all still sounded utterly surreal. What on earth was a Spiritchild? Until she'd worked out what it all meant, she didn't want him to worry any more than he already was.

Something jerked inside her chest, like someone had tied a ribbon around her ribs and pulled. She flinched in surprise. Ty raised a skeptical eyebrow. "Really," she said firmly, "I was just... lost in my own thoughts."

Suddenly, his expression changed. "Fae," he said, his eyes scanning her face. "Your wounds..."

"What?" she asked with a puzzled frown.

Instead of replying, Ty took her by the shoulders, and wordlessly steered her back to the mirror.

"Ty, what are you — oh!" Fae gasped softly at her reflection.

The angry, purpling bruise that had spread across her right temple before had faded to a yellowish, healing colour. The wound beneath it, completely disappeared. The stitches, gone.

She lifted her shirt up.

The marks across her ribs and torso had faded too.

"What the..." she murmured.

"Lost in your own thoughts, huh?" Ty said behind her.

Fae didn't know what to tell him. She lowered her shirt again, her mind whirling.

When she still didn't speak, Ty cleared his throat.

"Do you want to... talk about anything?" he said, treading carefully with his voice.

"No..." she said, her attention elsewhere. *Another path awaits...* A tug from within.

A spark ignited in her, and she knew what she had to do.

Ty was talking again. "The scouts are meeting to decide who will go on your quest..." he said.

"It's not *my* quest," she replied, distracted.

"Sheha mentioned taking the opportunity to visit the library at Alyla," he continued, turning back towards the living area.

"Wait." Fae dragged herself from her thoughts, and followed after him. "Sheha's going?" As long as Fae had known her, she'd never known Sheha to leave Arolynos.

"Yes," Ty said, absently squaring the already-tidy chairs beneath the kitchen table. "She seemed quite excited at the prospect. She's been desperate to browse their collections ever since she first heard of them." He began clearing the cups away, filling the basin with water.

His quietness held a note of solemnness, unsuited to him.

"Are you okay?" Fae asked.

"Of course," he replied, his back still turned to her. "There will plenty to keep me busy while my sister is gone, I have no doubt." Something about his tone bothered Fae. Something pointed...

She shook it off. She had more important matters to concern herself with.

"Okay," she said, still somewhat unsettled by his darker mood. "I'm going to see the scouts." She turned toward the door. "Care to join me?"

"Regretfully, I have other matters to attend to," Ty said, glancing at her wryly over his shoulder. "One of the joys of being an Eldra." He turned back to his dishes. "There is always something less exciting to do."

Fae shrugged.

"Suit yourself," she said, and stepped out onto the sun-warmed walkways of Arolynos, a new flame within her drawing her onward.

8

TO BRAVE THE WILDS

Fae's dancer's feet skipped softly along the sun-warmed walkways to the city stores, where she found the scouts already packing.

She hovered by the door, watching them as they bantered and exchanged quips among themselves; an easy joviality to their actions belying the urgency of their assigned tasks. Even now, Fae could feel the tension in the trees. The call that screamed to be answered.

She felt like a dream spectre — watching, but not quite a part of reality.

"Fae!" Fera's willowy figure moved to greet her, her burnished auburn hair catching the sunlight as it streamed in through the leaves above. She embraced Fae warmly and stepped back, a sharp glance all she needed to take in Fae's fading bruises. "You look like you've been in the human wars, my dear." A small crease marred her smooth forehead. "What happened?" She reached over to gently brush Fae's hair away from the yellowing bruise at her temple.

Hara must have left out her part in the scouts' latest assignments. Fae found she was glad of the omission. It was clear to her now that the visions had been meant for *her*, and her alone. Whatever that meant.

"Oh, this?" She touched a finger to her temple, thankful the gash had become something far more dismissible. "It's nothing. A moment of clumsiness, nothing more." She gave Fera a bashful smile, and hoped she would drop it.

Fera's eyes narrowed.

"She's fine Fera, stop mothering." Fae was rescued by a voice whose owner was bent nearly double, sifting through food provisions. Wil straightened from his task and turned to shine a roguish smile at them both. He was tall even by elvish standards, and appeared to have been hewn straight from the Great Tree itself. "You worry too much Fera," he said in his deep, smooth baritone. "This is why you are caretaker to our young. They need someone like you. But Fae—" he came over to place a hand on Fae's shoulder and gave her a wink "—she's a tougher cracker than most give her credit for, aren't you Fae?"

She grinned up at him. "Yes, I'm fine." She looked back to Fera and added gently, "Thanks for asking." She watched as the older woman gathered up a thick stack of paper, presumably for the school. "Do you need a hand with that?"

Fera adjusted her load and shook her head. "Thank you Fae, I'll be fine." She sighed. "I always forget how much we go through at the start of a new term!" Stepping past Fae, she turned back to the scouts. "I'll be off now! Don't go plundering all our resources while I'm gone!" Her voice held an edge, but her eyes twinkled all the same. Enough of the elves in the room had once been students under her watchful eye, and she didn't hesitate to use their habitual respect to her advantage.

Fae grinned as a few of them nodded obediently to their former teacher. She couldn't blame them; she'd been taught by Fera too.

Fae turned back to the group.

"So," she said, "who's going where?" Though she could guess the answer.

"Well," Thom spoke up, leaning a half-loaded pack against the wall and sitting himself down on a barrel of grain. "You know us. Elas, Wyn and I travel to Dvargra, to ask Lord Graem if they've noticed anything... untoward of late. Anything like the changes we've seen in Il'arys." He seemed to deliberately avoid naming the fading in the forest. As if voicing it would make the disturbing changes in their forest haven real.

Thom sighed. "It's been too long since we visited Graem's halls. I will be glad to see some old friends again." He rubbed a hand absently through the short, copper strands of his hair. Behind him, Elas and Wyn nodded in agreement. They were all shorter than average for elves, and had always been the first to volunteer for the long trip to the Edge Mountains.

"Yes, I'm sure you will," Zora said from the other side of the room. Her soft, dark hair looked almost black as she pointed a stern finger at the three scouts. "Just make sure you don't come back with a dwarven gut like you did last time. I know Graem's halls hardly want for rich foods, but that doesn't mean you have to eat it all!" Wyn's eyes widened in mock affront but Thom just chuckled, patting his stomach.

"A scout has to fuel a journey that long somehow Zora," he called across the room. "The dwarves are excellent hosts, what am I to say? Besides—" he stood again, looking back towards the travel rations available "—it would be rude to turn down their hospitality."

"So rude." Elas nodded, dark-blond hair sliding over his forehead as his clear-grey eyes twinkled. "It is a terrible insult to refuse a dwarf's kitchens! And they drink ale instead of water, to warm their toes in their cold halls." He spread his hands, upturned to either side and gave a dramatically woeful look. "We have no hope."

"Maybe I'll come back with a beard instead," Wyn said quietly, stroking his face longingly, his slate-blue eyes gazing into the distance. "I would like a beard."

Wil boomed with laughter. "You have as much of a chance growing a beard as Lord Graem has of growing an inch!" He chortled to himself. Fae couldn't help but laugh along with him — it was infectious.

"Here Zora, let me help you with those!" Fae said, moving to help the healer with a teetering pile of clothes and blankets from the laundry.

"Thanks Fae," Zora said. "We won't be needing as much as those three there." She started to split her stack into piles for everyone. "Sheha and I are only going to Alyla with Jal'ha." She indicated a half-hidden form that must have been Jal'ha, hunched over as he rifled through the camp supplies. "Sheha wants to search the archives there for any mention of anything similar to what we've been experiencing here. It should be warm enough this time of year, and the route isn't as demanding." Fae smiled — so Sheha was finally granted her wish. She was happy for her. But she worried how Ty would fare without his sister. They were partners in a lot of ways. Not only as siblings but as Eldra, healers, teachers.

A twinge of guilt pricked at Fae's conscience.

"Oh, yes!" Wil chose that moment to interject, grabbing a pile of blankets and rolling them up deftly to strap to his pack. "For I shall be daring the world of men to search for a trace of the fabled Peacekeepers of Arland with none other than the brothers Longstem at my back!" He gestured dramatically at Aren and Stef, who dutifully performed matching bows to Wil's tribute. Both brothers bore the same sun-warmed, ebony-black hair — Stef's cropped short, Aren's shoulder-length — but it was their eyes that stood out; Stef's gaze had the piercing sheen of polished steel, but Aren's was pure silver.

"We're finally being sent to investigate the current human condition," Wil continued. "If it's as dark as our esteemed Whisperers claim. It sounds as though the Peacekeepers are the most likely to be able to help." The team of three were perfect for the trip; Wil had been a scout at least a hundred years already, and Aren and Stef had spent their childhood exploring the forest with their father, who was a well-known and highly respected scout in his own right. The three of them knew Il'arys as well as Artimus knew the histories.

But now, they prepared to journey further than any of them had ever ventured before. "We will brave the wilds of humanity—" Aren took up the theatrics, stepping in front of Wil to trace an epic voyage through the air. "Crossing the Deadwolds, where not even humans dare to wander. Fording the river to avoid detection, and finally—" he paused "—stealing into the city of Throldon under cover of darkness!" He leaned in, and stage-whispered behind the back of his hand, "That's if it's even still there!"

"Don't be ridiculous Aren!" Zora scolded, batting him away. "Throldon will still be there, even if it is in ruins." She said the last in a quieter voice, as if to herself. "Besides, I wasn't talking about you! Thom, Elas, and Wyn have the much harsher journey, even if they are well fed at the end of it." She reshuffled the piles that had been knocked sideways by Aren's wild gesticulations. "They've the human trade routes, *and* the mountains and forests to traverse — and that's on top of your journey." She handed each of the Dvargra scouts a larger portion of warm clothing, and extra trail rations. "The only shame about taking more supplies is that you have to carry it," she added to them.

"Don't worry about us," Thom said, taking one of the bundles. "My stocky frame bears heavier loads better than your lanky ones." He winked at Fae. "Lower centre of gravity." But being short for an elf still meant the trio stood taller than Fae. "Besides, we'll probably be wearing most of it by the time it matters. The mountains will feel bitter cold after staying so long in these warmer climes."

"Complaining already Thom?" Wil jested. "I'd say these kind of trips are wearing on you, old man!"

"Old man!" Thom turned to face him. "I've barely thirty years on you! I'll wager you we get to Dvargra before you find the Peacekeepers, you cocksure youngster!"

"Ha! Done!" They shook hands on it, while the others shook their heads at them.

Jal'ha emerged, bearing an armful of useful items. "I don't know about you," he said as an aside to Zora, "but I'm glad we're bound for Alyla, and they are not. I think I'd fear for my life, traveling with them to the forest floor and back!"

Fae lingered while the scouts assembled their respective supplies. She joked with Wil, rolled eyes with Zora, and laughed at Elas and Aren's tomfoolery. She helped Zora fetch items from the stores, while Thom and Wil exchanged quips at each other's expense.

She noted what each of them packed, and where in the stores she could find each item.

There were boots, far heavier and sturdier than anyone ever wore around Arolynos. And long, fine cloaks with deep hoods; thick ones for Thom and his crew, lighter versions for Zora and hers. Travel rations, water-wraps — fashioned from the thick, shiny leaves of *yillre* lilies — and cooking implements for the road were among the essentials. Blankets, needles and thread, and oil cloths as well.

None of the scouts were going to the monument in those northern hills.

Where the whispers called for her.

Where the growing urgency inside her pulled her to go.

When the last of them bid her goodbye, Fae began gathering her own supplies.

Arolynos was a trusting city; no one would think it odd, Fae helping herself to an extra blanket or some spare sewing materials. She almost felt guilty picking a bag and stuffing it with the same items she'd seen the others pack.

But no one else had heard the gut-wrenching sound of the Aethyr's cries like she had.

No one understood the cold twist of fear at the darkness in the world like she did.

No one had seen that black stain spread across the world like she had.

The Eldra wouldn't understand the call she felt to follow her vision. Because it called to *her*.

And it was hers to fulfil.

Alone.

She returned to her rooms to retrieve the one item the city stores could not provide — her prized dancing swords.

There weren't many elven pastimes she'd shown an affinity towards, but she loved to dance. When she danced, her body and soul *sang*. Her limbs obeyed the ebb and flow of movement in a way that simply didn't happen under normal conditions. Her motions were lithe and graceful, where she was otherwise known for her clumsiness, the elegance of the elves escaping her. Which, she supposed, now made sense.

But her dancing was wild and deliberate. Abstract and beautiful.

When it seemed her only other strength was in the healing arts, dancing was a burst of fresh rainfall against the strength of an ancient tree — refreshing, invigorating, and alive.

She'd mastered the five primary forms of dance in an unprecedentedly short time, but Fae's true love was for the *Aleralys*; the dance of the fallen leaf.

In *Aleralys*, the dancer began surrounded by a forest of coloured streamers hanging from above, which were then cut away with long, slender blades, sharpened to an obsidian edge. One slice at a time, the dancer was revealed within, pivoting and turning with all the grace of a leaf twirling in the wind.

And her blades were magnificent. Long as a walking staff, and sharpened to the keenest edge, they sang through the air as her body sang through dance.

Most elves would be more comfortable keeping their distance and defending themselves with the haunting accuracy of a bow-and-arrow. Fae felt much safer with the notion of facing any opponents within reach of her blades.

Retrieving the swords from their place on her bookcase, she strapped them across her back in a long, wooden sheath.

She swung her borrowed satchel over one shoulder, packed with items inspired by those the scouts had gathered for their journeys. The cloak she'd selected was rolled up and strapped to the bag for now. She wore new boots, ready for a long, hard road, and the floor beneath her feet felt oddly less stable; she couldn't feel the curve and natural sway of the wood through her soles anymore. The disconnect felt alien and strange.

She looked back over her home, and at the things she was leaving behind. The view through the canopy from her bedroom. The musical trill of myna birds as they hopped from branch to branch. The hand-woven blanket Fera had given her as a housewarming gift. The warm, smooth wood underfoot, the gentle sway of the trees in the breeze.

For years she'd yearned for a connection to the Aethyr, for some hint of what lay behind the curtain in her mind. For years she'd known there was something more. Known she was meant for more. And the Aethyr had finally shown her the way.

She cast a brief thought to Ty and Sheha. And to Bek. Her family.

Her resolve wavered.

Eah waits for you... a breeze whispered through her open window, ruffling her hair as it passed. And the ache in her chest tugged at her, urging her on.

It was time to go.

As Arolynos went about its day, Fae had no trouble slipping down to the forest floor.

But, alone as she was, she didn't notice the tense quiet of the forest life.

And the soft, sure, footsteps of another.

9

SOURFRUITS

The hospit in Barrow was full to bursting again. Men and women lay on make-shift beds in make-shift wards, on chairs pulled together in the entranceway, even on blankets on the floors.

There had been another raid on the villages.

The Unity was getting closer.

Laina shook her head to clear her thoughts. She didn't have time to worry about it. Time now, was to focus her attention on the matter at hand.

She looked around her. Her apprentices dashed about. They were all busy with patients, sometimes two at a time. The older, more experienced healers were setting bones, fishing arrows out of wounds, or holding patients still while others did their work. The younger apprentices were washing wounds, stitching gashes, and distributing water among the injured.

Despite the overcrowding, everything seemed, at first glance, to be under control.

But Laina recognised the flash of distrust in more than a few eyes.

Every man for himself, the Unity dictated — their only law. And they regarded the Peacekeepers with a special brand of disgust and disdain.

Well, if those people wanted to leave this hospit — such as it was —

and treat themselves, they were welcome to. But most of them knew that meant risking their lives.

The problem was, being here was just as risky if they were found.

"Laina?" A tap on her shoulder was accompanied by a small voice. She turned to find one of the younger apprentices standing behind her, an unfamiliar young man at her side. He was tall, with dark hair, but he couldn't have been more than eighteen or nineteen years old.

"Yes Becka, who's this?"

"This is Ben. He says he wants to help," Becka said, her hands twitching restlessly. She was itching to get back to her patients, but waited for Laina's response nonetheless.

"Alright, thank you Becka," she said. While Becka bustled back to her work, Laina turned to face the newcomer. "Have you had any experience treating wounds before Ben?"

"No ma'am. But I can carry things need carrying if it helps. Anything I can do." He held her gaze as he spoke, his young voice full of sincerity. Laina eyed him up.

"Haven't you got any family to be taking care of?" she asked, although he was certainly old enough to have left home, to strike out on his own.

"No ma'am," he said.

"Don't you want to help rebuild?" she asked. Two villages hit in a relatively short time — there was plenty of work to go around for everyone.

"No ma'am," he said again. "I'm not needed there." He held her gaze, calm and firm. Laina narrowed her eyes. There was something about this boy — this young man — that didn't quite fit.

Someone called out across her ward, and one of her healers rushed over to assist.

Oh well, she thought, *can't be turning down help when it comes offering now can I?*

"Well I ain't no ma'am," she started, even if she was old enough to be this boy's mother. "You can call me Laina, just like everyone else does." She looked him up and down. "You've got a strong pair of arms on you — I'm sure we can find something you can help with." She waved down one of the other healers. "Donvan, this is Ben." She patted the young man on the arm, pushing him forward. "Ben here is willing and able to help. Can you find someone as could use it?" The healer nodded briskly and gestured for the young man to follow, and the two disappeared into the throng of people in need of help.

Laina watched them go. Something about him pricked at her, like a piece of dry grass stuck in her shirt, but she couldn't quite work out what it was...

"I told you I don't need your help!" An angry voice raised above the hubbub of the room. Laina looked across to where Jessica was trying to splint a badly broken leg, the owner of which was making the noise.

"Look, friend, why don't just let the lady fix you up, and then you can do us all a favour and be on your way?" another patient suggested wearily from a nearby bed.

"If you wanted me to do you a favour, I'd burn this place to the ground," the first man growled, eyes darting around the place. He took in the dozens of patients accepting help from Laina's Peacekeepers, and his face darkened.

Ah, Laina thought. *Unity to the death I see.* She sighed inwardly. No matter how far she travelled, no matter which corner of Arland she tucked herself into, the Unity's message always managed to reach her.

"'*Every man for himself*'," the man shouted, making eye contact with as many people as he could. "Don't you see the sense of it?" He glared wildly about. "You're all here, *dependent* on a stranger, because you couldn't stand on your own two feet!"

"I wouldn't start preaching about standing on two feet myself, in your position," another patient spoke up, and the man glanced down at his injured leg. A burble of laughter rippled through the hospit. The man with the broken leg glowered across the room, the laughter a spark struck to the kindling of his mood.

For a moment, Laina thought he might settle. But then, he braced one arm on the chair Jessica had used to lay out her equipment, and stood, bearing his weight through his one good leg.

"Now then," Jessica protested, hands outstretched as if she might steady him, "you'll only damage your leg more! If you just sit for a few minutes I can—"

But the man wasn't listening.

"I'll show you I can stand on my own — two feet or no!" he roared hoarsely, challenging the room to defy him.

Laina glanced over the patients assembled. Most of them wore expressions of incredulity. But there was a small handful who appeared to be galvanised by his words. Her heart pounded in her chest. Which way would this go?

"I depend on *no one*!" he continued to shout, waving a fist in the air. But the sudden motion was too much for his less-than-perfect balance, and he wobbled precariously. The colour drained from his face.

"Please!" Jessica squeaked. "Sit down before you do some serious damage!"

He back-handed her across the face.

And the room erupted.

The patients nearest the Unity man either scrambled to move out of the way, or dived at him. Not a small man himself, he pushed and shoved a few away before lifting the chair over his head, improvising himself a weapon. Jessica cried out as her equipment was sent flying across the room, and had to be pulled away by a young woman with strapped ribs before she could dive in to rescue the tools of her trade.

Eventually someone toppled the idiot man to the floor and wrested the chair from him.

"Be careful of his leg!" Jessica yelled above the commotion.

But even with a broken leg, the man fought and thrashed, throwing men from him in a fit of rage.

Fists flew, blood sprayed, and Laina heard more than a couple of noses crunch.

"THAT'S ENOUGH," a big voice bellowed. Men in the scrum found themselves lifted bodily from the pile and dumped unceremoniously to one side, where another man — tall, dark, and lean — escorted them either back to their beds, or outside to cool off. Robert worked the room as he went, exchanging jokes with patients, and easing the tension in the room. As one of Laina's Watch, he took his role in supporting the healers very seriously.

His comrade, Nathan, a burly man with the characteristically sandy hair of Seiner's Tarn folk, hauled aggressors from each other, pinning them with his intractable blue stare as he did so. He had little to no patience for fools, and loathed needless aggression.

Between Nathan picking people off each other like dander from a dog, and Robert dispersing them away from the fight with a quick word and easy smile, patients and healers alike got back to their business as normal. The reassuring hubbub of casual conversation filled the corners again, although everyone kept the big Seiner's man within their sights.

Eventually, Nathan reached the man at the bottom of the pile.

He lifted him by the scruff of his shirt as easily as a cat with her kitten.

The room paused to watch.

"These folk 'ere, are 'ere to be fixed up so's they can git back to livin'," Nathan spoke gruffly. "If you've no interest in bein' part o' that—" he swung the man towards the entrance "—there's the door."

The man's eyes blazed, but he wisely said nothing.

"Now," Nathan continued, "I think Jess 'ere was about to sort your leg out." He located the young healer in the crowd, an angry red mark flaring bright across her left cheek, "but I'd say it's up to her if she fancies finishin' the job." He brought the man's face up close to his own so that they stood — or hung — nose to nose. "I'd be a mite nicer to her if I was you," he said in a low growl.

The Unity man, despite his unenviable position, still looked as though he might refuse, until Nathan set him back on his feet. What colour had risen to his cheeks fighting, fled when his leg touched the floor.

He dropped onto the bed, silent as a scolded child.

Robert, finished with his task of keeping the peace, appeared at Jessica's side.

"Up to you Jess," he said, with a lop-sided smile that didn't quite reach his eyes.

Jessica looked over to the man on the bed, her face one of well-practiced matronliness.

"I won't force treatment on someone doesn't want it," she said, raising her voice enough so that those around could hear her too. "But nor will I refuse healing to them that need it." She walked over to her patient and stood beside him, waiting.

She waited until he looked up at her, a small grimace in his glower the only sign of remorse on his face.

Jessica's eyes narrowed. "Can I set your leg for you?" she asked. Her tone left no room for misunderstanding. If his answer was no, he could leave. Immediately. And likely assisted.

He looked around. Whatever he saw weakened his resolve, and his face unclenched.

He let out a sigh. "Yes ma'am," he said, eyes glancing to her face before flicking back down to study the floor. "Won't cause no more trouble."

Jessica nodded curtly, and fetched fresh materials for his splint. Robert and Nathan took up positions nearby. Robert kept up an easy banter with the patients and healers. Nathan scoured the room, his eyes resting longer on some men than others.

Good, Laina thought. He'd noticed the other Unity sympathisers in the room as well. She felt a swell of pride at her people. They looked after each other, so that they could in turn look after those that needed help.

She sighed deeply. Not that they should have to deal with this kind of grief. Nothing was ever simple.

But she didn't have long to dwell on it. She was called upon to help stitch a gaping wound where the vessels were pumping blood out of the tear so quickly it was near impossible to see what needed doing. Once the vessel had been sutured, she handed over to an apprentice to stitch up the wound. Then she had to set a broken leg, but doubted all the while if the patient would ever regain full use of the limb given the extent of the fractures. She prescribed oxroot, to draw impurities from the lungs of a child who'd breathed in too much smoke, and swallowed back tears at the sight of the small girl lying soot-stained and helpless on the bed.

So many people, she thought, *who didn't deserve this.*

She moved seamlessly from patient to patient, sometimes just to offer advice to the healer there, sometimes to take over entirely, sometimes just to comfort and reassure.

By the evening, she was exhausted, and not without good cause. The hospit was back in order again. Those who weren't so injured they couldn't walk headed back to their village to search for missing family members, or to begin the long process of rebuilding their community. Those who could, had gone home to comply with Laina's strict rest guidelines. All those she'd identified as Unity had chosen to take their treatment, and try their luck on the road, *"Beholden to no one."* The rest occupied the remaining beds at the hospit.

Laina walked a final round of her wards, ensuring everyone was resting well, before finally retiring to her study.

Wherever they were, Laina always had a study. Sometimes it was a grand room with a veritable library of texts covering all manner of topics. Sometimes it was just a small back room with a pallet to sleep on.

Sometimes it was a tent. This one was a cozy medium. No more than five paces across, there was a daybed up against the wall, a desk in one corner, and a sturdy bookcase next to the window.

It had become home.

She teased out her strawberry-blonde hair as she looked around the humble lodgings and sighed a long sigh. Perhaps they had stayed here too long.

Laina's little band of Peacekeepers were always on the move. One of many such groups, they never stayed too long in one place, skipping from village to village, helping anyone in need.

And picking up stragglers along the way.

Once there had been only five of them in her group — easy to hide, and quick to move on. Beside herself, there was Jessica, originally from Hapton, Robert, who mostly hunted and scouted for them, Nathan, who took it upon himself to be Laina's personal guard, and Kiel, an elderly preacher.

Now there were over fifty travellers, all banded together by her little group.

All of them wanted an end to the violence.

But violence seemed to follow Laina wherever she went. People travelled to seek the aid of a Peacekeeper group. And where there was news of Peacekeepers, Unity thugs followed.

They were extremely lucky to have lasted this long. But it was time to move on. She couldn't bear it if another raid found them...

Laina shook her head clear of memories best left buried. Absently turning the ring on her finger, she took another look around her modest study. One last time. Then, slowly and methodically, she began the disheartening task of packing her few belongings.

Packing always meant leaving.

Leaving always meant pursuit.

And pursuit meant violence.

She would spare these people that.

In the time she'd spent in this village, she'd been gifted many things, but very little was essential. She gathered up her healer's kit — the tools of her trade — a blanket, water skin, and spare clothes and bandages. Packing these items into her old travel satchel, she rested the bag against the foot of the bed, ready for the morning. She dusted off her travel cloak, which had hung unused for so long, and hauled her boots out from where they hid among the cobwebs beneath the bed.

Then she set herself down to sleep. She'd pass through the kitchens on the way out, and grab some food for the road there. But if she was going to be moving on tomorrow, she needed all the rest she could get.

As her eyes fluttered closed, the long day had her drifting off almost immediately.

And she dreamed.

At first, she dreamt of the mundane: the patients in her make-shift ward — a patchwork, stitched together from the many and varied versions she'd set up over the years; a patchwork ward with patchwork patients.

The apprentices she and the other healers had taken on, too many to count, their faces lost among the throngs of people seeking aid.

Her family, never far from her sleeping mind.

But then the dream turned to her past, and she was back in Woodnewton.

The two dreams overlapped, like she was watching two days at once.

With one eye, she saw sunshine and happiness. Children running joyously about, zigzagging between women washing clothes and kneading bread out in the fresh air. Men returning from their day's work with bushels of wheat, or armfuls of timber, grimy with dust and sweat, smiles on their faces.

The other saw fire. Screams. Horror. Bodies.

She thrashed in her sleep. Fought against the dream. Whimpered for it to stop.

She already knew that night too well. Did not need to relive it.

The night she lost her family to the Unity raid. The night she changed.

The flames brightened around her, moments from engulfing her completely...

The dream set her back in Barrow, back in her study, but distorted, as if seen through the oily sheen of a bubble from a washerwoman's tub.

Her dream-self walked the wards once more, found everyone sleeping. Then she was out in the night, two moons shining brilliantly overhead as her bare feet scratched on summer-dried grasses, her hair pulled back by the cool evening breeze.

The dream took her out of the village, heading west. She felt the grass pressed against the soles of her feet as she walked. It softened as she lifted, featherlight in the dream, her feet barely making an imprint at all. With a final leap, she left the ground altogether.

The land passed her by with impossible clarity. She saw the irregular town of Bredon, its many buildings in such varied state of repair that it was no longer recognisable as the prosperous market town it once was. The greatly diminished former trade hub that was Hapton flew past, and the haven in the hills known as Greneln was only distinguishable from the surrounding landscape by the small curls of smoke lifting gently over the hilltops.

And then, it was wild grasses alone, bending in concert, the wind rippling across the blades like waves on an endless sea. They stretched on for leagues and leagues in every direction. The plains became hills. And the grasslands became tundra. Finally, she came to a stop.

She stood atop one hill among many. The king of the hills, and it raised her up above the land.

From the top of this hill, the earth stretched out before her, laid out like a captain's map on a voyaging ship.

She saw all of Arland, leagues away, so small and distant.

Then there were others on the hill. Seven indistinct figures, standing together. And together, they watched as a shadow spread over the land.

It began in Throldon; it reached south over the river, west over the wastelands, east to the mountains, north towards the plains and the hills.

Swaying grasses blackened and died. Storm clouds rolled in. Bitter winds cut through her.

And the world darkened.

She was filled with a fear that was not her own. Felt the earth itself weeping.

Shadow surrounded the mount on which she stood, a sea of black, creeping ever closer.

The king of hills cowered at the onslaught. It shrank away from the advancing death until it seemed little more than a rocky outcrop in a raging sea.

Laina looked to the others, but all they did was watch. Waiting.

Panic welled inside her.

And the world around her was swallowed in darkness.

Laina woke, gasping for breath.

She sucked in lungfuls of air, beads of sweat rolling down her face, and waited for her racing heart to calm.

Her room was as she'd left it. Her pack leant against the frame of the bed, the study she'd come to call home quiet and still.

But the air in the room felt dense. Like a flock of small birds perched in the branches of a great tree, watching.

Waiting.

She glanced around the room. Nothing was out of place. But the heaviness in the room was familiar. The last time she'd felt it, in a moment of impossible despair, her grieving heart had found peace, felt hope. For a while at least. Time to heal.

Now, it was time for a change.

Something bigger than her was at stake.

When the pale light of dawn warmed the night's edge, and the moons were both well on the way to setting, Laina was already a mile out of the village.

She hadn't been able to get back to sleep. And she wasn't much for goodbyes.

Her small band of Peacekeepers would move on without her. They knew how it was.

It wasn't safe to stay anymore.

The make-shift hospit she left behind was well staffed, and the healers there, old and new, knew their craft well. The patients were in good hands.

So she hitched her pack high on her back, squared her shoulders, and placed one foot in front of the other.

Her worn, battered boots caressed her feet like old gloves, moulded to her over years of use. She would still need to take it easy. Comfortable shoes or no, it had been a month or two since she'd done any hard walking.

But there was something reassuring about having the wind kiss her neck as it whipped the hair from her face, and having nothing but open country in front and behind.

She smiled as the sun's rays began to colour the sky.

For the first time in a long time, no one needed her.

"Laina! Miss!" a voice called out.

Laina started. She turned. Looking back into the rising sun, she couldn't see much. She shielded her eyes against the glare.

A minute later, a shape emerged from the orange glow, running towards her.

"Ben?!" she called back when the features of the young man from the day before finally became clear. "What on earth are you doing?" The youth pulled up a few feet from her, and braced his hands on his knees, breathing heavily.

Laina marched over to him and hauled him upright by the arm. "*What*," she repeated, "*are you doing?*"

Ben waved his free hand at her, begging a moment. He gulped down a few breaths before he was able to speak.

"I was — up early — saw you walking." He gasped a couple more breaths. "Shouldn't walk alone out here." He gave a look that said she should know better, even as his chest worked like a bellows. "I went back to grab some things—" he shifted his pack on his shoulders "—but then you were too far away. I ran..." He took a final deep, gasping breath, blowing it out with a "*hooo*". He straightened fully, and waved his hands to indicate where they now stood. "And here I am."

Laina's face spoke volumes, and his confidence faltered. But something in his eyes told her he wouldn't be easily swayed from his decision.

She hadn't wanted *anyone* with her. It was no one's place to follow her feet but her own. And when her feet were taking directions from a *dream*...

On the other hand, travel could be lonely. And Ben had no one either — he'd said as much before — and likely nowhere to go.

She eyed him up. He eyed her back, a knowing twinkle in the blue of his eyes.

Well, when life gives you sourfruits...

She sighed. "Here you are."

10

NOT ALONE

The first thing Fae noticed about the forest floor, was the noise.

Up in the canopy, there was peace. The river was a quiet burbling down below, and the birds sang softly amongst the gentle whisper of leaves that shush-shushed softly against one another.

Down on the ground was a cacophony by comparison.

The river boomed past so loud and clear, she thought it about to crash down over her at any moment. Birdsong was raucous, involving species large and small, shrill and cawing. Animals darting under cover, rustling in the undergrowth and snapping branches with sharp *cracks*. The leaves of the lower canopy scraped against bark and branches in a sound that grated against her ears, while dry tree-limbs knocked together in the breeze like dry bones.

Fae tilted her head towards the sky, though she could see little of it. She already missed the feel of sunlight on her skin. She looked around her, and saw none of the delicate foliage she was used to; here it was all tough brambles and wide ferns. Reedy blades of wild grass stretched to meet the sun's rays as if to snatch them from mid-air. Dead leaves and bark chips littered the ground, and dark moss grew wet and green on fallen logs and tree stumps.

The gloom that surrounded her was suffocating, the air thick and damp.

It took every ounce of resolve, gathered up and held close, to walk away from the return route, to not turn around and head straight back to Arolynos.

To walk deeper into the darkness.

And north, to follow her vision.

The need of it hummed through her veins, tugging her onward with an urgency that eclipsed almost all reason. Almost all. She took a moment to check the straps of her pack, letting the small task ground her before she forgot herself.

The reality of her situation was far less romantic than it had sounded in her head. She trudged through damp undergrowth, swatting away low branches that sought to tangle her in their grasp. Twigs snagged on her clothes, roots caught at her feet, and there were just so many *bugs*!

She spat, propelling an ill-fated fly from her mouth.

Following my vision, she thought wryly, trying in vain to pull fly parts from her tongue. *Not exactly a glamorous escapade.*

The dark wildness of the forest floor had her flinching at every sound: every rustle of foliage, every snapped twig, every innocent bird-call. Eventually, she was so charged with tension that she found herself coiled, hand wrapped around her sword hilt, ready to spring at what turned out to be just a rabbit, who dived back under cover at Fae's shaky laugh.

But in the pause after her breath steadied, she heard muffled footsteps as they treaded through the carpet of dead leaves and bark chips.

She ducked behind a fallen tree trunk.

Her right hand gripped a sword hilt over her shoulder, her heart pounding in her chest so loud that she was sure it must be audible. She briefly relived the moment in her vision when she'd realised she was in plain sight of feral humans. The moment before she was beaten near senseless.

And she remembered that the forest floor was not as forgiving a place as it once was.

She closed her eyes and listened as the steps approached, preparing to leap out and defend herself.

The steps stopped. Her hunter breathed mere feet from her.

"Fae?" A quiet whisper. Her eyes flew open and she whirled around the tree.

"Bek?!" she near shouted. The boy stood rooted in front of her, blue eyes wide, as startled as the rabbit. "What are you doing here?" she demanded. By way of an answer, Bek ran towards her and flung his arms around her waist. She patted him on the head, then took him firmly by the shoulders, holding him at arm's length.

"You," she said firmly, her breath ragged as blood pounded through her body, "should be in school, little one!" She straightened, gazing over his head into the trees. "What on earth are you doing out here?" She glanced back down at him.

Bek's response was merely to cock his head to one side and raise one eyebrow, plainly saying, *I could ask you the same.*

She was about to respond when she heard more, bigger rustlings among the leaves behind her. Her head snapped up, and she ushered Bek to stand behind her. This time she did draw her swords, one in each hand.

I am going to have to toughen up, she thought to herself, *if every forest critter is bent on making me jump!* She assumed an easy stance, blades out to either side of her, ready for whatever else could be lurking in this place.

The noises stopped, and she strained her ears to find them again.

Probably just another rabbit, she thought with a sigh, sheathing her swords.

She turned back to Bek. But he wasn't looking at her anymore.

His head was turned towards the sky, his eyes focused above and behind her.

And he was wearing a smile.

A familiar chuckle accompanied a soft thud behind her.

Fae turned to meet eyes of darkest, storm-grey.

"Thank you Bek," Ty said with his usual easy smile, dusting his hands off each other. "I might never have found her if you hadn't made her shriek like that!" He had loose plant life in his short sandy hair, and streaks of green across his pant-legs. She glanced up and noticed the lower branches in the trees. They'd make an excellent path just above the forest floor — for someone agile enough to use them.

Fae's shoulders dropped, the tension leaking out of her like water from cupped hands. A part of her was glad to see him. Was always glad to see him. But today, she didn't want him here. Didn't want him pulling her off course.

He waited for her reaction, and she sighed, guessing his intentions.

"I'm not coming back, either of you," she said, addressing them both. "I have something I need to do, and I can't come back until I've seen it through." She pictured the stone monument from her vision, and the figures in the shadows there.

She'd not been able to shake that image. It stuck with her. That, and the unbearable sound of the Aethyr's pain.

And knowing that *she'd* been chosen to act on it.

She will carry us into the darkness...

Ty held his hands up. "I'm not here to stop you Fae," he said, a small frown creasing his forehead. "I knew the moment you said you were 'lost in your thoughts' that you'd decided to take things into your own hands." He sighed and stepped towards her. "The Eldra never did work fast enough for you." His mouth quirked up at the corner.

"It's not about that!" Fae protested. She folded her arms across her chest. "They're all going the wrong way! It doesn't matter what the other races have to say on the matter — the Aethyr want us to go north!" Her eyes dared him to challenge her. "They want *me* to go north." That vision had been for her alone; she *knew* it, with the same certainty that had her very bones yearning to follow it. It had been *her* stepping up to that dais; *her* destiny. Her... something more.

Ty went quiet, his eyes on hers, as if searching for more than she'd revealed. Her lips slammed shut, and she felt a scowl forming across her brow. How could he possibly understand it, when the Aethyr deemed fit to show only her?

Ty placed his hands over her arms and she had to tilt her head back to meet his gaze. Any other day, and she would take his hand and go with him wherever he asked. But though her breath caught at his nearness, today her heart pulled her elsewhere.

Her resolve must have been plain on her face, as he loosed a sigh, and smiled. "I'm not here to talk you out of it, Fae. I know better." He shot her a meaningful glance that coaxed a smile onto her own face. Then he sobered. "I just didn't want you to think you had to face any of this alone." Her eyes widened, and it was then that she noticed the pack on his shoulder.

A small hand slid into her palm, and she looked down to see Bek peering up at her. He nodded his agreement.

They weren't here to stop her. They wanted to come *with* her.

She shook her head. "I can't let you do that." They had lives here. And aside from following the pull within her, she still had no idea what she was doing.

Bek's hands cut the air. *You can't go alone,* he signed. He held her gaze unflinchingly, his jaw set. *We're coming.*

Fae looked at Ty. His lips kicked up at the corners, and he inclined his head as if to say, *What he said.*

Fae let out a breath, and with it, the fight left her. Her throat tightened with emotion, and her eyes burned. She blinked away tears and smiled at Bek, wrapping her arm around his shoulders.

Her relief surprised her. Alone, she had felt like a ribbon in *Aleralys,* waiting to be cut down. With them beside her, she felt like an elven arrow, flying straight and true. Like she could do anything. Yes, this quest was for her and her alone, but far from pulling her off course, their presence made her feel like she was sure to succeed. Her gaze turned back to Ty's, and the look in his eyes told her he understood.

He bent to touch his forehead briefly to hers, and her eyes fluttered closed at the contact.

"You are not alone," he said.

They made the best of the remaining light to find a suitable place to camp. But while Fae looked for an acceptably clear, dry patch of ground, perhaps with some shelter if they were lucky, Ty appeared to be searching for something more specific.

It was near dark when he finally let out a triumphant "Ah Ha!"

Waving them over, he guided them towards a rocky outcrop.

It turned out to be an enormous slab of stone, angling slantwise out of the ground. As it emerged, bracketed by two giant, fallen tree trunks, it formed a sort of small cave over the ground. The earth beneath was dry and compacted, and swept clear of the natural debris that littered the forest floor.

What Ty was looking at though, was the elven lettering carved into the surface of the stone, over the mouth of the cave.

It read:

"Ap nē Aro lea, rogh il saffeh y arys.
Shoto be'inta alach nē."

"To Those far from Haven, find here peace and shelter.
May safe journeys await you."

The symbols were beautifully hewn into the rock's surface, intricate and clear. They could have been carved only moments earlier, for all that they must have been there for years.

Beneath the slope of the listing monolith, a long shelf was carved into one side. Upon it stood three stoppered bottles of clear water, and a wide shallow bowl. Underneath, hung an assortment of dried herbs. A solid chest with metal banding hunkered against one side of the cave, while a neatly stacked wood-pile occupied the other. Built into the ground near the entrance to the cave, was a firepit lined with wide, flat stones.

"What is this place?" Fae said curiously as Ty began looking through the contents of the chest.

"It's a Waystop," he said from the back of the cave. He closed the lid of the chest, and selected some kindling from the wood-pile.

"Scouts use them," he continued, carrying the wood over to the firepit, "and restock them whenever they're passing." He arranged the kindling into an immaculate pyramid, and produced a flint and ferrite from one pocket. "Waystops are an invaluable resource for navigating the forest floor." He struck the flint across the ferrite. "There are a few scattered throughout Il'arys. It isn't the place of peace it used to be..." Flame caught on the dried lichen beneath the kindling, illuminating his face with a warm glow. He sat back on his heels. "And we're not scouts. It's been a while since I practiced any forest-craft. So we'd be wise to use the resources available to us." He smiled up at her from his fledgling campfire. She offered a small smile in return, but the shadows deepened on her face.

Fae turned to look out at the darkening forest, her thoughts swirling. She stepped from the cave to stand just beyond the orange light of the fire.

She was beginning to question the wisdom of throwing herself out into the world. She had no scouting skills, and no experience outside the safety of Arolynos. She stared out at the trees. Out there, where unknown dangers lurked, what use would she be? She quietly thanked Eah that Ty and Bek had decided to follow her. She had only the pull of her vision within to guide her. An inexplicable knowing. She had no idea what perils lay in their path. What awaited her at the end of it.

Still, when she was on her own, she had only her own safety to consider. Now, she was dragging others along on her blind quest. She worried about Bek, yet she understood his desire to follow her — they were both orphans of Arolynos; family, despite their differing origins.

What origins? she asked herself. It turned out she wasn't even elven. And Bek certainly wasn't human. *So where* did *we come from?*

Nothing about this journey is going to be normal, she decided with a sigh. Her mind was in turmoil, and she doubted every thought that passed through it.

She didn't notice when Bek padded over to stand beside her until he leaned his head against her side. She wrapped one arm around his young shoulders, and turned to look at him.

His face gazed out into the night. It didn't carry the heavy lines of worry, nor the sad, downturn of sorrow. He looked... content. At home. Lifting his head to meet her eyes, he smiled. And that simple gesture, the ease with which he stood at her side, settled some of the turmoil inside her.

The smells of simple cooking wafted out towards them; Ty and Bek had pulled up some wild onions and tubers on their way through the forest, and there was a bag of salt in the chest, kept dry. Together with the flatbread Ty had in his pack, dinner promised to be decent fare tonight at least.

Fae sighed. Campfires and foraged food — she had been thoroughly ill-prepared for her journey.

Bek tugged her back to the circle of firelight, weaving his fingers into hers. As she folded her legs to sit crosslegged on the ground by the fire, Ty passed her a torn-off hunk of flatbread. She looked up at him. He'd found them shelter, prepared food, and shared all this with her without being asked. He'd left the safety of Arolynos, the familiarity of his people, to be with her. To help her.

"Thank you," she said, and it wasn't just about the flatbread. He nodded his understanding.

For better or worse, they were in this together now.

She glanced across at Bek.

All of them.

11

BREAKING THE SURFACE

It rained in the night.

The rain here didn't fall with the steady, gentle pitter-patter that Fae was used to. It fell in loud, irregular sploshes. Gathered rain fell in drops the size of acorns, ricocheting through the layers of the forest canopy, and slapping against the cold stone of the Waystop. It added a non-rhythm to the base cacophony of sound, waking her at odd intervals.

When the dull light of dawn broke through to warm the damp ground outside the cave, Fae was already awake.

She was glad of the extra blanket she'd grabbed from the stores. It had kept her warm enough down on the cold forest floor, but she already missed home.

She snorted scornfully at herself. *Toughen up Fae, there's a long way to go yet.*

She thought of her vision, and her headlong flight over Arland. Of the rivers to ford, the plains to cross, and the leagues to cover. It all seemed so far away, her corner of the world so small. She'd only ever known Arolynos. And not only was she leaving Il'arys, she was also heading out over the human lands. Lands that Sheha had said weren't safe.

She turned her head to watch the sleeping forms of Ty and Bek across the cave, the rise and fall of their chests rhythmic with sleep. A gnawing guilt warred with her joy at having her family with her.

She blew a breath up over her face. Lying in the half-gloom, she waited for the light brightening outside the Waystop to reach her, willing it to stretch into the cave and chase her doubts away.

Bek woke abruptly, a guttural snore shocking him bolt upright in an instant. Fae laughed despite herself. The sight of Bek rubbing the sleep from his eyes, blinking in confusion brought a smile to her face that tasted like home. Ty pushed himself up onto one elbow in his bedroll, his eyes creasing in their familiar way.

"Good sleep, Bek?" he asked, lips kicking up at the corners. Bek brushed the last of the sleep from his eyes and nodded. A long fold pressed into his face from the fabric of his own bedroll served to make him look even more bewildered. Ty chuckled. "Good. We have a lot of ground to cover today."

They rose, packed, and began putting the Waystop to rights. Ty stepped out to collect wood and branches for the woodpile. Bek swept the firepit with a small, angled dustpan and a soot-covered brush made of switch, left for just such a purpose. Fae checked their supplies against what was left in the cave. She had a good stock of basic herbs in her sack; willowbark, florestem, and trickleroot, to name a few. The cave had an ample supply of these, and a few others, including some dried healer's helper. The elves had beautiful names for all the plants of the forest, but Fae liked the common tongue names for their byproducts; they made a simple sort of sense. She eyed the healer's helper — dried petals of the *lapissi* plant, known to accelerate the body's own healing process — and portioned off a helping to add to her own collection.

When Ty returned, bearing armfuls of stripped twigs and branches, he stacked them neatly in the corner beside the stockpile to allow them to dry, ready for the next visitor to the shelter.

With everything put back as it was, they shouldered their packs, and set off into the day.

With Ty and Bek walking beside her, Fae was far less twitchy than she had been the day before. And in the absence of her unexpected fear, she found herself instead mentally railing against how long it was taking to get through the forest.

After half a day of travel, she guessed the sun to be approaching its noon peak, but the light dwindled lazily, holding the forest in a perpetual twilight. The trees showed no sign of thinning; they crowded around her, impeding what little light might have made it down to the forest floor. Branches reached out to ensnare clothes and hair as the trunks leaned in towards them. Leaves and barbs clung to them as they brushed past. Fae used nimble fingers to tie her hair back in a braid that hung long down her back, but it felt as though the forest itself was clawing at her, entreating her to stay. It was unsettling, and she rubbed her arms against an eerie chill.

It was hard to imagine that these trees belonged to the same forest as her beloved Arolynos.

They finally came to a break in the oppressive undergrowth; a clearing of sorts where the ground sunk into a shallow bowl, the trees coming to a halt at its lip. Ty called a brief stop, and they sank gratefully to the ground, leaning cautiously against nearby tree trunks. Bek pulled an apple from his pack, and a small, folding knife from a side pocket.

"I had no idea the forest was so dark down here," Fae commented, straining her eyes into the undergrowth. Even more than her impatience, the trees themselves left her with a feeling of unease that made her want to leave the woods behind as quickly as possible. "Do you know how much further it goes on for?" She looked across at Ty, who was eyeing the canopy above them. He would have explored the forest in his youth, gathering and learning the plants it offered up. She was suddenly even more glad he'd come — without him, she would have had little chance of finding her way here.

But as she looked at him, even he seemed concerned. He eyed the surrounding trees warily, and his ears twitched in a rare display of agitation.

"It wasn't always this dark," he said, scanning around before bringing his gaze back to rest with her. "I fear this has something to do with your vision Fae." He indicated the trees around them. "The trees never used to grow so close. Once, you could follow the paths forged by creatures of the forest. Now..." he waved his hands in various directions around them. There were no paths to follow. And from a clearing like this, there should have been. "If only there was a sure and swift route to the edge." He clasped his hands together, resting his elbows on crossed legs, lost in thought. Then something caught his eye. He looked up, a small crease on his brow. Fae turned to follow his gaze.

Bek was making wild hand gestures. At first he made waves in the air, as if his hands followed the current of a stream. Or the wind. Then he made the hand sign for *"guardian"*. And then, *"forest guardian"*.

The confused lines on Ty's forehead deepened. Bek rolled his eyes. He put his fingers in the corners of his mouth, miming a whistle, and gave Ty a look of utter exasperation. When Ty's face remained blank, he threw his hands in the air.

"Rhiannonae," he said, his quiet voice plenty loud enough in the stillness of the clearing.

Ty stared.

Bek, apparently satisfied that Ty finally understood, sat back and resumed the methodical consumption of his apple, peeling away a slice at a time with his knife.

Fae's eyes flicked from one to the other, lost.

"How do you...?" Ty said, his mouth gaping slightly. Bek's shoulders came up in a half shrug, his head cocked to one side in a way that said he didn't know, or didn't care, and nor did it matter. He carved another slice from the apple.

Fae cleared her throat pointedly. "What?" she said, looking at Bek, before turning back to Ty. "What is '*Rhiannonae*'?"

Still eyeing Bek, somewhat suspiciously, Ty stood. He eyed the dense crowd of trees around them. Then glanced uncertainly back at Bek, who nodded a kind of encouragement, equating to an impatient flapping of his apple-wielding hand, while he bit into the slice impaled on his knife.

Ty took a breath, rolling his eyes skywards as if he couldn't believe what he was about to do.

He placed two fingers in each corner of his mouth, and let out a long, low, whistle.

It echoed sullenly into the trees.

Pure silence answered him.

As if the forest held its breath.

Eah waits for you.

Fae heard the words echo in her ears, and sat up a little straighter.

They waited.

After nearly two minutes, Ty let out his breath, shoulders slumping.

Still, he waited.

She could almost see the tension in his ears as they all strained to hear past the silence. It was like a blanket that smothered the air around them.

Then, like a faint heartbeat, they heard it.

A soft thundering in the distance, thrumming through the trees.

The leaves trembled without moving.

The ground shook beneath them, and didn't.

It was strange contradiction — the forest quivered in anticipation, but stood frozen in time.

Holding its breath.

Ty's eyes widened imperceptibly more, but, through a sheer effort of will, he stood tall and composed before the impending arrival of... *something*.

The faint heartbeat became a muffled drumming sound that seemed to rebound off the trees until it was everywhere, all around them.

Fae's eyes darted to Bek.

He was grinning from ear to ear.

What does he know?!

She turned her attention back to the trees.

The drumming was accompanied by the tell-tale rustle of something big moving through the undergrowth.

She checked herself; some*things* big.

Moving closer to Ty, she waved Bek to do the same.

She didn't feel the need to unsheathe her blades, but that didn't mean she felt any less nervous at the approach.

The chorus of bass grew louder; became thunder in the forest.

Then the thunder slowed. It neared.

Stopped.

A soft snort caught in the air.

And an enormous shadow loomed between the trees.

Ty backed them up to stand in the middle of the clearing.

And three magnificent beasts stepped into view.

Fae gasped as her eyes tracked up to take in the most unusual creature she'd ever seen.

They were similar to horses. In the same way that elves were similar to men.

Firstly, they were enormous. Easily thirty hands tall at the withers, they towered over the group. They were slender but powerfully built; strong, lean muscle apparent in every movement. Their legs, long and athletic, ended in delicate cloven hooves. And the faces that sat atop gracefully willowy necks were beautiful and alien and perfect all at once.

Their silky soft ears divided at the base, creating two petal-shaped openings on either side of their head. Their noses were long and tapered, with wide, curious nostrils that twitched as they scented the air. Their eyes were round and black in stark contrast to the pure, unsullied white of their coats.

In fact, it was more than just unsullied.

Fae squinted to be sure she wasn't seeing things.

Their coats *shone*.

They shone with the same glow Fae had seen before when her wounds had magically healed. It was the glow of Eah'lara — the realm of the Aethyr.

The Rhiannonae eyed the group warily.

Their gaze snagged on Bek, who waved happily.

Then their deep, black eyes came to rest on Fae.

Her face was streaked with muck from the trailing limbs of the forest, she could feel it caking on her skin. Her hair escaped her dirty, ash-blonde braid in wild, snarled tendrils.

She felt dwarfed by these breathtaking creatures.

The foremost of the Rhiannonae, a mare, stretched its neck forward, and sniffed the air around her. Fae froze. Long, soft whiskers twitched at the end of a downy soft nose. They tickled where they brushed Fae's skin, nostrils flaring delicately as the creature scented her.

Apparently satisfied, the great horse lifted its head, eyeing her.

Then, gradually, it bent its front knee, and lowered its body towards her. The beautiful, alien head bent too, and pressed forward to rest against Fae's arm.

Is she... bowing? Fae couldn't believe her eyes.

Still motionless with shock, she reached a timid hand up between the mare's ears. The fur that covered her neck was velvety smooth; she had no mane to speak of, just the same short, soft down that appear to cover her all over. The creature raised her head to Fae's touch, and levelled a look at her.

A small, accepting nicker rippled from the Rhiannonae, a sound that was echoed from behind. Then the other two creatures followed the mare's lead, lowering their heads and bending both knees to come to rest fully on the forest floor.

Fae's breath caught in her chest.

"Ty?" she breathed, eyes fixed on the face in front of her. "You mind explaining this to me?"

"The Rhiannonae are the guardians of the forest; they're spiritual creatures," he whispered back, as if afraid to disturb the creatures. "But they're supposed to be a myth." He paused, taking in the scene before him. "It's said they only appear to answer the call of an Eldra." His tone held a wry edge. "Although, judging by how they're reacting to you, I suspect that assumption might need amending." The mare in front of Fae blew a soft breath across her forehead as if in response.

"But..." Fae stammered, "before yesterday, I've never had anything to do with spirits!"

"Well," Ty said, "that's not strictly true, though, is it? The Aethyr are the ones that brought you to Arolynos. They *know* you, somehow." And yet they'd remained silent all this time. A spark of anger flared bright before fading just as fast. She'd wanted this for so long. But just as she'd come to accept that she'd never hear the Aethyr, they shouted so loud she'd come away black and blue. And now the spiritual guardians of the forest were *bowing* to her. She was finding it hard to reconcile her amazement with her confusion. Why had she been kept in the dark all those years?

Ty chuckled suddenly.

"What?" Fae asked.

"Well—" he looked at her "—I think we can safely say you're nothing quite as simple as human, can't we?" He shook his head with a smile.

But if she wasn't human, what *was* she?

Fae turned back to the giant, horse-like creature before her, mulling his words over in her head.

She held out her hand to the lead Rhiannonae, who dutifully nuzzled into her scent. She smiled as the soft nose-hairs tickled her palm, the breath warm against her skin, and her other hand reached up to stroke along the graceful line of the mare's jaw. The Rhiannonae watched her with big, black eyes, as if waiting for Fae to do something.

Fae cocked an eyebrow at the creature. The Rhiannonae huffed in response, as if to say, *you first*.

She wracked her brains. If these creatures were of Eah'lara, then their methods for communication were likely to be... spiritual. She closed her eyes, and breathed. She tried to picture the place from her vision; the warm, glowing white, the choral voices.

Listening, someone had once described to her, was like broadening your field of view, *beyond* the tangible senses.

Her vision was restricted by what lay within sight, her touch by what lay within reach. When Listening, the senses were supposed to travel outside of the physical body, perceiving the imperceivable. Sensing everything, all around. Completely unhindered.

Behind closed eyes, Fae focused her senses outside of her body. And *pushed...*

She almost cried out with joy at how easy it was. It was as if she'd always been able to, she'd just never had the guide. Before, her mind had been closed. Watched, but never capable. But now...

It was as if her visions had opened the door, and her senses had only to step through.

She stretched her mind. Pushed it past the boundaries of herself. Sent it outward.

Stopped. And breathed.

Slowly, the forest came to her.

She *felt* the leaves on the trees without touching them. Growing. Reaching. Twirling.

She *felt* the ground beneath her feet as if her boots weren't a barrier between them. Giving. Breathing. Nurturing.

She *felt* the creatures lurking in the shadows beyond their clearing. Watching. Waiting.

She *felt* the bated breath of her companions. Ty's awe and shock. Bek's cool composure.

And the stoic grace of the Rhiannonae beside her. Patient. Accepting. Protective.

Patient.

She smiled.

And opened her senses to the Aethyr.

It was like rising from a lifetime underwater.

The world was a vast ocean, dense and filled with endless life. Creatures and plants. Tall mountains and deep trenches. Storms and calms and booming waves and quiet caves. It pressed and pushed and made her belong.

But to see the Aethyr — to *hear* them — she had to leave the water.

And come up for air.

Fae's senses broke the surface.

And finally Listened.

The Aethyr were silent. Completely. Utterly.

Silent.

Watching. Waiting.

She opened her eyes, treading water, holding onto the silence.

Will you speak with me, Rhiannonae? She asked into the stillness, chest tight with hope.

The dark eyes in front of her widened.

And she *felt* the response.

There were no words of any language, but there was feeling, there were colours. There was intelligence there too; the age of the Rhiannonae felt like a chasm without end, and their unwavering devotion to the forest around them ached in its purity. There was a trepidatious uncertainty at being called. And a fast fascination in her.

Me? Fae thought. She was assaulted with a cascade of emotion. It began with fear. Fear of a dark force destroying the virtue of the forest they protected. Then came anger, helplessness, courage, sadness.

And in the midst of it all, a small, shining star of hope in the darkness.

Ageless black eyes bored into her.

Eah waits for you.

Fae blinked tears of joy from her eyes. And her mind became clear.

I think I understand now.

She looked over towards Ty, frozen slack-jawed in awe. Even Bek looked impressed this time.

She took in the gathering dark around them. The inhospitable forest all around them.

And turned back to the Rhiannonae.

Will you guide us? she asked.

12

FLY AND FLOW

R iding on the back of the Rhiannonae was the most surreal, yet
wonderful experience of Fae's existence.

Their movements were smooth, graceful, swan-like. They flowed over
the ground like liquid moonlight.

After hearing the thunder of their hoofbeats in their approach, Fae
had expected to feel every jolt and tremor as their hooves hit the forest
floor. But the elegant creatures skipped over the ground, delicately
skimming the undergrowth, touching down only feather-lightly before
surging forward again.

Judging by Bek's uncharacteristically joyful whooping behind her, Fae
gathered the boy was enjoying the experience as much as she was. Ty
appeared to be concentrating very hard on not falling off.

As they flew through the trees, branches and brambles and trailing
vines seemed to draw back, floating gently aside to let them pass. The
forest opened up before them, but there still lingered an edge of darkness;
a vignette of a chill, just beyond their little circle of energy. It was the only
thing to taint the experience for Fae; an ominous reminder of why she was
here.

At some point, the lead Rhiannonae came to a slow halt.

Fae had come to think of the mare as a queen. It was in the regal way she moved, her head held high and poised, and in how the other two followed her every lead.

They came to a stop in a wide clearing, where the darkness appeared to hold back just enough. In the centre, a small meadow of wild flowers bloomed. Above, a frayed edge of purpling sky could be seen high above, weaving in and out of sight through the swaying crown of the forest.

Ty dismounted gracefully, patting the sweeping curve of his mount's neck and gazing up at the sliver of sky above. At the trees that bowed in towards them.

He breathed a sigh of awe. "We must have covered at least twice the distance we would have on foot." He spoke softly, mostly to himself. He turned, reconsidered his assessment. "More, even." He took a step back, as if to get a better view skyward, muttering quietly all the while.

Fae smiled. She knew they'd come a long way. She'd felt it in the gentle bunch and stretch of the queen's back as she *flew* through Il'arys. Seen it in the flash of foliage as they coursed past.

And experienced it in the raw spiritual energy that flowed from the Rhiannonae themselves.

After so long feeling the absence of the Aethyr, the merest whispers at the fringes of her mind, the pureness of the Rhiannonae was a relief — thirst-quenching to a parched soul. A waterfall into the drought she'd been living. *This* is what she'd been missing all her life. This connection to spiritkind. She almost felt as if she *was* a spirit, isolated and alone for so long, finally coming home.

She didn't want to let go, half convinced that it was all a dream, set to evaporate the moment she blinked. She leant forward, stretching her arms around the neck of the queen, resting her cheek against the velvet-smooth hair that covered her neck.

"Thank you," she whispered, and her mount's petal-ears flickered in response, as if she knew the thanks was for more than just their guidance through the forest. The Rhiannonae bent her front leg, lowering herself gently closer to the ground so that Fae could dismount easily.

Bek, meanwhile, threw his legs over the back of his mount and slid down its flank, limbs flailing. "Wooeee!" he cried, his voice unbridled joy. The Rhiannonae bore his excitement stoically as he landed in a crouch on the ground, a wide grin splitting his face in half. Fae's mouth twitched at the corners. The lead Rhiannonae nudged her arm with the flat of its head.

Fatigue. Rest. The feeling of soft, lush grasses at her back. The scent of fresh flowers in the air.

Speed. Urgency. Wind brushing her face and whipping her hair. Pushing forward. Onward.

Draining. Energy sapping. Strength leaving her limbs. Like her body was a cracked cup. No... her soul.

Urgency.

Rest.

"Okay," Fae said, her head reeling from the way the Rhiannonae communicated, "I understand." She lifted her arm to rest a hand against the queen's tall shoulder. "Rest now, but not long." She looked around at the unnatural darkness that clung to the trees beyond the clearing. "We have to keep moving."

Ty, overheard, and nodded. "I don't like the weight to the air here," he said, clutching at the air with his hand to illustrate his point. "It feels ominous. Let's make it quick and be on our way."

Bek halted his flower-meadow frolicking long enough to join them.

Bad feelings, he signed, inclining his head towards the trees. *Go soon.*

Fae agreed. They stood in an oasis of natural beauty within the clearing. But all around it felt poisoned somehow. Suffocating.

They sat in the deepening gloom at the centre of the meadow, hurriedly eating from their travel rations and taking rushed sips from water-wraps, all the while casting uneasy glances into the undergrowth.

They didn't dally, but the light faded quickly until their only source of illumination was the faint glow from the Rhiannonae. And even that held a quietness to it. As if the air sat heavy upon them too.

The Rhiannonae pawed at the ground impatiently when it was time to go again, their cloven hooves combing through the grasses to paint delicate grooves in the soil beneath. The queen nickered softly, and the creatures lowered themselves once again to allow their riders to mount.

Speed. Urgency. The wind against her face. And the spine-tingling sense of being pursued.

The queen sent Fae a flash of her intentions, and then they were off.

The instant they left the clearing, the darkness plunged in around them again, a torrent drawn towards them, like water crashing over a cliff edge. And with the soft glow of their guides the only light to see by, the gloom of the forest seemed all the more menacing.

They all felt the urgency of the Rhiannonae. There was something in the forest that wasn't right. And it was getting worse.

Shadows whipped past their travelling circle, thrown into sharp relief as they passed.

Darkness nipped at their heels as they flew and flowed through the trees.

And then, out of the darkness, something darted out and snagged on Fae's ankle as they passed. It snaked up and around her leg with terrifying speed and yanked her from the back of the Rhiannonae before she even had a chance to scream.

She tumbled into the pitch-black, the light from her guide soaring away, without her in it. Whatever had pulled her from her mount retreated as soon as she hit the ground, and she was left scrambling to her feet on uneven, overgrown ground. She stood thigh-deep in thick undergrowth; unseen creatures scurried and slithered over her feet. Her breath caught in her throat. And deeper in the woods, other, bigger, things moved.

She was alone, and the darkness spread endlessly all around her. The silence was so thick that every sound cut through it like a spear through flesh, and set her heart pounding anew.

The dark pressed in on her, smothering her like a thick blanket. It stopped her from calling out. This forest didn't feel like the same forest she called home. If she called out to Ty and Bek, she wasn't convinced they were the only ones who would answer.

An instinctive fear caged her. She was rooted to the spot, unable to move while the darkness pressed in on her even more, until she was sure she would just become a part of it, crushed under the weight of the omnipresent gloom. Panic, despair, and other, overwhelming emotions crested over her, and she almost gave in to the urge to curl into a small ball and wait for the inevitable end to come.

In the darkness, muffled whispers hissed urgently into her mind, as if they knew she could save herself. But the dark was oppressive, it told her she couldn't. And the discord only served to unbalance her further.

Tendrils snaked over her in the dark, catching her arms in the undergrowth, pulling her legs deeper into the thick, crawling carpet of the forest floor.

The whispers shrieked in her ears.

And fear froze her.

Then the thunder and glow of the Rhiannonae leapt into the brush, and the queen of her spiritual escort landed beside her with a resounding crash, surrounding Fae with a light and warmth that chased the darkness away, both within and without. The sense of defeat that had wormed its way into her mind receded into the darkness, and she scrambled up onto the Rhiannonae's back as she stood sentry, glaring blackly at the bushes around them. Glancing down, Fae fought the bile in her throat when she saw that the forest floor was thick with crawling insects, twisting snakes, and vines that moved of their own volition. She reached down and batted spiders and beetles from her legs, and then threw herself over the queen's neck.

"Go!" she cried, and the mare's slender back bunched and stretched away from the sinister, black undergrowth.

Up ahead, the twin spheres of Ty and Bek's mounts loomed as dim as spent lamps, hopeless at beating back the endless dark that swallowed everything around them, flickering as tree-shadows flailed between their glow and hers. As Fae and the queen approached, the attempts of the forest to rip her from her mount intensified, branches whipping out to catch at her shoulders, vines lashing at her legs, and wide tree-limbs reaching out to throw her bodily to the ground. Fae pasted herself to the Rhiannonae's back, her stomach pressed flat along the spine of her mount, her body bunching and rolling with the creature that carried her from the darkness.

When they finally drew level with Ty and Bek, the queen let out a shrill whinny. Without hesitation, the other two Rhiannonae reared, and fell into step behind her as they tore past.

They didn't stop to rest again after that. Hours they rode. And in the dark those hours felt like days. Weeks. Forever. Every noise, every crack of a branch, every nocturnal call, spurred them to run faster; to outrun the dark.

And within their little sphere of light, it felt as if they travelled no distance at all; racing wildly in place, as if suspended in time.

A feral energy possessed Fae in those hours; she lost herself to it. Each minute stretched out endlessly, her senses strained to the limits of their endurance and beyond.

She felt as if her eyes were out on stalks, as if she might spear the darkness with them and see the path ahead.

Her ears stretched wide, to catch every sound.

Her nostrils flared, grasping at wisps of unfamiliar scents like ribbons to guide her.

Her every nerve was alert, on fire, ready to blare out a warning with her rapid, staccato heartbeat.

Even her new sense of the silent Aethyr was wide open, held above water, scouring the spirits for hints.

But they remained simple spectators.

She couldn't hold on like this forever. She could already feel her senses tugging at her, trying to haul her back beneath the surface of her mind.

She clung to the lifeline of the Rhiannonae.

Just a bit longer, she thought desperately, unable to let go.

Not yet.

By the time the sun illuminated the sky once more, she was exhausted. Beyond exhausted.

She was stretched so tight she could snap. So thin she might simply dissolve with a sigh of relief, and blow away like dust on a gentle breeze.

But the sun had risen, and they had reached the outskirts of the forest.

The sunrise chased the bolder darkness back into the shadows, and gave the forest back its charm. The canopy was thinner here, the forest crown not so high. The sky showed through the trees in frequent flashes, birds passing across the view with happy snatches of song. Small critters scampered through the undergrowth, which in turn had stopped reaching up to ensnare them.

The wildness that had crept into their expressions as they travelled through the dark hours receded, although Ty's face still held an undertone of grimness Fae hadn't seen before. The Rhiannonae slowed their pace to a more manageable canter, their hooves making soft pitter-patter sounds against the ground.

Despite the welcome arrival of daylight, their guides continued on without rest. And no one else called for one; they were all eager to be out of the woods.

Eventually, the endless forest of trunks and foliage finally opened up enough to see the tree-line. The Rhiannonae came to a halt just as the sun reached its zenith, arrowing bright yellow light straight down between the trees to warm the earth beneath. Wildflowers pushed up from the soil here, and they could almost forget the horrors that lurked behind them.

A journey that would have taken the better part of a week to navigate on foot unhindered, was over in little more than a day. All thanks to their guides.

But the Rhiannonae were guardians of the forest, and could not go beyond its boundaries. Coming to a halt, they lowered themselves for the last time to allow their riders to dismount. Even Bek's descent to the ground was more sobered this time. Fae reached a hand up to her mount's neck, and the queen brought her face down to a level with hers.

In the clear light of day, Fae could see that the Rhiannonae's eyes were not black, as she had originally thought. They were the darkest, endless blue of the ocean depths. Or a moonless, midnight sky.

She smiled, and pressed her forehead to the flat plane of the Rhiannonae's long face.

"Thank you," she breathed, infusing her voice with as much gratitude as she could, projecting it into the Aethyr as well.

Pleasure. Gratitude. A warm glow from within. A smile on her face.

The lead Rhiannonae stepped back, lifting her head high. And for a moment, the three creatures stood, gloriously visible in the full light of the sun. Magical. Magnificent.

And somewhere, in the background, a quiet murmuring caught on Fae's senses.

What...? She strained to hear it. It wasn't the "voice" of the Rhiannonae, such as that was. It was something else. Someone else. A soft susurrus of sound, barely audible, but there.

Then, as if by some silent cue, the Rhiannonae reared, pawing their hooves twenty feet into the air, breaking Fae's concentration. Their farewell cry was a hundred birdsongs, a sigh of wind, a chorus of falling rain. It was the groan of roots, the creak of the trees, and the flurry of a thousand leaves. And then they were gone, fading back into the forest as they galloped past; their passage a mere breath in her ear.

As she felt the brush of their energy pass, the anchor of the Rhiannonae was pulled from Fae's grasp, and her senses collapsed inwards.

Deprived of the spiritual tether, the part of herself that was stretched taut, Listening for the Aethyr, rebounded whip-fast, snapping back into her like a thunderbolt.

She cried out in dismay, just as Ty and Bek gasped at the swift departure of their guides.

That her exclamation was of a different nature, went unnoticed.

She was plunged back into her tangible senses and it felt like being submerged in ice-cold mountain-water. Her extended connection to the world was cut off, severed. After the hours connected to the life and spirits around her, she was left cold and alone within the thin, fragile shell of herself.

Fae wiped a tear from her eye.

"Are you alright, Fae?" Ty rushed to her. He held her at arm's length, looking her over with a worried, albeit practiced, clinical eye.

"I'm fine," Fae answered, her voice sounding distanced to her ears, as if she stood apart from her body.

"I still can't believe it," Ty said, seemingly satisfied with her declaration. He shook his head in disbelief.

"What?" she said, holding up an exhaustion as heavy as the mountains themselves.

"I can't believe they're real," he said, staring at her. His expression turned suddenly pensive. "That this darkness has already spread so far into Il'arys troubles me." His eyes flicked away, glancing back into the trees as he thought aloud. "Perhaps the influence of Arolynos has spared the forest around it..." He tapped his chin. "But still..."

It worried Fae too. Her vision hadn't shown the darkness affecting the Aethyr anywhere near the elves, focusing only on the humans. Had it spread that much farther? Was it that much worse where they had yet to go? She thought of the leaves that withered and fell where they should have been fresh and green. Of the solid, living wood of Arolynos breaking without warning. Of the oppressive forest floor. And it was only going to get worse...

Weariness washed over her, but the thought of staying another night in the forest sent a shiver down her spine.

"Let's get to the edge of the forest before the sun sets," she suggested, indicating the visible tree-line from their position with one hand, and rubbing at her face with the other. "We can set up camp there."

Shifting the weight of her pack, she waited barely long enough for the others to acknowledge her proposal before starting towards the vertical bars of sky visible between distant tree trunks.

Every step felt heavier than the last, as if her boots were filled with rocks.

By the time Fae collapsed to sit at the edge of the forest, the sun was halfway in its descent across the sky, with plenty of daylight left to set camp.

Ty dropped his pack and stared out across the land. Bek stood beside Fae, a hand on her shoulder. Born and raised in the trees, elves had few opportunities to see such broad swathes of open landscape. They stood, stunned by the view.

It was beautiful.

Vast plains stretched out before them. The I'dyll River exited the forest west of where they stood, flowing down to meet the Amedi River and eventually onward to the Great Fall, far to the east. The snaking form of the water glistened in the sunlight, but it lay far off yet. And the sky! Such vast expanses as she'd never seen before. In Arolynos, her world had been defined by the trees around her. But out here... the world was endless.

And she was to venture even further from the only home she'd ever known, out into this endless world, to do... what? If the darkness in the forest was only a taste of what was happening to the Aethyr, what hope did she have of making a difference? Of saving them?

Eventually, Ty shook himself of his reverie and turned to gather wood from the forest edge. Bek looked about for stones to line a campfire.

The sun continued its earthward journey while they worked. When it eventually kissed the horizon, it was with a song of gold, and pinks, and purples. In the sky above, graceful shadows danced across the clouds.

But Fae saw none of its beauty.

Instead, she stared blankly over the land.

This land that she'd never known.

Full of people she'd never met.

And a destiny she'd never expected.

13

FISH DREAMS

When Fae woke the next morning, it was to unfettered sunlight so bright it roused her as surely as the school bell to her ear, accustomed as she was to the softly filtered glow of Arolynos. She sat up squinting, and shielded her eyes until they adjusted to the glare.

The forest of Il'arys seemed to rise above the land around it, and the view from their vantage point laid the onward journey out like a map. The sky was a clear, uninterrupted blue, the sun a blazing orb suspended just above the horizon. Arland stretched out below, the Amedi River a lazy snake dividing the region, east to west. The plains rolled out and away for miles, the occasional landmark dotting the canvas like forgotten tableware on a smooth, green cloth.

After a cold breakfast, they descended into the valley of the Amedi River. There, they refilled their water-wraps and washed in the shallows of a wide bend in the river. The water was clear, but it tasted strange; earthy and metallic at the same time.

"The water in the Village is collected straight from the sky," Ty explained when Fae queried it. "Rainwater tastes fresher." He cupped a handful of water where it trickled over river-smoothed stones, and took a sip. "This has been filtered through rocks and minerals all the way from its source, to the valley here. It tastes of its journey." He smiled a wry smile. "As do all things."

Tastes of fish, Bek signed with a grin. He indicated a small school of slim, silvery fish in the deeper water, and paddled further into the river to get a closer look.

"Careful Bek," Fae cautioned as he waded towards the faster currents. "Don't get caught in the — oh!" she gasped as the boy plunged his head fully under the water, his legs still standing upright in the shallows.

After a moment, he emerged, his head glistening wet in the sun.

Sounds like fish dreams, he signed, then burst out laughing.

A small smile crept onto Fae's face as she watched him splash about, ducking his head in the water for a moment, and then moving along to repeat the process in a different part of the river. She looked over to Ty, who was wearing an inscrutable expression as he watched Bek's antics.

They set camp by the river that night. Bek managed to catch a slippery fish bare-handed, a feat which had Ty raising a questioning eyebrow at the boy. Fae spotted some edible waterroots at a point where the water eddied, and backtracked a little way to gather some. By the time she'd returned, Ty had a fire going and was gutting the fish.

A single, gibbous moon lit the countryside beyond their circle of firelight as they roasted the roots in the edge of the fire, peeling the blacked skins away to reveal sweet, tender flesh beneath. Bek proudly spitted the fish on a stick, and turned it over the flames until it flaked from the bones. Elves did not often eat meat, and the addition made the meal rich and filling. Stuffing the hot fish into warm flatbreads, and eating the roots straight from the skins, they enjoyed a hearty riverside dinner, all things considered.

"I hope we come across a village soon," Fae said, eyeing the supplies in her pack. "We've got plenty of hard rations." She lifted a hunk of dense, hard biscuit. Made from mixed grain flour and baked with candied fruits, it was made to last for long journeys and would sustain a traveller in the absence of anything else. "But we'll run out of flatbread in a couple of days."

"Don't worry Fae," Ty said around a mouthful of the baked waterroot. He gestured with his fish-stuffed flatbread. "We can forage a lot of food from the land. And I'm sure we'll find more supplies along the way. Just keep an eye out for more like these roots." As if remembering something else, he cast his eyes to the heavens. "Eah, may we pass by an orchard!" he said with a sudden wistfulness. "I would dearly love to fill my pack with a dozen apples!"

"Apples," Fae repeated flatly. They had apples in Arolynos.

"Oh not like the apples we know," Ty said, catching her tone. His face became serious and he leant forward. "In Arolynos, we eat the apples that grow naturally in the forest. But in Arland—" his voice took on a fervent edge "—they *cultivate* them! So many varieties, colours, *flavours!*" He rocked backwards, spreading his hands to indicate an endless choice. "It is hopeless to decide between them," he concluded.

"I didn't know you'd travelled in Arland," Fae said.

Ty looked at her. "Oh, I haven't," he replied.

"Then how do you know about apples?" she said, forehead creasing in confusion.

"Voren Longstem — Stef and Aren's father — used to bring them back with him from his travels," he explained dreamily. "Small, red ones, bright as berries and sweet as honey. Green ones as big as both fists and fresh as rainwater. Mmm," he moaned to himself, eyes closed. "What I wouldn't give to find an orchard, and pick some for myself."

Fae smiled. "Well alright then," she said. "I'll keep my eyes open for an orchard."

"Of course, humans grow more than just apples," Ty continued, his mind reliving stories told to him by his own childhood scouts. "Pears, and oranges, and grapes the likes of which we don't see in Arolynos. But for some reason grape orchards are called something different... I forget what..." he trailed off as he tried to remember.

"Okay, okay!" Fae laughed. "In between foraging, we will search for these orchards so that you can have your apples." She exchanged a glanced with Bek, who rolled his eyes as he licked his fingers of the last of his dinner. She forced a smile.

They'd both accepted the reality of their journey so easily. If only she could share in their optimism.

But all she could feel was the weight of her quest sitting heavy across her shoulders.

All she knew was to go north. The pull in her bones, in her blood, called to her whenever she paused long enough to feel it. But what was she supposed to do when she got there? How long would it take? How much worse would the darkness in the Aethyr be by then?

So many questions, each no more illuminating than the last, and no way of answering any of them.

And all the while, the Aethyr kept to their enigmatic silence.

The next day, Fae brooded beneath a heavy cloud.

The sun shone brightly on their journey, but her mood was black, and she spoke little.

Bek showed his concern plain upon his face, though she did not see it. Ty cast a worried look her way and quietly took the lead.

On the third day from the edge of Il'arys, he found what he was looking for.

A small wooden bridge perched over a tall but narrow gully that looked like an axe-wound in the ground. As the water flowed into the deep notch in the earth, it picked up speed, eagerly dashing headlong through the gap. An old village once shared both sides of the river, the bridge connecting the two halves while the long disused watermill balanced on the south side of the gully. When in use, there was no doubt the mill would have ground twice the wheat of any other, so fast was the water passing through it. But now, the wheel flapped uselessly back and forth in the water, its paddles long since rotted or broken. The bridge wasn't in much better shape, but it at least offered them a half-serviceable way across the Amedi, which would only get wider and harder to cross, the further they followed it.

But as they picked through the outskirts of the village, there were signs that the village hadn't just been deserted. The first house they passed was a mix of crumbling stone and shattered timbers. The next still wore blackened marks from an old fire. The door of the third was notched and battered, its neighbour's windows broken, the jagged shards stained with something dark.

The rasping caw of a crow rang out across the dead stillness, the only other sound that of the river rushing past. Running away.

Ty shuddered involuntarily. Bek's face was unreadable; his eyes were sad, his mouth grim, his jaw hard.

Fae saw it.

She saw even what the others did not.

She stopped. Looked up at the building husks.

She glared at the shell of a simple home. Its stout, stone chimney stack was collapsed in over burnt-through roof timbers, what remained of the front door in splinters.

And in her mind's eye, she saw her vision again, saw the chaos and violence that had brought about the destruction of this peaceful village, and so many others like it.

"Fae?" Ty called. He took a step towards her. Bek kept a wary distance.

Her face contorted with burning rage, her eyes blazing. Her hands curled into fists, and trembled with cold fury.

But her gaze was distant. Unfocused. Seeing past horrors as if they unfolded before her now.

"Fae?" Ty repeated, reaching a hand out to touch her arm. "Are you okay?"

His fingers brushed her skin.

And fire engulfed her.

Ty leapt back from the sudden blaze, and then almost jumped straight back at her to smother the flames that had sprung up around Fae's body.

Before he could, a small hand grabbed at his wrist. Ty turned to see Bek holding him back. When he went to pull away, the boy held on even tighter.

Look, he signed, pointing two fingers of one hand to his eyes, and then out to Fae.

Ty turned back, and looked again.

The flames had already receded somewhat, and as he watched, they retreated until they burned only in Fae's eyes, now glowing a molten orange, seeing something beyond what they could.

And she was *floating*.

Ty stopped pulling against Bek's grip.

The day had been a still one, but a wind came out of nowhere to circle Fae, whipping her hair into a frenzy around her head.

She looked... elemental. A being of wind and fire.

And then her skin began to glow.

The light within her intensified until it was almost blinding, and with it came a building pressure in the air, like they'd dived deep under water. Ty's ears popped, and the air crackled with static.

"Fae!" Ty called into the wind, his voice breaking with a nameless fear. Fear for her. And fear of her.

Fae heard Ty calling her name from beyond a roar of flame. The sound was secondary to what played before her eyes.

The ruins of the village in which she stood, blazing as hot and deadly as the day it was burned.

But it wasn't just the fire that held her enthralled.

She knew this village.

She knew what had happened here.

Pain lanced across her back and sides.

Echoes of those same wounds, as fresh as then.

The same fire raged unchecked.

The same screams rang in her ears; tormenting in their repetition.

But a new fire burned within her.

Before, she had felt fear.

This time, she felt fury.

She heard the humans — the vicious predators — working their bloody business through the homes of innocent villagers.

She found them in the village centre. Two men savagely beat a young woman. Another held her child by the hair, forcing him to watch.

The screams of the child pierced through her. The sobs of the woman tore ribbons from her heart.

Fury, raging unchecked beneath the surface, boiled over.

She was unaware of moving, but in an instant she was beside the group.

A flash of recognition shot through her as the first turned to face her. These were the men from her first vision. The ones who had beaten her too.

They crumpled before the inferno in her eyes.

An unnatural glow surrounded her. It felt... familiar.

She grasped at its energy. Wrapped it around her like a cloak.

Something whispered within her, just beyond her hearing.

She breathed deep, drawing the wind into her lungs.

The glow around her burned.

And she readied herself to unleash a force she had never before dreamed of.

She spared a glance at the woman and her child.

Their eyes were round with fear. The child peered out from behind his mother's protective embrace, and his eyes were filled with the same terror Fae had felt when confronted by these same men.

That terror stole the breath from her.

The wind stilled.

The fire calmed.

The child faded...

... Bek stood before her, wearing the same look on his face.

Her anger turned to ice in her gut as she realised what she had been about to do.

Although *how* she was going to unleash power the likes of which she had never known...

In the back of her mind, the whispers remained. Cocking her head to the side, she listened in to the sound. She'd heard it before — just a hint, before the Rhiannonae had returned to the forest. The sound brushed against the very edges of her senses, timid, and secretive.

She strained to hear it, to make sense of the whispers. And then...

She gasped. And *Listened* —

Then Ty was at her side, gripping her arm roughly and turning her to face him.

"What. Was. That?" he rasped, his eyes wide with a mix of anger, fear, shock... and something else.

But she didn't know. She'd felt powerful. She'd felt as if she had only to think it, and those monsters would have been dust on the wind.

But she was just a human. Wasn't she?

Suddenly the idea of having so much power in her grasp frightened her. What would it do to her? To have the power to wield life and death over others with no more than a thought? It sickened her.

She turned to Bek, opening her arm out to him. He hesitated only for a moment before walking into her embrace. Relief swept through her, and she wrapped her arms around him, squeezed him tight, praying it reassured him, that it salved some of the shock. The image of the terror in his eyes echoed through her mind. She couldn't bear the thought that he would be scared of her. She didn't ever want to see fear in his face when he looked at her.

Resting her chin on his head, she looked over the surrounding buildings, long since burned.

She breathed in deep, and blew it out long and slow. She glanced back at Ty.

"I saw this," she said, extending her arm out to take in the village. "It's the same village I saw before." He nodded in understanding. Her eyes swept over the ruins once more. "But this time it was different."

"You fought back," Ty said. It wasn't a question.

Fae frowned. "Yes," she said, not sure how else to describe what she had tried to do. All of a sudden, hot tears streamed unbidden down her face. She brushed them away angrily. "I became a monster," she answered herself. Bek's arms squeezed tight around her waist.

Ty stepped in front of her. "No," he said as his hands found hers. His skin warmed the chill that had settled in hers, and she found herself holding onto him like a lifeline. He ducked his head to look her in the eye. "Not a monster." He squeezed her hands and held her gaze, waiting for her to relent. Fae searched his face for the wariness he must surely feel of her now, but there wasn't any. Instead, he smiled. "You were beautiful," he said. He brought his hand up to show his thumb and forefinger a bare inch apart. "Maybe a little terrifying in your anger. No—" his eyes glanced askance, thinking. "Formidable," he revised, and nodded to himself, satisfied with his amended wording. His gaze came back to meet hers. "But I could feel the Aethyr's presence within you."

She frowned at him. The whispers. They'd had the feel of the Aethyr, the spirits that had never deigned to speak with her before the visions — were they starting to do so now?

"What did *you* see?" she asked him. Ty hesitated, and she felt a cold prickle as he weighed his words.

"You glowed," Bek whispered next to her. She looked down to find him staring up at her, not in fear, but in... wonder?... awe?

Ty cleared his throat. "Well first, you burned." He shot her a reproachful glare, a simple admonition that she should know better than to play with fire. "But then the fire receded until it was just in your eyes." His brow furrowed as he tried to put the sequence in order. "You were floating — just an inch or so — above the ground. You looked furious." This bit seemed to worry him, and his hand tightened around hers. "But then it's just like Bek said — you glowed." His eyes bored into hers, as if he hoped to glean something more than her nonplussed expression revealed. "The wind blew around you. Like a tornado, but just around you..." His lips pressed into a thin line and his face turned to puzzled worry. "There was power, building around you, like something was about to happen." He shook his head. "But then the light faltered, the wind dropped..." He half-turned, taking in the surrounding village as if to say, ...*and here we are*.

Fae was quiet. She hadn't just imagined she could destroy those people in her vision. She knew she *could* have, had they stood before her. If she hadn't seen the look in that child's eyes.

She squeezed her eyes shut to fight back more tears.

"I was a monster," she said again, her voice no more than a breath, the realisation of what she'd been capable of filling her with renewed horror.

"No." Bek spoke softly from her side. "Spiritchild."

Fae jolted from her melancholy. "Wha—?" She stared at the boy to be sure she'd heard correctly. She hadn't told anyone about that part of her vision. Ty did a full double take. Then he chuckled.

"Well," Ty said, a new smile upon his face, "I never did think you were 'just' human." He contemplated Bek carefully. "It's true though... Consider this..." He released Fae's hands to drop his pack against the still-standing portion of a nearby wall, and sat cross-legged beside it, patting the ground to indicate that they make themselves comfortable. Fae's hands clenched around the air where his had been, her skin tingling where his had warmed her. "We are, without a doubt," he began as they sat, "on a mission, bestowed upon us by the Aethyr." He ticked off one finger on his hand. "The legendary Rhiannonae deigned to serve us in our hour of need, when they haven't been heard of for generations." He ticked another finger off. "And you—" he indicated Fae with his counting hand "—are receiving visions in line with a destiny greater than any we could ever have previously predicted." He paused. "Not to mention the possibility of fire-wielding, spirit-glowing powers..." He scratched absently at his chin, then shrugged, ticking another finger off.

He spread his hands as if to invite questions.

Fae stared slack-jawed at him. She was shocked: both that his list of accolades all belonged to her, and that Ty had such faith in her. She had done nothing to deserve it, and yet here he was. Bek merely nodded and pulled out some hard biscuit to munch on. Ty plucked at the grass around him as Fae continued to gawp.

But Ty's list hadn't included everything. In that moment, she'd had the power to do anything. She'd been willing to harm with it. To kill. And that scared her more than anything.

"Mind you," Ty continued, pondering aloud, "This is all in line with Joa's Last..."

Bek laughed.

"Joa was crazy," he said matter-of-factly, "but right."

Ty eyed him. "You're talking more than usual today, Bek," he said, one eyebrow raised. "Any reason?"

Bek nodded, smiling. "Not so loud out here," he answered, and set to his food without further comment. When he was no more forthcoming, Ty shrugged, content enough that he seemed happier in himself, and looked back at Fae, still deep in thought. He leaned forward, steepling his fingers.

"Come on," he said firmly, "share. What's weighing on you? You've been lost since we left the forest."

She looked up at him, eyes wet. "How can I be chosen to be this... this 'one with the Spirit within', if I come from such a dark place?" she whispered, sweeping an arm out to indicate the village ruins, finally giving voice to her fears. She swallowed thickly. "If I was born of the most hurtful race known to the world?" A silent tear escaped her lashes and trailed a shining path down her cheek. She blinked her eyes shut and shook her head.

"I'm not the right person for this," she breathed, her voice breaking.

Ty reached over to wipe the tear from her face. Tilted her chin up to look her in the eye.

"I would entrust no other," he said, his gaze as immovable as stone. And in his gaze she saw the truth of his words, the faith he had in her. And she couldn't bear it.

Fae's face crumpled, and Ty gathered her to him as she sobbed silently into her hands. Alarmed, Bek crawled over to wrap his arms around her too.

Despite Ty's words, Fae couldn't shake the doubt, couldn't stop herself from wondering if the capacity for darkness lived inside her too. The burning rage, the cold fury, the force inside her that had been a heartbeat away from destroying...

Had the Aethyr chosen the right one to save them, in her?

14

THE DANCER

They crossed the bridge, and left the ghosts of the village behind.

The first night out from under its haunting memories, Fae danced.

Dancing had always been a sort of homecoming for her. After long days of learning, of healing the bodies and minds of others, she found the solitude and time spent moving with herself to be a kind of therapy in itself; tonic for the soul. No matter how peaceful the Village was, tending to the bustle of Arolynos was consuming. It was easy to lose a sense of self, of perspective.

She began with *Bin'dera*. Traditionally used to aid with contemplation, or meditation of sorts, the hypnotic movements of *Bin'dera* guided the thoughts inwards. She snaked her arms outwards in wide, arcing motions, before bringing them back to her centre. She stepped her feet out wide, making space to take in all that affected her. Then, balancing on her left leg, she swept the right back in to join it. Coming back to centre.

She repeated the movements on both sides, making them smaller and smaller until she barely left her centre at all.

Eventually, Fae stood in Mountain. Her hands at heart centre. Head bowed.

Inside, her mind was the flat calm of a lake. Not a ripple disturbed the surface.

The last few days had been a roiling storm of doubt, uncertainty, endless questions, and fear.

Now that all was calm, she allowed her thoughts back in. One at a time.

The first one was a single droplet on the lake. A single point of thought.

As the ripples spread across her mind, she moved into *Thallak*.

Thallak was the dance for logic. It was for objectivity. Evaluation. For finding solutions.

Thallak was often used in conjunction with *Bin'dera*, and the movements flowed seamlessly from one to the other. But while *Bin'dera* was graceful and hypnotic, *Thallak* was ordered. It had a pattern to it. A flow.

Finally, Fae finished with *Re'yal*, for strength.

Many partnered *Re'yal* with *Gestral*, the combat dance forms. But while *Re'yal* did contain moves to physically strengthen the body, it was primarily valued for its abilities to focus and reinforce the strength of the mind. Given what Fae suspected was yet to come on her journey, she decided a bit of mental fortitude wouldn't go amiss.

Her mouth twitched up at the corner as she finished, a fine sheen of sweat coating her skin. It had been a while since she'd had the chance to practice her dancing with such intent.

But then again, she supposed, she hadn't felt the need as intensely as she did now.

Every night after that, Fae carved out time to practice. After a few days, Ty and Bek followed her lead; spending a little time every day to do something for themselves. Something that had nothing to do with their enigmatic journey.

One such evening, Ty untied a long wrap of oilcloth from the side of his pack.

He placed the item across his crossed legs, and gently folded the edge of the wrappings back. Bek made a soft "ooh" sound, eyes wide.

Ty smiled at his reaction. It was a longbow, hewn of a single, sweeping length of *kewa*, a hardwood tree that grew strong, pliant timber. The gleaming wood had a well-oiled shine to it, the colour deep and rich. And around the grip, intricate etchings had been painstakingly inlaid into the belly of the bow.

Handling the bow with practiced ease, Ty held it out toward Bek, who took it with a reverent care. He ran his fingers gingerly along the length of it, tracing the etchings as they swirled over the surface of the wood.

"I can teach you if you like," Ty offered.

Bek's eyes darted up to meet his. He nodded so vigorously Fae thought his head might roll free of his neck.

Laughingly, Ty reclaimed the longbow. "Well first thing's first," he said, rewrapping it carefully, "you'll need to make your own." The look he cast Bek was flat and serious. When Bek's face fell, he yielded with a soft chuckle. "Don't worry, I will show you how." He clapped a hand on the boy's shoulder. "You would not expect to help yourself to my arm or my leg now, would you?" Bek's eyes widened with alarm, and he shook his head with the same alarming fervour as before. Ty smiled encouragingly at him. "Then I shall show you how to make your own to learn with, and care for as I do mine."

From that evening, with careful instructions, Bek kept an eye out for likely bow materials while out collecting firewood. On the third day of looking, he found a promising maple tree with long, straight limbs. He tugged Ty over to cast an eye over his finding, and Ty showed him what qualities to look for in the wood, what flaws to avoid, how best to harvest the limb, and how to treat it. Beaming with pride, Bek returned to camp that night with the beginning of his own precious longbow.

Next came the strings, and again Ty instructed Bek on what plants would yield good, strong fibres, long enough for a bowstring. He patiently fashioned five; Ty quietly advising that he would likely need more than one.

After a few days, Bek had a very respectable longbow, with a grip generously wrapped in twine, and even a few basic etchings around its belly.

Then their practice began in earnest.

The first night Ty took Bek a few steps away from the camp to teach him the principles of archery, Fae quietly brought her swords out of their sheath.

She hadn't performed the dance of the fallen leaf since her elevation to Senior Echa. Of course she had *danced* in that time. But *Aleralys* had always held a special place in her heart. Besides keeping her skills honed, she rarely practiced that particular form.

She sighed and put her swords away again. She had no need of a weapon today. And the empty plains of the Deadwolds, with its skeleton-villages, was no place for her *Aleralys*.

Nonetheless, with every passing day, Fae's spirits lifted, Bek spoke more and more often, and the edge of concern that had shaded Ty's face faded to nothingness.

A week after leaving the river behind them, they reached a wide, paved road running across their path from the eastern horizon, disappearing away to the west.

They stopped at its edge, peering at the stones as if they had no business being here.

Ty's gaze followed the road east, his eyes squinting into the distance.

"This must be the Southern Highway," he said. "If it is, it runs straight to Throldon." He turned, bringing an arm up to shield his face from the sun, setting low in the sky. "We don't want to be found anywhere near here if we can help it." His expression flattened, echoing the edge of concern he'd worn through Il'arys. He shifted his pack on his shoulders. "We'll find somewhere to camp further on." He nodded to the empty landscape north of the road. "Out of sight."

They walked until the sun was halfway below the horizon before stopping again. Bek quickly built up a small fire, while Fae and Ty dug through their provisions for dinner. Foraging across the Wolds had borne a variety of new food stuffs. In one deserted village, the inn's coldstore still held a good stock of supplies, from which they'd refilled their packs. And on the outskirts of another, Ty had found his orchard. They'd sat a while and eaten their fill of apples and pears in the dappled shade of the fruit trees; a rare moment of true peace and contentment in unknown lands. They'd found edible fungi, and plenty of roots and vegetables growing wild or in untended fields.

While the abandonment of the villages had made foraging easier, it also lent an air of otherworldliness to the land. They didn't come across another person in all the days of their travel; as if they were the only ones to walk the earth.

It gave Fae a creeping sense of unease.

She pushed some tubers into the edge of the fire to roast as the last sliver of sunlight disappeared behind the earth.

As night spread across the sky, and one moon chased the other from the horizon, the far-off calls of nocturnal creatures echoed across the plains. A short gust of wind carried the sound of voices toward them from the road. Ty's ears twitched, and he straightened to listen. After a moment, he relaxed — just a caravan stopped for the night. It was just as well they had chosen to camp away from the road.

Still, conversation that evening was quiet and halting.

A bare hour after darkness fell, a scream echoed across the land.

Fae's back jerked ramrod straight, her eyes darting to the other two. Ty's head snapped up towards the road, and Bek's brow furrowed into an uncharacteristic frown.

Another scream rose up from the road. Shouting, the shrill whinnying of panicked horses, then the clash of fighting.

With one glance, and not a single word exchanged, they jumped to their feet, grabbed their weapons, and sprinted toward the screams.

They'd only camped around half a mile from the road, and covered the distance easily. Coming over the crest of a small rise separating their camp from the road, the source of the noise became immediately apparent.

A sizeable group of raiders had set upon the caravan they'd heard earlier. They attacked weary travellers indiscriminately, tearing at men and women alike with rudimentary tools, nails, even teeth. The horses tried in vain to escape the smell of bloodshed. One, still half-hitched to a wagon, pulled wildly against its bearings. Eventually, the terrified animal tore off, heedless of the wagon still dragging at its side, and an opportunistic raider grabbed onto the wagon as it passed, leaping up to the driver's seat. Whipping the reins with savage glee, he hauled at the entangled horse to chase down those who thought to run. With eyes stretched wide enough to see the bloodshot whites around them, and flanks foaming with sweat, the animals were adding their own share of chaos to the melee.

One of the caravan men was attempting to hold his own against the raiders, but his opponents were too vicious, and had no quandaries about killing anyone standing in their way. He fell quickly.

A woman curled protectively around her child beneath the axle of the caravan, eyes wide with terror.

At the sight of them huddled together, anger swelled in Fae.

It burned within her.

But before her fury could consume her, she spotted one other figure. One who didn't belong to either group.

Seemingly apart from the travellers, a solitary human man danced between the raiders. He ducked and wove his way through the throng, dealing deadly blows to the aggressors with little more than a short dagger. The bow and quiver of arrows strapped to his back were useless at such close quarters; he fought fist and foot like the demons he faced.

Then, as he parried an unrestrained swing from one raider, another jumped him from behind. In a blink, he was outnumbered three to one. He was moments away from being overwhelmed.

Fae broke from her trance, drawing her swords.

They were not meant for such gruesome work.

But she hoped they'd forgive her.

"Cover!" she yelled over her shoulder as she leapt into the fray. She danced and dodged among the raiders, the embodiment of grace amidst chaos. She distantly heard the twang of Ty's longbow and a soft whisper as the answering arrow flew past her to take a raider in the throat. These monsters were deadly, but they were clumsy and slow. She flitted around them effortlessly; beautiful and far deadlier.

She leapt nimbly over the swing of a cudgel aspiring to take her legs from under her. Turning, she delivered a blow to the back of her assailant's head with the hilt of her blade. She swung her right sword in a smooth arc to take another thug in the chest, following it effortlessly with an upward slice with her other blade. She'd trained with elves. It was pure ease for her to assess the actions of these barbarous humans, and react accordingly, their limbs as slow as the ribbons she severed in her dancing.

But she was hopelessly outnumbered, even her fellow dancer was fighting three-to-one. The movements of her opponents were harsh and aggressive where the ribbons of *Aleralys* were floating and graceful. The yelling and screaming was loud in her ears. The smell of blood caught in her nose. Every movement jarred where it should flow. Her dancing did not belong in the midst of such violence.

She pivoted around another fighter, and caught sight of the woman and child clutching each other beneath the wagon. The anger that rose up in her at the sight reminded her why she danced with the violence. Why she fought. She remembered the woman from her vision, the way monsters just like these had held her child by the hair as they beat her.

Swinging one sword behind her, Fae gifted one thug a glancing slice across the face, forcing him to retreat, before taking another face-on. This one brandished a heavy metal bar — simple, but solid — and he blocked her swing with a blow that jarred her arm down to the bone. Her blades were sharp, but they weren't sharp enough to cut clean through metal. They bit, and wedged tight in the bar.

She wasn't expecting it. She was an expert in wielding her swords, but she was no fighter. In the split-second it took her to register her position, the thug twisted and let go of the bar, weighing down her swords and pulling them to the ground. With her guard down, he struck her full-force across the face, the blow sending stars across her vision.

The familiar *whoosh* of an arrow sped past, but not before a line of fire drew across her belly. As the man stumbled, Ty's arrow in his chest, the dagger he'd pulled on her dropped to the ground, wet with her blood.

She grunted in synchrony with him as he slumped to the ground, dead.

Taking a moment to retrieve her swords, she wrenched them from the ugly iron bar, and turned to the next assailant, ignoring the flash of pain across her middle for now. Even injured, she was faster than these men.

But the last of the raiders lay on the ground; unconscious or dead.

While she herself had been sure not to kill, Ty had not been so hesitant. And nor had her fellow dancer. She winced at the violence evident around the camp.

Glancing around for the other fighter, she spotted him tending to one of the wounded travellers. She scanned the area quickly. Of the eight that had made up the caravan when it set camp, only half remained. And not one of them was without injury.

If we hadn't camped so far from the road, Fae thought angrily, *we could have prevented much of this.* A mixture of fury and guilt churned in her gut. Ty appeared beside her, and put a hand on her shoulder.

"Are you alright?" he asked.

Without even looking at him, Fae could tell his eyebrows would be knitted, lines bracketing his mouth. She looked down, at the line stained in blood across her midriff. She fingered it gingerly and hissed. It hurt, but it wasn't serious.

The world pitched drunkenly for a moment, before righting itself again. No doubt from blood loss. Nothing she couldn't handle for now.

"Fae." Ty's voice was threaded with concern.

She nodded tersely, her gaze sweeping over the dead. "Fine," she said, "which is more than can be said for these people." She nodded towards the injured travellers.

Ty frowned, his hand tightening on her shoulder. "That needs stitching." He nodded to the slowly spreading stain on her shirt.

She shook her head, ignoring how the motion set her head spinning again. "It's clotting. It can wait."

Just as Ty opened his mouth to respond, the other dancer approached them. Bek ducked past him to join the small huddle of survivors.

"Well met," the traveller greeted them. Piercing blue eyes smiled at them over a scraggly beard in desperate need of a trim. He wiped the flat of his dagger clean on his trouser leg, the rest of his clothes already covered in gore. Judging his blade to be sufficiently bloodless, he sheathed it and raised his hand in a casual salute.

"Thank you kindly for jumpin' in just now," he said, mopping a mix of sweat, muck and blood from his face with his forearm. His country accent was thick enough to spread on toast, and Fae struggled to summon the focus required to follow his words. "Think that might just o' done me had you not come along when you did." He began wiping his hands as best he could on the seat of his slacks and inspected them closely. Judging them fit for purpose, he thrust out his right hand in a traditional human greeting.

"Name's Hal," he pronounced. Fae looked from his hand, to his earnest face, back to his outstretched hand again, and slowly extended her own in response. His grip was firm and strong when he folded his hand around hers, her own a hesitant reply.

Beaming a crooked smile, Hal looked to Ty, and his eyes widened when he noticed his hallmark upswept ears.

"Elves is it?" He raised an eyebrow. "Not seen the likes of you about, thought you were all dead. Or legend." He frowned a little. "What brings you out o' your woods?"

"We're on our way north," Fae said. Unsure of how to further explain their strange quest, she looked over to the other travellers.

"They'll need tending," she said, indicating the group. They were huddled closely together by the scant shelter of their miraculously undamaged caravan. Hal turned to follow her gaze. He cursed.

"Only four!" he muttered to himself as he strode over to them. He knelt by the youngest of the group, a boy no older than Bek, and placed a hand on the child's shoulder.

"How are you son? You hurt?" The boy shook his head no, though he bore a number of scrapes to his face. He huddled close into the side of the only woman of the group; presumably his mother. Hal stood and looked over the others, anger clouding his face. A young man hovered nearby, a deep rent in his shirt revealing a gash that ran almost the length of his arm. Bare-faced and tanned, he appeared to be on the fresh side of twenty, and his eyes kept darting about the place, as if expecting one of the raiders to rise and attack anew. The final remaining member of the band sat leaning against the spokes of one caravan wheel. He was a heavy-set man with the look and bearing of one whose word was usually heard and obeyed — likely the owner. Hal nodded to him. The man returned the gesture with hard eyes. It was a hard thing to see one's livelihood torn to shreds, not to mention the people who helped run it. His face was a grim mask.

Hal pointed out the odd angle of the man's leg, clearly broken.

"That'll need splinting if I'm a wagering man. That's for sure," he growled and mumbled to himself as he began rummaging through the wagon.

Fae and Ty moved through the ragged band, assessing each for their injuries.

They splinted the man's leg, the only sign he gave of his discomfort a deep grunt as they pulled it straight. The young man's arm needed binding, and Hal helpfully unearthed some bandages from the caravan for the job. The boy had a small head wound, but after a little cleaning it seemed well enough. The woman seemed the worst off, for all that her injuries were minor. She was covered in shallow scrapes and bruises. Her nails were clogged with dirt and blood. Her legs were grazed up to the thigh. She clutched her son tighter when Ty approached her to help.

Hal gripped his arm.

"I pulled one of 'em off her," he said, his voice lowered. "She was kickin' and fightin' back something wild. But he didn't get her." His eyes burned darkly, his voice dropping like rocks falling into a ravine. "I got him."

Ty eyed the dancer carefully, and nodded. He beckoned Fae over, quietly indicating the woman, whose eyes were still wide and distant, as if she was still somewhere else.

Fae knelt down beside her. She winced as the movement rubbed against her middle, and her vision blackened briefly. She breathed through it, until the world swam back into view, then slowly reached out to take the woman's hand. She smiled at the boy, who clutched at his mother still.

"It's alright," she soothed, "I'm just going to take a look at your mother's scrapes. Is that okay?" She kept her eyes on the boy, while holding the woman's hand. Small, round eyes nodded at her. She turned her attention to the woman.

"My name is Fae," she started gently. "What's yours?"

"Hannah," came the hoarse reply.

Fae smiled. "Hello Hannah. You look like you've got some nasty scrapes there." She nodded at the hands she held. "Would it be alright if I have a look?" She waited, and was rewarded with the barest nod.

"Okay," Fae said. She gently lifted Hannah's hand, turning it to check the grazes across her knuckles. One of her fingernails was torn from the bed, and oozed red and raw.

Fae repeated the process on the other hand.

"Some of these look painful," she said, looking Hannah in the eye as she spoke. "Can I wash these and bandage them for you?" She waited again. Hannah nodded wordlessly.

Fighting the ache across her belly, and the dizzying way her head swam, she worked with gentle, methodical care, and soon the woman's hands and arms were clean and bandaged. Fae sat back on her heels. Glanced down at Hannah's knees, skinned and filthy from the ground.

The rage swelled up in Fae again. How could humans do this to each other? What monsters were they? Then she thought of Hal, who'd pulled Hannah's attacker off her, who'd defended a group of helpless travellers with nothing but a short blade.

Not *all* monsters.

"Can I look at these?" she asked quietly, indicating Hannah's legs.

Hannah froze. Her eyes were wide as saucers when she glanced up to meet Fae's. For a moment, Fae thought she would clam up again. But then, she nodded. Slowly. There was still fear in her eyes, but it was a strange, trusting fear. And that was something Fae could work with.

Again, she worked carefully, talking softly to Hannah as she examined her legs. She cleaned them up, mumbling all the while, narrating what she was doing as she went.

The worst of the wounds on Hannah's legs were the grazes on her knees, a few layers deep, but they were easy enough to bandage. The rest were scrapes and bruises which, now cleaned, would heal on their own. Finished, Fae smiled at her, and looked over at her son, who had stayed silently beside her the whole time.

"Your mother might need a little help around the place while these heal." She gestured to the bandages. "Do you think you can do that?" She narrowed her eyes a little, feigning doubt. Just enough to coax the boy to straighten, and puff out his chest.

"I already help with lots of things," he piped up. "I can fetch water, and wash the bowls, and brush down the horses, and I'm the best at finding good firewood!" His face took on a determined scowl. "Mama doesn't need to worry! I can help!"

Fae laughed, stifling a wince as the motion pulled across her middle. "Thank goodness she has someone like you around!" She smiled at him. "What's your name?"

"Thomas," the boy replied.

"Well, Thomas," Fae said, holding her hand out the way Hal had done before, "I'm glad to have met you. And doubly glad you're here to help."

Thomas put his hand in hers without hesitation. "You can count on me!" he declared.

A small smile crept onto Hannah's face at the exchange. Then darkened again. Fae put a hand on her shoulder.

"You're okay," she said, meeting the woman's eyes. She waited for another nod before standing. The wound across her belly flared hot and painful, and she staggered slightly as the world tipped again.

"Do you have any willowbark?" she asked, ignoring it. She jerked her head — carefully — toward the caravan. Hannah nodded again. "Good. Those bruises are going to ache for a few days. Your hands too. Chew some willowbark for the pain, but not more than two thumbs a day." She held up her thumb, circling the length of it with the opposite index finger. "More than that and you'll start to get giddy. Okay?"

Hannah nodded mutely once more. Thomas nodded with more vigour. Fae smiled.

Between them, they'd be alright.

She turned to survey the campsite.

Where bodies of friends and foe alike had been strewn around like so many discarded ragdolls, the ground was a slippery mix of mud and gore. Ty and Hal had dragged the dead into two piles a little way from them. One for the raiders. One for fallen friends. A shallow grave was dug beside the smaller pile.

The travellers gathered to say a few words for their companions, before burying them in a roadside grave.

Fae averted her gaze from the intensely private moment. She glanced at the paved highway stretching from one horizon to the next. They were still too close to the road.

Fae located Ty. "We should move away from here," she said quietly, glancing along the road for signs of further visitors. Ty nodded. He eyed the dark stain on her shirt. She shook her head. "When we're away from here." His eyes narrowed, but he said nothing, and moved away to speak with Hal in lowered tones. In moments, Hal had recruited Bek to help soothe the horses before hitching them back to the wagons, Fae and Ty gathering up the ragged band of survivors. And together, they left the road.

15

WILLOWBARK TEA

The night's darkness was complete, with not even a star to break the infinite canvas. When their ragged band finally reached the safety of their tiny campfire, half a mile from the road, it seemed a mere candle-flicker in a sea of inky black.

The travellers peeled off to set up their own camp a few paces away. Concealed behind a low rise, they were hidden from the road, but still forewent the temptation of an additional fire. After unhitching and hobbling the horses, the four remaining members of the caravan turned in for the night.

Hal watched them go. "Guess we'll keep watch then, eh?" he grumbled, turning to fan his hands out before the fire.

"We'll take the first watch," Ty offered. "I have to see to Fae's wound yet, if she's finally finished playing the intrepid heroine." His eyes didn't leave the flames, but his tone spoke volumes that his face withheld.

Fae wasn't sure how she hadn't passed out yet — her head swam with every motion, but somehow, her feet had managed to carry her from the road without incident.

Hal eyed them each for a good moment, and then nodded. "Aye, I think that'd be a good call." He turned away from the fire. "I'll just set meself down over here." He hadn't much more than the clothes on his back, carrying only a hunting bow and a small messenger's pack worn tight across his body. He tossed the pack behind him, and shuffled back away from the campfire. When he lay down to sleep, it was with only the bag beneath his head. Fae wondered at the kind of person who had so little to his name and yet still risked life and limb to save a group of strangers.

Bek was quick to follow Hal's example, giving Fae a significant look that told her what she already knew.

Ty kept his cool silence until only he and Fae were left awake.

"Lie down," he murmured tersely, keeping his voice low and even. "And show me that wound."

Fae was too tired to try reassuring him, and did as she was told. The line across her midriff was burning hot and dull now, and it tugged in bright flashes whenever she moved. Lying down was easier said than done — the way her skin moved when she stretched out pulled the wound open again, and the fabric of her shirt stuck to the edges as she peeled it away. At least her head wasn't swimming so drunkenly with the ground solid beneath her. Finally, she was able to look at the damage done in the fight.

Firelight wasn't the best light in which to examine a wound, but even by the flickering glow of their tiny campfire, Fae could see that the gash created by her assailant's hidden blade had cut deeper than she'd originally thought. She hissed when she realised how close she had come to being disemboweled. The cut reached from just above her right hip to below the ribs on her left side. Either she had reflexively recoiled from the blow, or Ty's arrow had taken the brute just as he'd thrust with the knife. Whichever it was, the blade had been a hair's breadth away from penetrating into her abdomen, and wreaking serious damage.

A hundred thoughts sped through her head. A prevailing one was along the lines of, *I should have looked at this sooner.* She glanced guiltily up at Ty.

He avoided her gaze, focusing his attention on assessing the wound. His flat, seemingly emotionless expression told her more than if he had given her a full dressing-down in front of the whole school in Arolynos.

He was furious. But he said nothing.

He reached into his pack and pulled out a small, shallow bowl, the likes of which was useful for anything from mixing herbs to eating on the road; a roll of clean bandage material; a small bottle of florestem, a strong antiseptic; and a small sewing kit. He half-filled the bowl from his water-wrap, and placed it into the embers of the campfire to heat. Once wisps of steam began curling up from the surface of the water, he added five drops of florestem, a needle, and a few lengths of the bandage material into the bowl. Removing one of the bandages, he wrung out the excess water over her wound. Fae hissed quietly as the stinging burned across her middle.

Ty gently dabbed around the gash, repeating the process until the wound was pink and clean. The half-formed scabs that had developed over the last two hours finally came away, and fresh blood ran down either side of Fae's body. She bore his ministrations as stoically as she could, her teeth clenched against crying out.

Next, Ty washed a piece of willowbark in his florestem infusion, and then rubbed it directly onto the open edges of her skin. A warm, tingling sensation spread out from her middle, and the pain finally dulled to a manageable level.

Fae let out a breath.

"I'm going to stitch the edge closed now," Ty said, keeping his voice even. "There are at least three layers that need suturing — would you like more willowbark? I can make you a tea." Brewing the willowbark would release more of its analgesic properties, producing a soporific infusion in the process that would surely put her to sleep in no time.

She began to shake her head to turn down Ty's offer, and then caught the look on his face. His expression was flat, but lines bracketed his mouth, and he had a hard look behind his eyes. She wanted to apologise, to reassure him, say anything to break the tension. But she knew the best thing for it would be to just let him work.

She nodded mutely.

Ty shaved willowbark into a cup with some water and propped it up in the embers. While it brewed, he cut a length of suture from his kit and dropped it into the florestem solution to cleanse.

They waited in silence; Ty staring into the fire, and Fae staring at him.

Eventually the tea was ready, and Ty handed it to her, helping her sit upright enough to sip at it. When the tea was drained, Ty began stitching her wound. The willowbark worked fast, and all she felt was a gentle tugging as his needle pulled the tissues back together.

As the drug-induced fog settled around her senses, small details came into sharp focus. The slow lick of flame against the night. The kiss of its heat against one cheek. The hard earth beneath her fingers. The angle of Ty's brow. The tension in his jaw. The silver lining his eyes.

She frowned sleepily. "I'm sorry," she whispered to his stony face.

He started, his eyes finally flicking to meet hers. Just for a moment. Then he returned to his work.

"What for?" he said absently.

But the willowbark was quick to work its own brand of magic, and Fae could feel the fuzzy warmth of sleep folding over her like a familiar blanket.

Her eyes pulled closed. "For making you worry." Then sleep claimed her.

Ty paused long enough to watch her sleeping face. He brushed a wayward strand of silvery, ash-blonde hair from her face. And then finished his stitching.

The next morning, Ty checked everyone's injuries, including Fae's. Thanks to their combined ministrations, all were recovering well. Fae dug out a small portion of the healer's helper she'd picked up from the Waystop to brew a tea for the survivors, and Ty scowled her into drinking some herself. The stitches Ty had placed so carefully the previous night itched terribly, and she fought the urge to scratch at them. At least the discomfort meant the gash was healing. She was lucky.

Fae kept quiet while Ty inspected his work in the light of day, his lips pressed into a thin line. Other than needlessly instructing her on how to care for the wound, he refrained from lecturing her, for which she was grateful. They were both healers, she knew how foolish she'd been to ignore it.

She moved carefully after that, being sure not to stretch the stitches. She chewed willowbark, which aside from dulling the pain, also soothed the wound. She drank healer's helper.

After breaking their fast, they travelled back to the road.

They stopped to pay their respects at the low mound marking the final resting place of the other half of the caravan group, grim faces all around.

Then the travellers turned their wagons westward, towards Oresh. They were but one small band of many refugees fleeing the area surrounding Throldon, hoping for greener pastures. The burly leader of the group — whose name they had since learned was Smith — thanked them profusely for their help.

"You ought to come with us," he said, shaking Ty's hand. "There's nothing good out here for anyone, lone or otherwise." His eyes were sunken and tired, and when he shook his head, it was a motion heavy with grief. "Heavens know, we could use the company." His gaze flicked over to his depleted crew.

Ty gripped Smith's shoulder. "Thank you for the offer, but our path lies north, and our time is short." He smiled. "May fortune smile upon us, that our paths cross again one day."

Smith nodded his understanding. "Aye," was all he said. With a ragged sigh, he turned back to his people. Keen to leave this place, they wasted no time in returning to their westward flight.

Hal watched them leave, shaking his head occasionally.

Eventually, Fae had to ask. "What?"

"Hmm?" He turned to her, his face blank in the way of someone unaware of their actions.

Fae inclined her head in the direction of the slowly shrinking caravan. "Why do you shake your head at them?"

His gaze traced the road again, eyes distant.

"I only just met them yesterday," he said, "coming the other way. Told me 'bout the trouble in Throldon. I told 'em Oresh's nice this time o' year." He sighed, long and deep. Watched as the caravan finally dipped behind a rise.

He turned back to Fae and Ty, wiping the faraway look from his face.

"Guess I might as well head north with you lot, if you'll have me," he announced. "At least until we reach the Western Highway, over the Wastelands." He scratched at his beard pensively. "I'll make me own way east again from there. Greneln should be quiet. Not safe travelling on your own these days it seems." He frowned to himself. "Not safe at all."

"We'd be glad to have you along with us," Ty answered. Bek nodded beside him.

"We would," Fae agreed. He seemed a breed apart from the others — in spite of his rough appearance, he'd acted with the selflessness of any healer she'd ever worked with. And if they were likely to run into any more trouble, he'd be a welcome addition to their little band.

With that settled, and nothing further to keep them there, they shouldered their packs, and left the road once again to head north.

They shared small news between them for a while before running out of conversation.

"What about you Hal?" Fae asked in a lull. "Where are you from? What do you do?"

His lips curved up in a small, private smile.

"Well," he said, "ain't that a question?" He stretched his arms out in front of him as he walked, fingers interlaced, palms facing outward, as if preparing himself for a long story. In the light of day, his skin had the deep tan of one who'd spent plenty of time out on the road. "I grew up around Hapton, town north and east of us, or used to be. Long gone now. Da went to Throldon to fight when I was a young'un, never did figure out what for. Ma died o' the grippe when I was bare turned a man. Brother and sisters all got homes and families o' their own. So I went to Bredon looking for work." His expression blackened for a blink so quick, Fae wondered if she'd imagined it. "Didn't work out there, so I set out travelling. Seeing the world. Learnt a lot on the road." He smiled and jerked a thumb at his own chest. "They call my like rangers, on account of us ranging see." He paused, his face clouding over again. When he spoke again, his voice dropped, took a dark turn. His eyes followed his feet.

"Problem with people ain't just the Unity," he said. "Problem with people is people." He looked up at Fae.

"People is scared they're gonna do something wrong. Those lot we helped—" he waved an arm behind him, gesturing back the way they had come "—didn't know what to do with 'emselves. Just stood there dumb as rabbits and let themselves get killed by those things."

"The raiders?" Fae asked.

Hal nodded. "They ain't human. Maybe they was once but I ain't never seen a man eat another man alive. Not even a hungry one." He shook his head at the ground. "*Every man for himself* — ha!" he barked, a bitter laugh. "Shows a lot about some people when they take it to mean they can go about hurting people." Lines marred his forehead. "Not for me it don't." Something about his words weighed heavy with experience.

"What do you do then?" Fae asked.

"I help." Hal stated plainly. "Where I can. I help people with them sons o' demons." He ran a hand agitatedly through his hair. "Wish I could do more but people don't help themselves!" His hand formed a fist, his knuckles showing white under the skin.

"Them Unity bastards don't touch me though." He looked back at Fae, a wicked grin spreading over his troubled features. "I do my own thing, ain't bound by no one. Never part o' no travelling group; I make my own way." He paused, his eyes drifting askance. "I did think o' joining them Peacekeepers, but them's too damn obvious." He tutted, his gaze refocusing again. "Unity tracks 'em fast as anything. No—" he shook his head again, and then seemed to say more to himself, "I'm better off on my own." He mulled in his thoughts for a few paces, and then brightened.

"Anyway, enough about me! What about you lot?" He winked at her, returning Fae's questions. She smiled at him.

"We're northward bound," she said, "though quite why, we're not sure." She sighed a familiar exasperation. "We know it's related to the trouble you speak of, but quite how, and what we're to do about it, I don't know."

"I heard the elves talk to spirits and sorts," Hal mused. "You on a spirit quest, is it?"

Fae stared at him. As if in answer, the call that drew her north tugged at her chest.

"I didn't think the humans believed in the Aethyr!" She glanced at Ty, but he looked just as shocked as her at Hal's casual mention of spirits.

The ranger laughed. It was a laugh that was wide open, free and wild, deep in his belly.

"Calm yourselves friends!" He flapped his hands at them. "I don't know what this *'eeth-ear'* is you're talking about but you've long been held as folk who talk to spirits." He eyed them with the look of someone correcting a basic truth. "Don't worry, human folk still hold to the gods." He rolled his eyes and muttered, "Although we got too many o' them too."

Fae continued to gape at him.

"God — s?" she stuttered, emphasising the plural.

"Aye" Hal chuckled again. "There be all sorts o' gods in our heaven. Must be mighty crowded up there." He tilted his head back and spread his arms out wide to the sky. "And they all look after their own." He brought his gaze back to level with theirs, one eyebrow cocked. "So believe human folk anyways." His eyes flicked between the two dropped jaws before him. Then he glanced over to Bek, happily minding his own business as they walked along, swishing a long switch back and forth through the grasses.

He was clearly listening to their conversation, but showed none of the surprise so evident on Fae and Ty's faces.

Hal smiled. "I sure would like to hear your... *eeth-ear* stories though," he said, interlacing his fingers behind his head. His blue eyes twinkled. "Could make sittin' around a campfire a mite more interesting."

Fae smiled back at him, shaking her head. "It appears we have much to learn from each other, Master Ranger."

She decided she liked Hal. He had an easy way about him, and a trusting nature. He didn't have to travel with them, but after one shared fight and a night around a campfire, he'd decided to do just that. He didn't have to help those travellers, and yet had risked his life to do so.

She could think of worse company for the journey ahead.

16

THE BEST STORY-TELLERS

Laina picked her way through the bleak remains of a once-prosperous trade hub.

She vaguely recalled Hapton in its former glory, partly from her own childhood memories, and partly from the stories Jessica used to tell around campfires.

It was, or had been, a market town; districts upon districts dedicated to different trades and crafts. There had been a huge, sprawling farmers' market, loud with thick accents and passionately declared produce. The cloth market had been a bright and gauzy maze divided by every colour of silk, wool, and cotton, patterned and plain, sold by the yard or fashioned into beautiful cloaks, shirts, and dresses. There had been a timber district, selling everything from massive tree trunks hauled all the way from the lumberyards of Timbermill, to elaborately carved toys and trinkets. The stone district had boasted impossibly huge hunks of mountain rock, to exquisitely chiselled chess sets. Ironmonger's street divided the two, hot and glowing, ringing with the sound of farriers and smiths plying their trade. There had been a district for the sciences, and one for the scholars. Laina's favourite as a child had been the arts district, home to the painters, the sculptors, and the poets; her strongest memories of Hapton were of the colourful troupes on street corners, performing skilfully enough to captivate even the most sullen passer-by.

Now the town stood empty. Barren.

Market squares were wastelands, stalls abandoned. The cloth awnings that once stretched over the tables flew tattered and torn in the breeze. Doors to shops and homes alike swung absently in the breeze. Cupboards and drawers left open and empty.

Whatever had caused the citizens to leave, they had done it in a hurry. And it looked like raiders had swarmed through soon after; locusts, pillaging homes and livelihoods. Vultures picking clean the carcass.

Laina hoped fervently that everyone got out first.

She turned a full circle, taking in the complete absence of life in what should have been a beautiful, thriving market town. It may as well belong to the Wastelands now. The abandoned buildings seemed to fade into the dusty landscape, merging back into the dry grasslands that abutted Hapton's western edge.

It was the same everywhere. In the two weeks since leaving Barrow, she'd passed countless empty towns and villages, homes and livelihoods alike abandoned, as their people fled from an advancing tyranny. She'd thought Hapton far enough removed from Throldon's reach that it might remain at least somewhat unaffected by the changes occurring there. And that here, she might find allies.

She sighed into the wind. Not so.

But she *had* heard news from the travellers she had passed on the way.

Malcolm Stuart was gone.

Laina's personal feelings towards the Stuarts filled her with a cold joy at the news of his demise. But it accompanied worse tidings.

There was a new power in Throldon. One to be feared more than the Stuarts.

The Rebel Unity had been replaced by the Survivors, their leader known as "Lady Black". They were brutally elitist, and terrifyingly organised. And, depending on how much she chose to believe, there was black magic involved.

She couldn't shake the sinking feeling that the latter might have an element of truth to it.

And yet her dream pulled her north-west, *away* from Throldon.

What is *going on?* Laina thought, her brows knitting together. And what was her part in it all?

"Deserted," a voice startled her from behind. Laina fought to bring her racing heart back under control, and turned to face her unintended companion.

Ben stood beside her, glowering out over the town. "It's like every single one of 'em got up one morning, grabbed what they could carry, and got out as quick as they could." He eyed the empty shells that had once teemed with the hubbub of trade. Shuddered.

"D'you know why it feels so odd?" he said, angling his body towards her, even as his eyes continued to scan the buildings. "It doesn't even feel haunted or anything. It's like even the ghosts avoid it."

Laina agreed. There was an emptiness here that surpassed what she could see. Arland was becoming a dark place to walk.

She looked up at him, and frowned to herself. Barely grown into manhood, Ben was too young to be traipsing across the world with her on the whim of a dream.

"Ben," she began.

"Mmhmm," he replied absently, suspiciously eyeing a nearby window frame.

She hesitated, knowing what he'd say regardless, but she had to try. "You know," she started, absently picking at a perfectly trimmed fingernail. "Greneln is starting to sound rather nice." She tried to affect an air of casual indifference. "From what we've heard on the road, anyway." She gave a little shrug, as if it didn't really matter anyway. "You could always head up that way with everyone else, check it out." She glanced at him from the corner of her eye. "There'd be work there — I'm sure they've no end of options for an able lad like you..." Her mind drifted, and her gaze followed a leaf blowing out across their limited outlook. "You might find yourself a girl, maybe start a family..." She trailed off, as much from the look he gave her as from the pain of her own past.

He positioned himself in front of her. "Laina, we done talking 'bout this." The road they'd travelled together had cemented a solid friendship between them. He certainly no longer felt the need to call her "ma'am".

He ducked his head to meet her eyes. "I ain't going nowhere." Despite his youth, the look he gave her now reminded her a little of her husband. Gentle. Intractable. Stubborn. A small smile tugged at her cheeks. He grinned. "Besides," he carried on, knowing he'd already won, "what would you do without me? You wouldn't last ten miles out of here if I left!" His eyes twinkled playfully under a mock-serious brow.

"Dolt!" she exclaimed with feigned indignation. She aimed a swat at the side of his head which he dodged with practiced ease. "I've been traveling since before your mother was born!" she said as he danced away. While not quite true, their age gap had already become a running joke between them.

"And many a year before that too, I'd wager," Ben goaded back. "That ain't to say you don't appreciate a strapping young lad to be keepin' you company now though is it?" He laughed as Laina stuck her tongue out at him. Much though she misliked him being out here in this desolate place, she was grateful for his company. And his friendship. He had turned out to have a level head on his shoulders, an infectiously mellow outlook, and a wisdom far beyond his years.

A sigh escaped her lips as she surveyed her surroundings. She'd hoped to trade here; to pick up a few supplies on the way through. She hadn't expected to find Hapton flourishing, times being what they were, but nor had she expected to find it empty.

"I just can't believe there's no one here," she said sadly. "I had no idea." *I suppose there was no one to send word*, she thought. Anyone who came across this vista now would make as fast as they could in the opposite direction. There was an eerie disquiet about the place that permeated the silence, making the hairs on the back of her neck prickle constantly.

She shouldered her pack. "Right," she said decisively, "there's not much point lingering here. And I don't much fancy staying the night either." Ben nodded beside her. "It's not like I'll be picking up the supplies I was hoping for, so we'll just carry straight on through." And with that, she began picking her way down a debris-strewn thoroughfare, Ben falling into step with her.

"The gods must have seen something here they really didn't like to desert it so completely," Ben said casually, kicking at the dust as they walked past neglected houses and market stalls. The window boxes and flower beds hadn't even thought to overgrow yet; the exodus had been so recent, and sudden.

Laina snorted. "Gods didn't do this," she said. She gestured around them. "This is all the work of men and women, plain and simple. Nothing more, nothing less."

Ben looked over at her. "You don't believe the gods have any influence in the actions of everyday people?" he asked. She could have sworn there was something akin to a knowing glint in his eye, but it was there and gone again before she could even turn fully towards him. Laina smiled and shook her head.

"I don't believe there *are* any gods to influence them," she clarified. "Haven't done for a long time now." She glanced up to the sky and sighed. "Not since I was shown the wonder that exists within nature itself." Taking a breath, she looked back towards her companion, gone quiet beside her. "Gods are a relatively recent concept, did you know that?" she asked. "Mother Nature and the world around us has been here far, far longer. And She works far more honestly than any gods we might dream up."

Ben gave her an inscrutable look. "But the idea of Mother Nature is just a figment, made up to make the natural world easier to explain. It isn't real," he countered.

"I could say the same about your gods, Ben." Laina smiled back at him, long familiar with the path their conversation was taking. "The gods are just characters men made up to explain the world around them. To give them an illusion of control over it. If there is a god presiding over the seas, a sailor can pray to Him in the hope of improving his chances in a storm." She glanced at him askance. "But they're just stories. And the best of the story-tellers became preachers. And preachers have built some of the greatest religions from their stories, spreading their tales far into every corner of humanity." She flung her arms out to take in the vast expanses of the world. She laughed softly to herself as she lowered her arms. A tinge of sadness crept into her voice. "I've spent hours debating this with Kiel over the years," she said quietly. "Eventually, we each agreed to leave the other to their own brand of folly. He's entitled to believe what he will, as am I." She looked up at the young man listening patiently beside her, and shot him a quick wink. "Because I know the truth."

Ben smiled at her not-so subtle jab. "But what about the actions of gods?" he asked, clearly well-versed in his stories. "What about when crops thrive, or are blighted? When seas are calm or stormy? When good fortune shines down on us? Or bad? How do you explain that? Surely there must be a greater Being deciding our fates?"

Laina laughed.

"The crops and the oceans are all under Mother Nature's rule, and the good and the bad are all part of Her cycle. As for fortune, we make our own. I've always believed in that. There is no better luck than that which we make ourselves." She paused. When she continued, her voice lost some of its shine.

"We're all part of a larger cycle. Of life. You see enough births and deaths, or seasons come and go, and you'll start to see it." She looked over at Ben again, her eyes suddenly severe. "Gods are just humanity's scapegoat for things they don't understand.

"Nature takes care of us all in the end."

17

BETTER TO DIE

J ust south of the Amedi River, six elven scouts broke camp together
for the last time.

The cool light of dawn shone hazy through a thick layer of fog,
blanketing the countryside in an ominously serene glow, and hiding the
muddy outline of the city squatting across the water.

Thom eyed the fog suspiciously, absently passing a smoker's pipe
between his hands.

"What troubles you?" said Wil, coming to stand beside him.

Thom made a noise deep in his throat. He lifted the pipe to his
mouth, and chewed on the end.

"Can't say," he said, "but I mislike this fog." He narrowed his eyes
accusingly at it.

Wil gazed out over the river, and into the unrelenting curtain of white
hanging over the human capital.

The fog troubled him too. He, Aren and Stef were to cross the river,
through the unexpected fog, and enter Throldon in less than
advantageous conditions. It could only have been made worse if it were
dark.

Not that we would see any less if it were *dark,* he groused internally. Fog
limited visibility, muffled sounds, and hampered progress in all the worse

ways. It confused and misled. And it rolled in silently, without a moment's notice.

Not to mention, this hovering barrier had a sinister feel to it. Perhaps it was just a sign of what lay on the other side. Perhaps it was something else...

"When you two are done shooting the breeze, as they say around these parts!" Aren called from their meagre campsite. Elas grinned at his jest, the more level-headed Wyn cuffing him across the back of the head in rebuke. In Arolynos, "shooting the breeze" indicated a poor shot. A near miss. Or falling short.

Wil grimaced, running a hand through his hair. The coffee-brown strands were already getting too long for his liking. "Just thank the spirits that he's with me," he muttered to Thom, dryly. "I'm stuck with him, while you can carry on to Dvargra in peace."

"Ha!" came the reply. "You think Aren bad? Without him to juggle his jester's act, Elas will be talking my ears off all the way into the mountains. No —" Thom stroked at the beginnings of a beard feathering his jawline "—I think us equally matched for comic representation." He turned, removing the pipe from his mouth. "I'll show you shooting the breeze Master Longstem!" he called. "With you in the wind, my arrow could mark you a mile away."

"Oh please, there's no need for that." Aren shot him a lop-sided grin as he approached, his near-black hair swinging about his shoulders. "In any case, we all know you prefer the dwarven axe to an elven bow any day." He skipped a step back at Thom's answering growl, laughing all the while. "The camp is packed," he said finally, his grin faltering. "We're ready."

Wil gripped Thom's forearm in farewell; brothers in cause.

"Travel well," he said simply, leaving the rest unsaid.

"And you," Thom replied. To either side their brethren were doing likewise, wishing each other fair journeys.

Without further delay, the group bound for Dvargra, tucked away up in the north-eastern corner of the Edge Mountains, continued along the south side of the river to find a more remote location to cross. Wil and the two brothers walked a short distance to where the water was wide and shallow.

The waves lapped coolly around their calves as they forded, the sound echoing closely in the dense fog. When they reached the opposite bank, they found that it didn't dip politely down to greet them, but angled up sharply from the water, forcing them to climb blindly through the fog. Half-way up, Stef lost his footing on the cliff-like surface, kicking loose stones down to splash deafeningly in the water below. The three of them flattened themselves to the rock-face, waiting for the alert that was sure to go out. But there was no answering sound, no hint of discovery.

The fog enveloped them in a damp, wooly cloud, and gave nothing away.

Finally, they cleared the lip and leapt silently onto the bank. With a single gesture from Wil, they edged away from the river. Then crept through the white morning gloom, keeping low to the ground, ears stretched taut to catch the slightest noise.

Less than a quarter-mile, and what felt like hours later, the shapes of the city loomed into view.

The outskirts of Throldon were a litter of shanty housing and lean-tos, hastily erected in the shadow of the suburbs, which weren't much better off. Piles of manure burned outside rudely assembled tents and huts with a stench that watered the eyes. Men and women alike carried out their daily tasks with lost, empty looks, while children lugged about buckets of brownish water in bare feet. It had been years, decades, since these districts had had any sort of management, organised or otherwise, the residents forced to make the best of a bad situation.

Throldon was meant to be a thriving metropolis; the jewel in Arland's crown. But it hadn't been that since there'd been a king to call it a kingdom.

Wil led the scouts through the ramshackle, matchstick buildings as quietly as if navigating the forests. He wore a wide-brimmed hat and a bandana about his head to conceal his ears, Aren and Stef wearing matching headscarves for the same reason. They kept their heads down regardless — there wasn't anything they could do to hide their distinctive eyes. So they aimed to avoid notice altogether.

Wil, Stef, and Aren were tasked with locating one particular — very specific — human, which required that they kept a very low profile.

That human was Elisabeth Marl, the founder of the Peacekeepers.

The Eldra wanted information on the current human condition, and they had decided the head of the Peacekeeper movement was the best place to start. What complicated the matter, was that being associated with Elisabeth Marl was doubly dangerous in Throldon. Not only was the Peacekeeper movement a perpetual thorn in the side of the "every man for himself" Unity, but the Stuarts had made it a particular vendetta of theirs to find Marl, and if rumour was to be believed, they weren't being coy as to what they intended to do with her once she was in their hands.

Unsurprisingly, there had been no word of the Peacekeeper founder for years.

They were on the hunt for a ghost. For *rumours* of a ghost.

And the insistence of the Eldra that they find *this* particular ghost, had Wil thinking there was more to their reasoning than they were letting on.

As they picked their way across the muddy thoroughfares weaving between what passed for houses here, Wil silently hoped they *didn't* find Elisabeth Marl in Throldon.

May she be tucked away somewhere safe and hidden, far from here, he thought grimly. His attention snagged on the sunken eyes and haunted faces of a group of small children huddled by one foul-smelling fire. The breath escaped their lips in pathetic wisps of white, and their skeletal frames left little to hang their dirty rags upon. They didn't even shiver — as if they no longer believed it would make a difference. Or perhaps they simply lacked the energy to do so.

They're not children, Wil thought bitterly, *they're shells.* His eyes continued their vigilant sweep as they walked. It wasn't just the children bearing vacant, wide-eyed stares. *It's all of them.* It was like they'd all just... given up.

Aren hissed. Wil's head whipped round, his eyes automatically tracing the direction of the other scout's gaze. And what he saw had bile rising in his throat.

At first, it appeared to be an emaciated corpse. Most likely a woman. Abandoned in the street. It looked as if it could have been there for years, the flesh and muscle wasted away to almost nothing. And then she blinked.

It was only when Stef's hand brushed his arm in a deliberate reminder to keep moving, that Wil realised he'd stopped in his tracks, and was staring openly at the woman he'd thought was already dead.

"How is she still alive?" Wil whispered, struggling with his need to keep a low profile, and his disgust at how this human had been left to die.

"Keep moving," Aren breathed, keeping his head low. But Wil could see his hands were shaking too.

They were just about to duck between two storage sheds when the sound of desperate screams reached them.

Pulling up short, ears pricked, Wil whirled, working to pinpoint where the scream was coming from. Stef reached out to grip his shoulder.

"It would be unwise to interfere," he said gently. He tried to turn Wil away from the sound, but the heavy-built scout stood firm. That was not a sound he could ignore.

It was the bloodcurdling sound of someone screaming for their life.

Wil shrugged the hand away, altering his course towards the screams as they broke into ragged sobs. Aren shot his brother a look, silver eyes wide. Stef's jaw worked, the only sign of his concern, but he shrugged, and followed behind.

They rounded a corner, and found what they were looking for in the heart of the slums.

It seemed as though a fruit-vendor had been loading a cart of apples for market with his wife, when the group of Unity thugs had taken it upon themselves to entertain themselves at the couple's expense. The door to the couple's home stood open to the cold, the cart unhitched a short distance from it. One thug sat on the edge of the fruit cart, idly carving an apple with a wicked blade. Two more filled burlap sacks with the fruits, as if they had all the time in the world. Another restrained the fruit-vendor, with a strongly corded arm across his throat. The vendor struggled in vain against his captor's ruthless grip, his eyes fixed on a different scuffle, a few paces away.

The last man toyed with the vendor's wife while she sobbed hysterically in the dirt, bare feet away from her husband. She fought back, but what strength she had was exhausted, her arms clawing weakly at the man who pinned her to the ground.

Before anyone could react, Wil unsheathed his belt knife, strode into the scene, and ran his blade across the throat of the brute holding her. With elven-quick reflexes, Stef snapped the neck of the one restraining the vendor, and Aren drew a bead on the remaining thugs.

"Dare you," he invited, sighting them down the shaft of his arrow.

The remaining three hesitated, shock delaying their reactions as they eyed up their chances. One loosed a knife from a rude sheath on his belt.

Another pulled a double-headed axe from where it had been lying on the bed of the wagon. It scraped over the wood before he lifted it up and onto his shoulders.

Thinking quickly, Wil snarled. He grabbed the woman, hauling her off the ground with feigned roughness. Stef, following his lead, wrapped his hands firmly around the vendor's upper arms.

"My turn," Wil said, baring his teeth, trying to inject his voice with as much feral brutality as he could muster.

The thugs stiffened, and for a moment, he feared they would push for a fight. Then they slumped grudgingly, the tension leaving their bodies. The axe thunked down onto the ground. The knife slid back into its sheath.

This kind of challenge, they understood.

Clearly not wanting to spill any more blood over the issue, they cast one last, embittered look at their fallen comrades, hoisted their purloined sacks of apples, and slunk off to find easier prey.

The elves waited for them to round a corner before shoving the two hostages back inside their hut, closing the door behind them.

Wil and Stef released their captives, and the two humans backed into the furthest corner, fresh fear rounding their eyes.

The brothers ignored them, instead rounding on Wil.

"That was reckless." Stef levelled a flat look at his fellow scout.

Aren remained silent for once, pensive.

"That," Wil snapped back, "was necessary. The whole *problem* with humanity is that actions like that—" he gestured towards the door "—go unmanaged." He fumed quietly, but intensely. Then his shoulders dropped. He took a breath. Ran a hand through his hair. When he spoke again his voice had lost the rough edge of anger. Instead it was heavy, tired. "If anything, we've bolstered our cover as being part of this farce. Having blood on our hands will only strengthen our position." His eyes flared at his own words. "Besides—" he turned to the couple huddled in the corner "—we may gain some advantage here." He moved past the brothers and crouched down before the humans.

"My name is William," he said, adapting his name to a human equivalent. "My friends are Aaron and Stephan." He gestured to them. The couple continued to watch him with open trepidation on their faces.

With tension still palpable in the air, Aren came to sit cross-legged beside Wil on the floor, adopting a less threatening posture than Wil's coiled stance. He pushed his bow back over his shoulder and leaned forward, elbows resting on his knees.

"I'm Aaron," he said, pressing a hand to his chest to indicate himself. "It's been a while since we last saw Throldon." He cocked an eyebrow at Wil. "It seems we're a bit out of touch with things." He gave them a rueful smile, working his mouth around the human accent. "Would'ya mind catching us up?"

The couple stared at him a moment, before the wary look in their eyes started tipping towards one of curiosity. Wil, watching the exchange, dropped to join Aren cross-legged on the floor, pushing the tension from his body by a sheer force of will. Stef remained stationed by the door, keeping an ear out for further trouble.

Wil breathed deep, calming himself. "Are you hurt?" he asked finally. They shook their heads no, and he relaxed visibly.

"Who *are* you?" the woman whispered.

"Just travellers," Aren said with a shrug. He leaned back and made a lazy show of stretching his arms up over his head, yawning wide. "We're looking to find some Peacekeepers in the area if there are any," he said, peering at them from the corner of his eye as he made a show of casually inspecting the weave on a threadbare curtain. "Got a message for Elisabeth Marl." Their hosts' eyes widened, and he smiled to himself.

"Elisabeth Marl ain't been heard of for near on twenty year!" the man exclaimed.

"No, it can't be that long," the woman said softly. She paused, thinking. Then shook her head. "Still, she disappeared years ago. No one even knows if she's alive," she agreed.

Aren sighed loudly. "Ah well." He cast a glance towards Stef, standing tense by the door, his ears pinned back to catch anything important, inside or out. "Might as well catch up on current affairs while we're here then, eh lads?" He looked up at Wil who, at best, nodded a curt response. Aren rolled his eyes theatrically and shot the couple an easy smile. "Who rules in Throldon nowadays? Still the Stuarts?" He absently picked at one of his fingernails, listening intently.

"Mal Stuart never ruled." The man spat on the floor. "Just riled everyone up real good."

Wil's ears pricked at the use of the past tense. "You mean he doesn't anymore?" he pushed.

The man shook his head. "Nah, it's one of his most trusted rules 'em now. Ha!" His face twisted into a sardonic grimace. "She murdered him just like he murdered his daddy. And she rules proper like. Just not nice. Calls herself Lady Black, and she got a new motto: Survival of the fittest." He grimaced. "Just means the same for us. Them Unity bashers still treat the rest of us like cattle, still think they're better'n us." He leaned forward, holding Aren's gaze, his voice lowered. "But I hear that Lady is true fearsome. Bested some of their best fighters. She got herself a council of 'em, helps her rule the city with an iron fist like nothing the Stuarts ever managed."

"Now it's organised," the woman whispered with a tremor in her voice, looking into her lap.

Her husband nodded. "She says people who can't or won't fight don't deserve to live. Says we're 'diluting the human race' or something." He sat back again. "But them who fight against her she kills just as much." He held out a hand to either side of him, weighing them. "They either kill the men, or beat them into being slaves, and they rape the women before killing them too. They got harems of the ones they say's fit to bear their kids, but I hear that's worse, coz they live the horror every day."

"Better to die." His wife barely spoke.

The man's voice dropped to a whisper. "I heard Malcolm tried to take Lady Black to his bed, and that's why she killed him." His eyes flicked to the door, as if afraid someone might hear. "I'd say good riddance except she's no better."

Even Aren's easy manners faltered. He gawped at the couple openly.

"How has no one outside the city heard of this?" Wil asked in shock. Nothing had prepared them for this.

"The Lady works quick," their host answered. "She's only been in power half a year, maybe less." He looked to his wife, who nodded sadly. "But she had 'em organised before that. Musta done. They say she were Malcolm's best. And then everything changed overnight." He snapped his fingers, and his eyes darkened at the memory. "She's power mad and she wants everyone slaving for her. She don't want no one escaping to send word to Oresh or the dwarves until she knows she can fight 'em off. That's why they take the kids too. Soldiering."

"What about the Peacekeepers?" Wil asked. "The royals that disappeared? Isn't there anyone who could help?"

The man barked a humourless laugh.

"Ha! The royals?" He looked at Wil as if deciding whether or not he'd been joking. When it was clear he wasn't, the man shook his head. "You weren't kidding when you said you was out o' touch. The royals are long dead my friend. The Stuarts only made out they ran off first so no one killed 'em for regicide! And the Peacekeepers are in as much danger as anyone else in this city." He sighed. "They do better work in the villages, away from here." He shook his head and tucked his wife in closer against his side. "There ain't no one coming to help us. We've known that for a while." He looked up at the elves, as if seeing them clearly for the first time.

"Get out of the city friends," he said. "You won't find help here. Go, find strong allies. Spread the word, bring help." His eyes lost focus a moment, as if gazing into a different future. "Maybe then we can escape this madness." His voice trailed off at the end, but the words struck home with the elves all the same. Aren and Wil exchanged a glance and stood, each offering a hand up to their hosts.

"Come with us," Wil said. Maybe they could rescue at least two from their fate. But the man was already shaking his head.

"Thank you for your help today, but we stay." His gaze drifted to the side of the dwelling, where the sleeping pallets lay — four of them.

Realisation dawned on Wil.

"They took our children into their army," the woman said, an edge of iron beneath her soft voice. "We won't leave them behind." Aren nodded solemnly and held out his hand. The man grasped it firmly.

"We will come back," the scout promised.

"Time to go," Stef said from the doorway. "We've got trouble coming."

Outside, in the gloom of encroaching evening, torchlight approached, and what sounded like a small mob.

"Go! Quickly!" the woman urged. Wil hesitated.

"What about you two?" he worried.

"They won't be concerned with us with you to chase. Don't fret about us, friend, just go!" the man said, giving the scout a firm shove towards the door.

With one last backwards glance, the elves slipped out of the house and quietly back towards the river.

It was fully night again by the time they reached the river, the single sliver of a single moon outshone by the stars dusted across the sky. Rather than risk crossing in the dark, the elves tracked the lap of small waves west, putting distance between themselves and the city. Once it was safe to stop, they huddled around, and took stock.

One thing was clear, Throldon was in a far worse state than anticipated, and no help would be forth-coming from there. The Eldra had briefed them that Elisabeth Marl *was* likely alive, although they didn't say how they knew that, and had insisted that she was the human they needed.

But it was highly unlikely she was here. And turning back wasn't an option.

"What of the other human cities?" Aren said, casting ideas about in the hope that one might stick. "The problem is centred around Throldon, but what of Oresh? Or Greneln? Is Bredon still standing?" He tapped his chin, thinking.

Oresh was far to the west, so far in fact, that the culture was completely different. And Greneln was as far to the north.

Wil sighed inwardly. He stood.

"The cities are not where we're bound," he said decisively. "The humans mentioned that the villages are the safest place for the Peacekeepers to work. So we'll search there first." He shouldered his pack again, and the other two followed his lead, none of them keen to spend the night in the shade of the city. "We can bypass Throldon within two days," Wil continued.

"Then we head north. And begin our search there."

18

NEW NEWS

The Light and Way tavern was busier than usual.

The door banged open to admit yet another stranger; a traveller from the road most likely.

The innkeeper smiled a humourless smile. Business was good, days being what they were, but the reason behind his booming trade left a chill in his bones. That, and the sinking certainty that it wouldn't last.

The reason all these people were on the road in the first place was sure to catch up with him and his little inn eventually. Maybe even sooner than that.

He dried a tall glass with a rag, his eyes surveying the room. Sure, there were a handful of regulars, in from the village of Arnfeldt. There were even a few seasonals, midway along their journey between Dvargra and Greneln.

But the bulk of the noise in the taproom came from unfamiliar folk. People just trying to find somewhere safe. Or a way to profit from the troubles.

Against the far wall, a young family sat quietly around a table. Their packs were tucked away by their feet, and they clasped their drinks with the grip of someone holding on because everything else was lost. The two children watched the civilised chaos in the taproom with twinkling eyes. The parents stared blankly at the tabletop.

In the middle of the room, and causing the most noise, a group of seasonal travellers played fours with a band of off-duty mercenaries. Mercenaries were hard to find around these days, on account of how no man was supposed to be working for, or answerable to any other, but occasional bands passed through in between jobs based further afield.

"Bryant!" One of the seasonals hailed the innkeeper, jolting him from his vigil. "Another round for our friends if you please!"

"Coming right up Jessop," he answered, smoothly replacing the glass he'd been polishing and turning a tankard under the tap. He knocked on the side of the barrel. Still plenty in it for this night's trade at least. With practiced ease, he filled half a dozen for the group, all the while keeping an eye on the room. He nodded to himself. Raucous it may seem, but everything was in order.

He was setting the drinks down around the table when the door opened again. Tucking the tray under his arm as he placed the last tankard down, he looked up.

The door closed behind a young dwarf with brown, straw-like hair and eyes so dark they were almost black. She stood around average height for a dwarf, which put her at least a foot shorter than most people here. Beside her was a young boy, maybe twelve or thirteen, with bright blue eyes that saw more than they had any right to.

Bryant caught himself staring just before the dwarf's eyes caught his, and he quickly rearranged his face to wear his usual welcoming smile.

"Welcome! What'll it be for you?" he asked, making his way back behind the bar. He slotted the tray into its place and began running a cloth over the surface of the bar to mop up any errant drops. "A room? A meal? Or just a drink to chase away the cold?" He smiled at the two newcomers as they took stools opposite him. "Weather's turned a mite bitter these past few days."

The dwarf smiled. "An ale for me," she said, and then looked across at her companion through slightly narrowed eyes. The boy watched the clamorous group in the middle of the room intently. She turned back to the innkeeper. "And your weakest cider for him," she added dryly.

Bryant smiled an understanding. "That'll be twelve and four."

The dwarf counted out the coins; twelve copper pennies and four bronze cuits. She watched him deftly pour both her drink and a fresh cider for the lad, nodding her thanks when he placed them on the bar in front of her.

"I was hoping for any news, if you have it," she said, sliding the cider sideways to the boy, and wrapping her hands around her own mug. She stared into the ale, but Bryant saw the way she held herself. Still. As if coaxing a startled bird into her hand. Or as though she feared missing something important.

Bryant's eyebrow twitched. But he said nothing.

"Not much new news here," he said, returning to his idle polishing of already clean glasses. Standing, talking to customers made him feel as though he ought to be doing something; polishing gave him something to do with his hands.

The dwarf gave him a look before turning her gaze pointedly to the rest of the room. "Seem to have an awful lot of travellers for times with not much news," she said.

Bryant waved a dismissive hand at the taproom. "Not *new* news," he stressed the point. "People still running from down south. Traders still trading. Nothing new." He put down the glass and began wiping the bar.

"Anyone going north?" she nudged gently.

Bryant smiled to himself. *Everyone* was trying to go north.

"Oh aye," he said, "plenty looking to find better up north." He sighed dramatically. Like he'd said, this wasn't new. And it was a topic of conversation he'd long since worn out any interest in. But paying customers liked to hear news and gossip from their innkeep. "Not much north of here though," he continued, as if he hadn't said it a hundred times this week alone, "just wind and tundra and biting cold." He shook his head, as he had many times before. Maybe someone would eventually take the hint, and abandon this pointless dream of freedom in the north. "Greneln is about as far north as civilisation reaches," he added, "excepting Dvargra, of course." He inclined his head to her. Dwarves were known for living high up in the cold of the mountains, and were probably more accustomed to the harsh northern conditions than any of the others passing through Arnfeldt lately.

"Hmm," the dwarf murmured, taking a long, slow draw of ale. She put her mug down with a *clunk*, and went quiet.

She glanced across at the boy again, who hadn't taken his eyes off the room. But he too had a sort of stillness, as if he was listening all the while.

Bryant looked between them. But when the dwarf turned back to him, his face was a perfect mask of benign impassivity.

"Do you stock travel supplies?" she asked abruptly.

"Of course." He nodded at the room. "It's a good part of my trade." And that it was. All travellers needed provisions, and travellers made up a noticeable portion of his customers.

"Then I'll take a spread of travel rations for two for..." she tallied something in her head, "ten day's travel. No, make that two weeks." She began ticking off her fingers. "We'll need flatbread, hard cheese, any cold sausage you might have, apples if you have them—" She stopped as Bryant held up a hand.

"Like I said—" he put down his rag and brushed his hands on his apron "—travel provisions is part of my trade." He gave her an indulging look. "Let me put some things together, and you can tell me if it suits your needs."

The dwarf leant back on her stool. "Alright, Master Innkeep," she said, crossing her arms, a smile tugging at her lips. "Surprise me."

Half an hour later, the dwarf and the boy had their bags restocked with supplies and provisions for a hard journey—

"North," Bryant repeated flatly when she told him where there were headed.

"Yep, north," the dwarf said again, stuffing an extra blanket into the top of her pack, which was almost as big as she was. Alongside the edible supplies, Bryant had dug out some additional things to suggest for them, all of which they had taken. "Well, it's more like north-west, if I'm honest."

He was surprised. There was even less that way. The dwarf had seemed uncommonly sensible, and not at all like the foolish travellers fleeing the south that he'd become accustomed to.

She looked up, and he was just too slow to school his face in time. She smiled.

"I know what you're thinking," she said. She held up a hand when he went to protest. "No, it's okay. I know. Everyone thinks they'll find a better life north." She raised an eyebrow at him, daring him to deny his opinion on the matter. He smiled and spread his hands.

"I thought you not one for these ridiculous notions of freedom in the north and yet here you are—" he gestured at them both "—packing for the north."

"North-west," she repeated, shouldering her pack while her companion did likewise. "And aye, we go north, but not to find a better life. There is something I need to attend to." She glanced out of the window at the failing light. "We'll be back," she added, her voice far away.

"Well then," Bryant said, his smile back in place, "I look forward to seeing you pass through again on your return." He stuck a hand out. "Farewell, and fair travels."

She shook his hand. "Thank you."

She turned and left, the boy following wordlessly after her.

Bryant returned to his post behind the bar, and picked up a glass and a cloth.

He wondered how their journey would end. Just another traveller on the road north.

He reached across to replace the glass and select another, and felt the reassuring weight of coins in the purse against his leg. He smiled.

If nothing else, at least travelling flights of fancy paid well.

19

MOUNTAIN AIR AND METAL ORES

Thom called a halt.

Having reached the Rand, the sprawling forest dusting the foothills of the Edge Mountains, he, Wyn, and Elas were beginning to experience the inconvenience of snow. The wind had turned bitterly chill the further into the mountains their journey had taken them, and, as Thom had prophesied, they now wore most of the clothing they had with them.

Elas trudged up beside him. "What is it?" he asked, performing a quick scan of what lay ahead.

Thom gave a short shake of his head. "Nothing," he said, his grey eyes narrowing at the trees. "It's just..." His hands clenched and unclenched, grasping at something intangible but still somehow discernible. "It's too quiet," he said, finally figuring out what bothered him.

Elas gave him a look, then paused to listen. "The forest," he said simply, "is covered in snow." The snow in question made a reluctant crunching sound beneath his feet as he pivoted to indicate the mute whiteness that was the forest around them. "And everything with half a wit of sense is still sleeping through this intolerable cold!" He gave a pointed shudder. "Of course it's quiet."

Thom lifted a gloved hand in front of his face to make a shushing gesture.

"You're forgetting where we are." He glanced significantly at his fellow scout.

Elas paused. His eyes widened a fraction. "We're a stone's throw from Pomfritt."

Thom nodded. "Now listen."

They did.

"Nothing," Wyn said into the bone-deep silence.

"Nothing," Thom agreed.

They walked the remaining distance to the village normally raucous with dwarven life, now abandoned and empty. Picking their way to the open square at the centre, they stopped again. The only signs of habitation were their own footprints, following behind them.

"Gone," Elas said, searching the central cluster of buildings for some sign that he was wrong. When he saw none, he glanced back at Thom. "They're all gone."

Wyn nodded, approaching them. "Aye but it was done deliberately." He wiped clear the window of a nearby house. Everything was in order within. Nothing was upset or rushed. "The doors are locked, the homes are tidy, and nothing is damaged." He turned back to his compatriots. "They left voluntarily, and unhurried. We'll likely find them further north."

Thom nodded. They'd seen similar scenes in other villages they'd passed, but instead of lying empty, they'd been taken over by human refugees. Human refugees fleeing human raiders. The dwarves had given up their homes so that the humans might have somewhere to shelter from the cold.

Thom sighed. Such was the way of dwarves.

"I hope you're right," Elas said, trying, and failing, to shrug the strap of his pack from his many-layered shoulder. "I would dearly love to hear the full story of what on earth is going on here."

"And me," Wyn said with a nod. Thom had to agree. His ears itched to catch up with their friends in Dvargra.

Elas's constant movements caught at the corner of his eye.

"What in all of Eah'lara are you doing?" he grumbled.

Elas swore softly, hopping about in a sort of dancing shuffle to dislodge the pack from his shoulders. "It is well the raiders do not enter the forests," he said, jerking his arms in an attempt to free them. "I would hate to have to fight them on an equal footing, wearing all this gear!" He threw his hands up as far as they would go, tangled as they were in the straps. The extra layers clung to the fabric, stuck there with an added, half-frozen coating of snow. The pack wouldn't come loose.

Wyn chuckled softly at Elas's repeated attempts to extricate his arms from his pack.

"I wonder how the *Aly'sa* deal with it?" Wyn remarked dryly, referring to the legendary lost elves, said to live in the ice. Elas paused in his efforts long enough to give him a dark look, his clear-grey eyes flashing, before persevering with his shuffling dance.

A small furrow appeared on Thom's brow as he watched him, caught up in his layers. He too misliked being so swaddled — it made accessing his pipe and tabac so much more cumbersome, the habit one he'd picked up from the dwarves. Jax had repeatedly told him no good could come of breathing smoke into one's lungs, but Thom was mature enough even by elven standards to have cultivated a comfortable level of stubbornness he was unwilling to part with. He extracted his smoking kit from his own layers, and proceeded to stuff the bowl of his pipe with a particular dwarven brand of dried leaf that didn't give off any smoke; a perfect companion for a scout on the trail. Thom coughed at his first pull while Wyn took pity on Elas and helped him with his tangled straps.

"*Thank* you," Elas uttered profusely when his pack was finally free. Dropping it to the ground, he proceeded to rummage through it, digging out a selection of travel rations and handing them out.

"If they've any wit," he mumbled around a mouthful of spiced sweetroot-jerk, returning to the matter at hand, "they'll all have made straight for the city. This village won't stand empty long." He chewed thoughtfully. "The humans are running from something, and these villages appear to be the only safety they're able to find out here." He shook his head ruefully, and brushed the dark-blond hair from his eyes. "They owe the dwarves their lives. Otherwise, what would they do out in the wild with no shelter?" He paused, a slight sense of bemusement creasing his brow.

"What vexes me is this new source of fear." He gesticulated with another piece of jerk. "Humans have always been plagued by their own kind. Why are they running now?" Wyn nodded wordlessly and sat beside his friend. They fell silent, each pondering the question.

Across the statue-stillness of the snow, voices rang out.

In an instant, the elves were on their feet; the pipe was quickly stashed, the food put away. In the space of two heartbeats, they'd melted into the trees at the edge of the village.

Whoever approached made no efforts to hide their passage, the heavy crunch of boots in the snow echoing clearly out of the woods to ring out between the empty homes.

Then a thick, gloved hand shot out of the trees to sweep a branch from its path.

A hand that belonged to a dwarf.

The elves let out a collective sigh of relief, and moved from their cover to convene with the new arrivals.

A band of perhaps two dozen followed their leader from the trees, all looking worn and travel-weary. Upon seeing the elves, they slowed, eyeing them warily. Wrapped up against the cold as they were, the scouts would be hard to identify from tall humans given the state of things. But when the lead dwarf reached Thom, he smiled and extended a warm greeting.

"Welcome back to the Rand my friend! What brings you so far from your warmer forest dwelling?"

"Dohrldt!" Thom exclaimed, recognising the group's leader. Standing at little over five feet, he was tall for a dwarf, but still craned his neck to look up at Thom. He wore his beard long, braiding the ends to keep it tidy where it hung down towards his belly. His greying hair was a coarse, rusty colour, and from under heavy brows twinkled dark, intelligent eyes. He was already puffing on a pipe twin to Thom's, bringing a smile to the scout's face. The two clasped forearms. "How are you old friend?"

"Well, my friend, though I've been better," the dwarf admitted wryly. He indicated the group behind him. "I've been escorting villagers away from the overrun southern ranges." Pulling his hat from his head with one hand, he ran the other through the wild hair beneath. "The humans have nowhere else to go, but their plight is displacing many of our people." He blew out a weary breath, glancing back at the families clustered behind him. They hung back, unsure of what to think of the elves. Dohrldt rolled his eyes. Jamming his hat back onto his head, he grumbled, "A less seasoned lot, I have never seen. Even the men are a bunch of poltroons!" Raising his voice again, he declared, "It seems we are out of the worst of the trouble! It looks as though the humans haven't come this far north yet

— we should have a clear path to Dvargra from here." The villagers seemed to perk up at that.

"Yes, what of the humans?" Thom asked, as Elas and Wyn resumed their positions upon the ground. "We've passed many refugees, but we heard that the raiders do not enter the forests. Do you know why?"

Dohrldt pulled on his pipe, nodding. "Aye Thom, there's been a change in the Unity trouble. They're more organised now, and wreak havoc with irksome discipline. The innocents have been fleeing for their lives, and the closest refuge for many this side of Throldon is our forests." His lips twitched beneath his beard. "Perhaps the presence of your Aethyr in the woods is misliked by the raiders." His eyes twinkled as he gave Thom a knowing look. Thom smiled.

"Dohrldt you know the Aethyr are not 'ours' — they belong to no one," he said with the patient rebuke of one who is used to the same debate.

Dohrldt shrugged. "All I know now is that with so many human refugees in the villages, a lot of our people have chosen to migrate to the city. At first, our people welcomed them and tried to help as best they could, but soon the villages were overwhelmed and living conditions became cramped and overcrowded." He waved his pipe at the empty buildings around them. "Most of the families decided to move out, and leave their homes to those that needed them." He hooked his pipe back into his mouth, and puffed thoughtfully. He seemed deep in thought when he raised his eyes to regard his old friend.

"Long have dwarves had good relations with their human neighbours. Never before have we seen such disquiet across the country." His eyes darkened, troubled. "We're told the humans who haven't sought the shelter of the forests have made their way north to seek asylum from Greneln... The country is emptying." His gaze took on a distant quality as he spoke. "Either they seek refuge away from central Arland, or they're fated to supply the slave trade in Throldon." He shook his head, worry lines carving grooves in his face. "I mislike this change. This new order in the Unity means trouble. Their new leader rallies the thugs together like a rebel army. And there are dark whispers as to what it is like in the city." He shuddered. And looked back up at Thom.

"I hope you bear better news, friend," he said finally, shaking himself from his dark reflections.

"I fear not." Thom hung his head regretfully. Things were worse than he had been led to believe.

"We," Elas interjected from his position on the ground, straightening to affect an air of pomp unlike himself, "have been sent to consort with your Lord Graem concerning suitable actions to be taken in light of this new... problem." He shrugged when he couldn't think of a suitably eloquent word for what was happening in the world. "I miss Dvargra," he added simply.

"Well, we shall be there soon enough," Dohrldt said with a chuckle, tapping his pipe out into the snow, and stowing it with excessive care. "I judge it no more than a day's travel to the settlement outskirts. We'll be in our Lord Graem's halls by tomorrow eve. Your lot would most likely travel faster with your long strides." He winked ironically at them, knowing them to be of short stature relative to the rest of their race.

"Settlements?" Wyn queried.

"Since our village brethren have been flooding back to the city, we've had to expand our horizons somewhat," Dohrldt sighed. "Quite literally. We now have quite the metropolis up in Dvargra, even if most of the settlements are only temporary accommodation. The builders' guild is working to construct more permanent housing as fast as they're able." He shook his head to himself, and Thom noted how troubling these new developments were to him.

"Never have I seen the city in such a state," he confided in the scout before falling silent.

They sat in quiet contemplation for a moment before the dwarf stood abruptly.

"Well there's no use sitting here moping about it, I suppose you'll be wanting to get along. If you feel up to running, you'll make the settlements by dark, and the sentries will gladly escort you to Lord Graem." He glanced reluctantly back to his charges. "I must stay to guide the villagers. I don't think any of them have ever travelled so far from home before."

Elas and Wyn unfolded from their positions on the ground and shouldered their packs quickly.

Thom clasped Dohrldt's forearm again. "We shall see you shortly then," he said. The dwarf responded with a curt nod, and a twinkling smile, and then they were off.

The elves ran without argument. Time itself seemed to nip at their heels.

And there were sure to be hot baths and warm beds awaiting them.

The dwarven settlements were a vast network of temporary shelters that stretched around Dvargra in a wide arc reaching from one side to the other, bracketing the city against the mountainside. They had clearly been assembled quickly for the augmented populace, but there was a system to them that smacked of dwarven orderliness, and the speedy build had not been at the cost of robustness; to have your house fail you this far north was to risk your life.

Wide slabs of mountain stone had been laid out into walkways, keeping mud and slush from the paths. Family groups prepared communal meals around firepits set at the centre of small clusters of houses. Tiny children played in the snow on their doorsteps. The young helped the elderly carry provisions, and throughout the newly developed suburbs, there was a wholesome air of collaborative making-do.

In all, unsurprisingly, the whole operation seemed to be working rather well.

True to Dohrldt's word, the sentries placed at the perimeter of the settlements gladly sent a guide to lead the scouts through the organised maze, up to the city gates.

Huge monoliths of iron ore rose up either side of the main thoroughfare into the city. Mined from the mountain itself, and known as the Gatekeepers of Dvargra, the monoliths served to remind all of how the dwarves prospered; living on the least hospitable precipices of the world, they still came out strong.

Between the monoliths, a pair of huge, solid ironwork gates hung, operated by enormous gears below. Great, stone walls, a hundred feet tall, curved out from the side of the mountain to meet the Gatekeepers, caressing the inner city in a solid embrace of rock and iron.

And beyond, the city proper buzzed.

Hewn into the mountainside itself, at first glance, Dvargra appeared a carved tableau; a work of art, rather than a working, living city.

But on closer inspection, it was a hive of activity.

The scouts passed through the Gatekeepers and into the familiar Great

Square, a large open space bustling with the various activities of city life. Jagged fissures in the mountainside led away from the Square, forming the streets and lanes of the city, thoroughfares for trade, avenues and alleyways. And the deeper they dived into the mountain, the more the fissures fragmented, creating a labyrinth of rock only the dwarves fully understood.

Within the lanes, windows carved into solid expanses of rock marked homes, schools, and libraries. At ground level, doorways cut directly into the mountain's surface led into workshops, smithies and stores. Occasional stone stairways sliced into the rock face, leading to the upper levels, some barely wide enough for two people to pass sideways, others holding whole plazas on a single step. A handful of narrow stairs dotted throughout the city led all the way up to Dvargra's stark but ample farmlands perched on the inhospitable mountaintop.

About the Square, vendors hawked their wares from stalls, food-carts and merchant caravans, loudly proclaiming the quality of their goods, and adding to the welcome hustle and bustle of the city. Thom smiled, looking up at the carved face of the city. He breathed deep and tasted the sharp tang of fresh mountain air and metal ores.

This was home from home.

"Come on, old man," Elas said, ducking past him just beyond arm's reach. "We didn't run all the way here to stand and stare."

Thom grumbled something unsavoury under his breath, and fell into step behind the younger scouts.

Through the Gatekeepers, they passed the Guild Hall, a grand stone building constructed a hundred yards in front of the mountainside, and covered in enormous carved depictions of craftsmen and women working their various arts. Smiths, miners, engineers, farmers, weavers, carpenters, stonemasons, painters, and musicians; all manner of crafts represented on one enormous stone canvas. The Guild Hall was where the city's demands and resources were coordinated, but it was not where they would find the leader of the Dvargran dwarves.

Lord Graem's council halls were located within a plain, squat building behind the Guild Hall, and it was there that they headed.

As they neared, they turned a corner and nearly ran straight into a tower of books.

"Coming through, coming through," the books said, teetering

perilously from side to side. The elves stepped aside to let the books pass, and Wyn caught a glimpse of a face behind the stack.

"Stochell! How goes things?" he greeted the hidden dwarf warmly, and relieved him of half the papers.

"Oh, my thanks," Stochell replied profusely, appearing above the shortened pile. "Master Wyn!" His tired face broke into a wide smile. "It is good to see you! I am well, but all this building of the settlements has me running about like an apprentice again!" He shifted his papers, readjusting the weight in his arms. "And there's no imagination! Solid, sturdy, *boring* housing that is quick and easy to build." He rolled his eyes in a way that groaned "*boring!*" as clearly as if he'd bellowed it through the halls. He fixed Wyn with a suitably unimpressed look. "It's hardly stimulating work." Depositing his load onto a nearby ledge, he sighed deeply. The elves smiled. The Master Builder much preferred tinkering and inventing to the traditional applications of his trade.

"The settlements are certainly a mastery though." Thom attempted to pacify him.

Stochell waved away the compliment. "Yes yes I know." There was no arrogance in his words, purely fact. "But there's no challenge in it." He sighed again, and then caught himself, as if an idea had just struck him. He turned his attention back to the scouts, a sly glint in his eye.

"But you must have only just arrived!" he said, taking in their damp and disheveled appearance, his face lighting up. "You must avail yourself of some proper Dvargran hospitality before you seek out our Lord — he's out surveying the settlements in any case and won't be back for a few hours." His eyes twinkled. "And you have yet to experience my latest innovation!" He paused pointedly.

Elas obliged. "What's that?"

Stochell beamed with pride.

"I'm glad you asked Master Scout! I have produced a few prototypes of an ingenious — if I do say so myself — bathing system." He lifted a finger before anyone could interject. "I know, I know, you're not convinced — but hear me out! The water is sourced as usual, and feeds through the pipes as usual." He brought up his other hand, holding both index fingers in the air, his face bright with zeal. "But instead of filling a tub to wallow in, the water exits from a sprinkler in the ceiling, raining fresh and hot upon the user, before instantly draining away. Any waste is filtered and used to irrigate our crops!" He clapped his hands together and straightened, a smug expression across his face. "It is cleaner, more efficient and most importantly—" his grin seemed about to split his face in half "—brilliant!"

Wyn looked doubtful. He'd been looking forward to a proper bath for weeks. Thom's eyes twinkled with amusement at the dwarf's enthusiasm. Elas boomed with laughter.

"Lead the way Master Builder," he chortled. "I'm always ready to see what new innovations you have to offer!" As Stochell bustled away, Elas leant over to whisper to the others.

"Those bathtubs have always been too short for me! And in any case, Stochell has always been one for a fair test." He winked conspiratorially. "I'm sure he won't mind if I should require a tub as well to make a fair comparison!"

Elas met Wyn outside their rooms after a thorough testing of Stochell's new plumbing instalments. His skin was flushed red; first from the cold bite of mountain chill on the way into Dvargra, and then from the hot, steaming water that came from the taps in the dwarven city. The Master Builder took pride in his work, but making his "improvements" to the everyday mundane is what put the twinkle in his eye.

"*That's* better," Elas said, pulling the door to his guest room closed behind him. He glanced up and down the hallway. "Where's Thom?"

Wyn jerked his head towards the far end of the hall. "He went ahead," he said, turning to follow Thom's example. "Said he'll meet us there."

"Let's not keep him waiting then," Elas replied, falling into step behind him.

They found Thom, as expected, waiting outside Lord Graem's council chambers. He was washed and dressed in clean attire, but he paced agitatedly, giving him something of the air of a caged beast.

Elas hailed him. As Thom's bushy-browed eyes met his, a group of dwarves rounded the corner.

Lord Graem was of average stature for a dwarf, which put him at around five feet tall, but his presence more than made up for it. His auburn beard was neat and trim, and threaded with dignified grey. His face was ageless but for a spider's web of creases at the corners of bright blue eyes, glinting above a full moustache.

Those sharp eyes caught sight of the elf scouts instantly. His pace slowed, ever so slightly, enough that his entourage noticed, and looked up to see what had caught his attention.

He sighed. "I take your arrival to mean that our overcrowding problem is the least of our worries," he said, in a voice that was gruff and weary.

Thom's lips pressed together. "I'm afraid we have matters of an urgent nature to discuss with your lordship."

Lord Graem waved away his entourage, and stepped closer to the scouts. His face was grim.

"How many times have I told you not to call me that?" he said, his moustache twitching. Thom smiled a tired smile. "Come now, Thom," Graem said, reaching up to place a hand on the scout's upper arm — his shoulder was too high to reach. "Surely it can't be all that bad?"

Thom gripped his arm in return, his look turning sour.

"We have much to discuss."

20

A CAVE OF SIMPLE WONDERS

The Wastelands stretched for leagues in every direction; a blur of uninhabitable, dry, desert tundra. Nothing grew, not even grasses, the ground an unyielding mix of dark sand and loose dirt over cold, packed earth. Biting winds raced across the sands, picking up grit to cut mercilessly at anything left exposed. The air was thick with dust, obscuring anything beyond a dozen paces.

The Wastelands were aptly named.

Between the winds and Fae's wound, the going was slow, and she had to focus on putting one foot in front of the other, bowing her head into the sandy winds and pushing onward. Ty had a spare shirt wrapped around most of his face to protect it against the sands, and Bek held his arm up as an improvised shield.

Hal kept them going. He sang songs no one else knew the words to. Told jokes with a genuine smile. Kept them talking when all they wanted to do was mope and trudge.

Despite his best efforts though, the cold hostility of the Wastelands seeped into their very bones, sapping them of their strength. And their will.

Fae's wound dulled to a constant ache. She took it as a good sign — she had to, because this was no place to remove her bandages to check. She drank the tonic Ty made for her, and hoped for the best.

After five days, the ache had become one of many. Her belly ached and itched in its healing. Her back ached and stiffened after each day of pushing herself into the wind. Her legs ached from trudging across sandy ground with little to no purchase. Her *face* ached from its constant grimace, scrunched against the sand and dirt whipping around her.

And through it all, the call of her vision tugged at her still, pulling her onward.

After five days, numb to everything but the aches of the journey, Fae wondered if she would ever see an end to the seemingly *un*ending landscape.

When Hal let out a shout.

"Aha!" he exclaimed triumphantly. "About time too!" He ducked behind a rare rise in the land.

And disappeared.

Fae let out a desperate cry.

"Hal!" she called, fighting to keep the tremor from her voice. Her throat was dusty and dry from the sand and dirt tossed about by the unrelenting winds. She coughed hard.

Somehow finding a hidden energy reserve, she jogged towards the spot where Hal had disappeared. Her stomach pulled against its stitches, her legs burned, and her lungs protested the treatment. Her heart beat a rapid tattoo as she neared his position.

But Hal was nowhere to be seen.

"Hal!" she called again, hysteria edging into her voice.

From the ground itself, a head appeared beside her. She stared, not quite willing to believe her eyes.

"Come on now, no use standing there screaming," Hal said. "Follow me!" And he dropped out of sight again. If Fae hadn't been standing right next to him when he'd appeared, she wouldn't have known *how* to follow him. For a moment, in the blur of flying sand, it looked as though he'd emerged from the ground itself.

But she caught, just briefly, the swing of a door closing behind him. Moving an inch further forward, a narrow channel in the slope came into view. It was just wide enough, and deep enough, for a man to stand upright, sheltered from the hostile conditions of the Wastelands.

And somehow, Hal had disappeared into it.

Fae ducked into the space, and felt her body instantly relinquish its hold on the gruelling posture she'd had to adopt over the past few days. Her muscles screamed in new pain as they tried relaxing. But she had no time for that. Reaching out, Fae brushed her hands over the surface of the subtle incline she stood beside.

Hard, cold, ground scraped beneath her fingers. She gritted her teeth and persisted.

And then cold, compacted earth became smooth, and flat.

The flat of a rough-sanded table, of a smooth, classroom wall.

Of a door.

She groped around the flatness until she found an edge.

"Where did he go?" Ty panted roughly as he and Bek jogged up beside her.

She pulled, and the ground opened.

The narrow slot carved into the rise angled downward behind the door. Sparing a single backwards glanced, Fae filed in with Ty and Bek behind her, out of the wind.

The door banged shut behind them, a heavy latch falling into place preventing it from rebounding in its frame. Hal must have wedged it open for them.

In the seconds it took for her eyes to adjust to the darkness, Fae breathed her first unlabored breath in days. She coughed again, her lungs repelling the build-up of dust in her throat. Ty cleared his throat loudly too, the grit making it sound a painful process. Further in, a faint, flickering light was the only sign of where they ought to go.

They walked single-file along a narrow corridor, down into the ground. The walls were smoothed down, still holding the gritty character of the landscape outside, but without any jagged edges to snag them as they passed.

And then the passage opened out into a room. It was simple, but spacious. A long, scarred table leant against one wall, but that was the extent of the furniture. The hard, dirt floor was swept clear and smooth. Large, horizontal alcoves big enough for a man to lie down in were carved into the walls, and small recesses around the chamber held an assortment of oddities. One had a bowl and cup neatly stacked, another housed a small, ornate tinderbox. There was a carved statuette of a woman, her hands held together before her chest, and a wooden puzzle-box, of the type a child might play with. Most of the others held candles of various sizes, and in various states of melting, and it was these to which Hal tended as they entered.

He was at the far end of the room, holding a long, thin taper to the last of the wicks. The candles filled the cave with a warm, flickering light, the walls of the room rippling lazily in the candlelight. The ceiling was the sole surface that remained rough and unpolished.

Fae drank in their unexpected shelter, and sagged with relief. She almost cried. It was more than just a welcome respite from the barren landscape above. It was a marvel. A cave of simple wonders.

Bek casually arranged his bedroll in one of the horizontal alcoves, as if this weren't a wholly unexpected turn of events.

"How did you find this place?" Ty asked Hal.

The man studied his feet, but his eyes smiled. "I built it." Ty raised an eyebrow. Hal caught it, and the corner of his mouth twitched modestly. "It was before I became a ranger proper." He ran a hand through his dusty hair. "My first time crossing the Wastelands. I was making my way to Greneln from the South Road. Was going to Oresh and changed my mind halfway. Got caught in a storm." He shook his head, admonishing his past self. "Found myself as good a spot as any, and hunkered down against the hillock up there." He pointed to the narrow corridor, and the shallow slope above. "Thought to wait the storm out. Felt like I lay there hours. Musta fallen asleep though because I dreamed. Dreamt o' Greneln and them houses under the hills they live in up there. Musta been half buried in sand by the time I woke up but I started digging. Dug until I had a little hollow up on the hillside there. And that were enough shelter for that storm." He played a hand over his knuckles.

"Ever time I cross the Wastelands I do a bit more. Start with, it were just digging deeper. Then it were making the cave." He waved at the room around them. "Then the rest. I'm always adding to it." He looked around, as if seeing it for the first time again. Then he shrugged his shoulders, his narrative concluded, and went to gather timber from a small wood store in the back. Bringing an armload back, he began building a fire in the doorway.

Fae watched him, the details of Hal's bunker catching her eye as he worked. It was apparent just how much attention he'd lavished on the place since its inception. The slope of the tunnel and a cleverly thought-out groove in the ceiling served to funnel any smoke from the fire up and out. A small cold sink was dug into the ground in another corner. The sleeping alcoves were all carved into the same wall as the entrance, which kept them out of any drafts from the doorway.

For a place as inhospitable as the Wastelands, this shelter was a haven. It must have taken Hal years of travel to return often enough for the work that had gone into it. And it had clearly become more than just a shelter to him. There were blankets and spare clothing here, stored away against the need.

Once the fire was set and roaring, Hal retrieved some food from his stores, and worked on preparing a simple meal.

"Where did you find all this?" Fae asked, indicating the supplies and provisions stored in the cave. "And how did you bring it all here?" She sat down and began peeling away her sand-encrusted outer layers.

Hal shrugged. "When there ain't no need to be running between towns, I settle here." He began chopping root vegetables with a smooth-handled knife. "Sometimes I bring stuff with me, sometimes I forage for it. There ain't much out here to find, but you can if you're keen enough." He tapped his nose with a wink. Then he waved absently at the table. "That were the only difficult one. Found that in a caravan wreck strayed too far off the road. Abandoned." He turned back to his chopping. "Don't like to think too much as to why." They fell into an uneasy silence, broken only by Bek's soft snoring. He'd made himself comfortable in his chosen alcove, and dozed off.

Hal spared a glance his way. "Boy's got the right of it there," he said. He put his knife down and turned to Fae and Ty. "Didn't like to worry you 'til we was safe away." His eyes flicked to the doorway. "Don't know if you noticed, but the weather out there's getting a mite fickle. I'd wager there's a storm brewing. No need to panic," he added, seeing the unease cross both their faces. "Should only need to hole up here for a couple o' days, just 'til the storm passes." He gathered the chopped vegetables and dumped them into a pot. "Might as well make yourselves comfortable-like — we ain't going nowhere in this." He indicated the entrance tunnel again. "Not to worry, though," Hal said, moving a sturdy tripod over the fire. He hung his cooking pot from a hook at the apex, and covered it with a lid. "I'm sure we can find something to keep us occupied."

· · ·

The storm raged for three days, but as Hal promised, it wasn't time wasted.

Fae was relieved to see that her wound was indeed healing well enough, and gracefully accepted another pot of herbal tea when Ty brewed it for her. Finally out of the sand and wind, she dabbed florestem around the stitches to keep them clean, and wore her clothes loose to let the skin breathe.

Hal immediately set about using the time to work on his hideout, and Ty quickly offered his services. Fae volunteered with less strenuous tasks, keen to let her body heal as quickly as possible. Before long, they were all lending a hand.

Some of the timber in Hal's store had been set aside to make seating for the table. After much discussion, he and Ty agreed upon a design, and began disassembling other scrap, pulling useable nails out of old planks, and putting the resulting pieces back together.

On the second day, they rounded out the fireplace and lined it with broken half-bricks to stop the ash from blowing across the floor. Later, they all helped to chisel extra shelving and a long, wide work bench into the side wall, which Hal then lined with rough boards.

When they weren't working on improvements to the bunker, Fae danced — gently at first, testing out her still-healing skin. Hal and Ty exchanged fighting styles and tips, occasionally sparring to demonstrate. The ranger clearly had some skill in combat, his movements disciplined and precise. And while the elves weren't a typically aggressive people, Ty's grace and speed more than made up for a lack of fighting experience. His body was lean but strong, his movements river-smooth and whip-quick — Fae caught herself staring on more than one occasion. Bek certainly enjoyed watching them spar, applauding wildly whenever Hal won a bout.

At night, they discussed the land, the races, and their histories. When they exhausted those, they moved onto the old wives' tales that each race told of the other.

Hal laughed when Fae asked again about the human gods.

"We got all sorts o' gods — too many," he said, leaning forward to poke at the fire. "But you'll find different ones wherever you go. Seiner's Tarn folk pray to the Sailer. The Farmer's a favourite in the Wolds—" He stumbled to a halt, his eyes flared. He cleared his throat. "Anyway, there's the Mother, the Warrior, the Carpenter, the Judge... you get the idea. There's gods for everyone." He trailed off, staring into the fire.

Fae exchanged a glance with Ty. Was it coincidence, that the humans had a god called the Mother? He turned slightly towards her, his shoulder brushing past hers in a way that made her want to lean into him. She wondered briefly if he ever fought the urge to put his arm around her. She decided she wouldn't mind if he did.

Ty's eyes flicked to Hal, and he gave a short shake of his head. Fae followed his gaze — the ranger's eyes were glazed and distant, his mouth downturned at the corners. He seemed to have aged in an instant; a different man to the jovial, upbeat human they'd come to know.

"Who do you pray to?" Fae asked softly.

Hal smiled a small, rueful smile. "Don't pray much these days," he said. "Just go wherever my feet take me."

Fae nodded. There was the flavour of something more to Hal's story, but it was buried beneath years of aloneness, and sharpened by time. Like a splinter in his side, ignored, but it pricked him all the same. Fae didn't push. Left it buried. It would work its way out in time.

Sometime on the third day, the storm broke.

They hadn't heard it from within the bunker; the ground above had insulated almost all sound from outside. But when the weather finally calmed, they were surrounded by an eerie, grave-like stillness.

Ty's ears twitched.

"Aye," Hal said, picking up on the slight motion. "Storm's broken. I'll take today to put things to rights here, and we'll be off in the morning."

Fae had trouble sleeping that night. Her wound had almost fully healed thanks to the herbs and Ty's relentless ministrations, and, provided she didn't do anything else foolish, she'd no need to worry over it further. But the anticipation of continuing their journey north — and the relentless pull within her — served to keep her mind whirling as she lay awake in her bed.

Their time in Hal's hideout had been a welcome reprieve, but it was time to go.

They set out early the next morning, keen to get underway. After their brief sojourn, the Wastelands seemed even more barren and unforgiving. Even the sunrise was muffled by the cloud of sand that still hung in the air.

Fae felt herself slip towards the melancholia she'd suffered before the storm, when a break in the sand-cloud finally allowed a shaft of sunlight to fall over them.

The natural light and warmth on her skin was like water to a parched throat, and she lifted her face, closing her eyes to bask in the feel of it. Around her, she heard her companions breathe out a sigh.

"Right," Hal declared, "we're about halfway across this godsforsaken place. Only a few more days 'til we reach the Western Highway." He looked at them significantly. "It gets better from there." He nodded once, shouldered his pack, and set off northwards once more, the others trailing behind.

21

ONE LOOSE TILE

Just off the Southern Highway, a small camp fire burned brightly. Five figures sat hunched around it.

"Did you see the look on his face when he realised we weren't joking?" one man guffawed. He tore a chunk from the leg of roasted rabbit he held in one hand, the other wielding a crude club above his head. He brought the weapon down with a dull *thunk* as it lodged in the earth beside him.

"That weren't even the best part!" another countered. "Her screaming was the best!" He put on a cruelly high-pitched voice and held his hands clasped to his chest. "*No! Please don't! They're all I have! Don't hurt us!*"

The men around the fire fell about laughing. The youngest, closer to a boy, with delicate features, chewed his food quietly.

"What?" the second man demanded, thumping the boy hard on the arm. "Too wild for you?" He exchanged sneers with his fellows.

The boy shrugged indifferently. "Got what we wanted didn't we?" he said. He indicated the wagon and horse, standing hobbled off to the side. "Got plenty o' food. Some goods. New clothes. Even some coin." He took another bite. "Seems like a decent raid to me," he said around a mouthful of food.

The man to his right cuffed him on the back of the head. "Don't talk with your mouth full," he scolded roughly. The boy fell quiet. The man turned back to his companions. "We'll take this—" he jerked a thumb at the wagon "—to Oresh. We'll get the best price for Kingdom goods out West."

The men groaned. "C'mon, Rogan," one of them whined. "Throldon's closer, why don't we go there?"

Rogan fixed him with a glare. "You been on this crew how long, Jimmy?"

Jimmy swallowed thickly. "Near on six year."

Rogan nodded. "That's what I thought." He looked around the rest of the groaners. "Then you've been hearing the same rumours I've been hearing about Throldon." His gaze swung back to the unfortunate Jimmy. "Ain't that so?"

Jimmy nodded.

"And what rumours would I be talking about right now?" Rogan nearly growled, his voice went so low.

"Throldon ain't safe," the boy spoke up when Jimmy's tongue failed him. He dodged when Rogan's hand reached out to cuff him again.

"I'm teaching *Jimmy* a lesson here," Rogan said gruffly, "not you, Max. *You* listen." He turned back to the other men. "Throldon ain't safe," he repeated, looking them each in the eye. "And it ain't Unity either, the way I'm hearing it. Some whore's taken over and she's putting everyone through the wringer. So for now, we're on our own. Ain't no Unity message to back us up."

"Weren't we always on our own?" the first man asked, thumbing the edge of a notched blade.

"Aye." Rogan nodded solemnly. "But so was everyone else. There was a code. Now..." He trailed off.

The men fell silent. They finished their meal, sucking the juices from rabbit bones before tossing them into the fire where they hissed and spat.

The boy, Max, was the first to move. He left the campfire to set up his bedroll by the wagon. It was his job to watch the loot.

As he lay beside the wagon, he gazed up at the stars.

Max had been with Rogan's crew just under a year. They'd picked him up in the ruins of Hapton, where he'd been living off what little was left in the market town. If anything, the desertion of Hapton had made life easier for Max. The life of a street urchin was a hard one, only made more difficult by the presence of people objecting to your survival. Once everyone had left, it was easier to scrounge for food. There hadn't been many that had stayed, but Max had probably been the best at getting by.

When Rogan's crew rolled through a year or so ago, Max had decided instantly to avoid them. But one loose roof tile was all it took to fell that plan where it stood.

Max sighed. With blindly-chopped hair, a dirt-smudged face, and a figure too gaunt to be considered anything but scrawny, it was no wonder they'd assumed Max was a boy.

And she'd heard enough about what these sorts of men do to girls, to correct them.

She'd shown them where to find all the best loot, picking locks and scampering over the hollow husks of Hapton to get into buildings that were otherwise blocked. She'd impressed Rogan enough to stay alive. Because that's all she had left now.

So she watched the wagon.

She blew a breath over her face, watching it play with the growing strands of her hair. It needed cutting again. The last thing she needed was long, girly hair to draw attention to her feminine features.

She rolled over, putting her back to the fire, and closed her eyes. And rather than listen to the men's cruel stories from the road, she directed her hearing out into the empty wilderness.

The wind whispered through the grasses. A solitary bird called out with no answer. Firebugs hummed, and the occasional cricket chirped forlornly.

And through the darkness, something else.

Max strained her ears to listen. It sounded like the sails on a windmill. But there were no settlements for miles. No farms, no people.

She flicked through her mind to find another match for the sound.

There was no canvas on the wagon to flap, and no real wind to catch at one in any case.

The sound grew louder. *Flap. Flap. Flap.*

It had a rhythm to it. Like a slow, languishing heartbeat.

Now, even the men were commenting; she heard their questioning tones over by the fire.

It grew louder still. Until it was overhead.

Max squinted up into the night. But it was just dark. Not even the twin moons were out tonight.

And then fire spewed from the sky.

She threw an arm over her face, the sudden glare stabbing lances into her eyes.

Then she felt the *heat*. It burned against her face. Hot and sharp.

Then she heard the screams.

Amidst the roar of flame, and the crackle of fire, four men screamed wild, animal screams.

Max scrambled under the wagon, holding her arms over her face still. She screwed her eyes almost-shut, tried to shield them. Squinted towards the fire.

Three of them crawled blindly about. One staggered out into the darkness, his body blazing orange, his screams so piercing it made her stomach roil.

Then, one by one, they stopped moving.

The fire crackled happily in the calm that followed.

Max could do nothing but stare. She'd seen some things in her short life. But she'd never seen a man burned alive.

The smell of charred hair and flesh reached her nostrils, and she retched. Her stomach heaved over and over until she choked up nothing more than bile.

Then the ground shook.

She froze.

Sounds she didn't know the name for came to her from the direction of the campfire that was.

Slowly, agonisingly, she turned her head to look.

Outlined against the orange glow of the fire, a huge shape stood tall and black. Bigger than twenty — no, thirty — horse-carts, it lumbered closer to the fire, and a grey stream of cloud issued from where it stood. Where the cloud touched the fire, it dimmed with a sullen hiss, and soon the land was dark again.

Lights danced before Max's eyes. She was flash-blind, and she was frozen, trapped beneath the wagon. Through the ringing in her ears, she heard another distant *flap, flap, flap*. Her breath caught in her throat.

There's more than one...? Her heart pounded so loud she was surprised they couldn't hear it. A familiar tension coiled in her limbs, ready to run. But how did she run from *that*?

"What was that for?" a female voice sounded in the darkness.

A deep rumble answered her. Like the groan of a tall-ship in a storm.

"You know what. Why did you burn these men?" Max heard a soft *thump* — the sound of a boot against the dead weight of dead flesh.

The rumble came again, but within it, Max heard the words, "They smelled bad."

"'They smelled bad'?" the female voice repeated. "Remind me to wash regularly around you!"

"They smelled *wrong*," the deep rumble clarified. It sounded like a rock-slide down a mountain. Gravelly, and ominous.

"Right, well, now that it's done, shall we be on our way? Baev'ill's likely wondering why you took a sudden detour to the ground."

The sound of something big — huge — moving.

"There's one more," the rumble said.

Max's heart stuttered. She felt like the rabbit caught on the bead of an arrow. A huge, unmissable arrow. A cold sweat broke out along her spine.

"Does it smell bad?" the female voice asked sardonically.

"No," the rumble replied. "I will leave it for now, and the horse, and hope that they find better company."

"Good," the female replied. "Then let's go, and leave this dismal piece of nowhere behind."

"Indeed. The nomad awaits above."

The ground shook beneath her. A huge *whoosh* that set the wagon rocking.

Flap. Flap. Flap.

The sound of sails receded until Max was left in silence.

She didn't sleep. Max stayed under the wagon all night. She didn't dare move. For hours she sat hunched between the axles until her muscles seized up so badly she couldn't have moved if she'd wanted to.

When dawn finally breached the horizon, she breathed what felt like the first breath since fire shot out of the sky.

Slowly, painfully, she crept from beneath the wagon. Bracing a hand on the wheel spokes, she eased herself up, working the cramps from her muscles as she went. When she eventually stood upright, she looked around.

She regretted it almost immediately. Not a dozen paces away, the charred bodies of Rogan's crew lay blackened against the ground.

Swallowing bile, Max lowered her gaze.

The ground had been burned to ash, a huge swathe of black against the spring-green grass.

Except for a small circle around the wagon where she'd been hiding.

Max stared at it. That unmarked patch of grass. Even the wagon was unscathed, the only signs of damage on it the ones Rogan and his crew had inflicted the day before.

Dazed, and blinking in confusion, she looked around.

She spotted the horse. It had bolted as far as its hobbled legs had been able to, and was standing shellshocked a few yards away.

Max stumbled awkwardly over to the horse, trying to ignore the pins-and-needles all over, murmuring soothing sounds as she went. When she finally neared the horse enough to grab its halter, she turned to lead it back to the untouched wagon. But, try as she might, she could do nothing to convince the beast to come close enough to the campsite to hitch it up. Max blew out a resigned huff, and trudged back to pack only what she could carry herself.

She wrapped some clothes, food, and coin into a saddlebag. Thankfully, the horse was a docile cob, and she didn't shy once they were away from the blackened ground around the campfire.

Max slung her saddlebag over the mare's back. "What am I going to call you?" she murmured to the horse. Rogan's crew had stolen her along with the wagon. They hadn't exactly stopped to ask its name. Max glanced back at the sooty stain on the earth. Her mouth twitched.

"How about Firefly?" she said with a smile. She'd named a stray cat in Hapton the same once. She looked the horse over. The mare was a gentle roan, with an irregular white blaze on her face that looked almost as if it could be a flame. The mare nudged her with the flat of her head.

"Alright," Max said, scratching just behind the horse's jaw. "Firefly."

She pulled herself onto Firefly, who stood stolid and sure.

"Right," she grabbed the lead-rope, looping it around Firefly's neck to create basic reins, and gently eased her east. "Let's get away from here."

22

AN ENVIABLE ESTABLISHMENT

The trail of Elisabeth Marl had gone stale.

Wil, Stef, and Aren had stopped at every village on their way, teasing scraps of information from wary villagers; anything that might aid in their search.

Sometimes they were fortunate enough to chance upon someone who'd heard a credible rumour, but didn't trust the scouts enough to share it. More commonly they were left picking apart crazed suggestions and conspiracy theories that proved to be of no use at all. Occasionally, they were treated with open hostility, and answered with silence.

If there were Peacekeepers in the villages, they were well hidden.

"I think it might be time we re-evaluate," Aren said, the first to break the uneasy silence about their dwindling prospects as they trudged across open countryside to the next village. "We haven't had much luck with these people, and by the sounds of things, Elisabeth Marl has disappeared on purpose. She'll be hard to find just by asking around." He looked over at his companions, who considered his words silently.

"Why don't we try something new?" he continued hopefully.

Stef glanced up at him.

"The next village isn't far off now, brother," he said, his voice calmly controlled. "Let us see what they have to say. At the least we can rest there

— while we... re-evaluate." He shot Aren a look that told him to let it be, shooting another, more pointed glance at Wil. A storm-cloud brewed behind Wil's sky-blue eyes. Aren was not the only one chafing at their lack of progress.

True to Stef's word, it was only an hour or so before they reached the next village. From afar, it looked like all the other villages they'd passed through. As they neared, the hallmarks of recent raiding became apparent; the outer buildings were in a state halfway between ruin and repair, the people bandaged and bruised as they went about their business.

The public house was closed, so the scouts were directed to the village hall instead. There, they were told, they would find refreshments, although no one mentioned if they would be invited to stay.

The hall was filled wall to wall with stretchers and beds, forming a kind of make-shift physica. Most of the beds were occupied, although many of the patients looked to be recovering from their injuries.

Wil smiled for the first time in many days.

The physica — such as it was — was clean, and well-run, the patients clearly well cared for. The floors were scrubbed, there was clean water by every bed, and the sheets were all spotless. Bandages were fresh, patients chatted amiably with smiling healers, the atmosphere generally warm and wholesome.

All were signs of competent healers. The bulk of these people would return to full health, and soon.

The differences between places that had had the luxury of Peacekeeper care, and those that hadn't, were staggeringly obvious. Clumsy medical care was commonplace in rural, isolated villages. To be injured was often to be crippled. Sickness stretched on longer than bodies could tolerate it, and often resulted in chronic, debilitating illness. Death was a widely feared — even expected — prognosis.

But if a village was lucky enough to have a Peacekeeper group pass through, the range of treatable, even curable, diseases and injuries increased dramatically. Death rates dropped, and people didn't have to fear permanent disability. Small, remote villages rarely had anything but praise for Peacekeepers.

These were the stories the scouts were chasing.

They'd long given up on asking after Elisabeth Marl by her name. It was clear she hadn't used it for years. Instead they asked after a woman, in her forties, highly skilled, compassionate. Wherever these stories led, they found well cared-for villagers, and praise for the Peacekeepers.

Wil looked about the village-hall-physica they now stood in.

Aren and Stef noticed it too. It lifted their spirits to see, but they'd long ago learnt the importance of subtle questions in these times. Aren took the lead. He beckoned a nearby helper.

"Where can three weary travellers find some refreshments after a long day on the road?" he said, keeping his voice low. "We were told in the village that we might find something here." The girl nodded, her eyes fixed on Wil's towering frame, and pointed to a far corner, where pitchers of water and some simple fare was set out for patients.

"My thanks," Aren shot her a winning smile, inclining his head in a small bow. The girl blushed pink, and hurried back to her duties.

Retreating to the indicated corner, the scouts helped themselves to the water, and settled themselves on a nearby bench, all the while listening in to the conversations around them. There was the usual village chatter; updates on the repairs, and grumbling about the general state of things. But every now and then, they heard mention of a woman. A healer. One many credited as the reason they found themselves in such good health. Some of the villagers likened her to an angel, staying just long enough to ensure her charges would be alright before moving on to watch over another.

Then there were theories exchanged as to the nature of her disappearance.

Wil grumbled at these. "She's not here then," he said with a glower.

"No, but listen," Stef replied, his ears twitching.

The scouts were used to hearing stories of a mystery woman helping out at the local healing house or hospit, as the humans called their physicas. But she only ever stayed for a few days before moving on again.

The woman the villagers here spoke of, had arrived as part of a group, and only recently left after many weeks.

"Well that explains why we haven't found trace of her for a while," Aren whispered. "She's been here all along!"

"Let's not draw any conclusions just yet," Wil responded. "These tales don't quite match with what we've heard before of Elisabeth Marl's comings and goings. I don't want to start chasing the wrong woman." Aren snorted quietly into his drink.

"At least half those stories were volunteered too readily by the half-crazed, and the other half were hearsay." But he caught Wil's look and quieted, taking another token swig of water.

After a few minutes, a woman approached them from across the room.

Stef was the first to notice, and nudged at his brother. Aren straightened from the nonchalant slouch he'd taken to adopting in human company — "it's less threatening! And distracts from my tallness!" — and adopted a friendly smile for the newcomer. He noted her garb: a simple shift dress, sleeves rolled up, clean white apron tied around her waist, with hair fastened neatly at the nape of her neck — a healer's uniform.

"Greetings!" he addressed the woman. "You run a rather enviable establishment here milady, 'tis a rare sight to see." He waved an arm to the ward, then broadened his gesture to take in the food table beside them. "We are merely availing ourselves of the village's humble hospitality before we continue on our merry way." He tipped his cup to toast their generosity.

"I'm glad to hear it." The woman smiled back. "You're not from around here are you?" she said, eyeing Aren shrewdly. He had the good sense to look sheepish. "Visitors are welcome here," she continued, casting a glance across all of them, "albeit cautiously. These people have little to spare these days."

"Indeed," Aren agreed, nodding solemnly. "The same goes for far too many of late." He took a slow sip of his drink.

"It seems that there are still those who would help though," Wil spoke up, his thinning patience getting the better of him. "We've heard stories of travellers lending a hand where they can: fighting, building, healing..." He glanced significantly around the room before bringing his gaze back to rest on the healer.

Her expression still smiled, but it didn't quite reach her doe-brown eyes. She watched them with a wariness that belied her open demeanour.

Aren noticed it too.

"Excuse my friend his lack of subtlety," he said with a short glare at his companion. "We've been looking for such a group to join; to lend a hand where we can. Word was there was a group headed this way, led by a healer woman." He cocked an eyebrow at the woman before him. "Would that be you? Or if not, do you know who?"

The woman's eyes narrowed, considering them. Aren sensed she knew more than she was willing to share, and her understandable doubts about them was only serving to agitate Wil's impatience. After a quick calculation, he decided to throw caution to the wind. A final gambit.

He leant forward, resting his elbows on his knees, hands clasped before him.

"Is there somewhere we could speak more privately?" he said, voice lowered, his eyebrows raised imploringly as he met her gaze.

She looked at each of them. Squaring her shoulders with a sigh, she nodded for them to follow her. She led them out of the main hall, into a small side room. It was furnished plainly, housing only a bed, a desk and a bookcase.

"My name is Jessica by the way," she said as she closed the door behind them. "You don't have the look of trouble-makers so I'll admit, I'm curious." She took the seat at the desk and folded her arms, waiting.

"I am Aren," Aren replied. "And this is Wil, and my brother Stef. I didn't lie before." He took a deep breath, and ploughed on. "We're looking for Elisabeth Marl. We need her help." He glanced over at the other two, before slowly reaching up to untie the head-scarf he wore to cover his ears.

Jessica gasped, eyes darting from one to other. All three removed their headgear, revealing their identities in a single motion.

Aren placed his scarf on the desk.

His eyes met hers. "We *all* need her help."

Some hours later, Jessica sat agape at the figures arrayed before her.

"Well I never!" she exclaimed once they'd finished. "Elves! In our corner of the world." She sat back in her seat, holding a hand to her forehead. She blew out a breath. "And you need Laina's help? Madness!" She shook her head incredulously.

"Laina?" Wil asked. "So Elisabeth Marl *has* been going by a different name?"

"Oh aye!" Jessica nodded emphatically. "I mean, she never said as much but I had my suspicions." Her eyes slid off to the side, entertaining her own thoughts. "I could tell she had a story, but you see enough sadness in this line of work to know when to leave well enough alone." She sighed, and looked up at the elves again.

"She goes by Laina Woods. Has done for as long as I've known her. She's never been one to talk of her past though, so I'm afraid I couldn't shed any light on that for you." She leant forward over the desk, hands clasped on the rough wooden surface. "But I've no doubt that she was once Elisabeth Marl. You know they say she could be the last of the royals? But she's one helluva healer, as you can see from the — what was it you called it? — 'enviable establishment'." She smiled softly. "It was all her. Always was. She always knew what to do."

The elves exchanged a look. If the woman they were trailing was the last of the royals, there could be another reason why the Eldra had sent them after her.

"Do you know where she's gone?" Wil blurted, itching to follow as quickly as possible. They'd spent too much time traipsing from village to village for a lead like this.

Jessica shook herself free of her reminiscing, and stared at him. "Well no," she said, her eyes flaring in irritation. "She just disappeared one night, as you've no doubt heard." She waved towards the door, and the gossiping patients beyond. "She tended the wounded as usual, she went to bed as usual." She dropped her gaze. "The next morning she just wasn't here."

Out of the corner of his eye, Aren saw Wil's gaze sweep the ceiling in frustration.

Stef spoke next. "Did she ever speak of going somewhere after here?" he said. "We've heard she normally moved on more often. She stayed here longer than most."

Jessica nodded, lips pressed together. "Yes that's true. We normally move on as soon as the work is done." She smiled again, a small smile that belonged to a memory. "She always wanted to be there to help the next person as needed it." Jessica sighed, leaning back in her chair. "I think she was starting to feel at home here." She splayed her hands on the desk. "Once we'd set up here to help, the next village over was raided — I can't even remember the name of it. The people just brought their wounded straight to us here. So we stayed." She shrugged and balled her hands together.

"Was there a plan?" Wil pushed. "Was there anywhere you were heading before you stopped here?"

Jessica shook her head in response. "We go where we're needed. We came from the east — but you probably know that if you've tracked us this far. I suppose we may have continued westward..." She trailed off, scouring her mind for something more useful. "Laina always used to ask me about the markets in Hapton — she was desperate for a proper apothecary!" A smile escaped onto her face for a heartbeat; a burst of sunlight. "Every now and then, when a village had no supplies to speak of, Laina would go out into the woods and bring back handfuls of wild herbs." Her expression clouded again. "But I doubt she would vanish like this for the sake of a trip to the market." She began to shake her head again, frustration sharpening her features. But then she stopped. And seemed to check herself. She opened her mouth as if to say something, then pressed a finger to her lips, thinking.

"What is it?" Aren prompted.

Jessica clasped her hands in front of her and leant forward on her seat.

"It may be nothing," she began, "but I saw that young man — Ben, I think his name was — heading out early, the morning Laina disappeared. He said it was his time to move on, that his help was needed elsewhere. He was going with the wind, something his da used to say..." She trailed off again.

"What does this man have to do with Laina?" Wil asked, confusion making his impatience hard.

"Well nothing on its own," Jessica admitted, "but he seemed awfully agitated, as if he were desperate to be on his way. He was rushing. Like he were about to miss something. And he seemed very taken by Laina when he was helping us in the hospit..." Her voice meandered from point to point, echoing her train of thought. "Could be he was following after her. I know he didn't have any other family to speak of..." She seemed to think on it a moment longer before she straightened, and nodded decisively.

"If I were you, I'd follow that boy's footsteps. One way or another, he's following Laina too." She looked hard at Wil, who looked like a racehorse straining at a wagon's traces. "And he was heading west — no, maybe north-west."

Aren nodded and rose smoothly from where he sat cross-legged on the bed.

"Well it's the best lead we've had yet," he said. "Even if we don't catch him, we'll be able to track him cross-country." He looked over to the others.

Wil nodded. "North-west it is, then," he said.

23

EYES ON THE HORIZON

The low grassy knolls of the Northern Tundra eased over the Wastelands like gentle waves onto a sandy shore. The unrelentingly dusty ground gave way to short, stubby grasses, and then long, waving blades that rippled in the breeze. The smog of dirt and sand in the air thinned and settled, as greenery took over the ground.

Fae's body straightened little by little as they traversed the last few miles of the Wastelands. Between the wind and sand whipping around, her body had unconsciously hunched around itself, like a snail's shell, turning inward and ever inward. But once the air was clear of flying grit, she slowly arched her back, easing her body out of its awkward posture. She stretched towards the sky like a flower seeking the sun. It ached, sharp, prickling needles shooting across her shoulders and down her spine. But it ached in a good way. A good pain.

Finally unfurled, she squinted towards the northern horizon.

It was the same flat, featureless line in every direction. But the haze of sand in the air lay behind them, to the south. And the sun still rose in the east.

And the tug in her chest still pulled her unerringly northward. The hum in her veins had become so intense she felt as if her whole body was vibrating with the force of it. Closer, they were getting closer.

She drew in a breath of clear air, and relished the feel of it — a tonic for her airways.

"Aye," Hal said beside her, his voice as warm as the sun on her skin. "Like a breath of fresh air ain't it? Coming out of that cloud o' dirt. Huh," he chuckled. "Suppose it *is* a breath of fresh air."

"Mm." She breathed in deep again. "It's like waking after a long nightmare."

Hal nodded. Fae saw a small crease appear between his eyebrows. But whatever nightmare plagued him wasn't one he was ready to share; she saw that, too.

He turned to face her, and beckoned Ty and Bek over to join them.

"Western Highway is less than half a day's walking now." He grinned widely. "We'll be there for lunch."

Bek echoed the ranger's grin, his face creasing around the eyes.

Ty smiled with barely concealed relief. "I will be glad to get away from the Wastelands," he admitted.

Hal shot him a look. "It don't get much better in the Tundra," he said darkly. "It might be that the worst sandstorms are in the Wastelands, but it's unbearable cold up north, and just as barren too." He turned his back to the sand cloud and resumed walking. "Leagues upon leagues of nothing but grassy hills and cold. Bitter cold." He shuddered involuntarily. "I make a point not to go too far up that way." He rubbed his arms up and down, and gave a small shrug. "There's nothing up there anyways."

Ty's lips formed a thin line. "Well then, I'll be glad for a change, if nothing else."

"Hm," Hal muttered.

Just past midday, they reached the long stretch of compacted earth and stone that made up the Western Highway. Only the roads running directly into Throldon were paved. Centuries ago, rather than pave the miles and miles between the border cities, the royals had commissioned rubble be scattered over the route, and then compressed with wide, weighted wheels. It was simple, but effective, and the roads — such as they were — were easy to maintain and constantly in use.

That is, they used to be. But times had changed.

Stopping by the side of the highway, they broke out some food, and stretched out on the sun-warmed earth to rest. Their foraging was already better now that they were out of the Wastelands, and Hal had given them a quick run-down of which of the unfamiliar plants they could eat.

A companionable quiet hung about the group, each content to simply feel the sun on their skin, and the clear, unsullied breeze on their faces.

In truth, they lingered a little longer, savouring the break, and loath to part ways, as they knew they must inevitably do. They passed nearly an hour in idle small talk before Hal finally cleared his throat and stood, brushing the dust from the seat of his pants.

"Well, time I was on my way," he declared, gazing eastward along the highway. "There's a tavern not far up the way. Could be I make it before night falls, spend a night or two in a bed for a change." He smiled to himself and looked back at his companions. He seemed to consider his words. "Well," he said suddenly, "you've got your own ways to travel, so I'll let you get to it." He bent to pick up his pack. "Never was much for goodbyes," he muttered.

Ty stepped forward and offered his hand. Hal took it, his grip firm.

"It has been a privilege to travel with you Hal," Ty said as they shook hands. "May your journey onwards be swift and sure, that you arrive safely in Greneln." Bek nodded solemnly, then stepped forward to hug the ranger around the waist. Hal let go of Ty's hand to ruffle the boy's hair with one hand, the other wrapping around his shoulders, a pained edge to his smile.

"Travel well, Hal," said Fae, stepping forward to embrace him. "Friend," she added.

"Good luck in your adventures too, friends," Hal replied. He paused, lips parted, as if he were about to add something else. But he closed his mouth, and only nodded instead. His hand came up in a small wave. Then he turned, and walked away down the road. Continuing his lonely journey onwards.

Fae watched him go. She'd miss the plain-speaking ranger and his simple, easy ways. She wished things were as simple as he saw them.

When Hal's silhouette finally rounded a corner and disappeared down the road, Fae turned to find Ty and Bek waiting for her. She smiled an uneasy smile at them, and shouldered her own pack. Glancing over the endless grassy hillocks across the road, a rock settled in her gut. They still had a long way to go. In her vision, leagues and leagues of Northern Tundra had laid before her.

A nameless knowing told her the bulk of the journey was yet to come. But her blood hummed in anticipation.

"Shall we?" Ty said, breaking her from her thoughts.

She looked up at him to find deep, grey eyes watching her. Eyes that normally made her feel as though she could do anything. But she didn't know what came after this journey. The shadowy figures of her vision reared up in her mind. Who were they? What did they have to do with the Aethyr? The truth was, she had no idea what she was doing. All she knew was that she had to do it.

She dragged a more convincing smile onto her face.

"Let's," she said with a nod. A small hand slipped into hers. She looked down to see Bek gazing across the landscape. His smile was easy and innocent, but the look in his eyes was steel; unbending and resolute. Like he knew exactly where he was going. And he was more than ready to face whatever awaited them.

Something in that look scared her. But something in it gave her the strength to face the next chapter of their journey. She turned her face back to the north.

And stepped off the road.

The Northern Tundra was a cruel answer to the Wastelands. Harsh, serrated grasses snagged on their clothing, swaying in the breeze to catch at them no matter how they moved. Thick blades grew up through lichen, and hardy mosses covered rocky, unforgiving ground. The ground rolled away from them in every direction; earthy knolls were interspersed as often as not with hulking boulders camouflaged by spongy carpets of green that looked innocent enough, but stole their feet out from under them if they took a wrong step. The long-awaited kiss of warm sun upon skin kept spirits lifted, even if the unbroken tundra made every step seem like a drop in an endless ocean; the ripples sure to fade before ever reaching the other side.

They made camp in the shade of one hillock among many. And when night fell, even the campfire seemed fitful and uneasy.

The next morning, freezing mist enshrouded the camp. Only the knowledge of which side of the hill they'd settled on hinted at which way north lay. It felt like the Wastelands again, no one able to see more than a few paces in front of them. But the relentless sand, cutting into exposed skin and burrowing into their clothes, was replaced by the cold mist; tiny, biting droplets, stealthily soaking them through to the bone, and freezing in their hair. They broke camp quickly, eager to get moving.

When the midday sun finally burned through the mist, tired rays reaching toward the ground in smoky wisps, Ty called a break. The Western Highway had disappeared far behind them, and with it, the only landmark that might orientate them. All they had left to navigate by, was the position of the sun, as and when they could see it.

And Fae.

They climbed to the top of the nearest hillock, and collapsed at the top.

"You know," Ty said, breathing deeply to catch his breath, "it wouldn't be half as bad if there was a little elbow room between the hills." He glared at the tightly-packed, irregular peaks and troughs around them, one hand raised to shade his eyes from the sun.

Fae nodded. He was right — they were constantly having to weave between the mounds, or else be forced to climb every one in their path. Sometimes, they had to double back on themselves, but that was often safer than going over the hills.

Fae looked across at Ty. One arm was already covered in wide, jagged grazes where the treacherous mosses had caught him unawares climbing a particularly steep incline.

"How's the arm?" she asked.

He responded with a self-deprecating grimace. "Bruised," he replied. "Much like my ego." Her answering smile teased a smaller version onto his face. He stretched the offending arm out before him, scrutinising it. "It'll be fine," he said. "Just sore for a few days I suspect." He dug out some willowbark from the bottom of his pack to dull the pain, but Fae was glad to see that no lasting damage was done.

She squinted at the northern horizon, now bathed in bright sunlight, and clearly visible as a long, unbroken line.

In her vision, this endless tundra had been the last element of her journey. The monument on the hill had appeared in the midst of it.

There was no sign of anything but more hills around them.

Just how vast was it? How much further would it be? How long would it take?

Did the world have that long?

Fae squeezed her eyes shut against the sudden prick of burning tears, and the feeling of utter helplessness.

There was no doubt in her mind that she was *meant* to be here. That she was *meant* to walk this path.

But she couldn't deny the intimidating lack of any sliver of a plan for what came *after*.

The Aethyr hadn't exactly been forthcoming either.

They were still as mute as the tundra.

Fae pursed her lips in frustration. And determination.

She squared her shoulders and opened her eyes to the world again.

Even if this leg of the journey was as long as the rest of it put together, this was it.

The next milestone, would be where she was meant to be.

Fae dreamed that night.

She was one with the Aethyr. She spoke with them like old friends. She laughed and joked with wisps and clouds, trees and brooks, butterflies and birds. She flew.

She burst with joy at her union with them, and their oneness with nature. Her joy was a warm glow surrounding her.

The glow grew, and she felt power within it. She could do anything.

She could clear the clouds from the sky, still the waves on the sea, quiet a storm.

Burn and destroy.

The glow became the flames in the village as she watched it burn.

And the terror in the eyes of the child she had saved.

Days passed.

Miles passed.

Leagues lay behind them.

And yet still leagues lay ahead.

They'd run out of fresh supplies a week into the Tundra. All that was left was the trail rations. At least it left their packs lighter.

But with that lightness came the heavy knowledge that this may end up being a one way trip.

The mists that fell at night supplied them with ample water, which Ty collected by fashioning funnels of the wide grasses and slotting them into the necks of their water-wraps. Overnight, the mist beaded on the surface of the grass leaf, gathered, and ran into the wrap. By morning, their water supply was replenished in full.

Food, on the other hand, was scarce. Bek had tried chewing on the ever-present grasses, but he'd vomited it up less than an hour later, and suffered with fever and chills until the next day. They'd steered clear of testing any unfamiliar plants after that. Ty harvested lichen, but even that began to dwindle.

"You should eat something," he said, ten days into the Tundra. He handed a corner of hard biscuit out to Fae. "You're grey."

She *felt* grey. A shadow. A ghost. She existed only to put one foot in front of the other, and to scan the horizon for the monument.

"I'm fine," she said, hearing her voice as a distant echo. "Give it to Bek."

Bek looked worse. His young face was gaunt, his cheeks hollowed-out beneath the cheekbones. Something inside Fae twisted with guilt whenever she looked at him.

"I will," Ty insisted, shaking the biscuit at her. "But you need to eat too."

Fae looked at the small piece being offered. She knew she had to eat. But she also knew how much they had left. More precisely, how little.

She shook her head. "I'll have some lichen — I'm sure we'll see some more soon." It had been hours since she'd last seen the thin, white branches of edible fungus clinging to the barren rocks of the Tundra. She took a swig of her water instead.

"Fae—"

"I know, Ty," she said. That their hopes were looking smaller and smaller every day. That they might not come back from this.

The tug in her chest, the hum in her veins ebbed too, as if the Aethyr's call knew how desperate their situation was.

She glanced across at Bek. Her biggest regret was that he was here with her. When he could have been safe back in Arolynos.

But how long for? she thought. *How much longer will Arolynos be safe?*

She closed the door on the part of her mind that thought too much. The part that looked at all the painful truths and asked the difficult questions.

She closed her mind and went back to her only two purposes.

One foot in front of the other.

Eyes on the horizon.

24

WORSE COMING

W yn walked. He was restless. And he wasn't the only one.

They'd been availing themselves of Dvargran hospitality for a week. But they were no closer to knowing what to do about the human problem. Thom had spent every available moment in council with Lord Graem, debating the best possible course of action. He returned every evening more frayed and frustrated than the last. There just wasn't enough information about the human raiders to mount any kind of response.

And now there were rumours of refugees missing from the villages.

Wyn paced the streets of Dvargra. He was ill-suited to sitting in guest rooms, waiting for instructions. He turned to cut through a narrow passageway between two mountainous buildings that would bring him out onto the main thoroughfare across the Square. His brow was heavy, and his slate-blue eyes were dark and distant, as if the weight of the world's problems filtered through his head alone. The dwarves he passed along the way didn't offer their usual greeting. He understood. His sour mood was hard to miss.

Among the people of Dvargra, the unease of those who knew danger was on their doorstep was shared equally. No *dwarves* had gone missing — all the villages had now migrated into the city settlements — but humans were disappearing from the abandoned villages in alarming numbers. It was all just too close for comfort.

Finally, Wyn's feet brought him to his destination.

The Hammer and Anvil was a hugely popular alehouse looking over the Great Square, and one that Elas tended to favour when visiting the city.

Sure enough, as soon as Wyn ducked beneath the thick, oak doorframe, he spotted his fellow scout. His lips twitched. *Well, at least one of us is enjoying himself.* The twitch turned into a small smile as Elas boomed his infectious laugh. It felt good to smile. There had been too many days of worry, cooped up behind the mountain walls. A soul needed joy, needed laughter.

Wyn's smile faded, sliding from his face as easily as snow from a hot forge. They weren't here to reminisce with old friends.

Elas spotted him over the heads of the other dwarves assembled. It was high noon, and the innkeeper was serving the midday meal, which Elas enjoyed in the company of a group of dwarven fighters and scouts. He waved Wyn over to join them, his cheeks already bulging with hot pie, thick gravy flecked at the corner of his mouth.

"Wyn, have a slice of this!" he garbled, wiping a sleeve across his mouth. He washed down the pie with a swig from a tankard of ale. "It is quite possibly the best dwarven fare I have been offered yet! What did you call it again, Master Innkeep?" He paused and looked over to the dwarf behind the bar, who was trying to maintain an air of modesty, but it was clear that his pride at Elas's praise wouldn't allow it.

"It's only vegetable and bean pie," he mumbled humbly, but the mouth beneath his beard beamed. "My wife will be pleased to hear you thought so much of it, Master Scout. It would normally be steak and ale but, what with all the extra mouths to feed from the villages, beans is all we've got enough of." His eyes twinkled as he added, "Although if you ask my wife, it's the ale that brings the real flavour."

"Ale!" Elas exclaimed, serving Wyn his own slice. "And beans! Who knew? It really is amazing Wyn, you must try some!" He pushed the plate towards him before tucking into his own meal again. "Just as well really," he continued around another mouthful. "We elves don't tolerate meat well." He smiled blissfully. "Mmm! Is there potato in this?" He eyed the innkeeper, who nodded, pouring an extra drink for Wyn. Elas's eyes rolled into the back of his head in appreciation, and then he was too busy enjoying his food to say any more.

Wyn took his first bite of pie. Elas had not overdone his praise. The pastry crumbled and flaked apart in the mouth, and was sweet and buttery. It might have been too dry if it weren't for the ale-gravy, thick and bitter and soaked into the vegetables so that everything was moist and delicious. The beans rounded out the filling, and while Wyn would happily have eaten more, he found he was plenty full enough after his one slice. Washed down with a mug of dwarven ale, it was clearly food made to nourish the hardy folk of the mountains. He could see why Elas's rowdy group had fallen silent.

Most helped themselves to seconds; some even had thirds. Finally replete, conversation slowly regained momentum around the table.

"It's a good thing the settlements are finished," one dwarf scout said, picking up a thread from an earlier discussion. "Word is, the raiders are sneaking into the villages at night, and stealing anyone young enough to train into their army." His mouth made a harsh line. "Can't imagine how I'd sleep at night if Corinne and my little Ellie were still in Somenfeldt."

Another nodded solemnly. "Aye," he agreed. He wore the tabard of a city watchman. "The villages are no place to be for anyone right now." He wrapped thick hands around his mug. "Poor beggars," he murmured. "Those humans have run straight from bad to worse."

The group fell silent again, each contemplating the silent horrors in the woods. Wyn glanced across at Elas. He wore a neutral expression, his bearing easy. But for all that Elas had the look of the simple, harmless type, Wyn knew that look well. His comrade was listening intently, and seething beneath.

"I've heard worse," a third voice said, quiet as a thief in the night. It belonged to an unusually lean dwarf, dressed in forest greens. His eyes were fixed somewhere between his drink and the table, his slice of pie sitting forgotten to one side. He wore leather boots that were soft but thick; designed for long days and nights on his feet. The cloak that was slung over the back of his chair was a nondescript, mottled grey, but the silver pin that glinted from beneath a fold of the fabric was the shape of a winged boot. The sigil of a runner.

The first scout scowled. "What's worse than having your loved ones stolen away in the night? And having nowhere safe to hide them?" He spoke with the anger of someone who'd been perilously close to living that nightmare.

The runner raised a hand in a placating gesture. "Peace, friend, you misunderstand me," he said, his voice still barely raised above a whisper. "What I mean to say—" he knitted his fingers around his mug "—is that I've heard other tales. Of worse than bad men in the night." Dwarven runners travelled great distances, between the villages, gathering news and delivering messages between the people. He likely would have heard his news firsthand, or else seen it for himself.

"What have you heard?" The words were out of Wyn's mouth before he could stop them.

The only sign that the runner had heard him was in the slight flaring in the corners of his eyes. In the hard lines that bracketed his mouth. He took a long draught of ale, his gaze still distant.

He put his mug down on the table with a soft *thunk*.

"Spring is turning in the foothills. And yet the plants wither and die. The few forest creatures that wake from their winter sleep can't find enough food to sustain them. Some don't wake at all. Winter stores have rotted in the ground, new flowers aren't budding. Nothing grows. Everything is wasting. It's like a plague on the land. And it creeps closer every day." Just like in Arolynos. His voice was hollow and echoing. And the circles beneath his eyes seemed to deepen even as he uttered the words. His shoulders drooped when he finished, as if saying the words aloud had made the horrors real. He stared into his mug, and his gaze had a haunted cast to it.

"There is worse coming," he said, "and I don't think we can escape it."

Elas and Wyn finished their drinks, thanked the innkeeper, and left the Hammer and Anvil soon after the runner had finished his foreboding narrative. The tone in the alehouse hadn't improved any, and people had begun filtering away.

They returned to their guest quarters, and almost ran into Thom coming the other way.

"Good," he said upon seeing them. He beckoned them, his arm outstretched. "Come with me." He walked them past the door to their rooms and back outside, to the plain, squat council hall where Lord Graem was waiting for them. The Lord of Dvargra pored over a map of the region, marked with different coloured pins and pieces. Black markers made a broad swathe across the Rand, and red markers gathered around the pin at Dvargra. In between, were a scattering of yellow markers; humans stranded in the villages. There was no yellow behind the black line.

Lord Graem looked up as they entered. His hair was disheveled from constantly running frustrated fingers through the strands, and his eyes held the same haunted look as the runner's. The smile he greeted them with was stiff and brittle.

"Thank you for coming," he said, clasping their forearms in greeting. He turned back to his map, and the scouts took the wordless invitation to inspect it for themselves. Thom stood opposite; he'd seen it plenty over the past week. Graem wasted no time. He pointed to the black markers, forming a line across the south and west of his territory.

"The raiders advance into the foothills like ghosts in the night," he said, his voice harsh from days of talk, and nights full of the same. "And yet there are no signs of them where we know them to be."

"How do you know they're there then?" Elas asked.

Graem fisted a hand against the table. "There are too many signs to ignore." His face sagged in the way that only happened in the bone-weary. He ran his other hand over it, as if to rub away the fatigue. "Just not enough to find them. We know they're there. The humans flee an enemy, and then disappear in the dark. The land fails to prosper. Even the creatures of the forest flee." He hammered his fist into the wood, rattling the pieces not pinned to the board, his voice cracking with futile rage. "I *know* they're there and I can't do a damned thing about it. I don't know *enough* to track them down and put a stop to this." He turned to the scouts. "I need more information." His eyes bored into theirs, and in that moment, he looked twenty years older than the man they knew.

"We'll go," Thom spoke up, stepping up to the table. "We'll slip behind their lines without them ever knowing we were even in the field." His smirk told them how confident he was in their abilities to do just that. He turned to Graem. "We'll find the answers you need," he said fiercely. "Don't forget, Arolynos stands against this threat as well. We have envoys seeking help from the dragons, as well as the humans themselves. Between us, we will beat back the ghosts at your gate."

"I cannot ask that of you," Graem said.

"You're not," Thom replied simply. And Wyn wasn't the only one with restless feet.

Graem met Thom's eyes and nodded. "You have my thanks, I am in your debt."

"There is no need for thanks between us," Thom replied, with a tilt of his head. "We're glad to help."

Graem's thin smile was bursting with gratitude. "Can you set off at first light?" he said, with an anxious glance at his map.

The elves exchanged a look, but they already knew the answer.

"We'll be gone before dawn touches the Gatekeepers," Thom said.

25

GHOSTS IN THE NIGHT

As promised, Thom was already leading Wyn and Elas back through the Rand when dawn finally brushed its first edges against the mountain.

"Aah," Elas breathed as they set a pace through the trees. "I'm glad to be back on the move. I love Dvargra as much as either of you, but a week is too long to be cooped up in one place."

"Aye, well, don't get too comfortable," Thom answered over his shoulder. "We've got a way to run yet, and it won't be pretty when we get there, if the accounts are anything to go by."

Wyn recalled the voice of the runner in the Hammer and Anvil. The hollow ring of hopelessness in it.

"Well I shall be sure to enjoy the scenery while it lasts." Elas refused to let loose his silver lining. "It feels good to stretch my legs!"

While Wyn couldn't help but agree with the sentiment of his comrade, a cold ached in his bones that had nothing to do with the snow.

It took them two days to reach the line of black markers on Lord Graem's map. It was nothing so obvious as that, of course: the foothills were dusted with snow, the skies were clear above them, and all was peaceful and quiet. Too quiet.

They stopped at the edge of a small clearing.

No birds sang their springtime songs. No squirrels or flidgits scurried about, unearthing their winter stashes of nuts. No animal tracks stippled the ground.

The air felt too close. It stifled. There was no breath in the wind, no life in the trees.

Even Elas, ready with a joke at any occasion, looked uneasy.

"What *is* this?" Wyn said. He held himself stiffly, unsure of what to do with himself.

"It's unsettling," Thom said, his voice lowered as his eyes scanned the trees. He searched for a sign, any sign, of any being. There were none. "It's like Graem said. Ghosts."

Elas finally found a droplet of humour in their situation. "Ghosts?" he scoffed halfheartedly, his clear-grey eyes appearing almost white as they darted around the snow. "I never took you for a superstitious one, Thom." He raised an eyebrow at his fellow scout, but his expression lacked its usual joviality.

Thom didn't react, his eyes vigilantly surveying their surroundings. "How else would you describe it?" he said flatly.

Elas opened his mouth to respond. And shut it again. He had no response.

Wyn was the one to break the uneasy stalemate they held with the trees.

"Let's move on from here," he said with a sudden shudder. "We want to be *behind* the line, not caught this side of it."

Thom nodded, shifting his pack on his shoulder. "Yes. We stand a better chance of eluding them in territory they believe they've already cleared." He glanced warily at the statuesque trees. Elves were usually at home in the trees. But here, they were sitting ducks, with the advantage squarely with the raiders.

"Huh," Elas muttered, voicing the irony. "Whoever thought elves would ever be worried about *humans* tracking *them* in a forest?" He shook his head disbelievingly, snow-wet hair brushing against the tips of his eyelashes.

"Times changed," was all Thom had to say. "Come on, let's keep moving." He was keen to be out of these ill-fated woods. A week ago, they had trekked through here without a care for the human raiders nipping at their heels. But now...

The scouts wore their snow cloaks: thick lengths of woolly cloth that fell almost to the ground in a dappled, snow-grey sweep. The fabric kept them warm, but they were all the more grateful for the colouring, blending them into the snow-coated forest scenery as seamlessly as clouds against an overcast sky. They darted through the shadows of the trees, concealing their footprints as they went. It made for slower progress than they'd have liked, but in a perfectly surreal landscape such as this, they couldn't afford to leave a leaf out of place.

As afternoon turned to dusk, the silence finally broke.

Branches rustled off to Elas's right. He froze. Nothing had moved in the forest except them for miles. It was silent. It was irksome. Wrong. It was the reason they moved with such deliberate care. And it was all the more unnerving when it changed.

Wyn, to his left, sensed him halt, and glanced across. Elas raised a slow hand, one finger raised.

The rustling came again. Elas stared hard at the guilty section of woods, and cautiously moved into the shadow of a nearby tree. He felt Wyn do the same behind him, and knew that Thom would be following suit in turn.

Seconds turned into minutes, which felt like forever as Elas watched for the movement again. And when it came, it took his breath away.

Ghosts, they were not. It was much worse than that.

Black-clad humans dashed through the trees. They'd been trained, of that there was no doubt, their bodies whispering through the forest with barely a breath, making only the faintest disturbance in the trees. They paid no heed to their environment, as if they owned the woods, and had nothing left to fear here. Thom had been correct in his assumption — the raiders believed this section of woods clear already.

Elas counted each figure as they passed, keeping his eyes on the steady stream of bodies through the trees. Thirty-three... thirty-five... still more came. They watched the near-silent passage of human ghosts, speechless as much out of shock as out of need.

When at last it seemed the final figure had passed, there was a tap at Elas's shoulder.

Thom held a finger to his lips. *We don't know how many are in these woods,* he signed with his hands.

We have to get out of the trees, Wyn replied. *They have the advantage here.*

Agreed. Nods from both Thom and Elas.

Silent Passage, they all signed in unison. Ordinarily, they'd have laughed at the synchrony of their thoughts. But this was not the time or place for levity. With steely faces, they turned back to the matter of making their way through the trees as invisibly as possible, treading ever more carefully, but hastening their pace all the same. They could not linger here.

Dusk turned to night but they didn't stop. They passed two more groups darting through the forest in different directions, before they finally reached the edge of the woods.

The night was clouded, the landscape a flat dark. Skirting the tree-line, they finally set a cold camp about a mile south from the edge of the Rand, the sound of water gently lapping nearby. Thom took the first watch, Elas and Wyn not even bothering to lay out their bed-rolls before falling asleep on the ground.

So began the first of many restless nights to come.

Wyn watched as the sky lightened over the eastern mountain range. He hadn't slept. His mind was in too many places to sleep.

When the sun finally crested the ridge, flooding the sky with a blaze of orange and pinks, Wyn closed his eyes to feel the warmth of it against his skin, grounding him.

At least, he thought with a sigh, *in all the darkness, there is still light.* He opened his eyes and gazed across the landscape.

Then he turned his attention westward.

Nothing seemed amiss. They were camped on the north bank of Lake Beofar; fed by the Amedi River from the west, and pouring over the Great Fall to the east, down to the ocean beyond the mountains. The Rand woods tapered off just to the north of their camp, the Edge Mountains rising up at their backs, the plains of Arland stretching away, flat and uninterrupted to the north and west.

There were no camps. No smoke snaked up from the horizon. No signs of troop movements. Or prison camps.

Wyn put his back to the rising sun and stood, shading his eyes with one arm. The plains looked... peaceful.

Then what of these humans, ghosting in the night?

"Morning," a familiar grumble came from behind him. Then, "See anything?"

Wyn shook his head, then turned to face Elas, who looked as short on sleep as Wyn felt.

"It all looks as it ever did," he admitted. "I can't see anything obvious."

"Well, with the way those humans moved through the Rand last night, I wouldn't take that to mean anything significant," Thom said, sitting up from his bedroll, grey eyes heavy from not enough sleep.

Elas did nothing to hide the feelings showing clearly on his face. "That was unsettling," he said. "So many humans trained to move covertly like that — like a small army."

The grooves on Thom's forehead deepened. "Hmm," he muttered. He rubbed a hand across his mouth, as if he didn't want to give voice to his thoughts. He looked up at the other two. "I don't like to think what it could mean."

Wyn caught his hesitation. "But you have a theory." It wasn't a question.

Thom climbed from his bedroll, and began packing it away.

"Let's find out exactly what's going on," he said, dodging the question. "No use in tossing theories about." He left unsaid how badly something as simple as expectations could derail their mission.

They ate a quick, cold breakfast, munching on the dwarven equivalent of their hard travel biscuit, flavoured with barley and nutmeg. Then, retracing their steps back to the forest edge, they set about tracking ghosts.

It was as the day turned towards night again, that they finally found something tangible.

"Right," Elas said, as they lay in the grasses. "Well, at least we know they're not ghosts."

They watched as fires lit up across the campsite they faced.

It was huge — occupied by at least two hundred. Men and women went about their business in varying degrees of armament. Some wore knives openly on their belts, or in thigh sheaths. Others concealed a number of blades upon their person, noticeable only by the way they moved, or the occasional catch of clothing on a hidden hilt. There were a few bows present, and even a couple of axes being sharpened by the light of a campfire.

"I count two-fifty," Wyn murmured, scanning the camp. "Likely more. At least a hundred canvases, and they're not all sleepers." He pointed out the small, pod-like tents that lay squat against the ground, not much larger than two or three men laid abreast. Then he indicated a few larger, walled tents. "I'd reckon some of those will be mess tents. A couple will be for the leaders of this group." He stopped as Elas hissed a blue streak beside him. "What?"

"Look over there," the other scout said, pointing. "What does that look like to you?" Wyn and Thom's eyes traced the path his finger drew across the plain.

"Eah's Tears," Thom swore.

Towards one side of the camp, a large area of churned-up earth marked where lumber had been dragged in from the forests. Rainwater had filled the furrows left by its passage, turning the broken ground boggy, mud covering the bottom few inches of everything nearby. In amongst the mud, the lumber had been sectioned into irregular posts.

And lashed together to build a crude cage.

And inside the cage, were the missing villagers.

"They're all young," Wyn observed.

"And no cripples among them," Thom added.

Elas's face displayed his twinned disgust and horror clearly. "What do they want with them?"

"That type of prisoner?" Thom answered Elas with a thought of his own. "Only one reason you'd want young, fit prisoners. They'll be put to work. Or to fight. There are both men and women there." He nodded to one side of the cage, where two young women, barely older than girls, huddled together. "So it's not for sex." His expression darkened. "Or at least, not only that."

"No," Wyn agreed. "It's mostly fit and able men."

Thom nodded. "So they're wanted for work."

"But *what* work?" Elas spoke aloud what they were all thinking.

The three of them crept closer, keeping low to the ground to avoid detection. They approached as near as they dared, until they could just hear the conversation of the human guards above the drone of camp activity, and the crackle of a hundred campfires.

They stopped a hundred yards from the cage, tucked into a small, barely noticeable dip in the land. Beyond the notice of the humans, they were nonetheless well within range of their elven senses. One of the female prisoners was asking something of a guard. Water. His response was a cold laugh, and a sharp kick to the side of the cage where she stood.

Elas hissed in fury as the woman fell back from the bars.

"Peace," Thom breathed, shooting him a look. Elas glared daggers at the guard, but settled down to listen.

The humans spoke in harsh, guttural tones, and their laughter was cold and cruel. The sound made the small hairs stand up along Wyn's arms.

Eah, let us find out what's going on here so we can put a stop to it, and be gone from this cursed place, he thought, suppressing a shudder. Then, the humans were talking.

"—good job we're shipping them on in the morning," one was saying. "Ain't no room here for recruits anymore. They're all holing up in the dwarf camps now anyway."

"Ar," another replied, punctuating his words by loudly hawking up a gob of phlegm, and jettisoning it at the ground. "Anything to get me out of this godsforsaken, arse-end of nowhere." Hawk. Spit. "At least it's back to the capital next. No more camps and raids." Hawk. Spit. "*Gods*, what I wouldn't give for an actual bath, and a good, strong woman in my bed."

"Ha!" his partner barked. "You're just sour that Brendelle wouldn't sleep with you."

"Shut your trap!" the spitter snapped.

"Quit your pining," the other said. "Who knows? You might end up with one o' these beauties." He rapped on the wooden bars of the cage with the hilt of his dagger. The girls inside recoiled from his sneer.

"Nah." The spitter made a face. "Too scrawny. Besides, they've got to be processed first." He leaned in to shout at the prisoners. "You hear that?" he yelled cruelly. "You're going to Throldon to be part of our Lady's Survivors. And you'll be grateful for the hand fate dealt you." Hawk. Spit. Glare.

"Come on," his partner said, tugging his arm. "Here's the next shift. Let's get something to eat. And a stiff drink."

"That's if there's any left in this dump," the spitter grumbled, but he let himself be pulled away. The pair exchanged a nod with their replacements that was more of a chin-jerk, and then disappeared into the camp. The guards that took their place were not nearly as verbose. Although, when the young woman asked again for water, her answer was the same.

The elves backed away from the camp to a safer distance. They crouched in the shelter of a rocky outcrop, jutting proudly from the ground.

"We have to free them," Elas said immediately.

"No Elas," Thom said sadly. He held a hand up when Elas went to protest. "If we free them, those raiders will spend the next few days hunting both us, and them. And we will achieve nothing." He shook his head, his face grim, but determined. "No, we must follow them." He met Elas's hard gaze and held it. "We must follow them, and trace this rot to its core. In Throldon."

Wyn's face was resigned. Elas's went from outrage, to the same grim determination as Thom's.

He nodded fiercely. "Then we go to Throldon."

26

THE BRAVE AND THE STUPID

On the Western Highway, somewhere between Hapton and Oresh, Ben and Laina entered a small, remote village. The sort that likely started with the inn — the solitary, roadside variety — and expanded one household at a time to create a small community. Laina glanced about for somewhere to buy the provisions she'd been hoping to find in Hapton, but aside from the handful of tiny cottages, and one or two larger huts, the inn was all the village had.

The reasons became clear enough when they entered the inn itself.

Along the far wall sat a traditional bar, serving ales and liquors. In front of that, and filling the taproom to the right, were the usual tables and chairs one might expect.

But there, the expected ended.

The left arm of the room was entirely given over to — and crammed with — trade.

Bolts of cloth both plain and fine from the desert community of Oresh stacked neatly on a trestle table, ready to be unrolled for inspection. Leather goods and tack from the folk of Greneln rested on special racks bolted to the wall, buckles and bits and stirrups polished and shining. There were rich dyes, remedies and cure-alls, wicker baskets, even hunting gear and weaponry. Not only was the taproom full of exotic produce, but the tradesmen and women to sell it, too. The vendors heralded from all over the world; some were tall and dark skinned, others stockier with bright red hair, and none afraid to proclaim their wares at the top of their lungs, or denounce the usefulness or quality of the others'.

Laina, used to the quiet monotony of midland village life, found it all quite unnerving.

As her eyes moved around the room, she caught the eye of the barmaid, who beckoned them over.

"What can I do for you?" she asked jovially, once they'd successfully dodged and ducked their way to the bar.

"What's going on here?" Laina asked as a fresh barrage of abuse volleyed across the room between two traders. A group of men gambled loudly at one of the larger tables, and presumably the vendors wanted to ensure they were heard clearly. Laina flinched at the noise. "Is this normal?"

"Aw, don't mind them." The barmaid waved a hand dismissively towards the rabble. "They're always like this. You pay enough attention, you'll see it's all just talk. They'll sit down to a brew together at the end of the day, same as all the rest. Now," she said, leaning forward over the bar, "what can I do for you?" Laina eyed the supposedly organised chaos a moment longer, before turning back to the woman.

"We were looking for supplies for a journey north, and maybe a bed for the night, but I've not seen anyone selling food." The woman batted her hand dismissively again.

"Don't you worry about that," she said. "I keep all the edibles in the kitchen else there'd be times it'd be used as munitions between some o' this lot. You'd be surprised how tetchy Donnal can get about his baskets." She took out a stub of a pencil and a small pad of paper.

"What supplies were you needing?" She licked the tip of the pencil and poised to take their order.

"Well—" Laina paused. "We don't strictly know. We'll need food that'll last, on the road and off... and preferably light — we don't know how long we're going for..." She glanced at Ben. "Maybe a week, maybe two?" she asked. Ben shrugged in response.

"I don't know Laina, it's your journey," he said.

"Best make it two weeks' worth then," Laina said, turning back to the barmaid, "just to be sure." The woman stood poised with the pencil hovering over her paper, looking at Laina as if she wasn't quite sure that she was being serious. Deciding her client was indeed serious, and apparently sound enough of mind, she put down her pad and sighed.

"I'll see what I can put together for you. It'll be trail rations you'll be needing, like as not. We get a few seasoned travellers through here, as you might guess. I've an idea as to what you'll be needing. You said you needed a room?" Laina nodded confirmation. "Well I'll see what I can put together while you make yourselves comfortable. It's one silver a night, twenty coppers for feeding morning and evening." Laina agreed to the price for one room and paid the extra for them to have a proper meal before they headed off into the wilderness. She bartered a fair price of another two silver pieces for the trail rations and counted the appropriate coinage onto the bar. Their hostess raised her voice over the din, directing it towards a stern-looking man leaning against the far end of the bar. He watched the game of chance unfold with a sharp eye, as the players consumed more and more of the tavern's ale.

"Ernie!" she called across the bar. "Go fetch Tom and tell him to put a room together and show these two up!" The man nodded gruffly but seemed reluctant to take his eye off the group. Laina knew the look. These types of customers brought in good business, but they were a high risk to a proprietor's property. A call for another round of drinks provided a break in the game and a moment of calm for the landlord to slip off and see to his guests. Within moments, a small boy appeared from the back and scuttled upstairs to take care of their room. Ernie reclaimed his perch, and resumed his watch.

Laina and Ben took the opportunity to peruse the wares on sale. The vendors were all jolly enough folk, the verbal abuse hurled at each other often accompanied by a twinkle of the eye. Ben found some boots to replace his old, well-worn pair, and traded them in for a few coppers. No doubt the vendor would have them repaired in no time, and turn them around for a tidy profit, but Ben would feel the benefit of a new pair. Laina finally found the medical supplies she'd struggled for so long to get hold of, as well as some new, sharp needles and fresh thread. At one point, she found Ben eyeing up a bow and quiver of arrows.

"Ben, have you ever used a bow in your life?" Laina asked him, cutting off the tradesman mid-flow as he described in detail the qualities of his merchandise.

"No..." Ben admitted reluctantly.

"Then it'll be a waste of good money. And arrows!" she said, gently steering him away from the stall. As she glanced back, the vendor smiled. He shot her a wink and a nod of approval before turning to his next potential punter.

The boy called Tom chose that moment to reappear, and they followed him upstairs to a small, well-maintained room with two simple beds made up with freshly laundered linen. Holding the door for them, the boy asked timidly if they wanted their dinner brought up for them. They agreed upon dinner in their room, and settled in for a well-earned rest.

The longest part of their trek would begin on the morrow.

The next morning, Laina and Ben made their way downstairs to take their breakfast and collect the provisions they'd paid for at the bar. The traders from the day before were already back, seeing to their stalls. They shared hot drinks served by an Oreshian vendor with skin as black as the night, and laughed and joked among themselves. The taproom seemed more muted than the night before; calmer for the lack of raucous exchanges, but quietly warm and cheery. The sounds of breakfast being prepared echoed out from the kitchen behind the bar, accompanied by mouth-watering smells. Laina and Ben took a seat at a table out of the way of the traders.

While they waited for their hostess to emerge, Laina took pleasure in the relative calm of the morning; now that the ruckus had died down, there was a community spirit here, not so different to those she'd left behind.

As she watched the quiet coordination of the morning unfold, one of the drunks from the night before emerged from upstairs, heading straight for the Oreshian tradeswoman providing the steaming beverages.

"One of your finest *kahveh* if you wouldn't mind m'dear," he slurred slightly as he pushed three copper pennies over her counter, his accent the thickest she'd heard in years. "And may it be a strong'un." The woman handed him a small cup of hot, brown liquid. He took a careful sip and pulled a face that seemed stuck halfway between disgust and approval. He toasted the vendor.

"Just the job — my thanks." He paused to take another grimacing sip. "Although it'd be much improved, sitting in you home city, with sweets and cream to make it go down easier. That costs extra out here." He nodded towards the sounds emanating from the kitchen. "Just as well I paid upfront, else I'd be in trouble with the lady of the house this morning."

"Chance ain't got nothing to do with it and you know it! I know you lot better than that. That's why you'll always pay upfront and in full." The barmaid emerged from the back. She pinned an eyebrow high on her forehead to regard the man as he woefully sipped at his drink. The corners of her lips twitched and she turned away from him, spotting Laina and Ben at their table.

"Well good morning to you," she said cheerfully. "What can I get for you? I've got some eggs for frying up this morning, and some ham to go with 'em. Got some tea on the boil too, or if you'd like something a bit stronger, Amile has some Oreshian *kahveh* there for the brave, or the stupid." She shot a look at her other early-morning customer. "It's quite pleasant if you stir in cream and sugar, but those are extra."

"Just tea, thank you," Laina answered quickly, remembering the man's face at his first sip. "And ham and eggs would be perfect, thank you. Have you had a chance to put together our supplies?"

"Oh yes don't you worry," she replied with a wave. "I got that all sorted for you. I'll bring it out once you're fed, no need to fret." And with that she disappeared back into the kitchen. Laina glanced over at their fellow diner. He'd found a seat to slump in, looking only marginally more lively than before.

"Are you eating?" Laina asked him, aware that their hostess hadn't even asked him if he would.

"Aw don't worry about me," he said, his words already slurring less. "Lucy always takes enough off me for breakfast before I get to cards and drinks. She knows me better than that, like she said." He gave a little smile. "Good woman that." He paused thoughtfully while he took another sip of *kahveh*, his eyes glazed into the middle distance. Lifting his head to shoot Laina an apologetic smile, he caught sight of Ben.

Quick as a shot, he sat abruptly upright, working hard not to spray his drink across the table. He managed to swallow most of it, but coughed and spluttered to avoid choking on the rest.

Laina was halfway to her feet. "Are you alright?" she asked in alarm, about to leap to his aid.

He waved an arm at her, thumped a fist against his chest and hacked loudly to clear his throat. Even the barmaid was shooting him looks. But she returned to her business when he sat back in his seat, wiping tears from red-rimmed eyes. He took another sip of his *kahveh*.

"To all the numberless gods, boy! What're you doing here?" he croaked, a small cough escaping from the back of his throat. "I thought you was headed north, lad!" He stared unerringly at Ben.

Ben's expression was as puzzled as Laina felt.

"I'm sorry, you must have me mistaken with someone else sir," he answered politely. "We've never met before." The man started, his eyes narrowed, and he shot his drink a suspicious look. He glanced back at Ben, and shook his head in disbelief.

"I must have drunk more than my fair share last night then," he decided. He leant forward in his seat, squinting hard, as if to see Ben more clearly. "You'll be the spitting image of a boy I left not two days past. Bit older maybe. You got a brother?"

Ben shook his head. "No sir, lost my family in a raid near a month past. Ain't got no family left."

"Well I'm sure sorry to hear that," the man said. He seemed to consider something, then drained his cup in one gulp and stood, muttering to himself. He moved over to their table, and stuck out his hand.

"Name's Hal. Where you heading? There's a story here, I'd wager."

Laina looked at Ben. Ben shrugged back.

It's your journey, he seemed to say, with one, simple gesture.

Laina grasped Hal's hand. "Nice to meet you, Hal. I'm Laina." She indicated Ben. "This is Ben. And we're headed north, near enough." Before she could add anything else, the stranger's eyes creased, his mouth broadening into a wide smile. As if he was privy to a joke they weren't in on.

He pulled out a chair at their table and dropped into it, leaning back and clasping his hands behind his head.

"North," he chuckled. "Of course you are."

27

ALL AND ONE

Nine days after stepping off the Western Highway and into the barren wilds of the Northern Tundra, they saw it.

They were beyond exhausted, starving, and their pace had slowed to little more than a crawl. But it had become customary for them to climb the nearest hill around midday, to watch the freezing fog that plagued the mornings of the north clear. As the sun reached its zenith, and the final scraps of mist burned away, they were able to see much further, and take advantage of the unhampered view.

At the top of their chosen hillock, Ty eyed the fog with a weary, but calculating glare.

"What?" Fae asked, as Bek stretched out, star-shaped on the ground, his eyes closed in sunken sockets.

"I mislike this fog," Ty said plainly.

"Just now?" She arched a weary eyebrow. "It's been here every morning since we crossed the Western Highway."

"And yet, every day it has cleared by noon." He gestured at the thick blanket around them. "Does this show any sign of thinning to you?"

Fae forced herself to look at the fog. "No." Despite the brightness of the sun behind it, the haze remained thick and impermeable. "But it's okay," she said. "I can guide us." Ty's head whipped around at her certainty. "It's like there's a current," she elaborated, feeling the the call in her blood stronger than ever, the tug on her very bones, "pulling me towards it. It's been there from the beginning. Leading me to where I need to be." She pointed into the fog. "And that's that way."

She gasped suddenly. "There!"

She blinked a few times to be sure she wasn't just seeing the results of exhaustion and wishful thinking. But despite her efforts, above the unrelenting sea of fog, a king among hills loomed over the rest. And atop that hill, a structure that could only be what they had come so far to see.

Ty squinted at the structure, less than half a day's walk from them if they were lucky. "I wonder what it's for?" he mused aloud.

"I think it's a meeting place," Fae said without quite knowing where the answer had come from. Ty continued his distant scrutiny of the mount, then shrugged, allowing it to remain a mystery for now. He turned to Fae. "You seem more sure of yourself all of a sudden," he said.

A smile tugged at the corner of Fae's lips. "I suppose I am," she replied honestly. She gazed unerringly north. "I can get us through this fog."

Ty gave her an inscrutable look. "I suppose you can," was all he said. There was that unerring faith in her again, and it warmed her to the core. Fae shouldered her pack, which was considerably lighter than when she'd started out. Bek followed suit, dragging himself to his feet. Fae gave him a brief squeeze, and he smiled a strained smile at her.

Lifting his own pack, Ty swept an arm out in front of him. "After you."

With renewed purpose, they wasted no time descending their hillock and into the fog again, resuming their northward trek. They were all of them exhausted, ghost-like even, but they each found a hidden reserve to push on. Bek scampered over the rolling mounds and crags like it was day one, Ty stood a little taller, his eyes attempting to pierce the fog ahead, and Fae stepped a little lighter, as if she could get there quicker if she spent less time touching the ground.

They walked for hours. In the opaque cloud of fog that stretched out endlessly across the Tundra, every step felt the same. Every minute lasted forever. Any progress felt fleeting.

But Fae buzzed with the nearness of their goal. Perhaps she was dizzy from a lack of food for the past few days. But no, she was sure of it. They were close.

And then, the ground stopped undulating, and finally flattened. And slowly, gradually, it angled upward.

Out of the freezing white, the mountainous hill loomed.

Fae, following her unerring sense of direction, stopped at the foot of it. And the call within her vanished.

She nearly swayed on the spot. Her bones were silent. Her blood calm.

Ty and Bek pulled up beside her.

"Is this it?" Ty asked, peering up at the slope as it disappeared into the low-lying cloud ahead of them.

Fae nodded. "The pull — the compass arrow inside me — it's stopped." And its absence left her oddly empty. She looked up at the incline with them. The further it climbed, the steeper it angled, disappearing up into the ubiquitous low-lying cloud. It was smooth, where every other bump in the land was uneven, often treacherously so. And it was wide enough that they couldn't see the curve of it to either side.

Bek bounced on his feet, and then he was off, racing up the slope, and disappearing into the fog.

"Bek!" Fae cried. "Wait!" She turned back to Ty, who was smiling.

He shrugged. "I guess the only way left—" his eyes flicked up the slope of the hill "—is up."

Fae sighed, and set her feet again, finding somewhere within, some last vestige of strength to pull her up this last obstacle.

The fog was blindingly bright as they climbed, forcing her to squint into the mists. But, as they climbed, it finally began to thin, the air slowly warming around them, until at last, they emerged at the summit, the unfettered sun dazzling them with its brilliance. Fae threw her arm up to shield her eyes, blinking away tears to look over what they'd found.

The hilltop was bathed in sunlight, the fog stretching out every way they looked like a thick blanket; a rolling sea of smoke-like cloud.

And overlooking it all, was the monument from Fae's visions.

It was exactly as she'd seen it. The stepped, circular dais was edged by seven towering pillars, each thick enough that, were she to circle her arms around one, her hands would not meet on the other side. They soared thirty feet straight up, and met in a pattern of smooth arches that curved from the top of each stone column, the resulting lattice so intricate, it looked as if lace draped beneath the domed ceiling.

The steps that led up to the dais were weather-worn and smooth, the building undoubtedly having stood for centuries, but the detail of the engravings covering everything within the circle of pillars were as crisp as if the sculptor had left only moments before. Carved, flowering vines trailed down the columns, showing the beauty of changing seasons. In amongst the ceiling-lattice were symbols of weather and celestial signs. And woven through it all, intertwined around the leaves of stone trees that appeared to grow from the base of the pillars themselves, were clearly marked characters of a language unknown to Fae.

In the middle of the dais, a huge, rough-hewn stone the size of a horse-cart sat squat and unassuming. It held nothing of the beauty of the monument around it, but it drew the eye. Something about it wanted to be noticed.

Despite that, the structure wasn't what caught Fae's eye. After all, she'd seen it all before. What held her attention was the boy swinging his feet as he sat on the edge of the stone in the centre of the building. It was as if he was simply waiting for her outside the school in Arolynos, his small smile teasing her for taking so long.

"Don't run off like that!" she said, rushing towards him. Then she stopped.

Something about Bek's expression gave her pause. He was... changed.

His face had lost its gauntness somehow; his eyes were no longer sunken, his cheeks no longer hollow. He looked... fresh.

He smiled at her. But it wasn't a smile she knew. It was a knowing smile, like he'd posed her a riddle, and was waiting for her to solve it.

His blue eyes glinted with wisdom. His face was at once boyish, and ageless. The expression he wore held the serenity of a sage, and the calm acceptance of one who knew what was coming; who'd seen the circle of life turn a few times. Fae frowned ever so slightly.

What...?

Bek's smile widened, and he jumped down from his perch to stand beside her. He was taller, somehow, and broader. No longer a boy, but a man. *Impossible.* His body had aged, but his face still beamed with the same impish glee.

Everything about him seemed older; wiser.

And something in the way he smiled down at her — waiting for her to solve the riddle — made her stop.

And Listen.

She opened her senses to the world around her as she had with the Rhiannonae, and felt herself slip effortlessly into the place where she heard the Aethyr. It was easy. As easy as breathing.

She was met with silence.

She could sense the presence of the Aethyr, of all elements of life around her, with the clarity of a first-rung bell.

But the whispering that had plagued her since Il'arys, the murmurs exchanged just out of earshot, were silent. Now, it was like the world held its breath.

Hello Fae, a voice echoed in her head. Her eyes widened as she recognised it.

"Bek?" she answered aloud. The boy — the *man* — before her smiled. And when he spoke, it was in a deep, alien voice.

"You have questions," he stated without asking.

"Wha—?" Fae spluttered. "Who—?" She looked him up and down again, shot a confused glance at Ty, who appeared just as gobsmacked at Bek's sudden transformation. Shaking her head as if to clear it, Fae settled for the obvious question. "*What* is going on?"

Bek's smile twitched with an unfamiliar humour. "I'm afraid I must ask a little more patience," he said. "The tale is long in the telling, and I would have everyone here, so that I might tell it only once."

"Everyone?" Fae wondered. She looked around. Ty stood a few paces back, keeping a wary distance. There was no one else. Fae turned back to the man in front of her. She gazed intently into eyes she once knew, trying to understand him.

A flicker of memory crossed her mind, like the reflection of an old dream in the ripples of a lake.

In it, she stood on the steps of the dais, and watched as figures approached from all directions, their features veiled in shadow.

She blinked. Her vision hadn't yet fully played out.

There were others to come.

With nothing to do but wait, Fae and Ty settled themselves at the foot of a column whose base was carved into the likeness of an ancient elm tree. For every tree they recognised in the columns, there was another whose like they'd never seen before. The stone roots of the elm sprawled into the dais while the branches wove through intricate characters of an ancient language, unknown to either of them. Carved vines wrapped around the trunk of the tree, delicate buds and small, unfurling leaves captured in perpetual depiction of springtime.

They had nothing to eat, so they drank from their half-empty water-wraps. They tried drawing Bek into conversation, but he continued to speak only in riddles. Countless questions chased each other around Fae's mind, each one leading to a dozen more, but after Bek's cryptic responses, she resolved to hold her questions until more became clear.

The sun had begun its reluctant descent across the sky when the first newcomer climbed the dais, from the east.

She was short, perhaps four-feet-eight, with brown, straw-like hair and small, dark eyes. She had the strong jaw, and stocky stature, characteristic of the dwarves. On her back was a pack big enough that she could have fit herself inside it.

Fae nudged Ty, but he was already looking.

The dwarf approached Bek with a flat look. "So you aren't dead then," she said, dropping her pack to the floor with a heavy *thunk*. Her dark eyes narrowed as she regarded him more closely. She spoke as if she knew him, as if they'd met before. Her expression perfectly articulated how Fae felt looking at him — something wasn't quite right about him, but it was at the edge of her awareness, just out of reach. "Thought you must've been carried off by some creature of the wilds in the night, the way you disappeared," she continued, a small line appearing between her brows. Her gaze flicked to where Fae and Ty sat. "Who're they?"

Bek smiled, a twinkle in his eye. "All will become clear, Jesse," he said, "but I wait still for the rest before the telling of my tale."

Jesse grunted, shooting another disgruntled glance at Fae and Ty, before settling herself down at the opposite side of the monument. Her eyes traced the oak tree of her column, lingering on the script winding through the carved leaves, before settling on the horizon from whence she'd come.

They sat in silence for another half an hour, Bek happily kicking his feet over the side of the stone on which he sat, smiling to himself, and occasionally laughing with the changing wind.

Ty's ears twitched. The motion caught Fae's eye, and she looked up just as another silhouette appeared, this time from the northern aspect of the building.

Whoever it was approached in the shadow of the monument, and all Fae could see was the outline of a man. The man moved oddly, his body rolling like a fishing boat on the sea. And then the clatter of hooves on stone reached her as he climbed the stone steps.

Fae gasped. Ty gasped.

Bek smiled.

A centaur stood at the edge of the dais.

Standing easily nine feet tall, the centaur had a wild kind of beauty to him. His upper body was bare, displaying a strong, defined torso, with striking, black tribal tattoos circling his upper arms. But below the waist, his smooth, pale skin gave way to the rich chestnut colouring of a bay stallion.

His near-black hair hung to his waist, matching the strands of his tail, and up-tilted, dark-amber eyes blazed suspiciously at Bek from under a heavy brow.

"Well met, Immrith," Bek called, and it was like two beings spoke at once. One, in the common tongue, and another, in a rough, lilting language Fae didn't recognise.

The centaur's eyes widened, and in them was a mix of alarm and aggression. And the stare he fixed on Bek's legs was one of horror. Bek put both hands up, palms facing the centaur.

"Peace, friend," his dual voice soothed. "I know, I seem different." Fae arched an eyebrow at Ty. *I'll say*, she thought. Bek continued, "But I can see, you know it's me." The fire in Immrith's eyes faded, and he regarded Bek with open apprehension instead. Bek gave a wry smile, and lowered his hands. "All will be explained. Patience, please." He pleaded the last with more sincerity than he had with the dwarf, and it made Fae wonder if perhaps the centaur was prone to the opposite.

Immrith's hands clenched into fists at his sides.

"*Ach nu'ell ab sec'tar go doch be'dgal, Bravargh?*" The centaur's language came out guttural and harsh, but still held the same lilting cadence as Bek's second voice.

Bek pressed his palms together. "Patience, please," he repeated.

Immrith eyed Bek, then gave a curt nod, crossed his arms and stepped off the dais to gaze over the sweeping landscape, under the cover of nothing but open sky.

Fae turned to Ty. "*How does he know these people?*" she mouthed. The boy had arrived in Arolynos at barely seven years of age. How had he met a dwarf and a centaur before that?

A centaur! Fae marvelled. They were long believed extinct, even relegated to legend in some texts. But here was one, very much alive, not twenty feet from them.

Bek caught her eye, and gave her a look that seemed to say, *Phew!*

It was such a normal, joking expression from his almost-familiar face, that she couldn't help but grin in response. Then her smile faltered.

What had happened to her little shadow? The boy who spoke only a handful of words to even fewer people? She felt the same sense of agelessness from him now as she'd felt from the Rhiannonae, but that made no sense. He was just a child. Her brother in all but name.

Bek's face remained serene, understanding, even. "Not long now," he said, gazing out between the pillars on the south-east side of the monument.

A few moments passed before a solitary elf stepped onto the dais. She was dressed head to toe in hard-wearing riding gear, with thick boots that reached up to mid-thigh. Her knee-length, padded jacket split at the hip to show skin-tight leather leggings, and had overly long sleeves that hung over gloved knuckles. Her waist-length, black braid hung over a high, funnel-like neck which covered most of the lower half of her face, the visible skin a rich, creamy brown. Introducing herself as Aiya from Alyla, she glanced uneasily at Immrith and Jesse, but relaxed when she noticed Ty's upswept ears. Before she had a chance to find a place to wait, two humans arrived on her heels.

Ty recognised the first instantly.

"Hal!" he exclaimed, grasping the ranger's hand in greeting. "We thought you headed east!" Hal gripped his hand firmly in return, and stepped into the shelter of the monument, shaking his head free of the fog that had caught in his hair.

"Aye, well," he gestured to his companion. "I found Laina here making her way the same direction as you lot with a lad looked uncommonly like your Bek." An uneasy look crossed his face. "Thought maybe I might be of use to your quest after all." He glanced around at the other gatherers.

"Seems you weren't the only ones on your spirit quest." He eyed the centaur, still standing out on the grass.

Fae studied the woman he'd arrived with. Something about her seemed familiar as she walked over to where Bek stood in the middle of the dais. She had strawberry-blonde hair that was braided past her shoulders, and warm, brown eyes. She placed a hand on Bek's arm and spoke quietly with him. From the look on their faces, Fae sensed they were going through a similar conversation to the one she'd had with him.

She felt a flare of protectiveness over all these strangers approaching Bek — *her* Bek. But he seemed just as comfortable with the strangers as with her. Seemed to belong to them as much as her. She frowned as he smiled warmly at the human woman he couldn't possibly have met before.

Fae's eye was drawn to a ring made of wood on the woman's finger, and a glimmer of memory sparked distantly in her mind.

Then Hal noticed Bek beside her.

"There you are Ben!" he exclaimed, leaning around the woman to shake Bek's hand. "Thought we'd lost you out there." He paused and looked back to Fae and Ty. "Which reminds me, where's Bek?" His eyes darted between them and the man he'd called Ben. Fae, still not understanding, gestured to the man at the centre of all this so far. Hal frowned in confusion, and narrowed his eyes at Bek. Ben.

The man who was apparently both Bek *and* Ben — and somehow also known to the dwarf and centaur as well — chuckled a deep, rumbling laugh.

"Do not fret over it friends," he said, placing a hand on Hal's shoulder. "All will be explained, but I anticipate the arrival of one more." He looked pointedly at the elf, Aiya, who opened her mouth to speak, before something else made them all pause.

Something approached, but it wasn't on foot. The flap and snap of sails sounded above, growing louder and louder. The elves heard it first, the tips of their ears twitching at the new noise. Then the centaur and dwarf stopped to listen as well. Lastly, Hal and Laina stilled.

A breeze whipped up around the monument as the sound reached a booming crescendo. Immrith, the only one not standing beneath the roof of the monument, tipped his head back to see what approached. Fae saw his eyes widen, but to his credit, he did not move.

Suddenly, the light that was left in the sky was blotted out, and a huge shadow covered the whole of the structure they were gathered within. A great shock rocked the ground as the final member of their group landed. At once, Fae understood.

Two huge clawed feet stood at the base of the stone steps to the dais, and before she could move to get a better look, a giant reptilian head lowered into view through one of the great arches. Large dark eyes regarded them over a long, black, flat-nosed visage. A horned crest fanned out about the widest point of the face, black scales blending with dark green-gold at the tips, and tapering into dorsal ridges that stretched from the crown of its head to the end of its tail. If the head was anything to go by, this creature must be more immense than anything Fae had ever imagined. Aiya's presence here suddenly made sense to her.

Alyla was the elven settlement at the foot of the Hearthstone mountains, also known as the Dragontail peninsula.

The dragons had come to counsel as well.

The great, black head turned to Bek, and snorted indignantly. Bek laughed.

"You are welcome to remain in your true form, Kagos," he said in another dual voice that was half deep, rumbling boulders, and half his normal, yet unfamiliar voice. "But it would be nice of you to join us in here." He inclined his head somewhat deferentially. "If you please."

The molten black of the dragon's eyes swirled, and it snorted again. The head withdrew, and a great avalanche of sound reached them where they stood. It was as if a mountain collapsed just beyond the monument, the sound of boulders tumbling over one another accompanied by an earth-sundering roar.

Fae covered her ears against the deafening sound, but it reverberated through the very bones of the building, and through the soles of her feet, jarring her entire body. She gritted her teeth. The ear-splitting cacophony lasted only a few seconds, but when it had passed, its absence made her ears pop.

A new figure stood at the edge of the dais. Tall and naked, he graciously accepted the robe Aiya handed to him. Standing a few inches above Ty's already long frame, he had the willowy form of an elf. But that was where the similarities ended. His body, before he wrapped his robe about it, was covered in the same black scales as the dragon, giving way to smooth, ebony skin at the neck, hands, and feet. His neck was long and graceful, his face flat and expressionless, and his eyes shone liquid black. The green-gold colouration of the dragon's dorsal ridge was mirrored along the edges of his fan-shaped ears, and his nostrils were narrow slits cut into his skin, flaring open and shut as he breathed.

"Apologies." The figure that was, a moment ago, an unthinkably vast dragon, spoke in a rumble of a voice. The sound was like a quieter version of the tumult that heralded his transformation: rocks spilling over one another as they rolled down a mountain. His black eyes fixed upon Bek, one brow arching. "I trust this is important, Baev'ill." It was not a question. Aiya shifted nervously from foot to foot, and seemed to retreat turtle-like into the neck of her coat.

"Indeed, Kagos." Bek — or was it Baev'ill now? — inclined his head solemnly. "We wouldn't be here if it weren't." Kagos nodded once, and stepped further into the monument, Aiya stepping in close behind him. If Bek appeared different to how they had expected, neither of them said anything of it.

Bek nodded his gratitude, and turned to meet the eyes of everyone present.

"You all know me as someone different," he began, and his voice was at once deep and rumbling, rough and lilting, musical, toneless, young, ancient, innocent, and wise. It was one voice, and it was many. Fae's eyes widened at the person standing before her. She saw others do the same. "I am all those people," he continued, "and now I am one." He paused, a small, self-deprecating smile crossing his lips. "There is so much to explain," he said, and it was as much to himself as to the rest of them. "Well, now that we're all here..." He looked around at the group assembled.

"Let me begin."

PART II

28

IN THE BEGINNING

I n the beginning, was the Spirit.

Alone in the dark, the Spirit was tired and dull.

And then, the sun shone forth, and caught on a pearl in the dark.

A pearl of blue and green, swathed in soft clouds of white. And in the dark, it was beautiful.

At first, it was just water and rock and roughage. The only creatures that dared to carve out a life upon it were the mighty dragons.

But those dragons were the harbingers of more.

From the ground grew grasses, and bushes, and plants, and trees.

And from the rocks grew mountains, and ridges, and canyons.

And through the land wound rivers of sparkling blue, snaking towards a glittering blue-green sea.

And from the grass and trees and ground and mountains and rivers and seas, came forth *life*.

The Spirit watched in wonder as this quiet pearl, shining in the dark, became a loud and raucous world, teeming with life.

First insects and small shrimp, then fish and lizards, then birds and animals.

Life begot life.

As the world became home to more and more life, so the Spirit grew to love it more and more.

She loved the sky, and the way the sun and the twin moons shared in the lighting of it.

She loved the expansive seas, and how they caressed the shores.

She loved the way the land could be soft, hard, hot, cold, lush, or barren, and still be home to life.

She loved how the trees and grasses swayed in the wind, the way birds flew through the sky, the way even the smallest insect played a part in the circle of life.

As the world's creatures walked the earth, and swam the ocean depths, and soared the open skies, the Spirit's heart swelled within Her.

So great was Her love for the earth, that She plucked three of the brightest stars from the star-paved road across the heavens, and created children with whom She might share the wonders She beheld.

She became Aethyreomma, Mother of Spirits, and Her children were glorious.

Aethyreomma's star-children became the gods of the world, and though they were mostly unnoticed, they had their own part to play.

Eleyas came first, and to her, Aethyreomma gifted the forests, teeming with life. From the insects skittering over the forest floor, to the birds swooping through the canopy, Eleyas delighted in her domain.

Freya came second, and to her, Aethyreomma gave the mountains, rich with sparkling gems, minerals and ores. Freya was enthralled by the beauties offered up by the mountains, and the hardiness and tenacity of spirit in the creatures that lived there.

Anson was the Spirit's final child, and Her only son. To him, She gifted the wide, sweeping plains, and the snaking rivers that split the land with their wandering path.

Aethyreomma delighted in the earth, and was filled with joy to see Her children love it too.

Millenia came and went, the three gods tending to the earth together.

Aethyreomma oversaw the glittering oceans, while Her children watched over the land.

. . .

One day, Eleyas called to her siblings.

Among her bountiful forests, a new form of life was emerging.

Tall and willowy, and at one with the natural elements around them, these new beings demonstrated the same love of the land as their Mother Spirit.

Eleyas named her new charges "Elves", and gifted them a deep affinity with the wonders of the forest, and a respect for all life.

Filled with wonder, her siblings sought signs of such creatures in their own domains.

Centuries passed before Freya called upon her siblings.

Within the stone refuge of the mountain range that hugged the sea, a curious being with intelligent eyes appeared. Shorter and stockier than the beings of her sister's domains, Freya's people were hardy and sturdy, suiting their harsh mountain homes well.

Freya called them "Dwarves", and gifted them ingenuity, resilience, and an instinct for working with her most beloved mountains.

Yet more time passed, and Anson grew jealous of his sisters.

Eleyas's Elves and Freya's Dwarves crossed paths as they explored their world, sharing their love of the land from which they drew life, and forging strong bonds of friendship.

Aethyreomma counselled patience to Her son; life that took longer to blossom, She said, was all the sweeter for the wait.

Though Anson tried to take comfort in the varied creatures that roamed his lands, his jealousy grew bitter the longer it stewed.

When at last, Anson's lands yielded the bounty of men, his joy was clouded with resentment.

The people of his sisters' lands were graceful and wise, hardy and strong. The people of his lands were neither, shambling about with crude tools and rude shelters. Neither tall and willowy, nor short and stocky, the Humans, as Anson named his people, middled between the two, and he could see no remarkable traits from beneath his brooding cloud.

The Humans were young, and, after centuries of watching the elegant Elves and competent Dwarves, appeared rough and unfinished by comparison. Consumed by resentment, Anson did not offer his people a boon.

Aethyreomma, seeing Her son neglecting his Humans, took it upon herself to gift this newest race with great heart, so that they might love, as She did, the wonders of the world.

Time passed, and the Elves and Dwarves encountered the Humans roaming the plains and fishing the rivers.

While Eleyas and Freya delighted in seeing the people interact with the world and each other, the proximity of the races to each other only served to highlight how far Anson's Humans had yet to come. The Elves and the Dwarves had had centuries to learn and grow and develop. The Humans were a fledging race, and their constant demonstrations of inferiority maddened Anson.

But Anson had yet to gift his people a boon. And now he knew what he wanted for them.

He began whispering into the dreams of men. He whispered of his desire for them to prove themselves, to become the superior race; aspirations of greatness and a hunger for power.

But these whispers weren't selfless, like the gifts his sisters had given the Elves and the Dwarves. Anson's own yearning for his Humans to surpass the other races seeped into the dreams he bestowed upon them. And while the Elves and the Dwarves forged their own paths, unencumbered by the will of their gods, the Humans became aware of their deity, seeing him in their dreams, and feeling his will become theirs. They began to worship him, and laboured to fulfil his desire to rule as the superior race on the earth. They gave him many faces, so that all Humans could reach for greatness, whether they be fighters or farmers, sailors or builders.

With a desire for power and a thirst for dominance, some Humans clutched at leadership.

From leaders grew lords, from lords grew kings, and in a blink of time the world was covered in Human kingdoms.

Not content with dominating the land, the Humans hungered for more. They fought among themselves; for land, for resources, for people, for supremacy.

Eventually, their hunger spilled into the domains of the other races.

They challenged the Elves, and the Dwarves. And the hooks of war took hold.

The Elves fought to protect their forests, and all the life within them.

The Dwarves fought to save their homes and refuge in the beauty of the mountains.

The Humans fought to own the world.

Eleyas urged Anson to calm his people. They already dominated the land with their kingdoms.

Freya begged him to stop them. The Humans were killing and dying in equal measure in their quest for more.

Aethyreomma pleaded with Her son. Her treasured world was soaking in blood for the simple jealousy of one people. One god.

Despite the pleas of his Mother and sisters, Anson was gladdened to see his Humans finally take what he saw was rightfully theirs.

They were finally proving themselves to be the superior race.

They were even dying for it.

When it became clear Anson would not intervene, Eleyas and Freya confronted him.

And then, the gods themselves fought.

The winds galed furiously, rain and sleet and hail thundering to the ground. The earth bucked and heaved beneath. Rivers and lakes flooded alike, and lightning struck indiscriminately, lighting the sky in angry flashes, and sparking fires beneath.

The War of the Races raged on, even as the earth itself was thrown into turmoil.

As the gods clashed above, so the people fought below, infected by the wrath of their gods.

And all the while, the earth roiled.

People died by sword and arrow, by storm and quake.

And still, the gods warred.

Aethyreomma was distraught to see the destruction Her children wrought on the world She so loved. And so, She ripped the gods from the sky.

In grief and deepest sadness, She flung them from the earth, leaving Her once again alone with Her world.

. . .

When Aethyreomma looked back upon Her beloved world, She broke inside to see what Her children had done.

Death and darkness covered the earth.

People of all races lay broken and torn upon wasted battlefields.

Rivers ran pink with blood.

Deep gouges rent the land.

Forests were stained black from the passage of fire.

The Mother Spirit wept, Her tears falling to the ground in endless, cleansing rains.

For seven years, She washed away the sins of Her children with Her tears. And with every tear shed, a drop of the Spirit fell to the earth, soaking into the wounds of the world.

Plants grew anew from scorched ground, flourishing in the rain.

Insects and animals drank from the rivers and streams, fed by the fresh fall.

Before long, Aethyreomma, the Mother Spirit, inhabited all life in the world.

The rivers and streams were filled by Her sadness, and the sea became Her soul.

The ground and the mountains were soaked with Her sorrow, and glittered with crystals formed of Her love.

The earth healed and became fertile from Her nourishment, and brought forth fresh life.

And the creatures and people were finally cleansed of the blood and the rage of Her children. They drank from the rivers, and ate of the land, and so the Mother Spirit inhabited them too, with a bittersweet affection for the people of Her children.

When the rains finally ceased, and the sun shone clear upon the earth, the people of the world emerged to begin their lives anew.

The Elves continued to respect and protect their forests.

The Dwarves continued to prosper in their mountains.

And the Humans continued to grow. Both in heart, and in a quiet hunger for more.

For when Aethyreomma had flung Her children from the world, one had left a piece of himself behind.

Anson, loath to relinquish his hold on dominion, had held onto the world so tight that when he'd been ripped from it, the god had torn in two. A sliver remained, left forgotten on a precipice at the very edge of the mountains. A tattered shred, hanging over the endless sea, barely clinging to existence in the deepest shadows.

Split as She was, the parts of Aethyreomma became something different. She was no longer a single being, but many beings.

Many parts of many beings.

And so She was not the Mother Spirit, but many Spirits.

The Aethyr.

And each piece of Her developed its own essence. Spirits within the trees were different to Spirits within the mountains, and entirely different to Spirits within the clouds. The Spirit of a frog would be different to that of a starling, and again to that of a deer, or a bear.

But the Spirits of the people were slippery things, as if the souls of Elves and Dwarves and Humans were big enough already, and so these Spirits, rather than living *within* the people, lingered alongside them.

Together, the multitude of Aethyr formed the Eah.

And the Eah was the unified voice of the Spirits.

They whispered among one another, and their voices ranged across the world.

And they saw everything.

Even the fragment of an old, dead god, clinging to life on the outskirts.

Yearning for more than just a spectator's seat.

Wanting to play a part once more in the world.

To be supreme.

29

A LITTLE BIT BROKEN

For the most part, all was well. Humans kept to their lands, and governed their own people.

They formed treaties with the Elves and the Dwarves, and kept to themselves.

All the while, the part of Anson that clung to existence scraped and crawled its way into relevance.

It was nought but a fragment, a scrap; the god had been rent, torn in two when he was thrown from the earth, the wholer part of himself gone forever. What was left was a broken piece of a damaged god.

A piece that knew it wanted dominion.

But he couldn't do that in his current state.

Even he did not know how long he lay there, clinging to the edge of the world, gathering strength one iota at a time.

Seasons later, in the cool scent of ozone that came after a rainfall — a normal rainfall, not a torrent of sorrow or an onslaught of grief — he caught a sparkle that reminded him of something — a hint of... love... and life...

Mother...?

Broken, still a mere shred of his former self, the Anson that was left clawed his way towards it.

The sparkle turned out to be the point where a mountain spring burbled from the ground, crisp and clear, catching the sun's tentative rays.

The tattered remains of a god slipped into the cool waters, and let it carry him down the mountains to the plains below.

At some point, his essence washed up with the dregs of silt and flotsam of the foothills. He lay weak and alone until a grazing beast ventured near enough for him to cling to, to carry him further along his journey.

Anson spent years this way; drifting from place to place. Searching, ever searching.

In his fractured state, he did not have the strength to mould just any mind to his will. It had to be weak, pliable. It had to be a little bit broken. Like him.

Russel Stuart was the youngest of five sons in a poor family. His mother had died giving birth to him, so his father was left to raise his boys alone. He did the best he could.

In a family that size, in a village that small, there wasn't enough work or money to go around. Russel was a burden on his family. When his brothers weren't resenting him, they were pitying him, or trying in vain to hide their disgust. He tilled fields like a horse to earn his keep, and spent the little money he earned either gambling or drinking it away.

Russel often wondered who would care if he didn't appear to till the fields one morning. Would anyone notice? But there was no other place for him to go.

It was in one of these moods that Anson found him, and gleefully hitched himself to the young man.

As Anson whispered in his ear, Russel changed.

That day, Russel confronted his father. He was sick of playing fifth fiddle to his brothers. He wanted more of the family farm: more say, more share, more pay.

But, times being what they were, and at that, no different from any other times, John Stuart couldn't give his youngest son what he asked. And it pained him to see the anger in his quiet boy's eyes.

But Russel was not alone. And the whisper in his ear made so much sense.

Russel was not a bright lad, and had very little will to speak of. If he was told to mop the floor, he mopped the floor. If he was asked to chop the wood, he restocked the logpile. If he was asked to plough the fields like a farm animal, he did it.

But all of that meant he was uncommonly strong. And this strength made strangling his father as easy as if the farmer were but a ragdoll.

As his brothers returned from their day's work, he asked of them the same — he wanted more. They refused. And he killed them.

Eventually, he stood alone in the farmhouse.

Bury the bodies, the voice whispered in his ear. And he did.

See how easy it is? it said. *To take what is rightfully yours?* And he did.

With no more mouths to feed, Russel paid farm hands to do the work. And with a canny voice in his ear all the while, he thrived, taking on more land, and becoming a power in his own right.

Russel Stuart became a man. A land-owner. And a father.

The son of a tavern wench, Malcolm was the spitting image of his father, and no questions were raised when Russel claimed him as his own, although plenty wondered what on earth Russel Stuart would want with a child underfoot.

As it was, he was a cruel father. His own hadn't had the time or the instinct for nurturing him, and the whispering in his ear had interests in only one thing. But with a son by his side, Russel knew his power would be strengthened beyond doubt.

Malcolm grew up as cruel as his father, and before long, the scrap of Anson that whispered in his father's ear began to spend time with the son.

Between the two of them, the Stuarts schemed. The voice in their ears told them their land and power was paltry compared to what they could have. But, being of certain standings, there was a limit to how far they could go. To how much power they could grasp.

"There will always be lords and kings above who own the land," Malcolm growled one day to his father, already deep in his cups. "No matter how much we take on, no matter how many men we have to work it, we will always just be farmers."

"Rich farmers," Russel corrected his son, waving drunkenly about their home. It was warm, dry, and the crackling fire was stacked high, casting orange shadows about the place. Russel had never been so wealthy, and he was content with his lot, despite the whisperings in his ear.

"But farmers nonetheless," Malcolm insisted. "Even merchants pay their dues to someone. Even lords." He pushed himself to his feet and paced over to the fire, gazing into the glowing logs. "And what has the king done to deserve his lofty throne?" He turned to his father, a spark in his eye. "He was born to it. And what right is that?"

See how easy it is... the voice echoed in Russel's ear. It *had* been easy. Laughably easy when he thought on it, to change his fortunes.

"You could always kill the king," he mumbled absently, taking another long draw from his mug. When he put the cup down, the bottom clunked thickly on the wooden table. He looked up at his son.

Malcolm's mouth was curved into a grin.

"Exactly, father," he said.

With one simple thought, the Rebel Unity was conceived. Russel and Malcolm schemed all night, eventually concluding that no man should stand above another. No single person should be born to rule over others. Strength was to be earned — every man for himself.

The idea caught like a spark to dried thatch. And it burned across the Wolds.

Anson, or the broken piece that remained, was not whole enough of mind to recognise the error in their ideas.

All he saw was Humans rising up to claim what was rightfully theirs.

Village after village fell as the Stuarts "freed" people of leadership. They gathered an army of poor, mercenaries, and opposers to the monarchy. And Anson fed off their hunger for freedom, whispering sweet rebellion in their ears.

No Human should ever again be less than superior, he whispered. *Take what is rightfully yours.*

They called themselves the Unity, because they were united in a common goal, but the message was clear — every man for himself.

When the Rebel Unity reached the capital, Throldon was thrown into chaos. Anarchy ruled the streets, and Russel did eventually kill the king. He let the word spread that the king and his entourage had fled for their own cowardly lives, leaving the people behind to pay the price.

A lie, which only drew more to his cause.

In a day and a night, Throldon was under Unity control. Russel and Malcolm made the castle their own, and sent their people to ensure that no man, woman, or child was under the thumb of another.

Every man for himself, was their single dictate.

Anyone who wasn't, was taught the flavour of true fear under Unity rule.

30

SPIRIT-BORN

In Eah'lara, the Spirit Realm, geographical distance is reduced to a complex web of connections.

Aethyr float serenely through space. One Aethyr might witness multiple lifeforms on earth, miles apart, joined by seemingly tenuous links that connect them.

Equally, many Aethyr might inhabit one lifeform, like a tree, only looking to each other over the course of its life. Others interact constantly, weaving between the mortal world and Eah'lara a thousand-thousand times in a lifespan. The Aethyr carried in the wind and the rain will move into the ground and the grass, the insects and birds and the sky again.

The Spirit Realm is a peaceful melody of Aethyr following life through all its forms; an infinite canvas of light.

The manifestations of Anson's desire for a superior race was driving the already isolated peoples of the world apart, and with them, the Aethyr themselves. It was a subtle thing, hardly noticeable at first. But then the bonds connecting the web began to stretch, began to thin.

As chaos reigned in the world, and the twisted part of Anson continued whispering his dreams into the hearts of Humans, the collective Eah agreed intervention wasn't just necessary, it was essential.

A small group of Aethyr sought to enter the world as members of the mortal races. One for the Elves, one for the Dwarves, one of the Dragons, one for the Centaurs — overlooked by the gods — and one for the Humans. One would remain in Eah'lara to anchor them, to bind them together in the end.

These six were to guide the races together; to bridge the chasms wrought by Anson's insanity. They would retain their senses of self, their experiences, and their wisdom. But also their opinions, their prejudices, and their bias.

They needed another. New. Innocent. Naive even. Ignorant of what had come before.

One *born* into life.

A true *child* of Aethyreomma.

No Spirit had ever been born. They were each formed from the teardrops of the Spirit Mother, and were reborn in the never-ending circle of life on earth. Spirits did not have the capacity to carry and bear offspring.

They would need a seed to plant, and a mortal in which to grow it.

The Aethyr looked upon the earth for one to bear such a child. They searched for one whose goals aligned with their own. Someone kind of heart, driven by compassion, who wanted an end to the needless, poisonous violence of Humankind.

Eventually they found one. And they were surprised by her.

Among the Humans, the very race contaminated by violence and greed, there were a few who braved the blood and smoke to help others. To scrape together a peace, of sorts.

And at the centre of it all, a nobleman's daughter, burned out of her home, picked up the pieces left by Anson's corrupted puppets. She gathered preachers, healers, craftsmen, and others to help. And behind her, a movement of compassion grew.

Her, was the resounding consensus, a harmony of voices in the ether. *She will bear our Spiritchild.*

They watched, and waited. And as they watched, the Human woman Listened.

She heard them, and Listened.

Eventually, the woman found love with a man. And when new life took root within her, the Aethyr planted their seed within it, for a new Spirit to grow.

When the child was born, it burned with the light of Eah'lara, and the Aethyr were glad to see it — never before, had a Spirit been born.

Now, they were seven.

As the child grew, the Aethyr guides watched cautiously, quietly. They could not reveal themselves. Not yet. The child needed to grow into its own without the sway of their wishes.

She needed to be impartial, with mortal values and mortal needs. Mortal dreams and desires. Mortal loves and losses.

She needed to be one of *them*.

She would learn her heritage later.

And so they waited, and watched, as she grew.

Hushed as a whisper, unseen and unheard, they waited.

And they had hope.

And then the Humans came.

The ones that called themselves a Unity, but killed all who opposed them.

The ones that had let themselves be led into anarchy and violence.

They burned the village to the ground, and innocents died.

The Aethyr despaired. Years they had waited. And the dark influence of Anson spread a little more with every passing day. They did not have time...

Then, they heard a whisper. A prayer.

The mother, hidden in the midst of the destruction, cradling their Spiritchild, begged for her safety.

The Aethyr did not hesitate. They took the child through the Spirit Realm to a place where she could grow into what they needed. To Eleyas's peace-loving elves.

And, years later, when the time was right, that small group of Aethyr stepped into the mortal world to guide the races together, to the aid of their Spiritchild, who would save Eah'lara, and the world, from total annihilation.

31

DUST AND MOONLIGHT

Fae stared at Bek, agape.

Laina's eyes were wet with tears.

The being that was once a boy called Bek smiled, an apology for his deception.

When he spoke, it was a chorus of voices spoken together at once.

"I am a convergence of your companions," he said, continuing his story. He turned to the centaur. "To Equi'tox, we sent the one you knew as Bravargh." He turned to the dwarf. "To Dvargra, we sent the one known as Bran." He turned to Kagos, the dragon. "To Hearthstone, we sent Baev'ill." When he turned to Laina and Hal, he inclined his head with a hint of deference. "Into the plains, we sent Ben." His lips curled up at the corners, and he paused a moment before turning to Fae. "Bek went to Arolynos." For an instant, it seemed as though his expression bore the shadow of regret. But then his parental smile returned, and he addressed the wider group once more. "Another, known as Be'ella Tor, awaits to join us from Eah'lara — what you may know more commonly as the Spirit Realm. Our purpose is to unite the races, join together as one, and rip the broken remains of Anson from the earth. We mean to return our world to peace, as it once was." His voices took on a hard tone, and his lips pressed together in a grim line.

"The damage Anson inflicts worsens daily. He has found a way to push his influence outward, infecting more and more of Eah'lara and the Aethyr within it. Since we sent our emissaries into the world, he has found a new host in which to inject his poison. A former Unity thug called Tamra Walker. She titles herself Lady Black now, and her reach is destroying the very balance of life, such that we cannot stand to be near her operations."

"It hurts you," Fae whispered, hearing echoes of the Aethyr's cries from her vision. There had been a black stain on Arland; one that made the spirits weep. Had Bek known all this time? He always was so much more tuned into the Aethyr than anyone she knew. She missed her little shadow with a pang that arrowed straight through her. How much of the man before them was still *her* Bek?

Bek nodded. "Without our presence, the life in the region withers and dies, and the ripples are being felt across the world. It cannot be left any longer. We must act, and we must act now."

"Um—" the dwarf on the far side of the monument waved a hand in the air. "Just how are you proposing to act if you can't get near the problem?" she asked. "You just said it — you can't stand to be near Anson's new host."

Bek nodded again, and met Fae's eye. "That's where Fae comes in."

Laina's gaze snapped to her.

"Told you you weren't human," Ty breathed in her ear, his voice a wisp of awe.

"That's not entirely accurate," Bek corrected with a quirk of his lips. "You *are* human. At least, physically. But within you, there is a well of our power. You are human, but also Aethyr. You were born to take in our power, our experiences, our memories, and become better than the sum of our parts. To become better than us. To become stronger. Strong enough to tear a god from this earth. Well—" he chuckled, and his voices purred with the sound of it "—a piece of one anyway."

Fae gaped again.

"*Fae.*" A whisper came from her left. Barely a whisper. A strangled breath. "*My* Fae?"

She turned to see the human woman, Laina staring at her, tears running unchecked down her cheeks.

And she suddenly knew why the woman looked so familiar.

An image of a family frolicking in a sunny village.

A woman curled around the unconscious form of her child.
Distant, hazy memories of her own...

A thunderclap of realisation rang dizzyingly in her head.

"Mother?" Fae gasped, the revelation knocking the wind from her. She glanced over to Bek, the question shining from her eyes. He nodded slowly, a sad smile playing over his lips. When she continued to stare at him, the cogs of her mind locked up in shock, he held an arm out to Laina, inviting her to speak.

"Laina," he said gently, "this is your part of the tale to tell. You are in safe company here, if you wish to share it."

At his words, Fae's eyes slid slowly back across to her.

Laina ducked her head and twined her hands together. She took a step towards Fae, and stopped. She stood, eyes on the ground, fat tears silently painting the stone storm-grey at her feet. Then she pulled in a ragged breath, and raised her head.

Her lips were pressed together, and her eyes, now dry, were hard.

"When I was sixteen," she began shakily, "the Rebel Unity burned my home to the ground." She closed her eyes, her brows knitting together so tightly they made knots in her forehead. There was pain in her memories, but she breathed deep, nostrils flaring, and blew the air out, slow and controlled. She looked up, and when she spoke again, her voice had lost its faltering edge, and she spoke so that everyone could hear her.

"My father was Lord Gareth Marl of Bredon," she said, and this time her voice held sharpened steel. Hal's gaze snapped abruptly to her, but he didn't interrupt. "I was sixteen when Russel and Malcolm Stuart took offence to our home. The Rebel Unity descended like a pack of wolves, a thousand strong. They'd already sacked Throldon, so we had only our own garrison to defend against them. My father took them all, and any others willing and able to defend their homes." Lines bracketed her mouth. "They were slaughtered. Maimed. Or left to die on the field. The Unity raiders were savage, and ripped through the town like scythes to the crops. I escaped with my governess, Anna. She all but pulled me out of there before I could realise what was happening. I watched Bredon burn from the road." Laina paused, honouring the dead with her silence.

"We found a few others who'd escaped," she continued. "Aside from me and Anna, our family healer, Margaret, got out with a handful of women and children. We drifted for a day, or two — I don't remember —

and returned to Bredon after the raiders had finished picking the ruins clean." Her fingers, which had been fidgeting agitatedly, stilled. "There weren't many left behind. We didn't stay long. But that was when I knew I wanted to *do* something. I've never felt as helpless as I did the day the raiders attacked Bredon — I never wanted to feel like that again. I wanted to fight back. To make them pay." A derisive smile caught at the corner of her mouth, and she shook her head. "Margaret slapped me out of that delusion. She taught me healing. Taught me *that* was how I could fight back."

Laina looked up at the group, who were hanging onto her every word. "That's how the Peacekeepers began. It was just me and Margaret at first, and to start with I was next to useless. Anna helped in the ways she knew how to. And the other women too. We travelled from village to village, lending help where we could. Some chose to join us. I'm sure you know the rest." She waved a hand dismissively to the side, skipping past years in a single gesture. "Eventually, Margaret passed away. She was old when I was a child, let alone after fleeing her home and traipsing across half of Arland with me. I led the Peacekeepers alone for a time. We did a lot of good." She sighed, and ran a hand through her hair. "And then Andrew came along."

She smiled then. And it was a shaft of sunlight spearing through dark storm clouds.

"Andrew was calm, kind, and practical. He had a soothing presence, as if he hadn't a worry in the world. He used to make me laugh like I was a giddy teenager again." As Laina spoke, Fae saw them with her mind's eye, her memories lighting up one at a time, like fireflies in the night. "He would hold me and call me Lissa, like I was the most precious thing in the world to him. He didn't treat me as a leader of people, just saw me as I was." She looked over at Fae again. And although everyone heard her, her next words were for Fae alone.

"I loved him, *so* much." The words caught in her throat, snatching her breath along with them. "He was the light in my life. We were married in a village in the Wolds — Woodnewton, it was called. We settled down there for a time. We had a baby girl. We were happy." Her voice dropped to a whisper as she watched Fae. "You have his eyes."

"Then the Unity found us." Laina's own eyes glazed over, reliving hard memories. "I watched as they killed our friends, torched homes, did... *despicable* things... Andrew ran in to help, and they killed him for it..." She closed her eyes against the pain. Fae remembered her vision, and her breath caught in her throat.

Another memory flared. Of pure terror, the likes of which only a child could experience. Of being pressed close, her face buried against a mother's hair, the scent of lavender not quite masking the smell of fires running rampant.

A solitary tear rolled down Laina's cheek. "I ran away, and I hid. I feared for my life. I feared for my child." She breathed. "I prayed for the first time that day. To the Mother, to the Spirits — anyone who'd listen."

She looked up at Fae again. "It's as he says—" she nodded towards Bek "—when you were born, you glowed. Just for a minute, but I saw it. And I knew there was something special about you. Andrew taught me about the Spirits. He'd learnt about them from the elves he met in his travelling days — before me. He was a woodsman. Loved being in the trees." A shadow of a smile chased itself across her face, and Fae could suddenly recall the shape her father's body would make, curled over a piece of carpentry he was working on. It was like Laina's voice, her stories, were awakening memories her mind had buried to save her from remembering the pain.

"Margaret always used to talk about Mother Nature, and how She provides," Laina continued. "As a healer, it always made a kind of sense to me. But the Spirits... Well, I prayed to both. You *needed* to survive... *I* needed you to survive." Her gaze slid away for a second, before she gave a long sigh, and looked back up to meet Fae's eyes. "And then you were gone. In the same glow of light you were born into." A tentative smile broke onto her face. "I never expected to see you again. I just had to trust that you were safe. Away from the Unity's reach."

Fae's mind was awhirl. Her head filled with a white noise of questions, one piling on top of the next. A cacophony of information she couldn't even begin to process. Her visions replayed in her mind. The vision of the family in the human village — *her* family — and of the mother praying for her child — *her* mother. And in amongst the memories the Aethyr had shown her, were images from her own mind, dusty and unused, but there, caught amongst the cobwebs of her past.

Her parents dancing around the kitchen. Her mother singing her a lullaby at night. Her father carving a wooden pony for her to play with.

Out of the corner of her eye, Fae saw again the carved wooden ring on Laina's finger.

And she remembered tracing the whorls across that ring, feeling the swirls and edges beneath her fingers as if committing the pattern to memory. And with her other hand, tracing the smooth surface of its partner, on her father's hand.

Her heart stuttered. She wasn't ready for all of it yet. Ready to remember the terror of her home burning around her, the smell of smoke, choking and cloying. Ready to remember the love of a father lost to needless violence. To remember a child's fear at waking in a strange place to find her mother long gone. She didn't know if she could handle it on top of everything else. Not yet.

As it was, there was already too much to take in.

"So," she said, turning away from the painful memories, and back to face Bek, "you're saying I'm part-Aethyr?" *That,* she could just about handle. Outlandish and barely believable as it was, there was no pain there. No long-forgotten wounds ripped wide open. No reliving of memories her mind had papered over. Bizarrely, this felt like safer ground to tread. "And you want *me* to remove an ancient, broken god from the human race?" There was so much more, a dizzying tangle of emotions, but Fae forced herself to focus her mind on comprehending just these two points, or risk drowning. Laina — *her mother* — stood off to one side. Her face flickered between hurt, and a joy bruised by years of fractured hope.

"This is all very touching," the black-on-black figure of Kagos spoke up, his gravelly, avalanche-voice rumbling through the stone floor, "but what does that have to do with the rest of us?" He extended his arm in a lazy arc, taking in the assembled group. "From what you've said so far, you intend to imbue *this* woman—" he indicated Fae with a disdainful gesture that said exactly what he thought of that "—with the necessary abilities required to defeat Anson. It sounds as though our presence here is moot." He brought his hands back together, tucking them into the sleeves of his robe.

Bek humoured Kagos with a wry smile. "Part of the reason Anson has succeeded in infiltrating humanity so deeply — and unnoticed — is that the races stand leagues apart." He turned, deliberately meeting the eye of each member. All were standing conspicuously alone, in the manner in which they'd arrived. All avoided eye contact with the others.

"The races of this world live under the same sun, sleep under the same two moons. And yet you avoid one another so... *efficiently*." He gave them all a look of such utter exasperation, it was hard not to feel chastised. "You divide the land by race, and adhere to your boundaries like pages in a book."

"I still don't see your point, Baev'ill," Kagos rumbled.

Bek gave him such a withering glare that even Kagos faltered, only keeping hold of his cool disdain with a single raised eyebrow.

"Do you not think you'd have noticed, if a human under the influence of ill-omen walked past you in the world?" Bek asked him. The echo of his multiple voices scorned tenfold. He didn't give Kagos the chance to answer, turning instead to the dwarf. "Do you not think anyone in the close-knit community of the dwarves would have noticed a sudden change in behaviour in one of its members?" He whirled on the centaur. "Do you not think the elders would have noticed, if one among you could not stand to bear the *Ateth Legarrh*?"

Finally, he turned to Ty. "Do you not think a Whisperer would have noticed, if one among you had a suspicious *absence* of Aethyr about them?" Bek's hands curled into trembling fists, and Fae was reminded of the boy she'd known, scared and alone before he became family. He drew in a breath to calm himself.

"It is imperative that the races come together," he said with a sigh that seemed to say everything his words didn't. In that sigh was a hope that they would achieve more than just displacing a broken god. That they would bring the world together. "If they do not, we achieve the same end. With the division of the races, there is division in the Aethyr. We are stretched too thin, and we are suffocating for it. This world thrives on the diversity of its people; of life. Without it, spiritkind are dying. Anson is only a symptom. The disease is this segregation you have carved out for yourselves."

"But we've lived apart for centuries," Ty said gently. "Why now?"

"Anson," Bek replied simply. "He is a symptom, and also a catalyst. Simply put, the destruction he wreaks in Arland is exacerbating the problem."

The air in the monument fell silent.

Fae drew a deep, shuddering breath.

She believed it all. The thinning of the Aethyr explained the fading in

Arolynos, it explained the reluctance of spring to turn, the dwindling numbers of birds spiralling through the canopy.

She looked up at Bek. He was different, and yet the same blue eyes watched her, as he always had, waiting to follow her lead.

She believed in him.

"What do we do now?" she said.

All eyes turned to Bek. He stepped forward, taking Fae's hands, and enfolding them in his own.

She looked up at him. He wasn't the young orphan boy of Arolynos anymore. He was taller, older. His shoulders were broad, and he stood close enough to block her view of the others. His blue eyes twinkled knowingly at her, and the corner of his mouth turned up in a sad smile.

"We need to come together," he said, the additional voices fading until she heard her Bek above them all. "To become better than the sum of our parts."

Fae caught the trace of regret beneath his words. "What aren't you telling me?"

Bek's eyes dipped away, his jaw clenched. When he met her eyes again, his gaze bored into hers, severe, and deadly serious.

"Fae," he began, "you are a first. Aethyr can merge and part ways again, without any noticeable difference between them. We are parts of a larger whole; it is purest ease for us to do this. You..." He paused, as if trying to find the right words to say. "You are unique. You were born. Apart. An individual, not from our whole." He took a breath. "I don't know how this will affect you."

"Wait." Ty, standing the closest to them, stepped forward. "What are you talking about?" He stared from one to the other, demanding an answer.

Fae's power of speech seemed to have left her. Wading through everything she'd learned so far, her head was a buzz of white noise. But through it all, she knew one undeniable fact.

I was born to do this. To hold this power until it was needed. She looked up at Bek. *This was what was behind the curtain in my mind. This what what was missing.* He nodded — an almost imperceptible inclination of his head.

"In the same way that your travel companions have become one, in me," Bek said, holding Fae's gaze, while addressing the group, "so too, will we become one." He turned to face Ty. "It is our purpose. Fae is the host, the only one of us with a true corporeal form. But within her, the powers, experience, and memories of seven beings will reside. Six Aethyr and one Aethyr-born, in one body." His expression was tinged with unease as he spoke. "The intention is to gift Fae with abilities to take on a god. But power affects us all in strange and different ways, and I cannot say how she will emerge."

"Ty," Fae said softly, her voice coming back to her. "It's okay." Suddenly everything made sense. It all lined up in her head in neat little rows, and clicked into place.

Ty gripped her shoulders, turning her to face him. "There has to be another way." He turned to Bek. "There are six of you — can't you do it without Fae?"

Bek shook his head sadly. "The powers we hold are in the connections between living things. Connecting the sun to the flower, roots to the ground, pulling water to the sky. We remind baby birds how to fly, shake nuts from the trees, navigate the ocean's currents alongside sea-mammoths. Our powers are not meant for taking on gods. Only Aethyreomma was capable of that. Even with all the Aethyr together, we could not hope to achieve Her equal.

"We do not wield power, but we can connect Fae to it. She is a nucleus for the power within us. In planting a seed to grow with her, her potential is beyond ours. All she needs is guidance." Bek spread his hands. "Which is what we are for." His voice rang with the many again.

Don't you see, Ty? Fae thought, looking up at Ty as he stared disbelievingly at Bek. *It has to be me.* From the corner of her eye, she caught sight of Laina's face. The woman was fighting the urge to intervene, a mother's anguish pulling the skin taut across her cheekbones. But she kept her silence. She nodded at Fae; a jerky, hesitant motion. She understood better than Ty.

Or perhaps she simply accepted the situation for what it was.

Either way...

Fae squared her shoulders. She gently disengaged Ty's hands from her arms. Met his eyes.

They were storm grey, and it seemed as if the ocean itself crashed within them. A hundred emotions flashed behind his gaze, and it was all she could do not to look away.

Couldn't he see how hard this was? How much it was to take in?

Couldn't he see she didn't want to say goodbye?

She forced a smile onto her face, but she knew it wasn't convincing.

"I'll be fine," she said, injecting some confidence into her voice from somewhere deep within. "It's Bek." She glanced at the boy-turned-man beside them. "Plus a couple more." She squeezed Ty's hands. "We'll be fine."

Letting go of Ty's hands, she stepped around him to stand before Bek. Took a breath. Let it out. Stilled the turmoil in her mind. Or perhaps she stepped into the eye of the storm.

Either way.

"I'm ready," she said.

Bek's glance flicked to Ty, and back again. "Are you sure?"

Fae nodded. "I'm sure." The elves of Arolynos had never truly understood her. The Whisperers had dismissed her. But hadn't she always known she was capable of more?

Hadn't she always felt that she *was* more?

Bek took a step forward, until they were practically toe to toe. He angled his head down, touching his forehead to hers.

And in that moment, she stood with her fellow orphan from Arolynos once more.

A smile crossed her lips.

Bek's mouth formed two words, and she almost didn't catch them.

"I'm sorry."

Light surrounded her — particles swirling around them in a storm of stars.

Bek came apart, as if he were made of dust and moonlight.

And then pain.

Searing, unbearable pain.

32

BECOMING

Almost as soon as the pain began, it stopped.

Fae opened her eyes.

All around was a glowing white. Iridescent orbs floated about in a spectrum of colours, just a shade away from pure white. Shining spider-silk filaments spun through the air in every direction, visible only as the light caught them; gossamer-thin, glinting arrows of light.

At first, Fae thought there was no sound. But, when she listened, she heard a soft tinkling, like tiny bells, far away. It was warm. She felt feather-light, and half-asleep, thick-headed and fuzzy.

Hello, Fae. The same multi-voice that had spoken through Bek sounded in her head, but with a distinctly female tone.

She started. *Hello?* she replied, still in her head.

What you are seeing is Eah'lara, the Realm of Spirits, the multi-voice said. *It is where we reside, and whence we draw our power.*

This one's counterparts have drawn you here to complete the unifying of the seven. This one is known as Be'ella Tor. Be'ella Tor represents the Aethyr among the seven. Be'ella Tor will join the seven together as one.

Aren't we joined already? Fae asked. *Isn't that why I'm here?*

The seven are together, and reside within you. But to truly become one, you must open your mind to them. A pause. *It will be uncomfortable; to allow seven beings space within one consciousness has not been done before. But it is necessary.*

Fae hesitated.

There is no time for questions, Be'ella Tor continued. *You must open your mind. Let the others among your seven in. We will guide you. Let us in.* The multi-voice split out until Fae could discern the individuals within it. Be'ella Tor was there, and there were others she didn't recognise. And there was Bek.

Please, he whispered above the others. *Trust me.*

And she did. That little voice, seldom heard in company, was her brother by choice. And she would walk to the ends of the earth for him.

As he had for her.

Fae closed her eyes.

The seven reside within you, Be'ella Tor had said. So Fae searched within herself. It was opposite to how she'd first learnt to reach for the Aethyr — stretching her senses out and beyond herself. Now, she focused inward, listening to the rhythm of her breathing, and the flow of her thoughts.

It didn't take long to find them. The rest of the seven clamoured at the edge of her mind. Closing the distance between her conscious mind and the other six entities, she brought herself before them.

With her mind's eye, Fae saw her spirit guides in the guises they'd taken for their turn in the world. And she knew each instantly without introduction.

Bek looked, to her, as he had in Arolynos. Gone was the gauntness from weeks trekking across Arland, the hollowness in his cheeks, the bruised circles beneath his eyes. He waved at her timidly, smiling with the same dimpled cheeks that she knew so well.

The others were all cast from the same mould: same blue eyes, same brown hair, same jawline. But there, the similarities ended.

The human, Ben, was a few years older, approaching twenty, and held himself upright with the confidence of a young man making his own decisions in the world. He had broad shoulders, strong arms and sun-browned skin; the hallmarks of long days of hard labour. He stood with arms folded casually across his chest, his face holding an easy, neutral expression.

The dwarf, Bran, had the shorter stature of his race, and a face showing the first edges of adolescence. He watched her with a piercing gaze that seemed to perceive more of her than she was entirely comfortable with.

The centaur, Bravargh, towered over the group, his lower body that of a dark-brown horse. He wore his hair long, and black, angular tribal tattoos were inked down the right side of his torso. There was a hard glint in his eyes, like tempered steel, and Fae wondered at his nature.

The dragon, Baev'ill, appeared in his smaller, non-dragon form, like Kagos. While he had the blue eyes and brown hair favoured by the group, his embodiment into a dragon added a little more colour to his appearance. The skin of his hands, feet, and face was darker than that of that of his counterparts; closer to nutmeg. The scales that covered the rest of his body were a deep bronze, and the edges of his fan-shaped ears were dipped in bright, cobalt-blue. He oozed the same aloofness that Kagos had presented himself with, but the quirk in his mouth hinted at another facet to his character.

Be'ella Tor floated beside the others, giving off a distinctly feminine energy to the other guides' male manifestations. A soft wisp of floating light, her form was almost cloud-like, tapering to either end, imitating an indistinct ribbon that blurred into the surrounding space. From the lower end of the wisp, small, nebulous specks of changing colours trailed behind like ribbons on a kite string. And where the others might have shifted restlessly from foot to foot, Be'ella Tor alternated between curling herself into an orb, like the shapes Fae had seen floating throughout Eah'lara, and unfurling to reveal her ribbon-like form.

Ok, Fae thought, her former confidence wavering. *What now?*

Bek approached, closing the gap between them, an unavoidable sheepishness to his face.

We're not sure, he admitted, his fingers working to form the words even as he spoke into her mind. *Between the Aethyr, we just... open to each other.* His shoulders shrugged, hands spreading briefly before coming back together to hand-speak. *But with you, it's different.* He reached forward, and took her hands.

Bek's innocent, blue eyes looked up at her, and she felt a tug within her. She loved him as surely as any family. Trusted him implicitly.

A sudden thought occurred to her, and she shot him an accusatory look. *You knew all along that you'd be guiding me here, didn't you?* she teased him.

He caught her tone, and his lips kicked up into a wide smile. *Maybe,* he said, hedging. *We are Aethyr, but remember: for the last five years, we have been mortal as well, our true natures tucked into our mortal identities.* The look he gave her then was of the deepest sincerity. *I was, and always will be, your friend first, Niha. Your little shadow.* He leaned his head in towards her, and she reflexively bent hers to meet it.

Fae closed her eyes as her forehead touched his.

I trust you.

And somehow, she let them in.

33

A NEW WHOLE

Somehow, without quite knowing how, Fae opened herself to the six Aethyr waiting at the gates of her consciousness, and let them in.

First, of course, came Bek, gentle and familiar and welcome. He fit beside her like they were two spoons nestled together. He curled up beside her, guiding her through accepting the other five. In hindsight, he was probably the only reason she made it through the process.

Ben came next, easy and unassuming. He took up space. She didn't know him like Bek, and he pushed up against her, for all that he tried not to.

Then came Bran, impassive and cunning. He sidled into her mind with a lazy swagger, and took up residence in the corner, watching, ever watching.

Bravargh had an angry streak, and for all that he tried to ease in gently, his character took up even more space than Ben. And it was already getting hard to breathe.

Baev'ill was reckless and wild, and made no attempt to allow for the others. His personality was brash, and superior, and it took the will of all the others to force him to calm.

Finally the wisp of Be'ella Tor slipped in, knitting the doors of Fae's mind closed behind her. She was wise and whimsical; a child-like authority among the spirits.

"Uncomfortable" was how Be'ella Tor had described this to her. It was the understatement of the ages. If it was possible to be crushed within one's own mind, that was what was happening to Fae.

She couldn't breathe, couldn't move, couldn't *think*.

It wasn't discomfort, it was agony.

Hold on Fae, Bek's voice murmured from somewhere in her head, soothing. *It's about to get worse.*

Worse?!

Alright, Aethyr, the feminine tone of Be'ella Tor rang through, clear and assured. *Open up.*

Yes. Worse.

The skins that divided them into separate entities, dissolved.

This was it. This was the end.

If she felt fear, it was lost in the cacophony of everything else that became her.

Seven personalities, with all the attendant experiences, memories, and *power*, became one.

There was no more Be'ella Tor, no more Ben, or Bran, or Bravargh, or Baev'ill. No more Bek.

There was only Fae.

She was a river droplet. She'd been as far as the sea. Risen to the sky. Floated in the clouds. Rained upon the mountain. Flowed in the streams. Nourished the ground.

She was the earth, feeding life.

She was a seed. A sprout. A sapling. A tree. A leaf. A flower. A seed again.

She was the sky, and flew with the birds.

She was the ocean current, and swam with the fish within it.

She was the wind that drew the storm.

She was lightning.

She was thunder.

She was fire.

She was burning.

She was lost.

.   .   .

Ty saw the explosion of stars as Bek came apart at the seams. Tiny lights swirled around Fae until she was completely obscured from sight. The force of it pushed him back, and he saw the others in the monument do the same. They stood at the edge of the dais, each member between two towering stone columns, an impossible storm whipping around them.

And then, the wind dropped.

And there was just Fae.

For a moment, she just stood. Halfway between the pillars and the stone at the centre. Eyes closed. Hands down by her sides.

And then she began to glow. At first, it seemed only a trick of the fading light. But the glow continued to build, growing in intensity until Fae shone with power. It brightened, and brightened, forcing Ty to throw his arm up over his face.

Fae burned with a white-hot luminescence. It poured from her skin, spearing out from her nails and wreathing her hair in a magnificent crown of starlight. Her eyes flew open, and instead of ocean-green, sun-drenched rays of light shone forth.

Power licked over her like liquid fire, lifting her from the ground and whipping her hair into a frenzied dance, flickering scattered light-shows across the arced ceiling of the monument.

Cracks splintered across her skin, and light shone beneath.

And her face was pure torment.

Forcing his eyes closed on the spectacle of Fae's ascension to power, Ty hurled his senses outward.

The Whisperers of Arolynos were right, he and his sister *did* have a strong sense for the Aethyr. But neither of them had ever felt the need to test it further, until now.

Now, leveraging his abilities to their fullest, he Listened properly for the first time. And he felt tremendous, unimaginable power. It swirled and tore about, a tornado of energies, clashing and mixing and breaking and churning and spiralling endlessly, over and over.

And in the midst of it all, Fae.

She *was* the storm. Her essence whipped about; a tumult of power with no control.

Fae! Ty called into the chaos, energies crashing and tearing around him. *Fae!*

He clutched hope tight between his fingers, like a kite string that could be ripped from him at any moment in the maelstrom.

And he waited for her voice.

She floated.

In her ball of quiescent lightning, crackling electrical impulses zipped about, flickering quietly around her; not too close, but near enough that if she wanted, she had only to reach out and brush her fingers through the storm. Dancing afterimages burned across her senses. She drifted.

She was a haze of knowing.

She'd known a hundred homes, experienced a thousand lives.

What was life?

Who was she?

She *was...* someone... wasn't she? Underneath it all?

But her sense of self was obscured by countless lifetimes. She had been, she was, and she would be forever more. She was omnipresent.

She was all forces of nature, come together at once.

She was all living beings, past and present.

Who was she?

Fae.

A voice called her. It reached through the storm, lulled, and pulsing benignly around her.

Fae.

A name. She knew that name, didn't she? It felt... significant.

Was it hers?

Fae!

The voice was persistent.

It was... familiar.

It pulled at her.

Perhaps it was important...

The lightning storm sparked, and a flicker of something bright and sharp, licked across her senses. *Pain,* her mind supplied, dredged from a myriad of experiences. It was hot, and quick, and it ripped at the fabric of her.

The storm swirled on, uninterrupted.

A stray streak of lightning sliced through her, and she gasped in the wake of it.

Another burned a line of fire along her skin, and she tensed.

The storm crackled into life, picking up speed once more. It lashed out, a great, slumbering beast awakening with her senses.

Lightning bolts shot past in bursts, barely missing her. She cried out when one more met its mark, white-hot fire sinking into her, burning her through to the core.

The storm's aim became truer with every strike, until all bolts hit home, a barrage of lightning trained directly at her. And with every strike, she was more aware of the person beneath the power.

Of herself.

Until pain splintered it all over again.

Laina watched the spectacle of light in front of her, frozen; torn.

There stood her daughter, her only child, the one she'd thought was lost to her forever. And while she wanted nothing more than to go to her, they didn't know each other. And Fae hadn't shown any desire to rekindle the relationship they'd both missed out on for over fifteen years.

She was just overwhelmed, Laina told herself. *She was as blindsided by all of this as I was by her.* Because whatever she'd expected at the end of the spirits' sirensong, it sure as all things natural wasn't this.

Around the monument, the other members of this strange assembly watched as she did, with varying degrees of awe, distrust, even a droplet of fear. Even Kagos looked mildly impressed.

And in the middle of them all, Fae stood within a cyclone, bursting at the seams with fractured light. Wind whipped about her, pulling her hair in a tight spiral above her head. Light spilled out to cast dancing shadows over the pillars, bringing the stone trees to life. The arches lining the ceiling above were outlined perfectly in the brilliance of Fae's... becoming.

Fae's skin split in a jagged line up her neck, yellow-white light pouring through the gap. Her jaw was clenched, teeth gritted, muscles locked. And though her eyes shone with beacons of yet more light, they were angled harshly in pain.

Is this supposed to happen...? Laina worried, glancing around the others.

Not for the first time that day did she wish for Ben's stolid, pragmatic advice. She already missed his easy, reassuring manner.

But he wasn't here. Fae was.

She looked across at Fae's companion — the elf. His eyes were closed, brows knitted in concentration, deep lines creasing the skin above his nose.

Damn this! Whatever he was doing, he was no help to her right now. Laina pushed forward as far as the storm would allow, leaning into the wind. She planted her feet before Fae, one arm held up in front of her face. Even as she watched, her daughter's face twisted into a look of intense pain, her lips parting to let out an inaudible cry.

"Fae!" Laina yelled, the wind snatching her words away. "Fae—"

But what would she say? *I'm here?* She barely knew her. *You can do this?* Did any of them even know what "this" was? The truth was, she had no idea what Fae was going through.

Bracing her weight through one leg, she pushed forward again. One step. Then another. Until she stood at the heart of the storm. She reached out, grabbing a handful of Fae's cloak. Finally near enough, Laina threw her arms around Fae's shoulders, and gripped her tight.

There was power pouring from her, but it was just power. It had no purpose besides simply being. It did no harm, it just had nowhere to go.

Laina held on with a white-knuckle grip, felt Fae's body rigid with tension. With her face pressed against Fae's cheek, she could hear her teeth grinding viciously inside her mouth.

That she was still conscious, was a miracle in its own right. A body could only take so much...

"Live, Fae," Laina whispered into her ear. "You've got to live."

Ty couldn't say for sure when he noticed the change.

At some point, the storm in Eah'lara turned in on itself. It stopped swirling wildly above, and began to shrink. But it didn't diminish in strength; the power didn't lessen any. It condensed, became more savage — a sword, instead of a shield. A weapon instead of a wall.

The feral bolts of lightning coalesced. They folded inwards and ever inwards, packing into impossibly smaller shapes. Smaller and smaller, until the form began to resemble something recognisable.

And Ty's sense of Fae, swirling among the unfathomable swathe of energy, clarified.

The final motes of the storm gathered, and suddenly, Fae stood before him.

The gasp of air that escaped him when he saw her in one piece was more like a ragged sob. The tension he'd held within him escaped with it, and he stumbled a step towards her.

Fae blinked, her arms slightly extended, as if catching her balance.

She looked... fine. More than fine. She looked ethereal.

Her hair floated about her head like an aurora, luminous and pure and gleaming. Her eyes, usually a conspicuous ocean-green, shone emerald-bright, a halo of gold surrounding them. Her skin was smooth and glowing; the signs of their unforgiving journey north erased. And covering her, like a second skin, were thousands of tiny, hazy, shimmering orbs. They moved across her skin, languid and leisurely, seemingly of their own accord. Some hugged her body, as if basking in her warmth, while others appeared to hover, no more than half an inch from the surface of her. She glittered softly with their light.

Fae, Ty breathed, speechless. She looked truly spiritual. She looked as if she belonged here. Belonged to the Spiritual Realm.

Fae looked up, seeing Ty for the first time. Her face split into a beam to light up a hundred worlds. Then it faltered; the glow surrounding her dimmed a fraction.

Ty, she said, floating to him. Her eyes had clouded over, although the emerald sheen remained. The new gold ring around the green. *Thank you.* She met his eyes, and her expression wasn't one he recognised. *I heard you, and you helped me remember who I was.* Her eyes darted around, as if catching sight of numerous distractions. Ty tried to follow her gaze, but saw nothing but the endless purity of the realm of the Aethyr. *We must return,* she said. *I can see the threads again, the hurt being done.* She followed an invisible strand with her eyes, and frowned.

We mustn't delay. And then she was gone.

Fae opened her eyes, and looked around.

Seven shocked faces looked back.

She wasn't surprised. She finally understood the change in her.

Absorbing six of the Aethyr would have been a feat enough in itself, but the Aethyr that had selected themselves as her guides were among the oldest spirits in the Spirit Realm; those that had spent the longest in the world. They held eons of knowledge. And so much power that even they hadn't known what they gifted her with.

For a while there, she had lost herself in the midst of them, a tiny dust mote in a vast cloud of time.

And then not one, but two voices had called her. Her past, and her present. And she'd heard them. And they'd been just enough to remind the dust mote of who she was.

And why she was here.

She felt reborn. Before, she had been a grey, faded version of herself. Now, she was vibrant, full. She had a purpose, and the means with which to fulfil it.

She was no longer that songbird without a voice. She finally understood what she was always meant to be.

It was invigorating, As if nothing in the world could stop her now.

Fae's lips turned up in a smile when her eyes finally came to rest on Laina. Ty's voice had called to her. But somehow, Laina's had anchored her. She owed her mother a proper reunion, but now was not the time.

In the forge of her becoming, she'd undergone a kind of metamorphosis. She'd emerged deeper, sharper, and polished to a diamond shine. The well of power within her ran so deep, even the parts that made up her new whole didn't know how far it went. Her reach within Eah'lara was endless, the spider-silk webs connecting all life visible to her as clearly as her hands before her face. Here, in the cool air of the Northern Tundra, the threads of spiritkind sparkled into life before her eyes, laid over the world like a fine gauze, criss-crossing through the air. Most glinted healthily, shining bright with the life they represented. But a handful speared away to the south, heavy and black with death.

"Fae?" She turned to find Ty taking a tentative step towards her. He had an uncertain look about him, as if he wasn't entirely sure who stood before him. But there wasn't time to put his mind at ease.

She'd wasted too much time finding her way here already.

A part of her wanted to leave these people here, and skate straight to Throldon along the threads of the Aethyr. It would take her no time at all to evanesce into the Spirit Realm and follow the blackened filaments all the way to Anson. But the beings assembled here on the monument had been brought here for a reason. The Aethyr had guided them to her.

Though they didn't know it, they were here *for her*.

She let her eyes drift over them: two elves, two humans, a dwarf, a centaur, and a dragon. Seven. Her lips kicked up at the corners.

Of course. Seven companions, for the seven parts of her. And the seven parts of her already knew them. Kagos was aloof, condescending, and most importantly, bored. Bored of waiting with the rest of his race to die off. It gave him a sometimes unpleasant edge, but he was good underneath it all. Immrith was awkward and angry, an outsider even among his own kind. He was caring where many of his peers were brash, and it had made his existence a hard one. Aiya was a scholar, and dragonrider. She was timid and painfully under-confident, but had developed an unlikely backbone when it came to Kagos. Jesse was brooding and impatient, and didn't think much of others telling her how to act. But she hated the evil being worked in the foothills of the Rand, and had tired of waiting for a solution to appear out of thin air. Hal sought out the best in people, and always strove to do right by all. He was earnest, and saw the world in simple terms. And he had a personal thread tied to their cause. Laina, her mother, healed wherever she saw hurt, and couldn't turn a soul away. She worked herself to the bone rather than leave someone who needed help untended. And Ty...

She paused. She knew Ty. Strong, dependable, good. Always there. Good-humoured, except when she went out of her way to get hurt. Another healer, and not just in the literal sense.

Ty stared back at her. His eyes burned their dark, storm grey.

Fae looked away, letting her gaze scan out across the land. The fog had long ago cleared, and the sun now skimmed the edge of the world, pooling fiery orange on the horizon. She sighed. These people were a worthy team to have at her back, and hauling them along with her to arrive in a spiritual blackspot in the dark of night would do no one any favours.

She turned back to the assembled team. Her Seven. Her lips twitched again at the irony.

"Let's set camp," she said, and she heard more than one voice pass her lips. "We won't be doing anything this night." She met the eyes of each of them. "I know each one of you, but you don't know me yet. It's time we remedy that."

34

NEW FRIENDSHIPS

K agos was the first to speak up.

"And we're to just... follow your lead, are we?" he said with a sneer.

Fae smiled sweetly. He did not intimidate her.

"You followed Baev'ill here, did you not?" she reminded him. Baev'ill had chosen the form of a nomadic dragon, stopping briefly at Hearthstone before the next leg of his journey. He'd mentioned the turbulence spilling into the corners of the world, alluded that he might investigate it on his way past. "In fact, if memory serves," she continued, "he hardly had to convince you to come. *'Any excuse to get off this death-watch-peninsula,'* I believe were the words. Weren't you looking for just such a thing to combat your ennui?" She arched an eyebrow at the dragon. "A good battle to break up the century?"

Kagos's flat, black gaze narrowed. "But, as you say, I don't know *you.*"

Fae nodded. "You don't know *Fae.*" She indicated herself, in all her human glory. "But you know Baev'ill. He is within me." She swept her arms around. "All of them are within me now. Ask me anything. Anything that any one of them would have known."

Jesse threw down the first gauntlet. "The name of the last inn we stopped at," she challenged.

Fae smiled. "Easy — The Light and Way." She turned. "Next."

Immrith paced uneasily forward. "I once told you my worst fear. Name it." His words lilted easily through her mind, and the part of her that was once Bravargh provided her response.

"That the visions of your *Ateth Legarrh* are known by the elders of your clan," she answered softly, the guttural syllables of Equi'tox flowing effortlessly from her. The *Ateth Legarrh* was the Equiann coming of age ceremony, and the only time a centaur ever communed with spiritkind. She added, "They are not. Your elders speak truthfully, when they say the visions are for you alone." She held his gaze until he nodded acceptance. Then she turned to Kagos. "Next," she challenged.

The dragon answered her look with one of his own. He considered her for a long moment.

Then, with a curl of his lips, "Name me."

"Ha!" Fae laughed, a genuine laugh. It was very clever. No human could ever speak his true name. Because only a dragon in full form could speak Draconic. It wasn't a case of learning a new language, but rather of having the anatomy to do so. However...

She angled her face to glare at him from beneath severe eyebrows. And smiled.

It was all for theatrics, of course. She could do this from twenty miles away without a backwards glance.

Kaaghharr'ochsalith! she roared directly into his mind, anatomy be damned. It was the only way for her to properly speak his name.

Draconic, to hear, was a sound from the mountains themselves. It was all tumbling rocks and scraping landfalls. It was hard to hear, but held a wild beauty to those who understood its nuances. And of course, with no lips needed to utter the rough and rugged sounds, Fae was able to enunciate every tone.

Kagos, to his credit, showed no outward sign of having heard a thing. But he uttered a reluctant "hm", and buried his hands even further up the sleeves of his robes.

Fae could almost see Baev'ill dusting his hands off, a smug look on his nutmeg-brown face. The part of her that came from Bran was also enjoying this immensely — perhaps a bit *too* much. But her overarching feeling was her need to convince them of her authenticity. Time spent shooting down questions and doubts was time wasted.

I need them to trust me by morning, she thought, eyeing the puddle of sunlight throwing colours up into the clouds. *That's when I take whoever's with me to Throldon.* The last of the sun disappeared below the horizon, but the dark was held at bay by a soft light within the monument. Fae looked down, and saw that the glow was emanating from her own skin.

"Um..." She cleared her throat awkwardly, glancing at her luminous hands. She wasn't sure if she could control it — she wasn't even consciously aware she was doing anything. She wondered if it made the others uncomfortable.

"I'll get a fire going," Hal said into the uneasy silence.

"Yes." Laina leapt at the change of topic. "Let's have some dinner. It's been a long day."

Ty looked suddenly sheepish. "I'm afraid we don't have anything to add to the pot," he said. "We ran out of provisions a few days back."

"Figures," Jesse said blandly, throwing her pack onto the huge central stone. "The innkeeper I bought my supplies from was a bit overenthusiastic. I have plenty."

"Us too," Laina offered. "We'd be happy to share." Hal nodded his agreement.

Kagos made a noise halfway between a huff of air and a grunt. "I hunt my own food," he said, and stepped off the dais, into the night. His departure was appended by the earth-shuddering, avalanche-sound of his transition to full dragon form, and deafening wing-beats blew great gusts of wind through the monument before fading into the distant sky.

Fae glanced at Aiya, who remained behind.

"Don't worry," Aiya said, a blush rising to the visible portion of her cheeks at the attention. "He'll be back." She fidgeted where she stood. "You wouldn't believe it, but he doesn't like being the centre of attention."

"I hope it's not rude to ask," Ty said, "but why are you here with him?" He jerked his chin to the darkening sky into which Kagos had disappeared.

Aiya flushed an even deeper shade of red before she answered. "I'm Kagos's rider," she explained. "I was partnered with him when I turned twenty-one; we've been flying together for a hundred years. We're a team. It's... more efficient to have a rider assist a dragon than for them to have to change forms all the time."

Fae nodded her understanding, although Baev'ill had noticed the way

Aiya watched Kagos on the journey here. Seen the feelings that went beyond being part of a working team. Feelings that, by the looks of it, weren't reciprocated. And she sincerely hoped the rider wouldn't end up burned by something that fundamentally couldn't be.

She turned to Immrith, half expecting the centaur to follow Kagos's example, and disappear into the night.

"You're welcome to our fire," she said to him, switching to the language of Equi'tox. "If you would care to join us."

Immrith looked as though he might demur. Then Hal's fire flared into life, casting the monument in a more familiar kind of warm glow. Immrith's dark-amber eyes seemed to burn with their own fire as they flicked to the slowly growing flames. He inclined his head after a brief pause.

"I would be glad to share your fire," he replied formally. Then he stepped up to Fae, such that she had to arch her neck to look at him. "I understand your words when you speak, but these others speak differently." He glanced over at the fire, where Ty, Hal, Laina, Jesse, and Aiya were gathering. "I do not understand them." His face showed little outward sign of his unease, but Fae saw the characteristically small markers of conflicting feelings in his expression. The centaurs of the far Northern Tundra were not an emotional race. Back at home, one might have asked him why he was so upset. But here, among this group, no one would know the difference. Fae reached up and grasped his arm. Bravargh had travelled leagues upon leagues with Immrith. And so, had Fae.

"They speak a common tongue," she said, "but I can translate, if you'll allow it?" She refrained from speaking directly into his mind. The spirit quests of Equi'tox were a sacred thing, and she did not want to step on consecrated ground by emulating their methods of communication.

Immrith nodded at her offer. "That is kind. My thanks."

Fae chanced a smile, a rare thing for a centaur, and turned toward the fire. As she approached, Ty looked up. His face bore signs of fatigue, not to mention the beginnings of starvation, and dark hollows beneath his eyes. But he lit up when she smiled over at him. He opened his mouth to speak, and stopped dead. His ears twitched, and his head spun around to stare into the night.

Fae cocked her head, listening.

"Hello on the mount!" came a call from beyond the circle of firelight.

She glanced across at Ty, whose eyes had gone wide. His arm snaked out towards the long oilcloth, ever-present, strapped to the side of his pack. But he needn't have worried.

The flickering glow of firelight licked over three tall figures, striding towards them, the night's shadows obscuring their features until they stepped onto the dais. And stopped.

"Ty?"

Ty blinked. "Wil?"

Three elves stepped forward, looking as if they'd stepped into a dream. Wil's eyes were round and incredulous.

"What are *you* doing here?" he demanded with a little less decorum than was normally expected when addressing an Eldra.

"I could say the same to you!" Ty replied, although it was clear he hadn't thought any further ahead than that.

They stood, staring at each other, at a loss as to what else to say.

Aren and Stef stepped forward to stand either side of Wil, two dark sentries. Stef let his gaze sweep over the group, taking in the eclectic members without a word. Aren spotted Fae, and gave a little wave.

"Hullo, Fae!" he said. Then paused. "You appear to be glowing." Fae grinned at his attempt to lighten the mood, despite his own wide-eyed shock.

"Yes," she said. "And I'm not quite sure how to stop."

"Huh," he said.

"Weren't you supposed to be going to Throldon?" she asked, when further words failed him.

He looked around at those gathered, as if he might find the answer to her question among them. "Well," he began, "yes. But, if you remember, we went looking for Elisabeth Marl, didn't we? Turns out she isn't in Throldon." He scratched at the back of his head.

Laina rose one hand slowly into the air. Aren started, and stared at her. He pointed a polite finger in her direction, the look on his face asking, *that's you, is it?*

Laina nodded, lowering her hand.

"Huh," Aren said again, letting his own hand drop to his side.

"*We've* been following the trail of Elisabeth Marl since Throldon," Wil said, staring at Laina while still addressing Ty. His eyes flicked to Fae and quickly skirted away again. He turned back to Ty. "What are *you* doing here?" he repeated.

It was Fae's turn to raise a hand on the air. "That's my fault," she said, wondering where to begin. The whole point of waiting for her Seven to arrive was so that she only had to explain once. "It's a long story."

Jesse snorted. "Yes, apparently it goes all the way back to the birth of the gods themselves," she said dryly.

Fae burst out laughing. Bek would have found Jesse's dry wit hilarious. It had been lost on the overly observant Bran. Well, she *was* Bek now, as well as Bran, among others. The thought had her giggling all over again. She looked across at Wil and Ty to share the joke, but they weren't laughing. No one was. Sobering quickly, she cleared her throat.

"Um, yes, as I said, it's a long story." She glanced across at the fire that Hal had crackling merrily away to one side, and caught her mother's eye. Laina's lips twitched, her eyes sparkling with quiet mirth, coaxing a smile back onto Fae's face. "But it's late. Let's share a meal, and any questions you have, we can answer together."

Aren glanced hesitantly from his two companions, to the fire, skirting past Immrith, Hal, and Jesse in between. When it appeared no one was about to make the first move, he strode into the ring of firelight and dropped to the ground beside Hal.

"Well, I wouldn't say no to a hot meal," he said with a grateful sigh. "It's been a long day. Long month, in fact." He rummaged around in his pack. "I've some nuts and berries I managed to dry a way back, could add some flavour. I think Stef still has some apples he's squirrelled away—"

"Apples?" Ty's ears pricked up. He looked across at Aren's brother, still standing warily beside Wil. Stef's eyes bounced between his brethren by the fire, and the strangers still wearing guarded expressions.

Jesse came to her own conclusions, and gave a shrug that seemed to say, *do what you want,* before taking a place by the fire and pulling out her own contributions from her oversized pack. Laina waved Fae over. Hal began setting up a tripod.

Fae glanced up at Immrith, who still eyed Wil and Stef with a natural-born suspicion of the unknown. She placed a hand on his arm. Immrith stiffened, and then looked down at her.

"They are friends," she murmured. "Unexpected, but still friends."

The dark amber of Immrith's gaze held hers, and he nodded. He cast one last look at the new arrivals, and turned toward the fire.

Finally, Will and Stef approached. Wil gave her an inscrutable look, before walking past to murmur something in Ty's ear. Stef stepped up beside her, wearing his own thoughtful expression.

"Where did you learn Old Equiann?" he said eventually, his eyes of polished steel shimmering in the firelight.

Fae smiled. "A friend called Bravargh," she answered truthfully. "But it's not quite that simple." She indicated the fire, inviting him over. Jesse and Hal were chopping and throwing food into a pot, while Aren offered 'helpful' suggestions.

Fae took a seat beside Immrith, the better to translate for him. Stef sat with Wil, beside Ty and Aiya, who had kept mostly quiet during the proceedings. Aren was deep in animated conversation with Laina and Hal, Jesse occasionally tutting and rolling her eyes beside him.

"So," Wil said abruptly, "what *have* we missed?" Everyone fell silent. Fae opened her mouth to answer, to begin the whole story again, when Hal spoke up.

"Do you mind if I tell it?" he said. "Want to make sure I understood it right." Everyone looked at the simply-spoken ranger. Colour rose beneath his scratchy beard at the attention, but he waited calmly for Fae's response. Stunned, she nodded, extending an arm, inviting him to take the floor.

Hal cleared his throat. "So in the beginning, before all of us lot, before the gods even, there was a Spirit, and she loved the world..." His voice carried clear across the crackle of the campfire, and the group fell silent listening to his tale. Fae relayed his version quietly to Immrith, careful not to interrupt Hal's flow. He had a voice perfect for story-telling, deep and mellow, and Fae felt herself lulled by his words.

By the time he'd finished, the stewed mix in the pot was ready to share out. Jesse and Laina spooned some into the odd assortment of bowls or cups belonging to each individual, and they all sat back to eat.

"So Anson's the reason the Rebel Unity started?" Aren asked halfway through his meal. Hal glanced at Fae. She waved her spoon at him, indicating he was welcome to answer. He'd remembered all of it, including Laina's part in the story. She was glad. The ranger was easy to like, unthreatening, and all those assembled appeared to have fallen into an effortless rhythm with him already.

Fae smiled. The arrival of Wil and his team had eased some of the tensions in the group. And despite having to explain everything again, it provided the perfect opportunity for everyone to air any doubts, ask any questions.

Before they dived straight into the darkness.

Fae shook the shadows from her mind. Tonight was a time for new friends, new alliances.

Tomorrow was another day.

35

PROUD PEOPLE

K agos returned some time in the night. When they awoke in the morning, it was to find him standing between two of the monument's vast pillars, outlined in the glow of the rising sun. He stood with his back to them, paying no mind to the others as they rose and sat about discussing the evening's story.

"So," Jesse said, waving her water-skin about to emphasise her point, "you're saying humans don't even name Anson as one of their gods? Even now? There are loads of half-forgotten religions among humanity's 'countless gods' — surely he's in there somewhere?"

Laina wore a wry smile, shaking her head. "Not that I've ever heard of," she said. "We created the countless gods out of thin air to suit our purposes, or so I thought." She cast a sidelong glance at Hal. "I never believed in any of them, even as a girl. And I had to endure morning sermons in the keep." She lowered her gaze. "That was a long time ago."

"Aye," said Hal, scratching under his beard. "Always did say we got too many o' them. The Mother makes sense, but I never did see a mother need so much help looking after her children."

"Oh, Mother Nature is real for sure," Laina said. "You only have to watch a tide turn, or the birth of a new babe, or a flower turn to face the sun, to see it." She turned to Fae. "Or, I suppose that's Aethyreomma, the Mother Spirit?"

Fae shook her head with a smile. "Not quite," she said. "Nature goes about its ways regardless of spiritual input. It's different, now that the Aethyr live within the natural elements. But we simply follow its own inclinations." She shrugged an apology. "I'm sorry, but I've yet to encounter a 'Mother Nature'." She gestured to herself. "No one in here has. The world dances to its own tune. That's the beauty of it."

"Pfft." A snort of derision came from the edge of the dais, making them jump. Fae turned in time to see Kagos turn from his position at the pillars.

"Kagos," she said.

"The gods are a joke," he continued, as if she hadn't spoken. "They always were." He moved towards them, a storm brewing behind his eyes. He hadn't spared so much as a glance towards the three new additions to their group, and didn't bother now. "Dragonkind have called this earth home since before the time of the gods. We soared the skies and fished the seas when they were rife with creatures now only told of in stories. But these 'gods' you speak of had nothing to do with us. They didn't watch over us. Didn't gift us with any virtues. Didn't intercede when the mortal wars spilled dragons' blood." Kagos shook with rage, his face contorted with eons of pain and wrath. His voice rumbled like a mountain sundered, the depth of it vibrating through the stone of the dais. "We were born upon the earth when it was nothing but rock and rain. We've been around so long we're dying out! What say you to that? Where is our piece in the history?" His eyes gleamed obsidian black, his nostril slits flared as he stared Fae down.

She looked upon him, and her heart wept with sadness. Within her, the memories of Be'ella Tor surged to the fore.

"Dragonkind ruled before the Spirit Mother first saw the world. We know this. But in the beginning, She was content to watch. To witness. She watched the earth grow, and She marvelled at the magnificence of dragonkind. So in awe of your kind was She, that She let them be. To soar, and fish. To be." Unable to meet his eyes anymore, Fae's gaze dropped to the floor. A single tear rolled down her cheek. A wave of grief crested in her. She mourned for the loss of the dragons, who now numbered among the tens, where once they were thousands. She mourned for their solitude, for the freedom that was stolen from them when the mortal races warred. She *remembered* their glorious forms blotting out the sun as they filled the sky. Glittering wings of blue and green, scales of gold and crimson, they coloured a world that had yet to grow its own.

And the Spirit Mother had been filled with joy to see them. And so, She had let them be.

But now, with Kagos and all his fury standing before her, Fae could see that had been a mistake. Dragonkind were a proud people, and rightly so. And the slight had carried through the generations, almost until their end.

Fae straightened, squeezing the wetness from her eyes. She opened them to meet Kagos's molten obsidian gaze.

"We cannot change the past," she said. "I cannot take back what is done. And for that — for what it's worth — I am sorry." She swallowed as lines flared around Kagos's eyes. "But let us write a new line in history. Dragonkind have ever been custodians of this world. Let's have them remembered as such. Let's end this scourge on the earth, together. And rid it of the last tattered scrap of a god that wrought so much pain on your people." She paused, trying to read the face in front of her.

Kagos's eyes were narrowed to slits, the liquid black gleaming at her from behind an expression so guarded it could have been a fortress. She resisted the urge to glimpse at his energy from within the Spirit Realm; she needed him to trust her, to follow her. Taking a peek behind the curtain would win her no favours in that regard.

If possible, he narrowed his eyes imperceptibly further.

"Kagos..." Aiya murmured, imploring with a single word.

"I know," he snapped. Took a breath. He fixed Aiya with a look only a fraction softer than the one he'd gifted Fae. "I know."

He squared his shoulders toward Fae, drawing himself up. "I have already taken time to think on this," he said, "and I know my anger is not for you. You are right to say this poor excuse for a god was the beginning of all the ill that befell dragonkind. And you are right to say that he must be excised from the world." He paused, as if steeling himself for what came next.

"But I cannot help you."

Fae blinked. Aiya performed a full double-take. Her face displayed the same shock as Fae's.

"Did *not* see that coming," Aren whispered behind her.

Kagos sent him a withering glare. "It might seem surprising to you, whose people numbers among the thousands, but I have a duty to my own kind. One that comes before the wars of mankind."

"What duty is that?" Hal said quietly, but all heard him.

Kagos's eyes flared even blacker. He turned to the ranger.

"*What?*" His voice was frosty enough to chill even the Tundra air.

"What duty?" Hal repeated, with the open expression of one asking a simple question.

"The guarding of dragonkind, the First Ones, against the fate of this world. We are an ancient race, and the few who remain are old beyond compare, with eons of history in their very bones. I will not abandon them for the sake of a few humans."

Aiya stood agape at his words, as if she were hearing an entirely different person speak. Laina's lips thinned to a pencil-thin line.

Hal nodded. "Alright," he said. "Just wondered."

Ty was less satisfied. "But if Anson's influence carries on unabated, the very Aethyr within the world will perish — if it isn't already happening! The land will die around you. It will only accelerate the demise of dragonkind. You do your people a disservice if you *don't* help!"

"I will decide who I serve!" Kagos hissed dangerously. "And the land was fine before the Aethyr. It will survive. Besides," he cast a blistering look about the group, "it has champions enough without my input." His robe billowed and snapped as he turned. "Aiya!" he barked, and she jumped wildly. Without a backwards glance, Kagos swept from the monument.

Aiya gaped after him. She turned back, her eyes on the stones beneath their feet, and mumbled something apologetic into the collar of her coat before scurrying after him. The avalanche-crashing of Kagos's transition to his full dragon form seemed particularly pointed, and Fae had to grit her teeth through the bone-jarring vibrations of it. The sun darkened as a vast, winged silhouette passed before it, Kagos banking back south, towards the Hearthstone Mountains.

When his great, sweeping wings could no longer be heard beating against the cool, northern breeze, Fae swallowed a cold lump of disappointment, and turned to those that remained.

"I'd be grateful if any others not wishing to aid in our quest speak up now." Her eyes moved between each of them. "I intend to leave for Throldon today."

There was a moment of stillness; of silence.

Then, Jesse shrugged her shoulders. "I'm here aren't I?" she said simply, and turned back to her cold breakfast. She took a mouthful of oats, and waved her spoon in the air. "There's a reason a smarmy teenage boy convinced me to come out here and it wasn't his winning personality." The part of Fae that came from Bran smirked. "There are humans filling dwarven villages because they have nowhere else to go, and spring is ominously late coming to the Rand. Something's going on, and I didn't come all the way out here to turn back now."

"I'm with you," Laina said.

Hal nodded by her side. "Aye," he said.

Fae turned to Immrith. She'd forgotten to translate Kagos's final words for him, but he looked to have gotten the gist of it.

"The *Ateth Legarrh* showed me I would leave my clan's lands one day," he said, "for a purpose beyond any the elders would even know. I have never ventured beyond our borders before I met Bravargh, and no one I know has ever left Equi'tox. I felt fear." His face broke into a sudden smile, and in an instant he had the look of a man twenty years younger. "But now I have crossed the Barren Lands, and seen a dragon in full form!" He laughed, deep, and wild, and free. "I am no longer afraid of what is to come!"

Fae grinned back, raising one eyebrow. "Well," she said, "a little fear is healthy, eh? Keeps you thinking." She tapped the side of her head.

"Ha!" Immrith bellowed, as if what she'd said was the funniest thing in the world. He clapped her on the shoulder, and it made her bones shake. "I will come with you, *fae'yha* one," he said, using the Old Equiann word for 'of the spirits'. "Count on it." And he turned and walked away.

Fae watched him go, somewhat confused. Bravargh hadn't seen this side of Immrith in all their many weeks of travel. She decided it was good to see him smile.

"Fae." She turned to find Ty standing behind her.

He shifted uneasily from one foot to the other, and his eyes couldn't quite meet hers. He looked as if he was trying to work up the courage to introduce himself to someone intimidating.

"You don't have to look so nervous," she said. "I'm still me. Just... more." She shrugged, completely underprepared for how to explain her new enhanced state.

Ty's lips twitched with a shadow of a smile. "Then you already know I'm with you." He leant in, storm-grey eyes blazing. "If it were to the ends of the earth, I would still go with you."

The intensity of his words were such that Fae unconsciously took a step back. She parted her lips to respond, but no words seemed enough. Her mind was blank, for the first time since opening her eyes as seven-become-one.

"If there's room on your quest for extras, we'll join you." Wil stepped up beside Ty, dropping a hand onto his shoulder. "We were sent to find Elisabeth Marl," he added, mistaking the blank look on Fae's face for one of confusion. "It seems only right for us to assist her, especially when her goals align so perfectly with ours."

Aren came up behind Wil, pulling him to the side. "Wil! Can't you see they're having a moment?"

Wil frowned at the interruption. "*What* are you talking about?"

Aren shot Fae an apologetic glance, and dragged Wil away.

Fae turned back to Ty. "Ty..." she started, not in any way sure of what to say next. There was more between them than friendship — there had been for a while — and both of them knew it. But now wasn't the time.

Ty understood without her needing to speak another word. "It's okay," he said with a nod. He glanced at the unlikely team around them. "This takes precedent."

Fae nodded, relief plain upon her face. "We'll talk—" she said, seeking to reassure him.

"—After." He finished her train of thought. "Until then, we'll just continue as we were. Before." Before the Aethyr wept. Before she took six of them into herself, and became a new whole. The part of her that had known him most of her life bent towards him like a flower towards the sun, but there was more to her now, and bigger problems that required her attention.

"*Thank you*," she mouthed, and got a crooked smile in return.

Her eyes caught on one glittering thread, visible only to her, as it shimmered across her vision. Ty tried to follow her gaze. "What do you see?" he asked, turning his head slowly as if to track her line of sight.

She jolted from her reverie. "The threads," she said, tracing her finger along a pair that ran just past her elbow. "They connect everything. And they're everywhere. It seems so strange that I never saw them before." Ty nodded, still looking around, as if he might catch a glimpse of one.

She turned to the rest of the group, and conversations cut off mid-flow as all eyes instantly snapped to her.

"The Aethyr weep in Throldon," she said. She could feel it thrumming through her, her very blood diluted by the tears of their pain. "And the darkness that chases them is spreading. We know the recent acceleration of that spread coincides with Tamra Walker taking over the Unity. She is the new link to Anson, and she is where we must begin." Fae cast an eye about the group.

"Unless anyone else has a different idea?"

There was a pause. And then Jesse cleared her throat.

"Not to burst your bubble, or anything," she said, "but other than 'that's where we start,' what's your plan?"

Fae went to answer, and then realised she didn't have one. She looked within herself, scouring her seven source personalities for a scrap of a plan.

Come on guys, she thought, *you didn't have a plan before you dragged me into this?*

"What did the dwarf say?" Immrith asked. Fae translated. "She is right. Even the youngest filly knows you need a battle plan!"

"I know, I know!" Fae said. "I get the feeling that each of the Aethyr within me was hoping one of the others would think of it." But even Be'ella Tor had been thrown by Anson's jump to a new host. "Killing Malcolm Stuart would have unmoored Anson enough to dispel him. But it sounds as if this Black Lady will be much harder to get to."

"How do we get to her in the first place?" Wil asked. "We're hundreds of leagues away, and under-provisioned at that."

"I guess Kagos would have been mighty useful on that count if he wasn't such a pompous ass." Jesse grumbled.

"Actually," Fae said, "*I* was going to transport *him*. And all of you."

"How?" Immrith was the one to ask.

Fae grinned. "There's a little short-cut," she said.

"Through Eah'lara."

36

A THOUSAND TINY STITCHES

There was a moment of stunned silence.

"Aye," Hal said slowly. "That doesn't exactly sound like somewhere we can go." He gestured around at the flesh-and-blood beings assembled. "What with us not being spirits and all."

"Neither was I, when the Aethyr brought me to Arolynos," Fae said, with a slowly spreading smile. "But they did it."

"But you were already part-spirit," Laina pointed out.

Fae shook her head. "That doesn't matter. I was born human, with a human body. *That's* the part that needed transport." She shrugged. "Besides, that's not the only time the Aethyr have intervened in mortal lives. Regardless—" she changed topic switchblade-fast "—I will be the one to get us to Throldon." She plucked at the blackened threads that lay that way. "Or at least, as close as the web allows."

"The web?" Wil asked.

"Mm," Fae said. "The web that connects us all. All life on this earth is connected. Some of it directly — like a tree to the ground — some have to make a few stops along the way." She smiled at her own little joke. "But all, inevitably, connected." She lifted a hand to trace a finger along the path of threads only she could see. "These ones are sickening; I don't know how long the journey, but they represent the most direct route to the root of the problem." She chuckled. And grew somber again. "And time isn't a luxury we're blessed with."

Wil nodded. "Alright then. Aside from how we get there, what is it we actually aim to do once we're there?"

Immrith caught Fae's eye as the others turned to murmuring conversation.

"We're back to asking what the plan is," she translated, her mind filling with the chatter of multiple perspectives and opinions on the matter. The bold side of her from Baev'ill wanted to rush in and damn the consequences, the level-headed view from Ben and Bek urged caution and planning. All parts of her had differing points to make, and it made her head ache. She rubbed a hand against her brow with the exasperation of a mother trying to coerce a flock of children to cooperate.

"Do you want me to do that?" She turned to see Stef, ever the strong, silent type, standing beside her. He inclined his head to Immrith. *"Do eb'tal ichrar each sinch'ell Equith, go do no'ah sattr'ch?"* — "I speak a little Equiann, if I may help?"

Fae's eyes widened in surprise. "Where did *you* learn Old Equiann?" she gasped, repeating his own words back at him.

The corner of his mouth twitched so slightly she almost didn't notice, and he tapped the side of his nose with one long finger. "We learnt many things at my father's side before becoming scouts in our own right." He gestured towards Aren, who was talking animatedly with Hal and Laina. "I was always better at listening than my brother."

Fae suppressed a laugh. "I bet." She turned back to Immrith. "Would you mind if Stef translates for you?"

"Not at all," he said in his rough, lilting language. "It will be good to speak plainly with more than just one." He held out his arm, and Stef clasped it firmly. Fae eyed them for a second, and smiled to herself. Both strong, both men of few words. She couldn't have chosen a better match for either of them among this group.

Which gives me an idea.

"Okay," she said, addressing their group once more. "We don't know what we're facing when we get to Throldon—"

"It's not pretty," Aren chimed in. "Hovels and shanty housing. Gangs going around, beating on people just because they can. Hungry and hollow-eyed children..." He petered out, the shadows of horrible scenes playing behind his eyes.

"And that won't be the worst of it," Fae said gently, picking up his narrative. "I still don't know where we'll land, nor where Black is — other than the city — nor how heavily she's guarded. We may need to split up. We may become separated, despite our best intentions." Her eyes flicked to where Stef stood beside Immrith. "We should partner up, before we leave. Then if we get separated, everyone should have at least one ally beside them." Her eye caught on Hal, who was waving a finger in the air. "Hal?"

"...Eight, nine." He finished his headcount, ending with Fae. "There are nine of us," he said. "Pairs don't work."

"Three's a better number anyway," Aren said with a nod at his two fellow scouts. "But you're right. Trying to keep a group as big as this together is going to be tricky, and conspicuous. Smaller groups of three is a much better plan."

"Okay, three it is," Fae said. She did some quick thinking. "Every team should have a healer. So Laina, Ty, and I should divide ourselves between the groups." Ty and Laina made a poor show of hiding how they felt about being separated from her, but they kept it to themselves. "Stef and Immrith will stay together." They nodded their agreement in succinct synchrony. Fae looked about the group.

A couple of uneasy glances were being passed between people who'd only met bare hours ago. It was one thing to share a campfire and compare stories with a stranger, quite another to go into battle with one at your back.

"We'll split up too," Wil said with a nod to Aren.

Aren pulled himself up. "There are no senses keener than those of an elven scout," he boasted. "It would be senseless of us to hoard our skills in one team if we are to succeed together."

"I'll go with him," Jesse jerked a thumb at Aren. "Someone needs to keep him tethered to the ground."

"Good luck," Wil replied dryly. Aren shot him a short-lived scowl.

"I'll be their healer," Laina volunteered, taking a step closer to her newfound team.

"Ladies, please." Aren shone his most charming smile at them. "There's only one of me."

They ignored him.

"I'll go with Stef," Ty said, moving over to stand beside the scout and centaur.

Fae looked over them, the edge of something bittersweet welling within her. She felt a twinge of regret that she couldn't stick to either of them, like she wanted to so badly. But, glancing over the group, she felt a tapestry of pride for every single one of them, stitched together from years of donated experiences with each of them.

"Wil, Hal," she said, "that leaves us together."

"The best o' the bunch then," the ranger replied. Wil chuckled appreciatively. Fae grinned. Humour was good. It brought people together. And that's what they needed right now above all else. It was the only thing that would save them all.

Because she sure as Eah didn't have all the answers.

"Okay, so this is all very lovely," Jesse said, "with our cute little teams. But what are we actually *doing?*" She looked about for answers, her dark eyes coming to rest on Fae. "Eh?"

Fae sighed. She was the only one with any hope, any hints of what came next.

"Okay," she said, holding her hands out, palms forward. "Let me... have a word with myself." She cringed, then placed her palms together. "A moment, please." Turning her back on them, she walked to edge of the dais, and sat on the steps, looking out over the Northern Tundra. The day was uncharacteristically clear, and she breathed in a lungful of crisp, clean air, before blowing it slowly over her lips. She closed her eyes.

While her body sat on an ancient stone dais, as far from civilisation as mattered, her mind slipped into Eah'lara.

In her visions, and before taking in her Aethyr guides, Fae had experienced the Spirit Realm as an endless, purest white. Now, she saw diaphanous pastels rippling across it like celestial nebulae; millions of glittering spirit-particles drifting through space, interspersed with shimmering, star-like orbs.

The orbs — hazy, softly glowing balls of light; Aethyr *not* currently occupying the world — floated lazily through Eah'lara, passing time as Aethyr-in-waiting. Every now and then, one would start to shrink, fading slowly until it popped through the fabric of the Spirit Realm, and into the world. All that remained to indicate its presence was a tiny gap in a newly connected thread, like the smallest stitch in a hand-sewn quilt.

Fae watched the shimmer of thousands of spider-silk filaments as they hung poised between the Aethyr, tacked in place by the lifeforms they accompanied. The threads around her spread from the furthest reaches of her vision in one direction, to the same extent the opposite way, interrupted only by the tell-tale pinprick of an earthly life. Some shone bright gold, others verdant green. There were vivid crimsons and deep ocean-blues. All had the silvery edge of the most delicate, gossamer-thin silk. Those were the healthy ones. What they *should* look like.

But the threads that held Fae's attention were thick and blackened, the signs of an Aethyr trying desperately to hold on. When the lifeform connected to an Aethyr passed on, it was natural for the connection to drop, the filaments to fade, and a floating orb to reappear in Eah'lara. But if the lifeform yet lived, and the Aethyr in residence couldn't maintain the connection...

What on earth is going on over there? Fae thought, not for the first time. She traced the blackened threads south, running her senses along the line the same way a harpist plays her fingers across her instrument's strings.

There weren't many orbs around the monument — there weren't an abundance of Aethyr waiting around for grasses. But as Fae followed the path of the sickening threads, the number of orbs increased. The threads changed in colour from mostly greens and yellows and browns, to bolder, brighter shades of red, and orange, and blue. The nebulous backdrop reflected the carnival of colour in the threads, woven into a vivid tapestry; a diversity of life around her.

But the dark, sickly threads dived on, through the oasis of colour and on, further south.

Fae conjured a map of Arland in her mind before remembering that the web rarely had anything to do with real-world geography. She could have passed through an aspect of Oresh, or Greneln, or even shot north to Equi'tox before arrowing south again to Throldon — not the most direct path, but then the connections that bound people together never were.

She traced the black filaments through further greenery, on through sparsely populated regions, and past areas teeming with life — though not always human. There were points at which the life she sensed was purely plant, and others when it was clearly animal. The areas occupied by people were plain in their vitality, bursting with colours that rarely occurred naturally. But the black threads, too, grew in frequency, and in density. The further she traced them, the more she saw arrowing in towards her trajectory. The colours retreated, receding from the blackness like the tide from the shore.

And then the threads stopped.

37

DARK FOG

The threads of the Aethyr curled back on themselves, just short of a bank of featureless, dark fog.

They recoiled, as if revolted by what lay before them. The pastel colours stopped dead, and the murky, dark grey extended onwards.

There were no more threads to follow; none penetrated the gloom.

Fae backtracked to the last pinpricks in the threads, and extended her senses through the weakness in the fabric separating Eah'lara from the world. The part of her that came from Be'ella Tor knew exactly what she was doing — taking a quick peek at the lifeform that anchored the thread here — but she herself was astounded by it. It felt like ducking her head underwater, her face breaking the surface to peer at the ocean beneath. It was at once as natural as breathing, and utterly unbelievable.

I could just as easily be dreaming.

What she found, just the other side of the veil, were a handful of forest critters that had taken over an abandoned village. They chittered happily at the abundance of food left behind, and squeaked nervously at every sound.

Fae frowned. She had hoped to skate straight into Throldon, ideally right to Lady Black's doorstep, perhaps even the suburbs. *But my luck isn't that good, it would seem.* She poked around some more, peeking through at the world a few more times, but the closest Eah'lara took her to the city was a small settlement built up around a watermill, not unlike the village she'd walked through with Ty and Bek, what felt like years before.

It was a wrench, turning her back on the problem all seven parts of her had set out to correct, but she gritted her teeth and did it regardless, because she needed the others. They were important.

When Fae opened her eyes back on the world, it was with a dizzying sense of having travelled leagues in the blink of an eye. She swayed where she sat, and squeezed her eyes closed again, shutting out the lurching horizon. When she finally reopened them, it was to see that the sun had reached the apex of its slow arc across the southern sky.

I've been gone for hours! She checked herself. Not that many. It was early spring. Sunrise and sunset hadn't yet grown so far apart as to make strangers of dawn and noon. *Perhaps two or three,* she amended. That was good. That would work.

Fae stood, and turned back to the unlikely collection of people sharing a midday meal on the mount.

Immrith spotted her first, and raised a hand. "Welcome back," he said.

Stef turned at his words, nodding a wordless greeting. Ty watched her with worry lines carving deep grooves in his face.

"Find anything enlightening?" Jesse asked, handing her a plate of food from mixed sources. Fae took it gratefully and set it aside. She couldn't bring herself to think of eating.

"I can't reach the city," she said without preamble, "but I can get close. There's a watermill just beyond the suburbs — that's as far as I could reach before the dark fog."

"Dark fog?" Laina asked.

Fae nodded. "You'll see," she said. Describing it just wouldn't do it justice.

Jesse sat back on her heels. "Okay," she said. "So we've got to make our way *into* Throldon from the outskirts, then find this 'lady', get close enough to her, and then finally... what? Fight her? Then what?"

"Leave that bit to me," Fae said, speaking with a confidence of one of her Aethyr guides, but she wasn't sure which. It felt like Baev'ill: reckless, wild, and vastly overconfident. *But is it overconfidence, if it's rightly placed?* She rolled her eyes at her own thoughts. Definitely Baev'ill.

"Getting into Throldon isn't hard," Wil said, cleaning a pair of twin daggers. "We slipped in with no trouble at all. Just had to play rough to blend in." Lines bracketed his mouth at the reminder, an expression that was mirrored on Aren and Stef's faces.

"It's funny you mention the fog though," Aren said, tapping his finger in the air. "The place was thick with it when we walked through, wasn't it?" He directed the latter to his brother, who nodded in agreement. "I wonder if it's relevant."

Fae's brow furrowed. "We have no way of knowing at this point." She shrugged. "But Jesse's right. Finding Black will be our greatest challenge."

"Well, the residents of Throldon's *'suburbs'*—" Aren scowled, as if the outskirts of the city didn't deserve to be referred to in such a civilised terms "—they were happy enough to talk to us, weren't they?" He looked to his fellow scouts.

Wil snorted. "I'm not sure about 'happy', but they talked to us."

"They were scared," Stef added.

"*My point is,*" Aren said loudly, gifting his brethren with a glare, "that we could scout out the city easily enough and work out a fairly accurate picture of things once we get there." He feigned a nonchalant shrug. "It wasn't like the people shut us down; they were willing enough to tell us what was going on."

"Well it doesn't look like we have much of a choice in any case," Wil said. "But at least in that regard, it's no different from any other scouting trip."

"Excellent." Aren clapped his hands together with the air of a job well done. "So Fae will transport us to Throldon. Once there, we'll do a bit of digging around the city and work out where Black is located. Then, we'll fight our way in, and Fae can do battle with the *god* that's currently playing the Lady like a puppet." He looked around the group. "Sound about right?"

As Stef murmured in Old Equiann for Immrith's benefit, the centaur glanced about with an appraising eye, and frowned.

"There are nine here," he said, when Aren had finished. "And not all fighters. The one who rules a city with such an iron fist will laugh at us." He snorted. "Fires of Hell, *I'd* laugh at us." He shook his head firmly, long, black hair falling over his bare shoulder. "We should not fight our way in." Stef nodded his agreement as he finished translating.

"What would you suggest?" Aren put on a look of affront, but there was a twinkle in his eye.

"Steal in in the dead of night. Disguise as recruits." Immrith ticked off options on his fingers. "Anything *except* engage in a battle in the middle of your enemy's stronghold."

"We could enter as captives?" Hal suggested.

"No," Fae instantly said, without a moment's hesitation. She cast her eyes across the group. "No," she repeated. "No one goes in as captured. Intentionally or otherwise."

"I could go," Laina said softly. All eyes turned to her. "They're looking for me still, aren't they? I might draw Black out."

"Begging your pardon, Laina," Hal said, clearing his throat, "but it was the Stuarts out looking for you, not Black. And besides, that don't guarantee them raiders won't just kill you on the spot." He shook his head. "I don't think heroics is going to help us here." He looked over at Fae, his eyes ricocheting around the others. "I think it's as you say, we go in and hunker down. Do some digging. Quiet like." He shrugged. "We can figure out the rest when we've got some information to work with."

"One problem." Ty spoke up. He gestured to Immrith. "How do we sneak a *centaur* around Throldon, the human capital in Arland?"

"I've been thinking about that," Jesse said, shooting an apologetic look at Immrith. "But you're not going to like it."

Stef translated. Immrith's eyes narrowed. "Speak it."

Jesse gave a one-sided shrug that seemed to say, *You asked for it.*

"If you bent over a bit, you'd just about match the height of a large draft horse," she said, rooting around in her enormous pack. Drawing out a wide length of black cloth, she held it up. "I've seen some horses come through Dvargra with their heads covered on account of how they don't like the noise and close quarters of the city. Keeps them calm." She looked up at Immrith, who glowered at the black cloth while Stef murmured quickly. "I told you you wouldn't like it," Jesse said.

Immrith seethed. "It is a great indignity among my people, to be covered," he said, his voice dropping an octave. "You do not comprehend the gravity of the insult in saying this." Fae felt the reflexive recoil around the group at the acid in his tone. But Jesse stood fast, her face flat and unmoved.

"But we're not among your people, are we?" she said. "Nor mine." She paused a moment to give him a chance to hear her words. Towering centaur and diminutive dwarf eyed one another, each seeming to attempt staring the other into submission. "I'm not here to cause offence," Jesse said finally. "I'm just suggesting ways we might get you into a human city without drawing attention." She spread her hands. "The only way I see of us doing that is by hiding you, or covering you in some way. There's just no possible explanation for a centaur to be in Arland, let alone Throldon."

Fae looked between them. Immrith looked as if he was ready to hurl Jesse bodily from the dais. Jesse held his blazing amber gaze, implacable as the stone that surrounded them. But there was a hint of regret in her eyes, as if she wished she didn't have to be the one to state the point.

Finally, Immrith relented enough to drop his glare. He no longer looked as though he would do bodily harm, but Fae didn't think he was convinced enough to put a sheet over his head.

"Aye," Hal said, scratching under his beard and wearing a somewhat sheepish look. "Until yesterday, I wouldn't even have known your kind existed. Begging your pardon."

Laina nodded. "I've only ever heard of centaurs in stories and legends. I would never have suspected they were actually real."

"Hm." Aren tapped his chin thoughtfully. "We might be able to use that to our advantage." He spread his hands, palms down, setting the scene. "Imagine, if you will, two simple farm workers leading their skittish work-horse through the city, a blanket over its head to gentle his nervous tendencies. But these farmers aren't who they appear to be! They are Stef and Ty in disguise! But their disguises only take them so far, and before long they are stopped. Confronted. Surrounded. Their odds look slim." Stef openly rolled his eyes as he translated his brother's narrative. Ty wore a half-humouring smile. Immrith had already figured out where the story was going, and seemed to be thoroughly enjoying it. "The guards close ranks," Aren continued dramatically. He was standing in a half-crouch now, miming the men's readiness for a fight. "They're outnumbered at least ten-to-one. They take a step back to their horse, as if to cower behind it—" Immrith snorted, but Aren shot him a quicksilver wink "—and then Ty, whose longbow is useless at such short-range, whips the blanket from the horse's head, and up rears Immrith, the mighty centaur! The likes of which have never before been seen on human soil!" Aren leapt from his crouch, arms wide, near-black hair swinging about his shoulders. "The guards fall back — on their asses — and Immrith lays about with his mighty—" he quickly took in the centaur's lack of a weapon "—fists, taking down half their numbers in half as many blows. The rest are routed easily, turning tail and fleeing, so terrified are they of their impossible foe." Aren straightened and dusted off his hands. "Immrith dons his cloak once more, and the team continue on, their disguise back in place for the next challengers." He grinned. "Because what human would believe reports of a *centaur* in the city?"

"Magnificent!" Immrith bellowed. "And in this way I will single-handedly pave the way for our very own *fae'yha* one to defeat this poison god."

An uneasy silence fell over them. Fae swallowed nervously. This all hinged on her ability to wield the power within her, and prise Anson from his grip on the world. But as Bek had said, the power of the Aethyr was build from connections; it was for growing, and flowering, drifting, and flowing. It was up to her *human* part to shape in to their needs. She'd only experienced her own reservoir of power out of anger, out of fear.

How am I going to bring forth, and control *the full power of the seven within me?*

"We should go," Laina said quietly.

A murmur of assent rippled through them. Immrith nodded soberly.

Aren cleared his throat. "Yes. Right. I'll pack up." And he turned away to see to his supplies.

Planning a courageous take-down of the horrific regime in Throldon might be galvanising, but the reality was that none of them truly knew what they faced. It would be a mad scramble from start to finish, no matter what plans and contingencies they managed to pull together.

Fae tracked the path of the sun through the sky, one eager moon peeping over the horizon behind it.

It took them only a few minutes to ready themselves, and they assembled at the edge of the dais, looking out onto the bleak Northern Tundra. A bitter wind had picked up, and it pushed at their backs, as if to hurry them on their way. Fae found herself wishing for a coat, the likes of which Aiya had worn for riding the winds with Kagos.

Her mouth took a downward turn. She had been so sure the dragon would be a part of this. The man Baev'ill had gotten to know had been a good one, for all of his constant grumbling.

"So," Jesse said, interrupting her thoughts, "how does this work?"

38

SKATING

Jesse's question hit a weak spot in Fae's confidence.

"Um..." Fae stuttered. Because she didn't have an answer.

Her experiences of travel through the Eah'lara were mixed and varied. The Aethyr within her had inhabited all manner of life, but none of them had ever lifted eight living souls and transported them alongside, while skating from one point to another.

She closed her eyes, and tried to ignore the mutterings of her companions.

When a young Fae had been taken from a burning Woodnewton and deposited in Arolynos, it have been an act born of desperation, just like the vivid visions the Aethyr had sent her to remind her of who she was. Nothing of the like had never been done before, nor repeated since. Even Be'ella Tor hadn't been entirely sure *how* they'd managed to pick her up, and move her bodily across the world. Perhaps it had only been possible because Fae was already halfway to being Aethyr. Whatever the reason, they had counted their blessings that day.

From the veiled view within Eah'lara, Fae contemplated the faint auras of her allies. The strange, spirit-particles of Eah'lara gravitated towards the space they occupied, creating a wispy outline around them. Like silhouettes, outlined in shimmering dust against the gauzy fabric of the Spirit Realm.

Fae approached Ty's spiritual silhouette.

But the silhouette was just that — a glittering shadow backlit on a white curtain. She needed to reach *him*. His aura.

Feeling about for the threads that connected him to the world, she found the tell-tale pinprick in the fabric of the Spirit Realm, the anchor that would lead her to him. Reaching into his essence — his soul — was like tumbling into a cloud of pollen, and she sneezed despite herself. He smelled like fresh rain and sunlight. He tasted of sweet nectar and herbs. Her skin hummed at the feel of him.

Ty's aura felt like burying her toes into sun-warmed soil, and breathing in sweet, fresh air. She smiled. *Concentrate,* she reminded herself. *We're not here to play in the dirt and smell the flowers.*

Like Eah'lara itself, Ty's aura was made up of thousands — millions — of whisper-thin connections, each sparking softly as they relayed information in a language of light only they understood. She brushed her fingers along one of the fibres, a fraction of the width of their counterparts in Eah'lara. But instead of feeling the gentle bite of thread against her skin, she saw the thread part the instant her finger met its edge, the substance no more than finely-woven cloud. Fae's heart stopped as the two pieces floated apart.

She snatched her hand back, and pressed her fingers hard against her thighs, frozen. Her breath caught in her chest — how much damage could she do here?

The two ends of the broken thread drifted, caught in a lazy, swirling current. But as she watched, the current pushed and pulled at the fibres, snaring them in a dance meant just for those two, drawing them together, pulling them slowly in as surely as iron drawn to a lodestone. Closer and closer, each end spiralled around its partner, until finally, they snapped taut. One, glimmering, whisper-thin thread once more.

Fae breathed a slow sigh of relief. What would happen if she broke more than one thread? Would they all find their other halves to become whole again? Or would they become a jumbled mess of mixed messages? Or would they simply never rejoin, lost forever in a tangle of floating thread-ends?

And what of Ty then? She shook her head free of the thoughts. It didn't bear thinking of. Besides, she hadn't made it this far to fail now. She was *made* to do this.

She took a breath, calmed her breathing, and looked again.

The threads didn't appear to be confined by any tangible borders that she could lift. It was as if they were held together by will alone, just enough to form a vague outline of each of her companions.

If only she could move the pocket of Eah'lara *around* Ty's aura instead...

That's it!

Instead of focusing on Ty, she concentrated on the space around him.

Careful not to touch the delicate threads of his aura, she wrapped herself around the space he occupied in the Spirit Realm.

And all the connections that made Ty who he was, all the energy that held him together, came with it.

And her own aura expanded instinctively to accommodate him.

Yes, she cheered, as she tucked him carefully into a corner of her self.

When the Aethyr guides had stood at the edge of her psyche, they had known how to enter, how to merge with her, once invited. With Ty, it was different. He floated within his own little bubble, his essence nestled separately within hers.

Satisfied that she could repeat the process as necessary, Fae slowly — carefully — extracted Ty's aura from hers again, and replaced it back where she'd found it.

Opening her eyes back onto the grey Northern Tundra, she whirled to find Ty, a beam of elation across her face.

Ty looked like he'd been at sea for a month, and was struggling to rediscover his land legs.

He looked up at her. "Next time," he said dryly, "a little warning would be nice."

Fae's grin widened. "You're okay?"

"Of course I'm okay, it's just somewhat disorientating is all."

"Haha!" Fae clapped her hands, giddy with success. "That's amazing!"

"I thought you said you know how to do this?" Jesse said, suddenly very skeptical.

"Well," Fae said, backtracking quickly, "I do... in a way." She clasped her hands behind her back like a child caught in a lie. "But this exact set of circumstances is rather... unique to our situation." When Jesse didn't look particularly convinced, Fae swept the smile from her face, and met her eye.

"I can do it," she said, weighing her voice with the fullest expression of sincerity. *I must.*

"Well, let's get moving then," Hal said. "Can't stand up here all day waiting for the right moment."

"Even the moons cannot stop the sun crossing the sky," Immrith added, quoting an Equiann parable.

Ty and the other elves were strangely quiet, but they all nodded when her gaze turned to them.

"Alright then," Jesse said. "Let's get this over with." She levelled a stern finger at Fae's nose. "But if I end up with a centaur's backside and pointy ears, I will make you wish you had a second god to fight, so fierce will be my wrath."

Fae blinked, but nodded her assurance mutely.

To one side, Stef finished translating, and Immrith snorted his amusement.

Fae took a deep, calming breath. She closed her eyes.

One by one, she began drawing the essences of her companions into herself, tucking them safely away.

Ty, then Laina, and Hal, went without a hitch. Aren's aura bounced and jittered in his little pocket, echoing his character. It felt as if he might leap from her grasp like a frog at any moment. She took extra care not to jostle him. Stef seemed reluctant to come, his aura requiring a little extra "pull" as she lifted him through into the Spirit Realm. By the time she came to lift Wil, the corner of herself reserved for their safe passage was starting to feel crowded. It was like trying to carry a three-course dinner in a picnic blanket, only someone kept adding more cheese, and the blanket was already too small.

Immrith came readily enough, slotting in next to Wil. And then it was Jesse's turn.

Got you, Fae thought once everyone was finally in place. *Here we go.* Running her fingers harp-like along the blackened threads once more, Fae skated away from the monument, and off through Eah'lara.

The going was slower this time, weighed down with eight others, not all of whom were entirely comfortable being there.

About halfway — the distance only noticeable by how many more sickly threads were converging on her trajectory — Fae became acutely aware of the tenuousness of her grip on her blanket-parcel of auras. She held onto the corners by her fingertips, and she was beginning to tire.

Gritting her teeth, she adjusted her grip on her precious cargo, and pressed onward — if she had to set them down before reaching their destination, she wanted to be as close to Throldon as possible.

Almost there, almost there, she chanted to herself. The black threads were growing in numbers, until Eah'lara was thick with them.

She was just wondering if there were more black threads than there had been only hours before, when her grip on her make-shift parcel slipped.

"Eah's Tears," she swore, grabbing at the edges and gathering the auras back to her, holding them close.

But one, two, three of them tumbled from her grasp.

She had a split second to choose: drop them at the closest possible real-world position, wherever that might be, or lose them on the Spiritual Plane forever.

In the split second she had, she fumbled for a pinprick portal, and dropped the three auras through it.

She was about to follow behind, and lift them again, when the fabric of Eah'lara bucked. Heaving and rolling, it pitched her about, and ripped the portal from her grasp.

When everything settled again, the threads that criss-crossed around her were tossed about like leaves in the wind. The only thing she had left to tell her where to go, was her grip on the blackened thread that would take her to the watermill.

Fae lingered, torn.

It was like the map had been rewritten, and roads she knew were no longer on it, any sense of direction she'd had evaporating along with them.

The thought of abandoning her people made her sick to her stomach. She wouldn't. But she had no hope of finding them in this bird's nest of tumbled threads. Reluctantly, she knew she'd be better off setting down in the world, and tracking them there instead.

From the sheer weight of sickly threads pressing in around her, they couldn't be far from Throldon.

She hesitated a moment longer, loath to leave. Finally, she tore herself from the twisted weave of threads and upended nebulae and skated towards the crawling darkness of Throldon.

Clutching her remaining bundle, Fae traced her thread to its last viable exit before it curled back in revulsion from the dark fog around the city. One by one, and oh so carefully, she placed first Aren, then Stef, Hal, Laina, and finally Ty back into the world. And then opened her eyes.

Three elves and two humans blinked blearily in the fading afternoon light.

"Wait a minute," Aren said, looking around. "Didn't we come past here on our way round the city?" Stef scrutinised their location. The sun reached in beneath the cloud-cover to bathe the abandoned watermill barely a dozen paces away in a warm, orange glow. Rolling green countryside stretched away to either side, cut in two by the clear, slicing river beside them. Small wrinkles in the water surface caught the angled rays from the sun, and glittered back at them.

Fae doubled over, bracing her hands on her knees, her insides churning. She was exhausted, as if she'd run the distance, instead of skating through Eah'lara. She looked around.

Five of eight, she tallied again, her heart sinking. *Eah, I hope they're alright.*

Her eyes met Ty's; he was watching her, visibly checking her over. Then his gaze swept over the group. He frowned.

His eyes whipped back to Fae. "Where's Wil?"

The others all did a quick double-take, before their eyes settled on Fae. She felt sick to her stomach. "I lost them," she whispered.

The air stilled. Ty froze. As did the others.

"He's dead?" Aren asked, his face white as a sheet.

39

HOT COALS

"**N**o!" Fae rushed to clarify. "No, not dead. I had to put them down further back, or risk losing my grip on them completely. Wil, and Immrith, and Jesse." She hung her head, distraught that she had let them down so utterly. "I was about to follow, but something happened in Eah'lara, and... everything *moved*." Her hands fisted at her sides, helpless frustration building inside her. So much of what she'd faced already was new to her, despite her guides. How much use would she be in Throldon at this rate?

Don't be ridiculous. You are Spiritchild, the only one of your kind. And you were born *for this.* The self-assurance of Baev'ill bulled to the fore of her mind. She pushed it down. A little humility was owing, but wallowing in self-pity would do no one any good either.

"They can't be far," she said, straightening. She glanced up at the rapidly setting sun.

"But we won't be finding them tonight," Ty said, eyeing the same. "How far are they?"

"Hard to say," she said. "How far I travel in the Spirit Realm doesn't necessarily correlate with distance or direction out here."

"We should still look for them," Stef said, stepping forward.

Hal shook his head. "Ty's right." He pointed at the sun. "Unless

314

they're only over the next rise, we won't find 'em tonight. Best to hunker down and search in the morning."

"He's right," Aren said, laying a hand on Stef's shoulder. "It's Wil. He'll be fine."

"And Jesse's no wallflower herself," Laina added with a small smile.

"Argh!" Fae growled. Words didn't cover half of what she was feeling, and it was balling up into a hot, heavy knot in her chest.

Laina touched her arm. When Fae turned to her, she was faced with a look that was both gentle and firm; one that was used to comforting, but took no nonsense in return.

"You set them down the same as you did for us just now?" she asked.

Fae nodded.

"And they were definitely together?"

Fae nodded again. There was no doubt — it'd been quick, but she'd placed them back in the world through the same pinprick aperture.

"Then they are well, and have each other," Laina said with the tone of someone who considered the matter closed. "We'll look for them tomorrow." She turned to Hal. "Shall we see about some dinner?" She and Hal moved away to set up a cook-fire, and Aren pulled Stef over to join them, leaving Fae alone with Ty. Her hands were still balled into fists; she could feel the bite of her fingernails against her palms.

"Stop it," Ty said.

Fae started at his tone. "Stop what?"

"Stop dragging yourself over hot coals." He put up a hand to stop her when she went to deny it. "You still clench your teeth when you're mad at yourself, it shows in your jaw. And I suggest you relax your hands before you draw blood."

His words just made Fae want to clench her fists even tighter, as if she could throttle the defiance out of fate. She could *scream*. She was so mad at her failure to do one, simple task.

But he reached out his hand for hers, and the look in his eyes was so painfully tender. The anger in her gave way, just enough for her to relent. She extended her hand, and laid it in his. Ty turned it over so that it faced palm-up, and gently uncurled her fingers.

"Hmm," he said, ponderously.

"What?"

He looked up, and met her eyes, his own creasing at the corners.

"Nothing," he said. "I see the priceless hands of a priceless healer, and a close personal friend." His mouth curled upwards into a lop-sided smile. "I take great interest in the welfare of these hands, and of the person to whom they are attached."

Fae felt the frown-lines between her eyes unknit, and a small smile of her own crept onto her lips.

"Come on," Ty said, lowering his hand with hers still cupped within it. "Let's go and get some food. I can't think why, but I'm famished. Could be something to do with my unintentional fasting over the last few days." He arched an eyebrow at her. "And you look as though you've carried eight people at least a hundred leagues in a day."

Fae breathed a strained laugh, lifting her opposite hand to rub her eyes. "I *feel* like I've just had the monster of all shifts at the physica," she said.

Ty nodded his sympathy. "Let's take the rest while we can then. I'm sure there'll be precious little of it to come in the days ahead."

She sighed a long, resigned breath. "You're right," she said. "Eah, I wish this were simpler. And that the others were here." She aimed a glance at him. "Any ideas why Eah'lara would buck like that? Enough to redistribute all the connections in the area?"

Ty shook his head. "This is new territory for all of us," he answered ruefully, "and I'm hardly an expert in the mechanics of the Aethyr. I'm sure we'll have plenty more unknowns to speculate on as we go." Fae grimaced. The unscripted nature of this venture was wearing painfully thin, and the absence of answers to offset her growing pile of questions was fuelling her frustration. It was quickly becoming apparent that the added experience of six worldly Aethyr counted for very little in a novel — and completely unprecedented — crisis.

She grumbled low in her throat, and they turned to join the rest of their group. As Fae went to take a step, her hand slid from Ty's grasp. Without thinking, she twined her fingers through his, letting her palm lie snugly against his. It felt good. Neither one of them held onto the other, they simply... rested together.

"Huh," Ty breathed softly.

"Huh," she replied.

"Just like before, huh?" he whispered.

She laughed softly. "I guess not." She glanced down at their interlaced fingers. "But I like this better." Liked having someone beside her. Having *him* beside her.

"Good," he said. "So do I." He pulled her along gently. "Come on. Food."

They walked together over to where Hal and Aren had built two campfires: one in the traditional elven style, and one in Hal's own tried-and-tested method. Both blazed merrily away. Aren's was a neat teepee, the sticks angled upwards to support each other in a point at the top, with tinder and kindling beneath. Hal's looked more like the beginnings of a log cabin, with his sticks stacked atop each other in interlocking squares, the tinder shielded within the four walls. If Fae had to choose, she thought she preferred Aren's teepee shape, even though it was designed to burn out quickly, minimising the risk of spreading flames. There was just something unsettling about watching walls burn.

As it was, she didn't have to choose; both fires were being put to good use. A pot hung comfortably over Hal's campfire, while Stef was preparing something to bake in the embers of Aren's.

Dinner was a quiet affair, each member lost to their own thoughts. When everyone had finished, Hal stood, brushing his hands against his trousers.

"I'll take first watch," he said, putting his back to the campfire and scanning the dark around them. His gaze eventually came to the watermill, and his eyes narrowed thoughtfully. "Wonder if I can get up there..." And with that, he headed over toward the abandoned building.

"I'll turn in then," Laina said with an all-consuming yawn. She covered her mouth with the back of one hand, the other stretched out over her head. "I wake early most days, so I'll take the last watch if needed." She indicated her bedroll with a wave. "You know where to find me." And she too, left the ring of light around the campfires. Aren's had burnt down to not very much at all, flames licking across it quiet and sullen, while Hal's construction continued to crackle away, casting a warm glow over the four left.

"I'll take next watch," Stef grunted, flowing to his feet. "I'll let Hal know." As he left, he avoided her eyes. Fae pressed her lips together. She could well imagine why the scout might not want to talk to her.

Aren caught her look. "He's just worried about Wil," he said, attempting to comfort her. "Don't worry about him." A shadow passed over his face. "And I imagine he's not overjoyed at the prospect of going back into that slum of a city." He shook his head at the ground. "Couldn't get out of there quick enough. And we only saw a fraction. A slice of a fraction. But that was enough." He lifted his head, and stared after his brother.

"I'm sorry," Fae said in a voice barely above a whisper.

Aren shot her an easy smile. "Like I said, don't worry about it. Besides, you have nothing to be sorry for—"

A shout went up from the watermill. Hal. Another shout answered. Ty and Aren's ears twitched. A small furrow appeared between Ty's eyebrows. There was more shouting. And then they both visibly relaxed.

"What?" Fae asked, looking from one to the other. *How did I ever think I was truly elven when I can barely hear half of what they do?* She'd blamed the slow development of her ears for so much. She shook her head. What a fool she'd been.

Aren laughed and leapt to his feet, turning his back to the fire and looking out towards the watermill. Fae looked to Ty, one eyebrow raised. But he just gifted her with an infuriating wink, and jerked his head the same way.

Standing, Fae stood beside Aren, one arm raised needlessly to shade her eyes from the glare of the fire.

She spotted Hal's easy gait coming back, the bricks of the mill reflecting firelight behind his silhouette. There were four other vague figures walking beside him, indistinct against the deep black of the countryside, and it took her a minute to recognise them.

"I hope you've got some dinner left in the pot," Wil said as he walked into camp. "We've had to walk a fair way to get here."

"How did you find us?" Fae gasped, flinging her arms around his waist. "I'm so glad you're ok!"

Wil hugged her briefly, and exchanged a firm handclasp with Ty, and then Aren. "We passed by here before, on the way around Throldon to the villages north of here. As soon as we were back on solid ground, I recognised the area. You remember the standing stones we reached our first day out of the city?" Aren nodded, then snapped his fingers together with an enlightened "Ah!"

Wil continued, "When I saw those, I knew which watermill you were talking about. It's only a league or two north-west from here." He turned to Fae. "And when only three of us reappeared, I figured something must have gone not quite according to plan, so I convinced them to follow me here." He glanced over his shoulder to where Stef was talking to Immrith. "If you'll excuse me, I want to speak to Immrith in the presence of a translator. But Fae," he nodded his head surreptitiously over to where Jesse already sat cross-legged before Aren's barely-burning campfire, "you might want to go and speak to her. Tread carefully." He looked about to say more, but decided against it, opting instead to pat Fae reassuringly on the arm before heading back to Stef and Immrith.

Just then, Hal walked up to them. "I'll get this fire going again," he said, dropping some more wood beside it. "We'll get some supper sorted for these three. Good job they found us, eh?"

Fae smiled weakly, and made her way over to Jesse, leaving Ty with Hal. The remaining embers of Aren's fire cast just enough light to see by, but no more than that. Jesse stared into them blankly, not even acknowledging Fae when she folded her legs to sit beside her on the ground. They sat in silence for a while, Fae not knowing how to begin her apology, and Jesse not willing to prompt her.

Finally, it was Jesse who spoke first.

"Have you ever been carried across the Spirit Realm like that?" she asked, her eyes not leaving the embers.

Fae swallowed. "Yes, but I don't remember it."

Jesse nodded. "It's like you're asleep, but awake at the same time. You're floating. Have no control over it. Like in a dream, but you know you're dreaming. Only this time I knew it was real. I was completely aware that I had no control over my fate." She paused, and Fae wondered if that was all she wanted to say. "At first," she continued, "it was just that. I was just floating. And it was like I was in a glass bauble, the Spirit Realm just *there*, but out of reach. I was safe, but in the hands of someone else." Her eyes flicked briefly to Fae's crossed legs, and then back to the glowing embers again. "And then the bauble tipped. And I got that feeling you get when you know you're about to fall. That stomach-dropping fear, even though nothing had changed. I just *knew*." Then she finally did look up, and this time she met Fae's gaze. And Fae saw a wildness around her eyes, the kind of wildness only seen when one narrowly escapes with their life. "I knew you were going to drop me."

"Jesse—" Fae tried to find the words to comfort her. To apologise. "I never—"

"But you didn't."

"—would have... eh?" She stopped, heard Jesse's words. "No, of course I didn't." She didn't know how to tell Jesse how it felt to have eight people entrust they lives to her, to trust her to transport their bodies and souls across the world and deliver them safely.

What it felt like to have her ability to carry out that duty threatened.

What it felt like to know those lives were threatened.

"You didn't," Jesse said again, her eyes still fixed on Fae. "I knew I was going to fall, and then I was standing on solid ground." She blinked, and let out a ragged breath. She turned her gaze back to the fire. "I know something went wrong, or we'd have all landed here together. But whatever happened, you kept us safe." She looked back at Fae, and the wildness was gone from her eyes, replaced by her usual gruffness. "But I am *never*—" she looked Fae square in the eye "—*never* — doing that again."

Fae stared for a split-second before gathering her wits. "Understood," she said, slightly breathless. She'd expected the conversation to go an entirely different way.

"Good," Jesse said with a sharp nod. "Right, what's for dinner? I'm starving! Those two there—" she jerked a thumb over to Wil and Immrith "—don't know what it's like to have short legs. I practically had to run to keep up." She grumbled her way to her feet, and trudged across to Hal's newly-blazing fire.

Fae watched her go, still staring.

Ty approached cautiously. "Is she alright?" he asked.

Fae nodded dumbly.

"Good," he said, tugging her toward her bedroll. "Then sleep. Tomorrow is another day."

40

FORWARD, ONWARD

The next morning began much as the previous one, minus a dragon and his rider. This time, Fae turned to Wil over breakfast.

"Do you think," she said, "that you might help us navigate from here?" The new gold ring around her eyes glinted as she gazed north-east, towards the vague haze squatting darkly on the horizon that marked the city, just a few miles away. "I can't see beyond this point," she explained. "The web that connects everything stops here. The threads cut off, or veer away. Like spirit life just can't bear it." She swallowed nervously, her hands twisting together, the thought of what would affect the Aethyr this much sending chills down her spine. She turned back to Wil. "Without the threads to follow, I can't skate ahead, and the dark fog that covers this area blinds me."

Wil nodded slowly, glancing uneasily at Throldon's distant mass. "We can get you in," he said.

"But...?" Fae sensed something else in his tone.

Wil's eyes flicked to hers. "It's a warren in there. A maze of despair and hunger and no hope to speak of. We only skirted the suburbs, and that was bad enough. I don't know what horrors lie beyond that."

"Then we'll tackle that part together," she said. "But in unknown territory, without the advantage of the Spirit Realm, you're easily the best scout here."

"I heard that!" Aren called from where he sat, fletching arrows.

Wil didn't look convinced. "This is hardly my home soil," he said.

"No, but it was mine," Hal came up behind them and dropped to the ground opposite, folding his legs in front of him. "For a time anyways." He rubbed his hand across the back of his neck. "Not been back in many a year, but I reckon I could find my way around well enough."

Fae looked at the ranger properly for the first time since they'd parted ways on the Western Highway. Behind his rough beard and laid-back, easy manner, there was a weariness she hadn't noticed before. It was in his eyes; sitting in the circles beneath, and weighing down the creases at the corners. It gave him a strained look, as if he was pulling away from a path he had no choice but to walk.

"Thank you," she said, infusing her words with as much gratitude as she could muster.

Hal made a low grunt in his throat, and bobbed his head, for once short on words.

"Well, I don't know about the rest of you," Aren said, striding over to where they sat, "but I'm ready to get moving. Doesn't feel like I've done nearly enough walking recently." He shot Fae a wink.

"Speak for yourself," Jesse grumbled dryly. "Some of us enjoyed a lovely evening stroll last night." Wil smirked, Immrith's chuckle coming a second behind. She shot them a withering glare through narrowed eyes. "But we may as well make use of the light." She turned her back on them pointedly and asked Aren, "How far is it into the city?"

"Um..." He glanced at Wil, who stood with his arms crossed over Jesse's shoulder, doing a poor impression of hiding his amusement. "Six, seven, eight miles? Certainly no more than a couple of hours on foot."

Jesse snorted. "For you maybe," she muttered. "Best get a move on then, if you're wanting to get there while the sun is still high." And she trudged off to ready her oversized pack.

It turned out Jesse wasn't half as slow as she made herself out to be; they made it to the outer edge of Throldon with an hour to spare before midday. The journey through open countryside was blissfully uneventful, the track from the watermill providing an easy route to follow. The day was clear and bright, wide open fields stretching away to either side, wafting gently as crowds of barley crop bowed and scraped to the wind. The only strangeness was the quiet. No birds sang as they soared through the sky, and there was no rustling of small critters scurrying about in the long grasses. They might have been the only beings for miles around.

"It is too quiet here," Immrith remarked at one point. "Why is there no noise?" Stef replied that there ought to be, and that was the end of the talking for a while.

When the track finally breached the outskirts — a ramshackle collection of lean-tos and temporary shelters sprawling endlessly ahead, and to either side — Wil beckoned them off the road. A strange, low fog had begun to roll in, obscuring the skeletal "houses", until all but the closest were blurry outlines.

"This is how we found it last time," Wil said, the two brothers nodding behind him. "This fog never seems to lift. It grows thicker the further into the city you go, but never closer." He waved at the haze that hung around them. "Here, you can see three, maybe four buildings deep, the rest are hard to make out, but still visible." He nodded towards the city's centre. "But it will thicken, until beyond those first few houses, the air is a sheet of solid fog."

Stef frowned. "You might as well be standing in a village — that's about as much as you can see."

"It was easy to get turned about here on a good day," Hal said, eyeing the fog with a mix of suspicion and consideration. "This will only make it worse." He straightened his shoulders and adjusted his pack on his shoulders. "Well, nothing for it. 'Forward, onward,' as they say. 'If your heart is pure and your aim is true, fear not, and go on.'"

As he said those words, Laina froze in the act of tying her hair into a braid. Her hands dropped, and her hair unravelled.

"That was something my father used to say to his men," she breathed.

Hal winced.

"Aye," he answered gently. "That it was."

Laina stepped up beside him, her soft brown eyes searching his. "You knew him?" He nodded. "Why didn't you say something?"

Hal dropped his gaze. He shifted uncomfortably from one foot to the other, and rubbed at the back of his neck. "Ah, Miss Laina," he said, addressing his feet, "we all lost something the day the Unity razed Bredon. Sometimes I think it's best to leave the past right where we left it." He met her eyes briefly before resuming his study of the ground. "I don't like to remember what I lost. Figured you'd be the same, is all."

As he spoke, Laina watched him closely, as if there was something she'd noticed about him, but couldn't quite put her finger on it. Then her eyes suddenly went round, and a small gasp escaped her lips.

"Halbert?" she whispered.

Hal froze, a deer caught in the lamplight.

"Gods, it *is* you," she said with a cry, and without warning, flung her arms around the poor ranger. "I can't believe I didn't recognise you!"

Hal grimaced. "Aye, well, I've changed a mite since you last saw me."

"I didn't think anyone got out," Laina mumbled into his shoulder.

Hal patted her awkwardly on the back before gently disentangling her arms from around his neck. "There are times, Miss Laina, when I wish I hadn't," he said solemnly.

Laina went to rebuke him, and then seemed to remember herself. Her face dropped, and she sobered quickly. "Of course," she whispered. "I'm so sorry."

"Like I said," Hal said, making a gesture that indicated the conversation was over, "I don't like to remember."

A strained silence fell over the group. Fae itched to know more, but Hal specifically avoided discussing his past — something she'd noticed when they'd travelled together before.

Aren cleared his throat. "'Halbert'?" he asked, raising an eyebrow at the ranger, who carried a bow, not a polearm, as the name suggested.

Hal grimaced. "A, uh, nickname I was given a long time ago." He hefted his bow on his shoulder. "Used to favour the halbert. I learnt better, but the name stuck."

"Now now," Aren said with an airy tone. "No need to naysay the halbert, Halbert." He grinned. "It's a very versatile weapon. Bit brutish for my liking..." He trailed off, watching the ranger sideways.

Hal took the bait. "Brutish?" he said, his calm expression twisting into one of exaggerated affront. "I'll have you know I danced as well with the halbert as any of 'em peacocks with a spear! Better, most days."

"Oh really?" Aren drawled. "I'd like to see that some day, Master Ranger."

"You offering, Master Scout?" Hal goaded.

"It would be my pleasure," Aren replied. "After... this."

"Aye," Hal said, his face darkening again. "After this."

Jesse looked from one to other, and back again.

"Right," she said impatiently, "are we done? Shall we go?"

Wil cleared his throat loudly. "From what we saw on the way past, I'd say Throldon is no more than three or four miles across. But as I said before, it's a warren. I didn't see any straight routes through." He glanced at Stef, who seconded his assessment with a shake of his head. "The conditions are squalid, and the roads are in no state of repair, poor or otherwise." Reaching down, he snatched a dry stick up from the ground and began scratching a sketch of the area in the dirt. "We're here," he said, marking their location with a small "x". "If we keep heading east by northeast, we should hit the centre — if that's where we need to be."

"It's as good a guess as any," Fae said, having frustratingly little to contribute at this point. "None of the Aethyr in me knew anything about the current state of Throldon."

"That's ok," Aren said cheerily. "Gives the rest of us something to do." He shot her a quick wink.

"And what, exactly, *are* we supposed to do in the middle of the human capital?" Jesse gestured to herself and Immrith, towering beside her. "Not all of us are likely to blend in."

"I thought about that," Ty said. "With the exception of Immrith, we can *all* pass for voluntary recruits." He turned his best stern-teacher expression on Jesse, who looked about to protest, "Even you, Jesse. Humans have a closer relation with dwarves than any of the other races. You'll pass. We'll stand out—" he indicated himself, Aren, Stef, and Wil, standing at least a foot above Hal "—but if we cover our ears, the worst we should get is a handful of curious stares."

Aren cleared his throat. "The locals might not take too kindly to outsiders looking to join the Survivors' ranks." He exchanged black looks with Stef and Wil. "They've not exactly made an easy time of it for the city people."

"If we play the part of village workers, fallen on hard times *because* of the Survivors, driven to their ranks out of desperation, we should find a few sympathisers among the citizens."

"Alright, and then what?" Jesse said.

"Then we re-evaluate," Ty answered calmly. "There's little point in making a plan when we don't know the situation. Let's gather some information. *Then* we'll come up with a plan. If it all goes horribly wrong in the meantime, we'll meet back at the watermill to regroup."

Jesse seemed mollified enough at that, and grumbled something unintelligible that Ty took for acceptance, if not entirely agreement.

"Good," he said. "Wil, Stef, Aren, Hal — you take the lead talking to the inhabitants. You have the most recent experience of the area." The four nodded in unison, the scouts pulling well-worn bandanas and hats from their bags. "Immrith." Ty turned to the centaur. "I'm afraid now is the time for your disguise as well." Immrith scowled as Stef repeated Ty's words, but he accepted the length of black cloth Jesse produced from her pack without comment.

Fae began rifling through her belongings for something to cover her ears, when she remembered she'd blend in just fine. She was, after all, human.

Well, she thought, *on the outside at least.*

"Ready?" Ty whispered for her alone.

She nodded. "You've taken on the leadership role rather comfortably," she said, nodding to how everyone had jumped to his instructions without so much as a second suggestion.

"Ah," he said, noticing the same. "Yes, occupational hazard. They didn't make me an Eldra for my dashing good looks."

Fae grinned. "No, because those all went to Shae."

Ty gasped in mock horror, and clapped a hand to his chest. "You wound me!"

She nudged him gently with her elbow, and then turned her attention back to the group.

Appropriately garbed, they painted a curious picture. Varying in height by over two feet in places, they made an odd collection of individuals. Immrith would still draw a few stares, even covered as he was, but no one in the whole of Arland would suspect him of being anything other than an overly jumpy draft horse in need of gentling. Stef grasped Immrith's "lead-rope" — the other end of which the centaur simply held beneath his cowl.

"Right then," Ty said, regarding each of them. His eye caught on Hal, looking distinctly uneasy. "Onward then?"

The ranger squared his shoulders, and gave a resolute nod. "Aye," he said. "Fear not, and go on."

Together, the group stepped back onto the road, and followed it through the fog, and into Throldon proper.

41

OLD FRIENDS

"This is useless," Aren said when they reconvened hours later. "They're all clammed up tighter than father whenever we asked him about something we 'weren't ready for'."

"Really?" Jesse said flatly. "That's the best example you've got? How about, 'they're all clammed up tighter than a flidgit's nut-sack'?" She sniggered at her own double-entendre; the tiny flying marsupials were known for using their pouches for storing nuts when scurrying around the treetops. They were also known for being difficult to distinguish between males and females on account of the male's ability to retract its testes fully into its abdomen when threatened. "Or even better, 'clammed up tighter than a —'"

"Okay, I think we get the point," Fae interrupted, although at least Aren was smiling again. He was right though, they'd had precious little luck in getting anything useful from the residents of Throldon thus far. "They're scared," she said. She didn't need extra senses to see that. These people were absolutely terrified; for their families, for their livelihoods, and for their lives.

The standards of living improved the further into the bowels of the city they ventured, although barely. Homes and businesses were mostly stone-built, with thatched or even tiled roofing, and patched with timber. And for the most part, they were kept in good order... up to a point.

There were still signs of neglect even here: paint peeled from sills and doorframes, broken window-panes were boarded over rather than replaced, weeds grew in window boxes, and paved paths were chipped and damaged.

"Yes," Wil said, a frown dividing his brows. "But that's no different from last time we were here, and we found someone then who was willing to talk to us at least."

"You're wrong," Hal said darkly. "It's changed. People were scared under the Unity, but at least they knew how to stay on the right side of the thugs." He shook his head as if he couldn't believe how much worse it was. "Now, it's like they're scared to breathe wrong. Like anything they do could be their last act." He paused, watching a couple walk past with glazed expressions. "Like they've given up hope of ever being safe again."

They'd passed more groups of hollow-eyed children, huddled together while haggard and downtrodden common folk went about their business with monochrome necessity. Hunched shoulders, grey faces, wary gazes, heavy steps. A market, which should have been raucous and loud, was muted and limited to the most basic essentials.

"You'll find your luxuries over Castleside," one man told them, when Hal asked where he could find a blacksmith for arrowheads. "We got a smith here—" he waved down the twisting lane "—but he don't do weapons." He gestured to Immrith, still hidden beneath his improvised cowl. "You'll get your farriers down that way too. Ironmonger Street's your best bet. Next to Mercy Square."

"Been to Ironmonger's before," Hal said, his accent thickening even more as he spoke to the locals. "Never used to be a Mercy Square beside it."

The man gave him a searching look. "Well it's there now." He narrowed his eyes. "What d'you say you was here for again?"

"A second chance," Hal answered, cutting over Aren, about to launch into his rehearsed tale of destitution and hope for a better life. The man eyed their packs and assorted weapons, and worked out the rest.

"Don't know what sort of second chance you're wanting," he said, "but I hope you find something better than what's left here." He waved up the road again, only this time it was more of a shooing motion. "Blacksmith's up that way." Hal nodded his thanks, and the group moved on again.

"What was that?" Aren whispered as they turned onto another dusty lane.

"Seen him before," Hal murmured under his breath. "And he weren't scratching a living in Throldon's scraps. Must have been in one o' the villages."

"But I thought most of the villagers fled?" Laina said.

Hal shrugged. "Guess not all of 'em."

They kept their heads down as they weaved through the shops and homes, some little more than hovels. The buildings might've been an improvement on those in the outskirts, built during the reigns of monarchs, but they were still far from palaces.

Rounding another corner, Hal led them through a wide square, the ever-present fog lingering at the edges to lend the place an ominous, hazy gloom.

He took no more than four steps, and stopped.

"Did you happen to make any friends on your last visit, lads?" he asked. Up ahead, two figures peeled away from the shadows, and stepped into the centre of the square.

"Eah's Tears," Wil swore.

"I told you it was foolish drawing attention," Stef murmured behind him.

"What's done is done," Wil snapped. "There are only two of them. What are they going to do?"

"Bring more friends," Hal answered, as more figures trickled from the edges of the square to pool in the middle, "and make things difficult for us, I imagine."

Stef was muttering in rapid Equiann beside the hulking form of Immrith. Ty put out a hand.

"Wait," he said softly.

"Well well well," the voice of the leading figure rang out. Even given the browbeaten undertone they'd noted so far, Fae thought the square was suspiciously empty; the man's voice echoed within the walls of the square, and the fog around it. "I couldn't believe our luck, when Jimmy said he spotted four bean-poles strutting across our patch, asking questions." He took three slow steps forward, swaggering more with each one. "And imagine my *pleasure,* at learning three o' them be the same bean-poles jumped us last month, leaving us two men down." The man stopped half a dozen paces from them. He was wiry and lean, standing a few inches shy of six feet tall, with straw-like, dark-brown hair that stuck out sideways. The skin around his pale brown eyes was deeply lined, although Fae put him at only around thirty years old. When he sneered at them across the empty square, the gaps where two of his teeth should have been glared out from behind a crooked smile.

"Do you remember him?" Aren muttered to Wil.

"*You* should," Wil muttered back sharply. "You're the one who had a bead on him last time we came."

Aren considered the man standing before them now, legs shoulder-width apart, his arms open in what appeared to be a welcoming greeting.

"Ah yes," he said after the briefest pause. "Thug number four."

"Well apparently, he's thug number one now," Wil hissed.

"Where's the one with the axe?" Stef asked.

"You mean that one?" Hal answered, with a nod to a second man stepping up to join the leader. He hefted a long, double-headed axe, and swung it up to rest on his shoulder.

Jesse snorted. "What a display." She jerked her chin to each of the two men in turn. "That one plays the magnanimous host, while the other one plays the bruiser. And both thinking it makes their piece out to be the bigger one." She rolled her eyes. "*Men.*"

Wil turned to level a scowl at her, but then the man started talking again.

"We didn't get the courtesy of exchanging names last time you was here," he continued. "So let me start us off." He brought one hand in to his chest, leaving the other extended. "I'm Mickey, but these boys here call me Boss." He indicated the axe-wielding individual beside him. Closer to six feet tall and sturdily built, he looked the more imposing of the two, despite not being the one that went by the name "Boss." "This fella here is Jimmy. They call him Headless, on account of how he likes to leave his enemies." The half-toothed grin slammed shut and took a downward turn. "And the two you killed were Joe and Pete." He scowled, his face screwed up into an expression of pure hatred. "Way I see it, you owe us two back."

"Gods," Laina breathed.

"Well they ain't gonna help us," Hal whispered back, without taking his eyes from Mickey and Headless Jimmy. He took a step forward, and addressed the leader of the mob forming in the square. Close to a dozen angry-looking men and women now ranged behind the two they faced, with more lurking in the shadows.

"Mickey, look, I'm sorry two of your boys came off badly. It weren't personal. All we want is—"

"I don't give a shit what you want!" Mickey shrieked, a vein popping at his temple. "Your boys killed two o' mine! My own! What *I* want, is their heads." Jimmy hefted his axe, and dropped it into his palm with a heavy *slap* to emphasise his boss's point.

"Something tells me, we ain't getting out of this without a fight," Hal murmured.

"No kidding," Aren said sourly, as the mob began to advance around Mickey.

"Back up, slowly like," Hal said in a low voice.

"Would if I could," Jesse said, "but it doesn't look like they'll be so happy to oblige."

Fae turned at the tone in her voice, and found the exit down the street they'd come from blocked.

Seeing the same, Mickey smiled a triumphant, feral grin.

"Alright boys," he snarled, "let's have 'em." And the mob broke into a run, charging towards them.

"Now?" Fae heard Stef ask Ty desperately.

Ty had a resigned look about him, as if he'd really hoped it wouldn't come to this.

And then the first thug reached Hal, and swung a hefty club at his head, which the ranger dodged deftly.

"Yes," Ty sighed. "Now."

Stef uttered some quick Equiann to the hooded Immrith, and whipped the cloth from his head.

To Immrith's credit, he made quite the jaw-dropping entrance, rearing up on his hind legs, his front hooves wheeling in midair, as he flexed his heavily-muscled arms out to the sides. His near-black hair rippled wildly behind him like a cape, his amber eyes flashing dangerously as he scanned about for an opponent. He bared his teeth in a wicked grin when he saw the numbers that faced him.

Mickey's boys pulled up short in their headlong charge, but it was too late. Immrith's hooves caught one unlucky thug in the mouth, sending blood and teeth spraying, and gifting him with a smile to rival his leader's. Stef blocked a right-hook that had stalled in shock, batting it aside and shoving his opponent towards Aren's waiting fist. Wil was circling another in a half crouch, his twin knives out to mirror the man opposite him. The man lunged, and then Wil was weaving around his knife, jabbing and slashing at the openings he left. Hal dodged and ducked around the two who'd decided to take him on, while Jesse used her height to her advantage and punched out their kneecaps.

Ty and Fae fought together in the middle of the group, with Laina between them. Fae's mother was not a fighter, and they worked hard to keep her out of the fray. Fae pulled her swords from their sheath, separating them with a metallic *swish*. Ty yanked his bow from its oilcloth, and brought it to bear from behind the ragged line the others held. With surprising accuracy in such close quarters, he buried arrows in legs, arms, shoulders, anything to slow the human mob.

Fae stood ready, her swords held high.

When one of the thugs charged past Stef and made it inside Ty's reach with the bow, Fae struck. She snaked out with her right blade, slashing a line of red across the man's chest. He stumbled backwards, and was knocked from view by one of Immrith's swinging fists. The centaur appeared to be thoroughly enjoying himself, laying about blows left and right that left recipients dazed and reeling. Occasionally he'd throw in a heavy-hoofed kick for good measure, and send a thug sprawling in the dirt.

Fae's erstwhile opponent was replaced with another, racing in through the gap left by his comrade. Fae had just enough time to register that this one swung a rusty shortsword from one hand before she was forced to parry and dance out of the way. Pivoting sideways, she cast a sidelong glance to make sure Laina was still defended, and was relieved to see that she stood back-to-back with Ty. Aren had also positioned himself nearby, grappling with a thug with one eye, and covered her on the other side.

Turning her pivot into a pirouette, Fae brought her swords whipping around, like the seeds of a sycamore tree, hoping to force her opponent back. But instead of whistling through empty air, her left blade struck the unyielding edge of steel, sending shockwaves up her arm. Swinging the right blade underneath the left, she sliced at the hand gripping the shortsword. There was a yelp, but the sword was released only long enough for it to be passed nimbly from the injured right hand to the left.

Fae looked up, and found herself looking into the eyes of a woman around the same age as her, with a hard-edged hatred in her gaze. She had the air of an untamed beast, twitching restlessly, but her eyes were steady as stone.

Fae raised her swords once more, suddenly wondering if she had it in her to kill when it came down to it.

The woman before her raised her sword, holding it at an angle across her body, and bared her teeth. Her muscles bunched, readying to launch herself at Fae. She opened her mouth to scream her battlecry...

And a roar levelled the square. Windows rattled in their panes. Roof tiles slid from their perches to shatter on the ground.

The fighting stopped as combatants instinctively ducked their heads and covered their ears, some even dropping their weapons in their haste.

Fae's opponent curled into a crouch, head whipping around to find the source of the noise.

And still the roar rumbled on, shaking each and every one of them to the bone.

Mountains sunder and boulders break. An avalanche of sound.

Ty's ears twitched beside Fae. Shallow creases appeared around the corners of his eyes.

Fae smiled. *I knew it.* Then she heard it too.

Wings the size of a tall-ship's sails were flapping nearby, hidden in the fog, but getting closer and closer with every furl and snap.

Then they stopped. There was an ominous, echoing crumbling sound. And then silence.

A roof tile shattered on the cobbles somewhere in the daylight gloom.

Mickey and his "boys" unconsciously backed up together until they were huddled around their leader again, necks craning fruitlessly as they scanned the foggy sky.

Out of nowhere, a line of fire spewed from the fog above them to burn a wall of flame into the ground between the two sides. Shrieks went up from the Throldon thugs, and Fae just about made them out scrambling back from the fire, panicked, but unharmed.

As Mickey's mob beat a chaotic retreat, Kagos appeared out of the fog. His enormous figure loomed out of the murk, crouched atop the buildings lining the far end of the square. His vast wings reached across the full length of the terraced row on which he perched, and his legs, the size of tree-trunks, stood upon crushed chimney stacks. He dwarfed the buildings, let alone the people beside them. His huge head was easily the size of two horse-carts, and his green-gold dorsal ridge shimmered in the firelight, quivering threateningly as he rumbled deep in his throat. He made a terrifying picture, his pure black scales making him look like the embodiment of evil, while the liquid black of his eyes burned with reflections of the flames below.

He roared again, in his earth-rending voice, and Fae saw more than one of Mickey's gang lose control of their bladders.

Aiya stepped out from behind one of Kagos's giant forelegs.

"I'd be nice if I were you," she called, effecting an air of nonchalance. "He has a habit of judging people by their smell." She wrinkled her nose. "And by the looks of it, a few of you aren't exactly smelling of roses right now."

Kagos rumbled menacingly, and it was the sound of rocks tumbling into a bottomless ravine.

Without hesitation, the mob broke rank, racing from the square in a frenzied scramble.

The dragon sent the occasional sadistic gout of flame at their heels, to encourage a rapid departure, and then finally the square was quiet again, the only sound coming from the crackle of flames across the cobbles.

Kagos lifted away from the roofline, before dropping to the floor of the square, his landing shaking the ground beneath their feet. His head snaked back and forth, and a stream of grey cloud spread across the square, obscuring Fae's view of him. The cloud dampened the flames, until they were nothing more than a charred scar in the stones, hissing and adding to the fog-mired air.

The ground shook again with a familiar avalanche of sound, and if Fae hadn't known better, she would have believed the city crumbled to dust around them. Then, Kagos strode through the grey cloud, his robe of heavy, black silk billowing around his bare feet as he stepped across still-hissing cobbles. Aiya appeared close behind, and Fae noted the thick soles on her thigh-high boots, presumably for just such a situation. She was digging through her pack, and finally pulled out a pair of simple, but fine sandals. Placing them on the ground at the edge of the char, she stepped back to allow Kagos to step into them, so that his feet would not touch the filthy ground of the city.

"You came," Fae said, with a smugness she hadn't owned two days ago.

The look Kagos gifted her with appeared withering at first glance, but she knew him now, and she saw the smirk hiding beneath.

"So it seems," he rumbled, his voice grating stone. "It would appear as though you need my help."

"*Men*," Fae heard Jesse mutter behind her.

"You ran them off just as we had the better of them!" Immrith protested, a bloody spatter decorating his torso. He wore a feral grin, and looked as if he had actually been enjoying himself.

"Actually," Hal said, scrubbing his hands down the sides of his trouser-legs, "they had a pretty decent handle on us too." He straightened, wiping the sweat from his brow. "And they, like as not, have fresh fighters in the wings." He looked Kagos in the eye. "Thank you for coming when you did."

"What changed your mind?" Fae asked.

Kagos flicked a glance at Aiya, who was looking quietly smug beside him. "Aiya suggested we fly over Throldon and the surrounding area, to prove the state of the land is not as bad as you said." His lips thinned, slit-like nostrils flaring slightly. "It is worse." Aiya's expression grew somber to match his. "I have a duty to watch over my brethren," he continued. "And today, that duty involves defending our world against those who would poison it from within."

He dipped his head to Fae. "We're with you."

PART III

42

SKY-ROADS AND MINIATURE WORLDS

Max crouched in a small space where two roofs and a dormer eave met, providing an ideal spot to watch events unfold below.

In the ten days she'd been in Throldon, she'd made it her business to get to know as much about this miserable city as possible — and that included learning to recognise the key players. When it came to who ran the streets, the gang of unsavoury characters filling the square above which she was currently perched, was one of the worst — generally best avoided.

Today, Mickey and his goons were facing off with an unfortunate group of newcomers, and had them pinned in Old Gallows Square. Max winced. It looked like Mickey had brought half his crew with him, and Headless was clearly fixing for a fight. The way she'd heard it, they'd taken the loss of Pete and Joe hard, and were looking to return the favour if ever they saw those "tall-folk bean-poles" again.

Well, apparently they had, and here they were.

Max sighed. Hapton had been just the same. There were always gangs who grouped together, thinking they could own the city by being the meanest, and it always went the same way. She'd seen enough blood spilled in back allies to know she was better off on her own.

The man at the front of the newcomers stepped forward, trying to calm Mickey down, his body language easy and unthreatening. But the gang leader's eyes nearly popped out of their sockets.

"I don't give a shit what you want!" Max heard him shriek.

Well that's it, Max thought, *he's lost it.* She'd not yet seen Mickey reach this level of rage and walk away without leaving someone bloodied. She reached behind her and pulled out the apple she'd snagged on the way here. The second she'd seen Mickey marching through the streets of Throldon, rallying his troops, she'd known a sizeable fight was in store.

She took a big bite of her apple. *And good entertainment is so hard to come by these days.* She looked forward to the day someone big enough and strong enough could finally teach Mickey and his goons that they weren't the top of the food chain.

But, Max thought morosely, looking down at the eight strangers and their gentled horse, *doesn't look like it's gonna be these poor sods.* She spotted Ali Quickfingers and Andy the Hammer sneaking into the square behind the newcomers, cutting off their retreat. She sighed, and settled back into her little nook between the roofs. This wouldn't take long.

Then all of a sudden, one of the bean-poles whipped the cowl from his horse, and an extra fighter appeared in the mix. He was bare-chested and strong, and he reared up on the horse like...

Wait... The bite of apple in Max's mouth fell to the roof tiles underfoot. *What, in the name of the countless gods, is* that?

The fighter wasn't *on* the horse, the fighter *was* the horse, his torso merging smoothly into the chestnut horse-hair of a bay stallion. He reared up, one flailing hoof cracking Wilfred Rangle hard across the jaw.

After that, the fight was chaos. Max leant forward, gripping the edge of the dormer with white-knuckled fingers, biting the inside of her cheek to keep herself from whooping whenever the newcomers got one up on Mickey's goons.

Wilf was only the first to go down. Soon after him, Louis the Fist was knocked clean out by one of the bean-poles, then it was Tyra the Bitch, kneecapped — by a dwarf of all things — as she rushed one of the newcomers with Kimmy Righteous. Kimmy ducked the swing coming her way and managed to dodge the kneecapping, but was taken out by one of the horse-man's flailing fists.

He's a liability! Max fought back a laugh as the horse-man lay about, apparently heedless of who he might hit.

In the middle of the group, one of the bean-poles aimed a longbow with haunting accuracy into the fray. At his back was a woman wielding dual blades that sang through the air. They were the most beautiful weapons Max had ever laid eyes on: polished to a high shine and razor sharp, they curved only just enough to slice through the air like a hot knife through soft butter. But they were nothing compared to the woman who commanded them. If the blades sang, she *danced*, ducking and dodging and weaving as if the motions were moves she'd practiced and perfected a hundred times before. She sliced Lance Lacoste across the chest and he stumbled back into the path of the horse-man's erratic swings.

And then she faced Hannah.

"Shit," Max hissed.

Hannah was the third sibling in the Three 'Mares. The other two had been Joe and Pete.

"*Shit,*" Max said again. She rose up above the edge of her hideout, craning to get a better look. The Three 'Mares had been so called because they were a notorious nightmare to deal with, whether you were on their side or not. Thick as thieves, those three had been loyal to the death to each other above all else. The way Max had heard it, Mickey had come to a very complex arrangement with them to bring them on side. She cast a furtive glance across at the leader, and saw the look of surprise she expected; Hannah hadn't been invited to this particular fight.

Looking back at the 'Mare, Max could see why: the woman was wild with grief. She slashed with her sword, something she was well-practiced with. The sword-dancer spun away, flicking one of her beautiful blades out to catch Hannah's hand under the hilt. But the 'Mare just tossed the weapon to her other hand, screaming something no doubt vulgar at the other woman.

And then the square shook, and a roar so loud it rattled her head filled the air.

Caught off balance, Max fell back into her little nook, instinctively grabbing at the eave of the dormer so she wouldn't slide down into the street.

No. Her eyes went wide, but she wasn't looking at the square anymore. She was looking at four men burning alive from beneath the wagon where she hid. *No no no no no no no.* She curled into the smallest shape she could make, and pressed herself against the wall of the dormer, squeezing her eyes shut so tight stars blinked inside the lids

She heard the flapping of sails. *Wings.*

She felt the rush of heat against her right arm. *Fire.*

She heard the shrieks of Mickey's gang, and prepared herself for the smell of charred flesh that was sure to follow.

But instead, she heard the same female voice she'd heard before.

"I'd be nice if I were you," she called serenely. "He has a habit of judging people by their smell."

They smelled wrong, the gravelly voice had said when they'd burned Rogan and his men.

There was more rumbling, more whimpers, and then the yelled retreat of over a dozen men and women scrambling from the square.

The flap of giant wings. The thundering boom of giant feet on the stones below. The hiss of dying fire.

When her arm no longer felt the prickle of heat from below, Max finally raised her head enough to peer down into the misty gloom that had filled the square.

A dark figure emerged from the murk. Max squinted her eyes but all she could make out was someone tall, dressed all in black. Beside that one was a woman wearing some kind of long coat that covered her from her lips to her knees.

"You came," the sword-dancer said.

"So it seems," the black figure replied, and his voice held the echo of gravel and rock-slides and mountains crumbling.

And then the black figure said something about the land being poisoned, and Max's interest piqued. Things hadn't been right for a long time. Not here, not in Hapton, and not on the road with Rogan's crew either.

When the newcomers eventually left the square, she trailed behind them, hopping from roof to roof and following the sky-roads most people knew nothing about. Throldon was even better than Hapton had been for these, the city having reached the architectural milestone of solid roofing far before the market town, and the topography that resulted was as varied as if Throldon was a miniature world in its own right. There were valleys that ran between sloping roofs of buildings built so close together that they may as well have been one, and mountains of steep, precipitous tile that even Max hadn't attempted to summit. There were soft, rolling hills of thatch — which made for wonderfully warm basking spots on a sunny day — and smooth, slippery sheets of green copper that were treacherous to cross, but sometimes unavoidable.

In the central, wealthier districts of Throldon, the buildings were proud and upright, with covered footbridges between them allowing the gentry to move across the city without ever having to set foot on the filthy streets. Of course, what benefitted the overtly affluent, also worked to Max's advantage beautifully.

As the sprawling network of sky-roads branched out into the city's poorer streets, buildings began to lean alarmingly towards each other, so that Max had only to step from one roof to another. Sometimes, she was forced to leap, defying gravity and risking one of her numerous, cat-like lives in the process. She had yet to fall, of course — at least, not in Throldon. Hapton had been the backdrop to her last loss against gravity, and that had left her with the questionable hospitality of Rogan and his men. She wasn't keen to repeat the process.

In any case, the group she was following now clearly had no idea where they were going. At one point, she sat at the centre of a cruciform building, and watched them walk around it twice before veering off in a seemingly random direction. They were heading vaguely towards the centre of the city — bad idea — but with no logic to the path they chose.

The horse-man was covered again, plodding along like the gentled draft horse she'd initially taken him for. The black figure had a deep hood pulled low over his own face, his hands tucked into his sleeves. He looked a lot like a preacher of the Judge, the final adjudicator of all souls as they pass through the gates of death. Max gave an involuntary shudder. All the preachers gave her the heebie-jeebies.

She couldn't get over the fact that this person, this unassuming black figure, had been the one to rain down fire and death on Rogan's crew.

I was sure it was... bigger, she mused. But then, a wall of flame in the dark and the sight of four men burning alive could do funny things to a person's perceptions. As she followed the group of strangers through the city, she found herself creeping nearer, and nearer, peering into the shadows of the hood, angling herself to get a better look at the monster that had set her free, then left her alone.

She was so consumed with getting a closer look, that she didn't notice when they led her into a dead-end.

In the secluded alley, the black figure turned, and looked straight at her.

Black-on-black eyes of liquid obsidian pinned Max to the spot.

On any other day, she might have scrambled up to the roofline, or dropped to the moss-covered balcony below to duck behind the balustrade. She might have fallen.

But she was rooted in place, hanging precariously as she gripped a rusty drainpipe in one hand, and the lip of the roof with the other, her heart beating a thundering tattoo against her chest.

Why don't you come down from there, Little Phoenix? a deep, rumbling voice sounded in her head.

She did lose her grip then.

Her hand slipped from the drainpipe, and she clung desperately to the roof with the other as she swung out over the alleyway, perilously close to the extent of her fingers' ability to hold on to the roof-edge.

She scrambled for better purchase for a second that felt like minutes. By the time she got her feet back under her, gripping a shallow half-ledge where the floor below stuck out a couple of inches, the whole group of newcomers was looking up at her. She was about to clamber back up the drainpipe when an older woman in the group called out to her.

"What are you doing up there?!" she cried. "Get down before you kill yourself!"

Max almost laughed out loud. It was the kind of thing her mother would have said. That was, back when she still had a mother. The pain of that loss had dulled to a quiet ache a long time ago, but this woman's maternal air still gave her pause. Kind eyes looked up at her, a mixture of scolding and worry.

"Come down, girl," the one accompanying the black figure called calmly. "We won't hurt you."

"Like you didn't hurt Rogan and his crew?" Max found herself yelling back.

The woman stilled. The black one's flat lips curled up in a very small, amused smile.

Would you deny the world is better off without them? the rumbling voice asked. Max's lips clamped shut. She couldn't deny it. They'd been awful, cruel men. The voice continued. *You will not be harmed, Little Phoenix. I did not burn you then, nor will I burn you now.*

"How can I trust you?" she yelled from her perch, which was already slippery with her nervous sweat, and the dampness of persistent fog. She would have to decide soon: up to the roof, or down to the street?

"You're the one spying on us!" the dwarf argued back. The only normal-looking man there put a hand out to interrupt her.

"You don't," he called up simply. "Until you can."

Max considered. Then carefully shifted her weight, slotting her fingers and bare toes into the cracks in the mortar, until she could safely make her way down the wall.

43

ENEMY OF MY ENEMY

The girl that dropped to the ground after climbing down the crumbling townhouse wall like a spider was no more than a waif. Her roughly-chopped hair hung just past her shoulders in lank, tangled ropes, and her dark brown eyes, when she turned to face them, were wide and round, set in a thin face. Fae judged her to be in her early adolescence but, lacking any girlish curves to soften her frame, it was hard to tell; she could have even passed for a boy.

"Are you alright?" Laina said as soon as her feet were on the ground. She eyed the girls' scraped knees with open concern. "Are you hurt?"

The girl shifted from foot to foot, and folded one leg behind the other. "I'm fine," she said self-consciously.

"How long have you been following us?" Ty asked.

"I'd guess at least since the square," Aiya said, stepping forward. She shot Kagos a look that held a spark of anger within it. "Is this the other one from the plains?"

"What one from the plains?" Ty asked. He looked from Aiya to Kagos, and back again.

"She hears me," Kagos said, ignoring Ty, as if the fact held significance.

Aiya's eyes widened, and flicked to the girl. "She hears?" she repeated.

"She speaks as well," the girl muttered irately.

"You know her?" Fae asked, barely keeping up with the fragmented conversation.

Aiya winced. "Not exactly," she said.

"They burned the men I was travelling with alive, and left me alone on the Southern Highway," the girl answered for her. She turned a withering glare on Kagos. "I thought you'd be bigger," she spat with surprising venom.

Kagos flashed her a smug, toothy grin. "You should see me on a good day."

Jesse elbowed her way forward. "Okay, not that this isn't *delightful* and all, but might I remind everyone of why we're here?"

"Yes," Aren agreed, "we don't exactly have time for tea with the locals." He look down at the girl with an apologetic grimace. "No offence." She shrugged.

"She's coming with us," Kagos said, as if it was obvious.

"What?!" came a chorus of voices.

"She hears Draconic," he said, tapping a long finger to his temple. "That's a rare gift, and one that belongs with the dragons. Not wallowing in human filth."

"Hey!" the girl protested.

"I thought your kind were dying out?" Hal said.

"Perhaps," Kagos answered enigmatically.

"Do I get a say in this?" the girl asked.

"*Of course* you do," Aiya said quickly, shooting Kagos a glare.

He sighed. "Of *course* you can choose." Aiya rolled her eyes at the edge in his tone. "You can choose between coming voluntarily, or being carried back to Hearthstone."

"*After* we defeat Anson," Fae reminded him.

Kagos stilled, as if weighing it up.

"Thought you were with us," Hal said.

"Who's Anson?" the girl asked.

"Okay, stop!" Jesse raised her voice above the tangle of questions piling over one another. "Everybody, stop." Everyone looked at her, quieting their rabble. In the momentary lull, Jesse took a deep breath, and levelled a glare at each of them.

"We're not here for this—" she waggled a finger between the girl and Kagos "—we're here for one job, and that is to find this damned Lady, and do whatever it is that needs doing to fix the Spirit Realm and restore natural life so the humans can go back to their villages, and the forests can get back to waking up. *Not*," she stressed, "to pick up recruits on the streets of Throldon." She marched up to stand toe-to-toe with the girl. There wasn't much difference between them in height.

"What's your name, girl?"

"Max."

"Right, Max, nothing personal, but we're in the middle of something rather important right now and we don't really have time to babysit. So why don't you run along your way, and we'll do the same."

Max nodded, and turned to leave. "Looked to me like you could use some help though." She gestured to the roofline from where she'd apparently been watching them.

"How's that?" Jesse scowled.

"You haven't got a clue where you're going," Max said. "I saw you walk around the same building twice earlier."

"You can't have been here that long," Aiya said. "We crossed paths, what, two weeks ago? Even if you rode straight here, you've only been in the city twelve days at best." She narrowed her eyes at the girl. "You're just as new as we are."

Max gave her an indulging smile. "You're very naïve for someone who sees the world from above." She levelled a finger at Kagos. "I may not know what you are, but I know you fly."

"How do you *not* know what I am?" Kagos said, his ebony brow forming a shallow dent in the middle.

Max became suddenly reticent. "It was dark before..." she mumbled.

"What about today?" Aiya pushed. "He hardly made any effort to hide, *in broad daylight*." She shot Kagos a look of utter exasperation.

Max was examining her feet with unprecedented interest, and mumbled something unintelligible under her breath.

"Speak up, girl."

"I hid, okay?" Max burst out. "I was scared, so I ducked behind the roof and hid. I didn't see anything."

Kagos smiled a rare genuine smile. "A wise course of action in both circumstances," he said gently. "Well, no need to live in ignorance any longer. I am a dragon, Little Phoenix. So yes—" he smirked quietly at Aiya "—we see the world from above."

"Why do you keep calling me that?" Max asked, her face wrinkled with confusion.

"What?"

"Little Phoenix."

Kagos's smile broadened. "Because you walked away from my flames unscathed, little one!" he answered with laughter in his voice. "There are precious few who can make such a claim."

Max regarded him as if he was the crazy man on the street everyone went out of their way to avoid, then turned back to Aiya.

"Anyway," she said, picking up where she left off, "there's not much for a street urchin to do in a new city except get to know the place." She pointed to the roofs again. "And there's no better place to do that than from above. There aren't many who choose the sky-roads on account of falling being a terminal problem." She beamed proudly, and jabbed herself in the chest with a thumb. "I never fall." She glanced askance. "Well, almost never. Anyway, that makes it safe from the territorials, like Mickey. And it's easy to listen in, find out who's who around a place. Besides—" she paused, suddenly looking uncomfortable "—you don't want a local."

"Go on," Jesse said, looking decidedly unconvinced.

Max's eyes hardened again. "Trust me. The longer they've been here, the more likely people are to be a bit..." She snapped her fingers, searching for the right words. "I don't know, a bit dead behind the eyes." She shrugged awkwardly. "It seems worse when they're on their own. Like the street kids. None of them have anyone else. So they all just... drift. Like street ghosts."

Fae exchanged a glance with Ty. Another sign of the spreading influence of Anson? Of the absence of Aethyr here? She looked over to Hal, who had taken the lead so far in Throldon. He caught her look, and gave a shrug, as if to say, *Your guess is as good as mine.*

"Okay," Ty said aloud, casting a look at the darkening fog above the nearly-touching rooflines. "Seeing as you're so familiar with the place now — we'll need a place to lay low tonight. Got anywhere for us?"

Max grinned wide, as if she'd been waiting for that very question.

"I know *just* the place."

. . .

By the time they reached Max's hideaway, sunlight had well and truly given up trying to infiltrate the pervasive fog, and the city dwellers had replaced its reluctant pall with tall, oil-lit lamps at every street corner. The light they cast was a sickly yellow, and clung in pools at the base of their posts, barely illuminating more than a foot of street. The dim lighting suited Max well, as she strode easily through the streets. She didn't skirt the edges, nor strut confidently. She blended in, melting through the shadows like she was one of them.

Max ducked down an empty street, took them though a rusted iron gate, and on through a further warren of narrow alleyways and small, dark yards. She navigated it all with impressive night-vision, leaving the rest of them to stumble along after her.

And tucked away at the end of the labyrinth, the walls opened up to reveal a wide, open dead-space between two buildings. The walls to either side leaned so drunkenly close that the roofing above overlapped, offering an effective shelter from the elements. At the far end, the walls and floor ended abruptly, giving way to the sputtering yellow light of the street, now two-storeys below them.

"Where are we?" Fae asked. She didn't remember climbing any stairs to get here.

"Nowhere," Max replied, affecting a ghostly voice, and waving her arms before her face. She grinned at their blank faces. Walking across to the left-hand wall, she slapped the bricks that made up its surface. "Brownstone Place—" she crossed to the other wall, covered in a crumbling render "—meets Grenauld Avenue." She patted the stone affectionately, then pointed down. "There's a corner shop on the ground level, and the owner lives above that." Spreading her hands, she cast her eyes about the space in which they stood. "Throldon's a funny city," she said. "It's mostly flat. Or at least, that's what the people who built it wanted to believe. If you look closely, you'll see all the buildings are on a level, even when the ground ain't." She brought her hands back together. "There are nooks like this all over the place, but most of them are occupied. I got lucky with this one." She jerked a thumb to the conjoined roofs. "Dry." She indicated the entrance. "Hard to get into." Then, pointing to the open view of the street, "Easy to leave." She grinned. "If you have the right skill-set, of course."

Fae was impressed. "Thank you for sharing it with us," she said.

"Yes," Jesse added with a suspicious glint. "Why *did* you?"

Max shrugged. "Said you wanted to take down Lady Black. Even Rogan was scared o' her. At first, I thought, you know, the enemy of my enemy... but then I got here..." She hugged herself, suppressing a shudder. "Ain't nothing good, does this." She moved across to look out of the open wall, careful to stick to the shadows. Down on the street, a woman scurried along, pulling her young child with her, all the while casting furtive glances over each shoulder. Opposite them, a young couple shuffled from one sickly pool of lamplight to the next. Their eyes were empty, devoid of life, like the walking dead.

Max turned back to Jesse. "The Unity destroyed a lot in the name of the little guys." She indicated herself. "But they was just selfish. Made a lot of things worse for most of us. Throldon's the only city left with anyone in it for a hundred leagues, and now the Lady's pissin' all over that too." Max sniffed, and drew herself up. "Figure it's time for the slate to be wiped clear. And if you're the ones to do it—" she shrugged again "—that suits me fine."

"Then our interests align," Kagos said, his black eyes gleaming in the reticent glow from the street.

"Yeah," Max said uncertainly. "I don't get what *you* want from me, but I'd like to help get rid of Lady Black." She looked up at Fae. "If I can."

Fae exchanged a look with Ty, who mirrored the girl's signature shrug.

"We *could* use a guide," Hal said, eyeing a deeply frowning Jesse.

Jesse narrowed her eyes at Max. "Do *you* know where Black is in this steaming pile of dung you call a city?" she said.

Max nodded. "I know where the training complex is," she replied. "The whole bailey's 'Survivors Only'. I can take you there. Makes sense she'd be there too."

"Fine," Jesse said, convinced at least for now. "Now someone take that damned hood off Immrith, he's giving me the creeps, just standing there like that."

Immrith emerged at a word from Stef, and threw the cowl to the ground. He uncurled his hunched spine, arching backwards and shaking out his great mane of hair.

"I will not be walked around like a blind crone anymore," he declared vehemently. "I will not cower beneath cloth while being spoon-fed conversation out of context." His eye caught on Max. "Who is this?" And then took in their surroundings with distinct discomfort. "What is this place?"

"This is Max," Fae said, her multilingual voice allowing everyone present to understand at least one side of the conversation. "And this is somewhere safe to lie low for the night. Max has agreed to guide us to Black's stronghold in the city." Immrith snorted, as if skeptical such a tiny little thing could be of any use to anyone.

"It is suffocating," he said, about their locale. "I have never known anyone to be safer than under the open skies."

"You could always continue stumbling about in the dark," Max suggested airily. She didn't understand Immrith's words, but his derisive tone was unmistakable. "But," she admitted, "I'd rather you succeed. The last team of tall-folk weren't lucky enough to find someone like me before the Survivors found *them*."

Fae, Ty, and the scouts stilled.

"What do you mean, 'the last team'?" Wil asked precisely.

44

THE LAST TEAM

"There was another group of 'em," Max said. "Only arrived a couple days ago." She pointed between Wil, Aren, and Stef. "Thought you were them when I first saw you in Old Gallows — got the same look about you."

"Describe them," Wil said, employing a great deal of willpower to keep his voice even.

Max glanced uneasily from him to Aren and Stef, who were staring at her with just as much intensity. She swallowed.

"Three men, one older than the other two. About five-eleven, maybe six foot, one was a bit taller... all had something wrapped round their heads." She eyed Aren's head-scarf. "They wore cloaks — don't see that much around here. The older one had a pipe." When still no one said anything, she looked Wil in the eye. "Look, I've lived in either a big town, or a bigger city my whole life. And I'll tell you, a woodsman stands out in a crowd of people more than if he wore court motley and danced a merry jig. These three, like you lot—" she indicated Ty, Fae, Wil, Aren, and Stef "—were woodsmen. Or near as makes no difference."

"What happened to them?" Wil asked.

"They were sniffing around the complex," Max answered. "Survivors don't take too kind to outsiders sticking their noses where they're not welcome. Saw one of 'em get grabbed by red-bands but I don't know more than that." Wil fell quiet.

"Thom smokes a pipe," Stef said softly.

Aren nodded. "But what would those three be doing here?" he asked. "They're supposed to be in Dvargra." Stef shrugged. "Can you take us to the place it happened?" Aren asked.

Max nodded. "Of course." She hesitated. "You should know, it's crawlin' with red-bands."

"What now?" Jesse asked.

"Survivors," Max replied. "Patrols. And they don't wait for a reason to snatch someone off the streets." She jerked her chin at Immrith, "Might want to leave him here." Then shot Kagos a look. "And him."

Kagos looked affronted. "I can be discreet," he said. Aiya's eyebrows leapt an inch closer to her hairline, but she kept her opinions to herself.

Max shook her head. "Even with your hood down low, it's obvious you're not from around here. You stick out just as much as him." She nodded towards Immrith, towering over them all and looking distinctly unhappy about their hideout arrangements. "Besides—" she turned back to Wil and Aren "—the fewer people come, the better. Can't exactly expect to take a group of—" she did a quick head count "—eleven, plus yours truly, to spy on Lady Black's heavily-guarded complex and *not* get caught."

"I'll go," Aren and Wil chorused.

"I'll go too," Fae said. "I would like to see what we're facing."

"Well, there ain't much to see," Max warned, "but I can take you there." She glanced between the leaning walls of her little dead-space, out at the deepening gloom. "Probably best go now, if you're keen." She turned back to Fae. "No time like the present."

Exchanging a quick look with Wil and Aren, Fae nodded. "How far is it?"

"Through these streets, a couple of hours, and that's if we don't bump into any patrols."

"Two hours?!" Fae cried in dismay. "Just how big is this city?" And then she noticed the sly grin creeping across Max's face. "What?"

"We won't be taking the streets," she said.

. . .

Max's "sky-roads" took them out from under the eaves between Brownstone and Grenauld, and up onto the top of the city skyline. Finally able to walk more or less in a straight line for the first time since entering Throldon, they *flew* the mile-or-so to the outer bailey wall.

It was raining a fine, grey mist that soaked them through in an instant. Even so, from on top of things, Fae could see why Max's best guess at walking the distance had been so long: the streets of Throldon wended back and forth with the confidence of a drunkard who in truth neither knew nor cared where he was going. In some instances, getting from one building to its neighbour on the other side of the same wall involved a mile-long round-trip — it would be easier to break through the wall and rebuild it again after. Labyrinthine alleys snaked between wide thoroughfares that narrowed until they were nothing but spy-holes between walls.

There were places where the sky-roads were just as tricky to navigate, even treacherous, but Max proved a very able guide, and before long they were perched across from the walls of Lady Black's "complex".

The old bailey walls towered over the city by at least fifty feet, throwing the surrounding streets into a perpetual gloom.

The four of them crouched like gargoyles atop a two-storey baker-shop, watching the empty stretch of wet cobbles below.

"They were snooping around down there," Max muttered under her breath, indicating a section of the featureless wall opposite them, interrupted only by an unassuming, wooden door. "Sounded to me like they were thinking of going in." Her eyes slid sideways to meet Fae's. "Sounded to me like they didn't all agree on the subject." She shrugged, an involuntary shiver catching her halfway so that the motion looked more like a nervous tic. "Anyways, they got unlucky 'cause that's when the red-bands came out and spotted them. They ran, but one of 'em got snatched, like I said."

"When did this happen?" Wil asked, staring intently at the door below them.

"Night before last," Max replied with a sniff. The misty rain had begun to gather in her tangled mass of hair, and was now running down her forehead in slow runnels. She wiped a dirty forearm across her face, eyeing their cloaks jealously.

"Is there another way in?" Fae asked.

Max shook her head like a wet dog, sending out a spray of water that no one could escape. "Not unless you fancy trying the main gates." She gave an ugly snort that articulated exactly what she thought of that option. Then she froze. Her eyes darted to the street. "Get down!" she hissed suddenly, waving them back and dropping to her belly on the flat roof, heedless of the shallow pool of water that had formed there. Fae, Wil, and Aren swiftly followed suit, peering over the edge with their hoods pulled low.

Within seconds of Max's warning, three men, dressed in mismatched, dark clothing appeared at the far end of the row. They wore no uniform to tie them together, except for a wide band of red cloth fastened around their upper arm.

They ranged in age from around eighteen to thirty, but where the city dwellers they'd seen so far had all had the look of people living day to day wondering if there'd be any food on the table, these men all appeared strong and fit. They walked from the end of the street to the door opposite the four watchers with sure, even steps. When they reached the door, there was no knock, no lock, no call for identification. They simply opened it, and disappeared inside.

Max relaxed visibly.

"Not very secure," Wil noted scornfully.

"They don't need it to be," Max said.

"Who are they?" Fae asked.

"Red-bands," Max answered. "Survivors. Broken-in enough to do the job, and bad enough on a good day. If you ever see a red-*belt*, run. They're the ones that compete — and win — in the Lady's fighting ring. I've only seen one of them so far. The red-bands are just the goons, like Mickey's boys." She shook her head. "They're bad enough," she repeated.

"*There*," Aren whispered suddenly.

Wil nodded. "I saw."

"What?" Fae asked. Aren pointed down the to the mouth of a darkened alley, visible as the road curved further up the street.

Tucked into the shadows, two hooded figures lurked.

"Knew they wouldn't leave one behind," Aren said with a cold smile. As he spoke, the figures detached from the shadows, and traced the route of the red-bands. From their size and bearing, they appeared to be men, but Max was right: they walked with the easy grace of elves. They skirted the walls, dodging the shallow pools of lamplight as they went, heading straight for the door.

"They can't go in there!" Max hissed, panicked. "There's a reason there's no lock on that door!" But that's exactly where the cloaked figures were going. A hand reached out for the door-handle. Max sucked air through gritted teeth. "They must have a death wish," she muttered.

A duskowl's call pierced the misty gloom, making Fae and Max jump a mile. The cloaked hand jerked back from the door below.

Fae's head whipped around to find Aren lowering his cupped hands from his mouth, his eyes fixed on the street, and the only figures in it. The two hoods swivelled left and right below, searching for the source of the sound. Aren called again. The sleepy hoot of a duskowl travelled softly through the rain without echoing against the walls of the city.

Finally, two pale faces peered up at them. Thom, and Elas.

Aren immediately began hand-signalling, weaving his fingers in clear gestures that all Arolynos scouts were drilled in until they knew them better than their native tongue.

"Where can we meet them?" Aren asked of Max.

"Tell them to head back to that alley," she said, climbing to her feet. "I'll meet them there." And she was off through the rain, skipping barefoot across rooftops made glassy-slick in the wet. Aren relayed her message with quick fingers, and waited to receive the appropriate acknowledgement. Thom responded with the customary flat-palm that indicated he'd seen Aren's signal, and he and Elas returned the way they'd come, back to the shadows of the alley, where a Throldon street-urchin awaited them.

"So Wyn has been taken," Wil muttered darkly.

"So it seems," Aren replied. Fae watched as the two scouts below disappeared back into the gap between two brick buildings.

"What are they doing here?" Wil asked no one in particular.

"Let's get them back to the others," Fae said, getting to her feet. "I'm sure their reasons are as unfortunate as ours."

They stole silently through the night like red-handed thieves, following Max's nimble steps exactly as she led them back along the sky-roads.

Both Thom and Elas showed signs of a less than auspicious journey so far: Thom's face was a mottled purple from his left temple almost down to his jawline, and Elas winced whenever the sky-roads led them through a change in elevation. Out of the corner of her eye, Fae noticed him favouring his right side as they leapt from rooftop to rooftop, occasionally pressing a hand against his ribs, but he made no mention of it, his expression as dark and brooding as Thom's.

Neither of them had spoken a word since climbing up from the alleyway, Thom signing quickly that they should talk out from under the bailey's shadow. So they ran. Back to the relative safety of Max's hideout.

When they finally dropped into the dead-space between Brownstone and Grenauld, Immrith was standing in the alleyway behind. His neck was craned back to stare at the narrow sliver of sky above, for all that it was only the flat grey of night-darkened fog. He nodded to them as they passed, his body a picture of tension. His jaw was clenched, the muscles of his arms bunched where they folded tight against his chest. His silent discomfort at being sandwiched between two buildings in the middle of a foreign city was clearer than if he'd raged and broken through the walls brushing against his broad shoulders. Fae reached a hand up to touch him lightly on one arm in a gesture she hoped he found comforting, and moved into the strange corner space occupied by the rest of her mismatched team.

Ty had fashioned a pair of torches somehow, and their light glowed softly above the sickly yellow cast from the street. He met her at the entrance, his fingers knitting with hers briefly.

"I worried," he murmured by way of greeting, the relief in his voice clearly audible.

Fae squeezed his hand before letting go. "I'm fine," she said, turning. "These two, less so." Thom and Elas appeared behind her, followed by Wil and Aren.

"Thom! Elas!" Ty greeted them warmly, gripping the forearm of each as they came in under the eaves. "What brings you to Throldon?" He took in their appearance. "What happened? Come. Sit. Let us have a look at you."

Thom batted his hand away. "It's nothing, don't mother over us." Ty pulled up short, surprised by Thom's tone.

Fae, having expected an element of ill-temper from their mood on the way back, took over.

"Your eye might look worse than it is," she said, nodding to the ugly bruise covering a good portion of his face, "but Elas at least has broken ribs, if he isn't hiding more." She gave the scout her best intractable-healer glare. "Sit." Elas sat gratefully on an upended crate, and pulled his shirt up over his ribs without prompt. While Ty stepped forward to examine Elas, Fae stood opposite Thom, arms folded.

"What, on earth, happened?" She said it gently, but firmly. They'd lost one of their team, but what they were doing in Throldon was still a big question that needed an answer.

Thom scowled. "It's a long story," he said, "and it led to us trailing a *slave* caravan into this damned fog-encrusted city." He hung his head, his scowl deepening further until it ran grooves into his face. "We've seen some dark things this past week. And sought answers." Lifting his head, he met Fae's eyes with deep, painful anguish in his own. "Lord Graem is ready to move against a strange human force moving through the Rand. He's grinding his teeth down to nothing with how hard he champs at the bit. But he can't find anything to act on beyond rumours and ghost stories. We thought, who better to scout out an unknown force than a small, covert group of short elves?" Thom's lips curled in an ugly expression of self-disgust. "The more we found, the darker it became. And then we made it here." He shook his head, berating himself harshly. "Stupid really. We should have turned back at the city limits."

Elas straightened with a wince. "That would have meant leaving those people to their fates." Now it was Elas's turn to shake his head, but it was a gesture of vehement denial. "We're not those kind of scouts, Thom." Thom fell silent. "We followed the caravan into the city," Elas continued. "All the way up to that gated inner wall. It's too well-guarded even for us to slip past. So we started looking at other ways in. We found the side door..." He trailed off, then sucked in a breath as Ty began wrapping his ribs with a length of thick, woven cloth. "It was like they were watching for us before we got there. Those men, wearing red on their arms..."

"Red-bands," Max supplied from a corner.

"Original," Elas said flatly. "Well, they came straight at us, straight down the street. We didn't even have a chance to find cover. We were outnumbered." He glanced down at his strapped ribs. "A couple caught up to us. They're strong: one got Thom in the face, another threw me into a wall. But we got away from them. Wyn was helping me over a fence when they caught us again." He exchanged a solemn look with Thom. "We only just got away. Because of him."

There was a moment of contemplative silence, and then Elas eased to his feet.

"So we found somewhere to lick our wounds, and were just looking into how best to attempt a rescue, when you showed up." He looked askance at the assortment of characters tucked into the dead-space, and arched an eyebrow. "Now your turn," he said. "What are *you* doing here?"

Aren stepped in. "Why don't I introduce you to everyone? I'll do my best to explain as we go."

"In the meantime," Ty said, turning to Thom, "we'll work out how to rescue Wyn." Thom's scowl lessened somewhat, and he gave a gruff nod of gratitude.

"Max," Fae called. "Would you lend us your expertise?"

"Never heard it called that before," the girl said, unfolding herself from the floor. "But sure, Wha'd'ya need to know?"

Fae gifted her with a smile of pure, distilled determination.

"How do we get into the Survivors' complex?"

45

THE GRANDMASTER

They talked long into the night, until dawn brightened the city's eternal murk to a lighter shade of grey.

Max was clear: there was no way into the complex that wasn't under constant watch. The walls were too high, and patrolled in any case, and the only entrances through the solid expanse of vertical stone were heavily guarded.

"How many Survivors are inside?" Wil asked at one point.

"I don't know," Max answered truthfully. "At least a few hundred. Maybe a thousand." She spread her hands to either side. "It's the only part of the city I haven't been able to check out."

"So, horribly outnumbered however we look at it," Ty said.

Max nodded. "And there always seems to be a lot of 'em round the entrances." She shrugged. "Could be they're just packed in there like fish in a barrel. But I think they just like to stick to the edges of the complex for some reason."

"So either we get lucky," Hal said, "or we die finding out."

"We're not dying here," Fae said with rock-solid, completely unfounded confidence. "I didn't come here to fail." She cast her eyes around at them all. "None of us did."

"True," Jesse said, drawing the word out. "But a lot of this hinges on you." She levelled Fae with a significant look. "Didn't you say you can't connect to the Spirit Realm here?"

Fae closed her eyes to look upon Eah'lara as it was here.

It was dark, the nebulae that made up its fabric swept far from this place. Fae cast her senses out, and found a distant glimmer of spirit-life, like the tiniest sparkle of sea on a distant horizon.

She smiled in the darkness. And opened her eyes.

"It's there," Fae said. "But the connections are severed, out beyond the city. I can't reach it from here, but it's there."

"Doesn't that limit your power?" Jesse asked.

Fae tipped her head to one side, considering. "Yes," she answered. "But only as much as the sea is limited by how much it rains." She reached inside herself, and pulled the merest fraction of her power into her breath. It was like drawing her aura into her lungs, and letting it shine through her skin, her eyes, her hair. It warmed her. Made her feel *strong*.

"Woah," Max breathed. Fae smiled, and let the glow fade. Before the other Aethyr had joined with her, she hadn't even known that sort of control was possible. But Be'ella Tor was a wonderful, whimsical genius when it came to aura control. And now, so was Fae.

"Alright, point made," Jesse grumbled, grudgingly impressed.

"I have power *in* me," Fae said, looking down at her splayed fingers, "but none of me have ever used it to fight." She clenched her hands into fists.

"But you can," Ty said gently. He reached across and eased open her hand. "Remember the village? With the watermill?" Fae looked up from her hands to meet his eyes. They were grey and warm and *safe*. And she remembered. Remembered seeing the destruction in that village that had brought about her relocation to Arolynos. Remembered the outrage she'd felt. The fire within her.

Ty smiled as she remembered. "You were a power in your own right, even then," he said. "You'll find what you need within you, when the time comes."

"We could always go in the front door," Kagos said casually, inspecting his nails as he leant back against one wall, looking out onto the street.

"Are you crazy, old man?" Max said, scowling. "That's the *worst possible* option we haven't even discussed. Even if we did want to go in all hooting and hollering, the front gate is *crawling* with red-bands." She glared at him, daring him to argue.

Instead, Kagos smiled. It started as a self-satisfied smirk, and turned into a grin, just short of laughter. He looked... excited.

Aiya's expression was as baffled as the rest of them. And then her eyes widened, realisation dawning across her face.

"You can't be serious," she said. Everyone's eyes swivelled to her.

"What?" Fae asked.

"My dear Aiya, why else would I be here, if not to make use of my singular talents?" Kagos said, ignoring Fae's question.

"You are not invincible!" Aiya argued, her face a picture of incredulity.

"I, like our Spiritchild, don't intend to die here," he replied calmly.

"The hundreds-to-thousands of humans inside those walls will likely feel otherwise!" Aiya was all but shouting now, her face flushed.

"They often do," Kagos said wistfully. "But I think we can agree that this variety of human likely deserves my attention."

"Will somebody please let us in on the other half of this conversation?" Jesse interjected.

"I think I get it," Max volunteered. She shot Kagos a shrewd glance. "You said you're a dragon right?" Kagos nodded, a roguish glint in his eye. Max leant back and folded her arms across her chest. "You want to blow down the gates."

"Exactly." Kagos clapped his hands together with glee. "And so well put as well. You are very astute for a human."

The part of Fae that came from Baev'ill approved wholeheartedly with Kagos's intentions. Every other part urged caution.

"A lot of people could get hurt," she said. "If they've been bringing in slaves to work in the complex, then there could be innocent lives at risk."

"All in the name of remaking the world," Kagos replied. "What better death could one wish for?"

"That's not what we're here for," Fae growled.

Kagos patted the air with one hand. "Peace, Fae, peace. I can adjust my fire so that it does not burn. It's not all death and destruction at the hands of dragons, you know." His voice contained a hint of injury, as if offended that she thought so little of his abilities.

Ty hesitated. "Really?" he said. "That's possible? You can just... turn it down?"

Kagos smirked again. "It's not quite that simple. It takes centuries of discipline and even then some never master it. I—" he brought a poised hand to his chest "—am quite the grandmaster of fire control. The fire you saw in the square earlier was not for burning. Sometimes fear will do the job far, *far* better than death."

"Well that's disturbing," Jesse mumbled to herself.

"Indeed," Ty said, his elven ears picking up her words regardless. "But it also opens up a lot of possibilities we haven't considered yet." He turned to Kagos. "How precise is your control?"

Kagos drew himself up. "To within half a degree," he said haughtily. "Not that that means anything to you." He bent and picked up a piece of scrap wood from the floor. Holding it in one hand, he pressed his other to the bricks that made up Brownstone Place. He held up the wood. "In one breath, I can turn this to ash—" then patted the wall "—and leave this barely scorched. I can burn a fire that won't catch, one that inflicts harm but little damage. I can burn away contaminants and poisons, while giving a person little more than sunburn. It is an art form at which I am *singularly* well practiced." He tossed the stick into the corner and dusted off his hands.

"Won't the humans notice if they're not burning?" Aren asked, holding one finger in the air.

"Ha!" Kagos laughed in a single, short bark. "The mind controls the body, friend. No, they won't notice. They will be far too occupied with the flames around them to worry about whether or not they burn."

"That still sounds awful," Jesse muttered.

"It is," Aiya said. "But it's far better than the alternative." She let that sink in for a moment, and turned to glower at Kagos. "Which is not to say that it's a good idea! What if they've got archers? Or, Eah forbid, crossbowmen?"

"I will not be flying so close that such a weapon could reach me," Kagos replied archly.

"You'll have to, if you want to see what you're burning!" Aiya waved out of the open wall at the fog. "You can't see more than a dozen paces in this. You'll be the biggest target they've ever had the good fortune to practice on!" She planted her hands firmly on her hips, and dared him to disagree with a glare.

Fae watched their stand-off with a mixture of amusement and

concern. She couldn't tell if Kagos was oblivious to the care behind Aiya's protests, or if he was playing dumb to avoid dealing with it.

"My dear Aiya," Kagos said calmly, as he walked over to stand in front of his rider. Her breath hitched, almost imperceptibly; there was no way he could have missed it. He leant forward, until they were all but nose-to-nose. "You worry too much," he whispered.

He straightened, and turned, leaving Aiya blinking in confusion behind him. "So," he said, continuing with his plan, "I'll deal with the monsters at the gate. But I'm afraid I lack both the subtlety and the patience to comb through a castle looking for two among hundreds." He waved a dismissive hand, as if brushing something bothersome to the side. "That, I leave to you."

"I might be able to help with that." Laina spoke up for the first time. "My father was cousin to King Reginald. We visited the castle almost every year when I was girl."

"Tell us what you know," Thom said immediately.

From what Laina remembered, the bailey housed the stables, workshops, and the barracks, all arrayed around the training grounds and a wide open space for gathering troops, back when there were armies to speak of. The castle keep itself had begun as a traditional stone quadrangle construction with circular towers at each compass point, but the original fortress had been expanded over the decades by almost every king as they added modifications according to their moods. The resulting construction within the bailey was as sprawling as it was vast.

Laina worried her hands together. "I can only guide us around the buildings as I used to know them. I can't speculate as to where anything is inside now."

"It's an advantage we wouldn't have without you," Fae reassured her.

"It's also highly likely the whole place has changed since I last saw it," Laina continued. "It's been longer than I care to think about since I was a girl. And the city has seen two radical changes in management since then."

"Aye." Hal's rough voice came from where he perched on an upended wooden crate. "The bailey was a mess when I saw it in the Stuarts' time. Rubble everywhere, like they'd torn it up just for the fun of it. But then, the gates were open back then." He gave a shrug. "Could have changed again by now."

"So all we know really," Wil said, "is that we don't really know anything."

"I think that's fair," Max said. "I once heard talk that the Lady was pushing for some remodelling."

"Then let's just get in there, and work out the rest as we go," Elas snapped impatiently. "That's how we've always had to manage before. It's part of the job."

"Peace, Elas," Ty said gently, placing a hand on his shoulder. "You know we're trying to make the best of a bad situation."

Elas pulled in a long breath through his nose, making his nostrils flare. He let the air out slowly again, and dropped his head, nodding reluctantly.

"Well if you're looking to go in the front door and make the most of some mayhem," Max said, with a sidewards glance at Kagos, "then I'd suggest you aim for the dusk guard change. You'll be able to catch more of them in the chaos that way."

"Sounds like fun," Kagos said.

"There's something wrong with you," Jesse grumbled with a confused frown. Kagos smiled, and mimed tipping an imaginary hat.

"So we must wait another day to rescue our comrade?" Thom said through gritted teeth.

"You must wait a day to maximise our chances of a successful rescue," Ty corrected him with a stern look.

"We wait," Wil said, backing him up.

Thom glanced towards Elas, whose head remained bowed, his bound ribs a stark reminder of their last encounter with the Survivors. He nodded, his jaw silently clenched.

"We wait."

They passed the following hours in a sullen silence. What little conversation was shared, was done in lowered tones.

Fae spent a portion of the day watching the street from the half-shadows cast by the walls of their hidden space. The more she watched, the more the sense of disquiet festered within her, until she had to look away. It was more than just a feeling of an oppressed people ruled by a merciless leader, the sense of lost hope pervaded everywhere. Like they'd given up on life. Like they didn't even know they were waiting to die.

Finally, the light began to dim in the pervasive fog. Max had been out on top of the city to keep an eye on the complex for any complicating factors, and she dropped into the alley behind the dead-space just as they were readying to leave.

"Time to go then," she said. "It's a shame we can't use the sky-roads." She sent a pointed look towards Immrith, who was too restless to notice. "Luckily, I know the shortcuts. Just mind the people." And she led them back through the labyrinthine alleys, and out into the street.

Immrith and Kagos wore their hoods long and low to cover their features. The elves donned their travel cloaks and did likewise, lest they draw attention by matching the description of a group of strangers that were chased by red-bands two nights before. They stole through the deepening gloom, skirting busy streets and cutting through alleys until they reached a roofed arcade of abandoned shopfronts, boarded up and forsaken to the advances of time. Opposite darkened doors and empty windows, the arches of the arcade opened onto a wide square overlooking the bailey's front gates. The group tucked themselves into the shadows to watch.

"Here comes the guard changeover," Max whispered. As the words passed her lips, a team of twenty red-bands exited the wicket gate and fanned out to take up their respective positions.

"This looks like my cue," Kagos said, clearing his throat and striding out into the open.

"Kagos!" Aiya hissed desperately, multiple emotions warring across her face. But Kagos only shot her a parting wink over his shoulder. The sigh of frustration that escaped her lips was almost a growl. "This is the *worst* idea he's ever had," she muttered to herself, and then jogged after him.

At the centre of the square, Kagos turned. His gaze flicked to the approaching Aiya before fixing on Max. Her eyes widened, and then she nodded fervently. Across the square, Kagos nodded once, and turned back to the gate.

And then, he changed.

Fae was transfixed. Not even Baev'ill had had the privilege to witness this — it was a very personal process, and not all dragonkind were willing to share it.

The sounds of boulders crashing and mountains breaking as Kagos changed, it turned out, were not entirely misplaced.

At first it seemed as though his body opened up: great, black limbs unfolding from deeper within himself like a giant, midnight flower unfurling in the middle of the street. Then came the boulders, rolling outwards from the centre. From a delicate framework of darkest petals, huge, jagged hunks of rock thrust up into place over his extended body, jutting out and expanding to fill the gaps.

It all happened impossibly quickly, making Fae doubt what she was seeing. Within two heartbeats, a man barely taller than Ty had become an enormous, hulking dragon, formed of black boulders and seemingly forged of the mountains themselves. His wings peeled away from his back last, at first appearing as flimsy as a butterfly emerging from its chrysalis, then solidifying into thick, black, leathery sails stretched across a bony scaffold that continued to elongate until his wingspan reached nearly the full width of the square.

Fae barely noticed Aiya climb up to sit between two of the fins that made up Kagos's dorsal ridge line, only spotting her when the dragon reared up his wagon-sized head to let out a mighty, earth-sundering roar.

The men guarding the gates immediately flew into a frenzied panic, falling over themselves as they scrambled about, apparently without any remaining mental faculties. The dragon gave a short, chuffing sound. Max chuckled beside Fae.

"He says maybe he won't have to burn anything, the way they're running scared just at the sight of him," the girl said. Fae turned to look at her in astonishment.

"He's talking to you?" she asked.

Max nodded. "Told me to be his mouth and your ears on account of how I can hear him..." The girl looked uncomfortable. "Don't know how I feel about that," she admitted.

"Well," Jesse said, overhearing, "maybe we can agonise over it another time, yes?" Her eyes were glued to the scene of chaos before them. Fae followed her gaze.

Kagos looked to be making fun of the situation, bobbing and weaving his head around in a strange, giant version of peek-a-boo, spooking one group of guards after the other. Fae could just hear Aiya's yells over the noise, and eventually Kagos spread his enormous wings and took to the sky in a surprisingly agile leap.

The square fell deathly silent, the only sound that of sail-ship-sized wings gathering air and beating downward. *Furl, snap, furl, snap.*

A call went up from the wall, one guard pointing into the fog above.

And then the flames fell.

The screams were instant, men throwing themselves over each other to get away.

Fae watched with a kind of disturbed fascination as the fire caught on the stone and wood of the ramparts, but didn't touch the men at all. She didn't see a single guard fall to the ground, rolling to put out flames licking across his body. Instead they ran, like ants from a damaged nest, swarming about in frantic panic.

"Let's go!" Elas yelled.

And then they were running. They ran around the arcade, keeping to the flickering shadows cast by dancing flames.

Then dashed the last paces to the gate.

46

SOMETHING POINTY

Passing beneath the burning arches of the bailey's gatehouse, Fae was hit with a wave of heat.

"Stay away from the walls!" Max called as they ran through the short tunnel. "Kagos says his flames won't burn us, but once caught, the buildings burn just like any other fire." Fae glanced around at the rapidly spreading flames.

That's all of it then, she thought, a bead of sweat running cold down her spine.

But then her attention was pulled away from the fire as two figures appeared ahead. Two red-bands rounded the far end of the gatehouse, racing to the aid of their comrades. They were only a few paces away, and on course to barrel straight into Elas and Aren, leading the charge. The elves made to pull up short, reaching for weapons, but a hollered battle-cry echoed through the tunnel, and then Immrith was galloping straight through them. With fists flailing, he sent both unfortunate red-bands flying with a single swing of his powerful arms.

Jesse dodged as one of them soared past her. "Hey!" she protested. "Watch where you're throwing people!" While Immrith may not have understood her words, he caught her tone well enough, and responded with a small half-bow, and a proud smirk. Jesse huffed, and rolled her eyes.

They burst out from under the gatehouse just as a mighty roar came from above. Behind them, damaged stones fell from the crenelations above to smash upon the ground, sending rubble spraying at their feet. And in front, a whole different battle was erupting.

The huge, black shape of Kagos flew in low, swooping across the courtyard to deliver his theatrical flames. Red-band reinforcements sprinting towards the gatehouse fell back instinctively, blocked by a wall of benign fire. Task completed, Kagos banked harshly, pumping his enormous wings, barely clearing the bailey walls as he exited his new arena. He disappeared into the fog above — now glowing a pulsing, angry orange — and Fae could hear his ominous wingbeats circling, watching for his next opportunity to strike.

Fae surveyed the courtyard in which they now stood. It was a wide, open space, perhaps three-hundred feet long, and half as wide, and lined with an assortment of workshops and smithies. In the centre, what appeared to be a fighting ring had been marked out on the packed earth of the ground with a length of thick, white rope. And just beyond that, before the castle proper, was the largest cage Fae had ever seen.

Constructed of timber poles wide enough that she doubted she could fit her hand around one, the structure stood easily eight feet tall, and spanned almost the full width of the yard.

And it was stuffed full with humans.

Thom and Elas caught sight of the cage immediately, and their gazes hardened to granite. Without a word, they skirted the edge of the courtyard, heading straight for the captive humans.

"Wait!" Ty called, jogging after with a quick look behind to check the others were following.

Just as they neared the cage, a group of Survivors — marked by their red bands and feral snarls — came rushing around the side of it, heading straight for them.

"Ah shit!" Max exclaimed. Following the direction of her gaze, Fae saw the reason for it. Ten feet behind the advancing Survivors, a stairway led up to the ramparts. And at the top of the stair, were more archers.

"Eah's Tears!" Ty swore beside her. The archers nocked their arrows, drew back, and took aim.

Fire poured from the sky to light the wall in flames. Screams pierced Fae's skull as the red-bands atop the wall fled instinctively. Two bodies toppled from the ramparts, flailing like rag-dolls. Kagos roared his earth-shuddering roar as he flew low overhead. But the red-bands on the ground continued to advance on them.

Don't burn the cage! Fae arrowed after Kagos desperately. The prisoners would not be able to escape if the wooden bars caught light.

I am not a monster, came the affronted reply.

And then the Survivors were upon them.

Fae drew her swords in a single smooth motion, and held them before her with arms slightly bent, the blades angled towards each other like lovers leaning in to kiss.

The first Survivor that came at her held a single longsword, and swung it in a wide arc designed to knock her blades aside. Fae leapt back, letting her right sword drop down while the left parried the longsword, leaving an opening for her to strike with her free blade. Her opponent twisted away at the last moment, spinning to bring his sword back into play. But Fae had two blades to his one, and she was a *dancer*. She spun and leapt and twirled, leaving the Survivor slicing at nothing but air. The moment Fae's right sword bit flesh, his fight was over. She twisted her blade free, and whirled to face the next red-band.

Ty and Hal stood back-to-back, both of their bows useless in the fray of such close combat, even for Ty's impressive skills. They each held a long knife, fending off their attackers with vicious skill. Immrith faced four red-bands to himself, and laid about ruthlessly, taking full advantage of his greater height and ability to kick out with lethal effect, as well as making good use of his fists. Aren, Stef, Wil, Elas and Thom fought together in a tangle of friend and foe. Scouts did not typically carry combat weapons, and they were having to make do with their knives like Ty and Hal. Laina and Max hid, tucked between a blacksmith's and a carpenter's workshop. Jesse was nowhere to be seen.

Fae was about to jump to Immrith's aid when she heard a shout.

"Let us out!" a young man with bright green eyes called over the pandemonium in the bailey. "Let us out! We can fight!"

She hesitated. She looked at the bars of the cage. There was no way her swords would be able to hack through them with any speed. The only option would be to open the hatch. A quick glance at that revealed a hefty chain locked firmly in place around the bars. Fae whirled, scanning the red-bands fighting in the courtyard. There was no guarantee any of them even carried the keys.

"I got this," Max said, appearing beside her in a blink. She pulled three makeshift iron picks out of her tangled mess of hair with a grin. "I can't fight for toffee, but this, I can do." And she darted away to take up position crouched on the ground by the hatch, trying to make herself as small as possible.

Fae turned back to the fight. They'd been outnumbered to start, but the scouts were gaining the advantage against their group of Survivors. Ty and Hal were holding their own. Immrith was sporting several nasty lacerations to his flanks. Fae threw herself to his aid, knocking the blade from the hand of a red-band who'd been about to slash at Immrith's hindquarters again. Using the advantage of surprise, she quickly beat the woman back, finishing with a sharp blow to the head with the pommel of her sword.

And then a man wearing a brown canvas tunic, belted at the waist with simple rope leapt into the fray, jumping onto the back of one redband, and wrapping a thick arm around his neck. Another tackled the Survivor facing Hal, throwing them both to the ground in a tangle of limbs, the red-band's knife skittering away across the ground.

Prisoners poured from the cage. There must have been at least two or three-hundred men and women, all in the prime of their lives, all looking like they'd been dragged halfway across Arland to be here.

The red bands' simple uniform made the prisoners' task of identifying who to target doubly easy, and despite being armed against half-starved captives, the Survivors were outnumbered. It wasn't long before they were subdued.

Hal pulled a man from the ground beside him. "Thank you, friend," he said, as the fellow dusted himself off. "What's your name?"

"David," the man said. "Been wanting to do that for weeks." He looked about at the burning bailey, the red-bands unconscious on the ground, and finally the freed prisoners leaking towards the gatehouse from the open hatch of the cage. David's lips pressed together, but he nodded with a look of grim satisfaction.

"Thank you for coming along when you did," he said. Hal nodded, and opened his mouth to reply when Jesse appeared from behind the cage. She hauled a duffel almost as big as her travel pack behind her, which clattered when she let it fall to the ground.

"Good," she said, surveying the scene. She looked at the scouts.

"Thought you might like something a bit more fit for purpose." She kicked the bag, and it clanged metallically. Bending down, she peeled it open to reveal half an armoury stuffed inside. She looked up to meet the eyes of a handful of freed humans gathering around. "You looked like you could use something pointy too." With a heave, Jesse pulled a sword from within the bundled weapons. "Looks more your size than mine." She passed it to a tall man with nothing on his feet. The man hefted the weapon, turning it in his grip to admire the blade from all angles.

"I've always wanted one of these." Fae turned from the ragged congregation of humans to see Thom lifting a great, two-headed axe from the duffel.

"How did you carry all this?" Aren said, lifting a crossbow from the sack.

"I'm stronger than I look," Jesse replied neutrally.

"I'm impressed," Aren said. "Ooh, what have we here?" He grabbed at something deep in the bag, and shook it loose. "Could this be...?" He drew a long pole-arm from the tangle of weaponry. Atop a long shaft of polished wood was a small, slender axe-head opposite a wicked, claw-like hook. Above the axe-head, the smooth, narrowed point of a spear glinted in the fire-light. Aren shot Jesse a roguish grin. "Is this a halbert for our Halbert?"

Jesse affected a look of indifference, but there was a glint in her eye.

"Ha ha!" he laughed, and tossed the weapon to Hal. "I wanted to see this!" Hal caught the pole-arm deftly, twirling it briefly and planting the butt on the ground by his feet. Fae thought he stood taller, straighter. In an instant he was less of the wandering ranger, and more the disciplined soldier.

The rest of the weapons were passed about in short order. Immrith selected an intimidating war-hammer, setting it across both palms with an appreciative grin. With the exception of Aren's crossbow and Thom's axe, the scouts chose long knives, much better suited to close combat. Jesse chose a pair of curved daggers, slotting them comfortably into her belt.

Fae and Ty stood to one side with Laina.

"I'm not a fighter," Laina said, when Ty asked why she chose no weapons. "I'm here to help, and heal. Not hurt." Her voice dropped to near a whisper. "There's been enough hurting." Fae regarded her mother with growing respect. Even after everything she'd been through, everything she'd lost, there was no desire for vengeance in her. Only peace.

"Not that I'm not grateful or anything—" a voice interrupted her train of thought. She turned to find the man with the green eyes approaching. He gestured to the stream of humans fleeing the bailey "—but why *are* you here?"

"We're looking for a friend," Fae said. "And then I need to have a conversation with Lady Black."

Something in her eyes made the man raise his eyebrows, his lips forming a soft *oh*. "It's like that is it?" he said. "Your friend, they a prisoner too?" Fae nodded. His face darkened. "They say it's worse inside." He gestured to the cage that he'd inhabited until a few minutes ago. "This is just a holding cell." He pursed his lips, looking up at the castle. Turning back to Fae, he said, "Good luck to you. I hope you find your friend." And then he followed the line of ex-prisoners heading towards the burning gatehouse, and freedom. A cry went up from the ramparts, but the prisoners were armed now, and had a score to settle.

The billow of giant sails whooshed above their heads, and Fae glanced up in time to see Kagos's green-gold tail-ridges flash past.

"Another friend of yours?" David asked, a sword resting across his shoulders. Above, Kagos banked, and worked his huge wings to bring him to perch atop the gatehouse into the castle itself.

"Something like that," Jesse said, kicking the now-empty duffel to one side.

"Uhuh," David said, awestruck, as he watched the great beast.

"Kagos wants to know if we need him for anything else?" Max said, dodging the last few fleeing prisoners to stand beside Fae.

Ty eyed the castle gates, and swept the bailey with his gaze. "I'd be grateful if he could dissuade any reinforcements from following us in," he said, nodding at the keep. "I have a feeling we'll be hard-pressed enough inside."

Max nodded, and went quiet. Then she snorted, her hand coming up to cover a smile.

"What?" Fae asked.

Max's face turned red, visible even beneath the dirt layer. "Nothing," she said quickly. "He says that's fine." Jesse shot her a suspicious look, but said nothing.

"You *talk* to that thing?" David asked, eyes bulging.

"Yeah." Max shifted uncomfortably, her face going impossibly redder. "It's new to me too."

"David," Fae said, "you should go. Get out of this place."

David snapped back to his senses. "Yes," he said. "Yes, I will." He paused. "I heard you're looking for a friend." He glanced at the tall, leggy figures of Aren, Wil, and Elas huddled nearby, their headwear still covering their ears. "Heard the red-bands talking about a new prospect last night. Said he was a tall feller. Said he was taken straight to solitary, on account of how much trouble he gave 'em on the way in." He pointed up to the tower at the northern-most corner of the castle. "Solitary's up there." He shot a glare of bitter hatred at the red-bands on the ground. "They liked to tell us things, to scare us." He tore his gaze away, turning back to Fae and Ty. "Told us there's more jails inside. Plenty of work to do, they said. Said there's places they take the kids to train 'em up to be soldiers. Places for 'promising' prospects. Places for the women to work. Only they made it clear it weren't work any of 'em would choose." He spat on the ground, his face twisting into one of revulsion. "Didn't think we could do worse than them Unity bastards, but here we are."

"Well," Fae said, "we aim to end this. Now."

David nodded. "That's right good to hear." He hesitated, a guilt-stricken look crossing his face. "I'd join you, but I got a wife and two girls at home. At least, I hope..." His brow knitted with a mix of dread and unthinkable possibilities. "I need to make sure they're safe." He fidgeted, conflict contorting his features.

Ty reached out a hand, and rested it on David's shoulder. "Go. Be with your family. Come back when it's time to build Throldon anew."

David met his gaze with a grateful smile. "Thank you," he said, relief plain upon his face. "May the Mother guide you!" And he turned, and jogged over to join the last of his people leaving the castle grounds.

"Can we go now?" Immrith said, brandishing his new war-hammer back and forth in a few easy practice swings. Max danced out of reach of the weapon, and Jesse gave him a look as if she thought he'd gone mad.

"He says can we go now," Stef translated, slotting his newly-acquired belt-knife into its sheath.

"If he can stop swinging that damn hammer so close to my face, then yes," Jesse replied testily. Immrith gave one final swing before bringing the weapon up in a pendulum arc to rest across his shoulders.

He grinned. "I start to understand you now," he said, in a faltering common tongue. "You always angry, little girl."

Jesse looked about ready to explode.

"Immrith!" Aren said quickly, before Jesse could open her mouth. "You understand us?"

Immrith tipped his head to one side. He lifted a hand, his thumb and index finger half an inch apart. "Little," he said. "I understand little before. Getting better. I listen." He smiled smugly at Jesse's impression of a gasping fish out of water.

"That's great!" Aren exclaimed with an open smile. "When we're done here, I'd love to pick your brains about the north." Immrith's expression changed to one of confusion. Stef quickly translated, and his face morphed again into understanding.

"Ah!" he said. "This is strange words. Sound like you want to stab me in head." He mimed being stabbed in the head.

"Alright," Fae said, as Aren opened his mouth to reply. "Immrith, I'm glad you're catching up with the language. That makes things a little easier." She turned to Laina. "Now, how do we get into the castle?"

Laina swallowed nervously. She looked around the courtyard, then closed her eyes.

"Around the south wall, there's a serving entrance," she said, her brow furrowed. "It leads to the bakery and the kitchens."

"Won't that be busy?" Jesse said.

"Are there any others?" Fae asked.

"There's one more on the east wall that leads to the laundry," Laina said. "Or, it used to."

"Let's try that one," Ty suggested. "Kitchens are always busy, especially if the castle is full of troops."

"Alright," Laina said. "That's on the far side of the keep." She indicated a narrow passage that led behind the workshops, eventually disappearing between the castle wall and the outer bailey.

"Of course it is," Jesse grumbled.

47

DUTY

They skirted around the castle in pitch-black between the two looming walls.

The ramparts were quiet, the majority of the red-bands having raced away to deal with the blaze at the gates.

After long minutes stumbling through the dark, they finally came upon a modest wooden door set into a recess in the base of the castle wall. A small, sputtering torch was its only ornamentation.

"Someone uses this door, if they've bothered to light it," Hal said, nodding at the torch.

Thom nodded soberly. "Agreed," he said. "We'll go carefully." He dropped his axe into his hands, holding it across his body.

"I'll go first," Hal said, fumbling with his sleeve. When he finally dropped his hand, a red strip of cloth was tied around his upper arm.

Laina sucked in a breath. "What are you doing?" she asked.

"If they're recruiting as quickly as it looks, they probably don't all know each other," he explained. He gestured to the visible flash of red. "This makes it easy for them to identify allies. Which makes it an easy disguise for us." He turned his attention to the scouts. "I know it's one of your own in here. But I'll lead. If I'm the first face one of 'em sees, we'll have one more second to react than they will."

Thom nodded again. "Understood," he said. "Thank you."

Hal batted the remark to one side with the back of his hand. "Makes sense is all. Laina, you guide me as best you can. I've been to Throldon before but never inside the keep. Everyone else, follow behind." He looked around the group, and when no one argued, "Alright then. Ready?" A series of nods. "Let's go."

He pushed open the door.

There was a pause.

"I will stay," Immrith said. One look into the narrow, low-ceilinged passageway that lay beyond the door had everyone nodding in agreement. Navigating the keep with limited space to manoeuvre would be a trial for all of them, more so for Immrith with his tall and broad frame; it would be a liability. "I help dragon. Fight red-bands." He tapped his upper arm, and pointed to Hal's own red band. No one argued.

Hal held out a hand. "Thank you, Immrith, for getting us this far," he said solemnly. They grasped forearms firmly, and released. Fae reached a hand up to touch Immrith lightly on the arm.

"I can still reach you." She tapped the side of her head. "If I have your permission."

Immrith's eyes widened. "You mean, like spirits? *Ateth Legarrh*?"

Fae smiled. "Not quite." She gestured from her head to his. "May I?" Immrith hesitated, then nodded slowly. Fae closed her eyes, and opened her senses to where the beauty of Eah'lara should be. Instead of glowing nebulae and shimmering threads, thirteen shining auras surrounded her; Kagos and Aiya set slightly apart, but still there. There was another, paler aura with them all, and Fae identified Max's essence, somewhat faded, but still there. Looking closer, she noticed that everyone's auras had lost some of their luminosity. They shone brightly in the darkness of Throldon, but they were not the dazzling, glittering lights that they had been even two days earlier.

And Fae remembered Max's words about how the locals seemed dead behind the eyes. Would the same thing happen to her friends, if they stayed here too long?

Pushing her rising dread aside, she located Immrith's wildness, and reached out to him.

Immrith, she said gently into his mind. *Can you hear me?* The centaurs' dialogue with spirits was a sacred thing. She didn't want to overwhelm him.

I hear you, came the response.

I can speak this way with you, even when you are not beside me, she continued. *So you will not be alone.* Sensing a sort of acceptance from Immrith, she turned her attention to Kagos.

Kagos.

Yes, Spiritchild.

The passageways here are not built with centaurs in mind. Immrith will remain outside with you. Can you reach him?

I can only commune with those who hear Draconic. Aside from Aiya, the girl is the only other among your group with whom I can speak like this.

Fae opened her eyes to the others, still bathed in torchlit gloom.

"I'll go with Immrith," Max said, before Fae had a chance to speak.

She frowned. "Kagos?"

Max nodded. "It makes sense. Apparently you can reach him anyway. So I act as go-between for him and Immrith." The girl shook her head. "This day just keeps on getting weirder and weirder." She looked up at the towering centaur. "That okay with you?" Immrith grunted his assent. "Alright then." Max looked around the group. "It's been nice knowing you all." She raised her hand and gave an awkward little wave. "See you on the other side."

"We'll come too," Aren said, indicating himself and Stef. He gestured to the open door, and the narrow passage beyond. "Too many at once in there will be more of a hindrance than a help. We can do more good out here for now." He turned to Wil. "That alright with you?"

Wil clapped him on the shoulder. "We'll all go," he said, gripping Stef's shoulder with his other hand. He turned to Thom and Elas. "You go and get Wyn." He looked up at Immrith, his gaze hardening. "We'll guard the gates."

Immrith nodded with a quirk jerk of his head. "Can you run?" he asked, including the three of them in his question.

The corner of Aren's mouth twitched. "We'll just see who has the right to ask that question, shall we?"

Immrith looked as if he might say something when Max abruptly jerked upright. "Kagos says there are more red-bands moving into the courtyard." She looked up at Immrith. "Time to go."

Immrith extended his hand to her. "Get up," he said brusquely. "Quicker like this." And he hauled the girl onto his back in one swift motion. Once in position, Max sat stiffly, unsure of where to put her hands. Immrith twisted, grasping his long, black hair in one fist. "Do not touch hair," he said sternly.

Max nodded fervently, in a way that reminded Fae of Bek, and a ripple of grief swept through her. She would never get to see his face again, even though his spark still lived within her.

Fae blinked back the sting of unexpected tears as Wil, Aren, and Stef spared barely a second to grasp arms with Ty, Thom, and Elas.

And then, they were ready.

"Hold on," Immrith said. And without warning, he plunged away into the darkness. Fae saw Max throw her tiny arms around his waist, before they all disappeared into the shadows.

"Alright, let's get on with this," Elas said, bouncing impatiently on the balls of his feet.

"Agreed," said Jesse, eyeing the open doorway like it was a coiled snake, waiting to strike.

Then, one after the other, the seven remaining entered the castle.

Out in the courtyard, Kagos identified the barracks. It was the small outcrop of the lower castle wall from which dozens of the infernal banded humans were pouring. Apparently, they'd been alerted to the presence of intruders stealing in under the cover of the fires. They also seemed to have worked out at least some of the properties of his fire, unless their sudden refusal to take cover had always been a part of their battle plans.

He blew a great burst of flame at the nearest squad. Instead of scattering like scared chickens, they stood fast, waiting for his fire to cease.

He roared his annoyance, and found a small sliver of satisfaction in watching the ground tremble beneath their feet, throwing several off balance.

Now that the innocents are out, do you think our Spiritchild would approve of lethal force? he asked Aiya, who watched events from astride his neck.

I think we may be left with little choice, she answered. *They've brought archers.* And that they had. Behind the first wave, a line of men and women carrying anything from simple bows to heavy crossbows were moving into position.

Girl, I hope you're not dawdling, he arrowed at Max.

We're nearly there! came the reply.

Tell her to come out swinging, suggested Aiya dryly.

Down below, and off to his left, the press of Survivors broke, like the surface of a lake disturbed by a hound leaping into its waters. The crowd erupted on impact of something large and violent into their midsts, the ripples shattering outward, knocking more than a few humans flying. Then the centaur came into view, wielding a war-hammer the size of the person astride his back.

At that moment, true horror, the likes of which he had not felt in eons, flooded through Kagos.

Girl, what are you doing? he demanded. The human girl was important. He hadn't believed it at first, but there was no longer any doubt in his mind what she was. And he may not ever find another with her unique abilities again. But Max was too busy holding on for dear life to reply.

He gave another mighty roar, and spread his wings.

What are you doing? Aiya cried out with her mind as she lurched for balance.

My duty, he replied, and launched himself from the castle roof.

If he was grounded by one of those archers, so be it.

Aiya would know what to do.

48

SITTING SOLITARY

They heard Kagos's second roar like a hammer strike to their very bones. Brick dust loosed itself from the walls to shower down upon them.

Fae went to reach out to the dragon, but Ty placed a hand on her arm.

"Let them do their job," he said. "Let us do ours."

Pressing her lips together against the urge to be in two places at once, Fae turned her attention to the room they had entered.

That it had once been a laundry was evident by the neatly stacked wash-tubs and boards lining one wall, but it had clearly not been used as such in a long while; a thick layer of dust coated all but a single strip of floor through the middle of the room. At the far end, worn stone steps climbed up and out, twisting away into darkness.

"That'll lead up to the servants' areas," Laina whispered. "It's like a warren, connecting the staff to any part of the keep." She paused. "Or, it used to be."

"Don't suppose you know your way around the warren," Jesse said doubtfully, "being the daughter of a lord and all?"

Laina shook her head. "No," she said regretfully. "I got myself lost down there once and was forbidden from exploring below again." Her brow creased in concentration. "I could guess at navigating it but I have a much better chance with the upstairs layout."

"Let's see what we find down here first, shall we?" Ty suggested.

Moving further from their only exit point, Hal led them across the room, pausing at the foot of the stairs, listening. He signalled an all-clear, and began climbing.

The passageway at the top of the stairs was empty. As were the hallways that branched away from it.

"Where is everyone?" Thom growled under his breath. "They can't *all* be outside."

"I don't know, but I don't like it," Hal said, his eyes darting uneasily from side to side.

"To get to the north tower," Laina said, "we'll have to go upstairs. The servants' areas aren't directly connected to that wing." She pointed along the corridor. "We should be able to follow this to the end, but it won't reach the tower."

"Alright," Hal said. "Let's make the most of this—" he gestured to the empty hall "—and go get your friend. Wyn, was it?" Elas nodded, his face set with dark determination. "Let's get Wyn first, while they don't know we're here. He might've heard something in here we could use."

They stole along the empty hallways like shadows, stopping periodically to check they were still alone.

Eventually, they reached the end, where the corridor split into a T-shape, each branch leading to more stairs upward.

Laina pointed right. "It should be that way."

Creeping up the stairway, Hal slowly pushed the door open a crack, peering through the gap while the others waited below with bated breath. A minute passed in tense silence, Hal's arm held outstretched towards them, palm out. *Wait.*

Then he waved them up, letting the door close again behind him.

"I can hear people," he said as Ty reached the top of the stair, "but they're not close, and they're not getting closer." Thom's ears twitched behind Ty, listening intently. He nodded in agreement.

"Laina." Hal waved her forward. He opened the door a fraction. "Do you recognise anything?"

Laina put her face to the gap, and nodded instantly. "Yes," she whispered. "The tower wing is just a short way down the hall." She turned back to Hal. "But this is one of the main galleries through the keep. Unless the castle is empty, we'll almost certainly bump into someone here."

Hal nodded. "Thought as much," he said with a grim scowl. He exchanged a look with Ty. "This is the part where we run through the castle and hope for the best."

"Then let's get on with it," Elas growled impatiently, halfway down the stair.

"Peace, Elas," Thom told him firmly. "We would not have gotten even this far alone." Elas grumbled under his breath, and fell silent.

"He's right, though," Jesse said.

"Yes," Hal agreed. "No point waitin' here." And without further delay, he pushed open the door, and stepped into the hallway beyond, striding as confidently as if he belonged there.

They all filed out of the stair to follow Laina's directions along the gallery. Skirting the walls, Fae marvelled at the space they ran through.

Painted ceilings soared high above, framed within ornately carved roses of plaster and wood. Columns as tall and thick as trees ran up the walls to splay into sweeping arches across the ceiling. Curtains fell from twenty feet high to pool in puddles of silk and velvet on the floor.

But floor level was where the opulence faded, sullied by the events of the last thirty years. The fine fabrics of the curtains were dirty and ragged, sometimes torn off at head-height. Flocked and hand-painted wallpapers were ripped and slashed in places, as though a wild animal had been released into the halls. Once-thick, luxurious carpets were stained and threadbare, or missing entirely to reveal cracked, neglected tiles beneath.

"Well," Jesse muttered, "I suppose we should take comfort in knowing the Unity treated *all* their things like crap."

As they jogged through the fractured opulence, the sound of people gathered in raucous revelry echoed through the keep. Yet still, no one stepped into the gallery.

"Why does that sound make me queasy?" Laina whispered, her face as pale as the delicate plasterwork above.

Fae couldn't shake the feeling that the noise of so many Survivors enjoying themselves was unlikely to be a good omen either. "One thing at a time," she said.

Laina nodded, brown eyes darting up and down the cavernous hallway. Suddenly, she stopped.

"It's this one," she said, standing opposite a pair of carved, wooden doors. Inlaid into the panels were depictions of a single, tall tower, with a single, small window. Inside the doors, an equally grand, albeit smaller hallway extended past half a dozen dusty studies, before coming to an abrupt end at a spiral of stone steps leading up.

Fae leapt from her skin at the sound of voices ringing down the tower stairs. Heart pounding, she allowed Ty to pull her into one darkened study, leaving Hal as the only one visible.

The stone of the walls conspired to make the voices sound closer than they were, until it seemed impossible that the owners weren't on top of her, shouting in her ear.

Finally, the cold, echoing quality gave way to flat, harsh tones.

"Oi!" one voice shouted at close range. "Who're you? Why aren't you watching the trials?"

"There are intruders in the castle," Hal answered calmly.

"Wha—?"

Jesse flew out below eye-level of the two men standing at the foot of the tower, their attention diverted by Hal's unexpected presence. Moving quickly, and with a merciless flick of her wrists, she drew her twin daggers across the back of their knees, slicing the tendons there.

Elas revealed himself at the same time, lifting his knee to take one crumpling guard in the face, while Hal wrapped his arm around the other's neck, squeezing until the guard lost consciousness.

It was over so quickly Fae had barely had a chance to blink.

"Nice doing business with you," Jesse said, wiping her blades on the back of one guard's jerkin, and sheathing them again with a nod to Elas and Hal.

Hal nodded, eyeing the stairs darkly. "Onward, then," he said.

They crept up the seemingly endless spiral, past arched doorways leading to black, uninhabited floors.

Finally, on the thirteenth floor, the doorway was lit, the single torch flame casting flickering shadows between the stones. Inside, two red-bands sat opposite one another across a barrel, a set of well-worn playing cards laid out between them.

"Can't believe our luck," one groused. "Sitting solitary duty when they're running the trials downstairs." His companion grunted noncommittally. "It's cruel, is what it is," the first continued. "Seeing what fresh blood's joining the ranks is all part of the excitement!" He blew out a frustrated sigh. "And we're missing it!" The second guard grumbled something incoherent, punctuated by the snap of cards being laid down. A bark of laughter came from the first. "Ha! That's nothing! Those piss-heads on the walls wouldn't know how to piss straight without help. Probably someone just dropped a torch and threw oil over it instead of water. Least it'll keep them busy for a while." He chuckled to himself. The second voice grunted something more emphatically, as though arguing a point.

"Oh Samuel, there's no such thing as dragons! Listen to yourself! Like I said, someone got piss-drunk, set fire to the gate and started making up stupid stories. Apparently couldn't think up something better than a bloody dragon! Ha!" The sound of a hand slapping against cloth cracked loudly through the empty space. "I'll bet it was Carlson. Incompetent arse!" Samuel grumbled something more, which seemed to pacify his partner enough to play through another round of their game, the snap and flick of cards against wood the only sound punctuating the silence.

Hal held up one finger. Then two. Three.

Ty, Elas, and Thom flowed up and around him, slipping through the door, to take the guards by surprise.

It was instantly apparent which was which, the talkative red-band being tall and upright where Samuel was hunched and hobbled, with a stump of a tongue visible through a handful of yellow teeth as he gave a yelp and pitched backward. He fell off his chair, tumbling back to come to a stop in a crumpled heap against the wall. His partner leapt to his feet and drew a sword.

"Who, by the countless gods, are you?" he demanded pompously, holding his steel uncertainly before him.

"A stupid story," Hal said, advancing from behind Elas, his weapon held casually at his side, "that doesn't exist." He thrust his halbert, engaging the red-band without warning. His opponent parried, bringing his blade back around to swing at Hal's right shoulder. But Hal twirled his pole-arm in a figure-of-eight to smash into the guard's nose from below. The blow set the man flying, clipping a stone pillar on the way past. He landed in an awkward shape, his head resting at an unhealthy angle.

Samuel had survived his topple, and was frantically trying to push himself into the wall itself, trembling hands up in front of his face, his eyes screwed shut. Thom looked as if he still wanted to knock him out, but

Laina stepped forward. She knelt down before the crippled guard, and laid a gentle hand on his arm. One eye cracked open.

"If you won't trouble us, we won't trouble you." She turned to glare up at Thom, still standing menacingly over the guard. His eyes narrowed a fraction, but he stepped away nonetheless.

"We should at least tie him up," Ty said. Laina frowned, and turned back to Samuel. The guard nodded, and held his hands out, wrists together.

"You don't have to do that," a familiar voice called from down a barely-lit passageway. Thom and Elas rushed towards it, and found a door of solid iron with a small, metal grill just big enough to show Wyn's face within.

"Wyn!" Elas cried with a mix of elation and relief. "Are you alright?"

The portion of Wyn's face that could be seen, smiled. "I am well, Elas. Aside from being shut in here, I've been given no further attention. How are the ribs?"

Elas grinned sheepishly. "Healing, thanks to you. And you'd never guess who else."

At that moment, Ty and Fae reached the cell, with Samuel in tow.

Wyn's eyes flicked to them. "I thought I heard our esteemed Eldra come to save me," he said. "What are you doing here? And... Fae?" He frowned. "Isn't this a little out of scope for you?"

A small laugh escaped Fae. "Less than you'd think, Wyn," she said. "But that's a long story. Let's get you out of here first."

Samuel stepped forward, fumbling with a jangling set of iron keys on a ring so large he could fit his fist through it. Selecting one key among dozens, he slid it into the well-oiled lock of Wyn's cell, and turned it smoothly. Wyn stepped from the cell, and grasped Samuel's hand.

"Thank you Samuel," he said, to the confusion of everyone else. "Will you be safe up here?" Samuel responded with unexpectedly deft fingers, signing much like the elven scouts did.

"Why are you thanking him?" Thom asked, his face one of complete puzzlement.

"Samuel is the warden of sorts here," Wyn explained. "But ostensibly, one with a conscience. He took a liking to me, and we got talking." He raised his hands to shape the words, "*do you sign?*" with his fingers. "Human signing is slightly different to ours, but once you know one form it's easy enough to decipher another." He turned to Ty. "Samuel is as much a prisoner here as I've been. Because of his physical limitations, if he was to enter the trials, as all Survivors do, he would undoubtedly be killed. As prison warden, he has found a way to survive."

Fae looked at the crippled warden again, the part of her that came from Bran spotting an opportunity.

"Samuel," she said, "how long have you been warden here?"

Samuel's hands moved.

"Fifteen years," Wyn translated. "What does that have to do with anything?"

Ty, catching on quickly, hushed the other scout.

Fae continued. "So you were here when Lady Black took over." She didn't phrase it as a question, but Samuel nodded anyway. Fire flashed in her eyes. "Tell me about her."

Samuel swallowed.

"She's only been in power a few months Fae," Wyn said. "And Samuel has been stuck up here the whole time. What do you think he's going to be able to—" He stopped when Samuel laid a hand on his arm. And then he began to sign.

"Prisoners talk, guards even more so," Wyn spoke for the warden. "And Lady Black turned more than a few heads when she arrived. They found her in a brothel in the city. One of the rough types. The kind that breaks people. They say she was half-mad, cut up the Madame in charge, half the working girls dead behind her. But she went, calm as anything, straight to the Unity — to fight. Even the thugs were calling her ruthless. She was feral, like a wild animal that refused to be put down, and she fought and killed her way to the top — where Malcolm Stuart himself noticed her." Samuel's hands paused. "They say she became even crueller when she started working with him. They say she... enjoyed the work. And then, she killed him too. He had a reputation for taking what he wanted — never did bother with asking first."

Fae could do the maths — a woman driven to killing in the most sadistic forge would see only one way to deal with a man who thought to lay his hands on her. She felt a twinge of sadness at the thought of the woman Black might have been before... before fate had taken the threads of her life and twisted them into a cruel fist. Then that sadness hardened into cold rage when she remembered the cages — *cages* — of people outside, the hollow-eyed children in the streets, and the darkness spreading across Arland, poured from a cauldron already blackened by cruelty. Anson had *chosen* Black over Malcolm Stuart. He had not done it because she was innocent.

Samuel was still signing. "The next day, she renamed the Unity as the Survivors, and no one batted an eyelid. The trials started a week later."

"What are these trials?" Fae asked, fire coiling around the rage in her gut.

Wyn's face hardened, his eyes flashing like an impending storm. Even Samuel's expression blackened.

"The trials are how the Survivors rank their 'prospects'," Wyn said in a voice gone deep and foreboding. "They bring humans in from all over Arland and force them to prove they're worthy. It's like a livestock market, only they make them fight. Even children." He turned abruptly and began walking from the cells, his strides long and purposeful.

"Wyn!" Fae called. "Where are you going?"

Wyn whirled at the entrance, barely sparing a glance for Jesse, Hal, and Laina.

"This is where those prison carts have been bringing all those villagers," he growled at Thom. "We can't waste time reporting back to Lord Graem. We need to do something about it here. Now."

Thom gripped Wyn's arm. "Peace, Wyn, why do you think there are so many of us here?" He waved a hand to where the others were waiting.

Fae turned to Samuel. "Would Black attend the trials?"

Samuel's fingers flew into their nimble dance once more, Wyn's eyes tracking their motions.

"He says the Lady always attends the trials, to fight the strongest herself." He looked over at Fae again. "What exactly are you planning to do?"

All seven parts of Fae shone fierce through her eyes.

"We're going to take back the world."

49

THE LIBRARY AND THE TRIALS

S ounds from the trials echoed through the empty halls as Laina guided them back along the gallery towards the cacophony of shrieks and jeers.

"It sounds like they're in the Great Hall," she said. "Which would make sense if there are as many attending as you say."

Wyn's face was dark. "It's all they've talked about since I got here. A new caravan of 'prospects' means trials. Which means fresh blood for their fighting, and fresh bodies for their harem." He snarled.

"The Hall can hold up to five thousand," Laina said, her eyes flicking from Wyn to Fae. "What are you going to do?"

A bolt of power flashed behind Fae's eyes.

"End it," she said.

"Wait," Wyn stopped suddenly. His face twisted with conflict. "There's something else we have to do first."

"What else is there?" Fae asked.

Inside, all seven parts of her were pulling at the reins that her mortal body held. The pieces that came from Baev'ill and Bravargh were like caged animals, pacing and growling at the bars of her mind. The pragmatic, analytical sides of Ben and Bran watched, waiting with impatiently gritted teeth. Even the gentleness in Bek and serene whimsy of Be'ella Tor had hardened in anticipation of what was to come.

And then there was Fae, holding all of them inside her. Power crested within her like a wave, ready to break. Like a storm about to hit land.

She was ready. Ready to take on the force that had corrupted humanity and torn her from her family. The force that had deprived her of a father, and of knowing her mother. The force that made the Aethyr themselves weep.

"They do more than fight each other here," Wyn said. "Samuel said they train children to fight too. Take them from their families and bring them here to shape them into fighters for their trials."

The storm inside Fae went deathly quiet.

Take them from their families.

"There are children here?" she said, and her voice echoed with a distant rumble of thunder. Wyn nodded, his face dark. "Show me."

"Samuel said they were in the west wing..." Wyn turned about, trying to orientate himself.

"This way," Laina cried, and took them back the way they'd come. They passed the innocuous door down to the serving levels, and followed the still-deserted gallery to its conclusion. The corridor chicaned, and they ran straight into a group of Survivors guarding the entrance to the east wing.

Hal didn't even break stride, swinging his halbert in a wide arc that sent one guard flying into another. Before the other four could draw breath to shout, Ty loosed an arrow across the short distance to take one in the throat. Thom jumped past Hal to engage two more, swinging his double-headed axe about like whirlwind. Elas and Wyn threw themselves into the fray, catching the two that Hal had knocked over as they struggled to their feet.

The last guard seemed not to like the odds, and turned to run, only to find the tip of Fae's sword at his throat. The ocean-green of her eyes flashed dangerously, the new ring of gold around them blazing.

"I dare you to run," she said.

The red-band backed away from her a step. Two steps. Then suddenly, he was stumbling backwards, tipping over to land sprawled across the floor. Jesse stepped out from behind, and drew a line across his throat with one blade.

She turned to Fae as the guard gurgled his last, wet breath. "Don't think I haven't noticed you don't like killin'," she said, wiping the dagger on her trouser-leg. "But I think that might be something you're gonna have to get friendly with, don't you?"

Lines bracketed Fae's mouth.

"By the Mother..." Laina gasped at the door. "This used to be the library."

Beyond the high, arched entrance rose towering bookcases as far as the eye could see in either direction. Rows and rows of solid shelving stretched so high above the floor that narrow ladders hung from rails above to reach the upper levels.

But there weren't books on the shelves.

They were occupied by children.

The oldest couldn't have been more than fourteen. And the youngest was a tiny scrap of a girl who looked to be around four or five. Most of the children stared at the newcomers with glazed, vacant eyes from their narrow ledges, while others drifted around ground level like ghosts. Some even bore chains around their ankles.

Wyn, his slate-blue eyes darkening to storm-grey, turned back to the hallway with a hiss of disgust, and Fae heard him rifling through the pockets of downed guards behind them as she stepped further into the room.

"This must be what Max was talking about," Laina whispered, her eyes darting from side to side, and up and down. In all, around a hundred children lay or sat precariously perched on shelves, a further twenty or so roaming the floor. In the middle of the room, a white circle was painted on the polished wooden floorboards.

"What's wrong with them?" Jesse said, eyeing the drifting figures warily.

"Their souls suffer the absence of the Aethyr," Fae answered, and in her voice was the authority of Be'ella Tor. Her eyes drifted to the night-dark windows, where rain had begun lashing at the panes. "The spirits are barred from here by the corruption Anson cultivates. These children—" she swept out an arm to include all the youngsters lining the shelves "—have had their Aethyr ripped from them, and their souls starve for them. They are lost, adrift." She turned to Ty. "But we can fix it."

"Hey! Kid!" Jesse walked up to a child of around twelve, who stood staring at them with hollow eyes. "What do you do here?"

The boy's eyes moved slowly to fix Jesse with a not-quite-focused gaze.

He fidgeted, as if he was nervous. "We... we train," he said uncertainly. "She says we have to be strong."

Jesse frowned. "What—" she pointed to a boy of no more than six, curled up beside an older girl "—even him?"

The boy nodded. "We must all be strong," he said, his voice gathering momentum, as if reciting words that had been rehearsed a hundred times. "So we can fight. So we can be Survivors."

"Who do you fight?" Elas ground out between gritted teeth.

"The Survivors."

"They make you fight grown men?" Hal growled.

The boy nodded again. "Then we earn our bands. Then they take us away from here..." His eyes fluttered up through the shelves. "I don't know what happens then." The fear that edged into his gaze was loud enough to echo through Fae's mind. She scanned the narrow ledges, and saw that, vacant or not, every one of them was lost, alone, and deeply, utterly, afraid.

"Well—" Wyn stepped forward, a small set of keys dangling from his hands. "We're going to get you out. The halls are empty, you can run now while they're all at the trials."

The response to his words was heart-breaking. Every single child scurried back to the shelves to lie prone in their cubbies like corpses in caskets.

Laina took the keys Wyn had found among the bodies of the guards, and approached an older boy whose shackles had worn angry welts around his ankles, tears in her eyes. But when she went to unlock the manacles, he kicked out as much as his chained legs would allow, and scrambled up to a higher shelf. She approached another, a girl of around ten or eleven. This time, the child lashed out with her nails, hissing as she followed the boy's example.

It was as if the only thing they knew beyond their vacant stares was fighting. As if the ability to understand anything else had been beaten out of them.

"What are you doing?" Elas demanded, storming forward. "The guards are dead. Go! Run!" But the too-small figures stayed where they were, like toy soldiers. Soldiers trained to know that the price for defiance was pain.

What have these children endured, to fear even escape? Fae's rage swirled in a pool at her centre.

"We can't leave," an older girl said from a lower shelf. "Leaving before we earn our band is death." She turned her strange, empty eyes to Fae. "We never know whose."

Elas's glower darkened, and he scanned the shelves.

"There are too many of them," he muttered angrily.

Wyn nodded, arriving at the same conclusion. "We can't take them if they won't come," he said, jaw clenched.

"We should have brought some of the prisoners from outside with us," Ty said. "They could have led the children out while we continue on."

Thom shook his head. "We didn't know this is what we would find," he said. "And those people have a right to their freedom just as much."

The group scanned the vacant expressions lining the bookshelves, at a loss as to how to proceed.

"We'll come back for them," Laina said eventually, a promise as much to herself as to the listening children.

"We'll have to," Jesse said. "We can't waste Kagos's distraction on ferrying this lot out. We're already wasting time as it is." But even she seemed uncomfortable with the notion of leaving children unguarded. Then she added, "Someone mentioned that there are woman locked up in this hell-keep too," and her voice was the cold granite of the Dvargran mountains. "When this is over, we free all of them."

Fae's eyes swept the shelves, her gaze tempered steel. Her control over the parts of her that wanted to end Anson and his corrupted command over the human race was slipping; waves of power crashed against the inner walls of her mind.

The children weren't going anywhere. And somewhere in the castle, there were countless other captives being held for one twisted purpose or another.

They couldn't get any of them out without first dealing with the rot at the core of this place.

She turned to the door.

"Let's go and pay Lady Black's trials a visit," Fae said, her voice a deadly blade.

"Let's finish this."

. . .

Racing back along the gallery, they had only to follow the sounds of the trials until they turned a final corner, and were at last faced with the entrance to the Great Hall. The huge double doors stood open, allowing the riotous clamour out into the gallery. A raucous cheer went up as they approached, vicious, and cruel.

Hundreds of Survivors gathered around a central spectacle, with their backs turned to the doors. Most were red-banded. Some were red-belted. All were goading and jeering whatever, or whoever was in the middle. More than once, Fae saw money change hands. The smell of stale sweat and the iron tang of blood scented the air, hot and humid and heavy.

Power crackled through her veins, under her skin. To either side of her, the others wore stony faces with a resolve that could fell mountains.

Laina swallowed. "This is going to be bad."

Hal nodded. "Aye," he said, staring daggers at the crowded room. "Maybe you should stay back. Like you said, you're not a fighter."

Laina shook her head. "I'll stay out of your way, but no. These are my people too. It's about time I stopped running from it."

Fae's ears were filled with the shouts and insults being flung around the trials. Her hearing seemed to extend preternaturally past the crowds, allowing the sounds of flesh striking flesh to reach her. Grunts of pain. A cry of anguish. A thud, and silence.

Laughter from the crowd.

Fae bared her teeth.

"Stand back," she said, and strode into the room, her power curling around her fingertips.

The Survivors watching the trials were too caught up in the action to notice Fae as she moved through them, eyes blazing golden-green. She circled around, until she could go no further.

Blocking her way, was another cage, smaller than the one that had been outside, but still fully occupied by captive humans. Some were beaten and bloodied. The ones that weren't, wore looks varying from open terror, to fierce determination, and utter resignation. One woman knelt sobbing beside a figure lying prone and unmoving to one side of the cage.

Fae scanned the captives, and stiffened.

There were children in the cage too.

To the rear, four or five children no older than ten huddled behind the others, trying to stay hidden. A small group of adults stood between them and the spectacle, shielding them as best they could, to keep them from seeing, and from being seen.

Another sickening cheer went up from the crowd, and the door to the cage was wrenched open.

"Right," the red-band at the hatch yelled, "let's have one of the small-fries now. We got some of our trainees for you to prove yourselves against. Come on now, don't be shy." He leered. When the children didn't step forward, his smile turned sour. "One of you get out here right now or I'll send my boys in to get you, you hear me?" The woman kneeling with the injured figure glanced frantically to the back of the cage. The red-band glared around the sullen faces, then shrugged, and turned to call his lackeys. A small voice piped up.

"I'll go." A little girl stepped around the men trying to shield her. She was smaller than Max, and looked twice as breakable. Her bright, flame-red hair was tied back in a rough plait, and her chin trembled, despite the stubborn look in her eye.

"No—" one of the other prisoners gasped.

"Shut it!" the red-band snapped. "Come on then." He waved her along. "Hurry it up."

As he shoved the girl through the throng, Fae began to push her way through alongside them. She was barely aware of what she was doing, moving more by force of will than by intention. Finally, she came to a point where she could see what the crowd was watching.

Like in the courtyard, a thick white rope was laid out in a circle in the middle. Or at least, it had been white once. Now it was smeared and stained with blood and... other things. On the opposite side of the circle, was another cage. Every person in it was bloodied, but at least they all stood on their own two feet. Beside the cage was a bench lined with banded fighters, barefoot, and with their knuckles wrapped in strips of cloth.

In Fae's mind, the pieces were coming together. The first cage she'd seen was for the "prospects". The cage opposite for the successful ones. The line beside it, for the challengers.

The little girl stepped into the circle, and she looked like a doll among mercenaries. She was barefoot, like the challengers, and wore only a simple shift dress. She stood, looking as if she'd never clenched a fist in her life.

Her challenger stepped forward; a boy, only two or three years older, but honed by constant training. His arms were thin, but muscled, and he bounced on the balls of his feet, waiting for the command to start.

But for all that he looked the part, Fae noticed something else about him. He had the same ghostliness she'd seen in the other children. The same somewhat lost and vacant look. And there was something uneasy in his eyes when he looked at the girl he was to fight. He glanced nervously to his left.

Fae followed his gaze. And found that above the crowds, on a raised platform, stood a group of red-belted Survivors, all battle-hardened and scarred. And in their midst, stood a woman dressed all in black, with dark-blonde hair slicked back into a tight, waist-length rope, blue eyes rimmed in kohl, and lips a thin, cruel line.

Tamra Walker — Throldon's Lady Black.

"Begin!" she commanded, and the boy in the ring jumped to obey. He jumped with the same responsiveness of a dog that knew disobedience led to a beating.

He lunged at the girl.

And suddenly, without knowing how she got there, Fae stood between them.

The boy barrelled into her, and fell back.

There was a roar of protest from the crowd. It swelled and grew as each voice that joined it became more offended by her presence. But no one stepped in.

Above the tumult, a single clap of hands was heard. Then another, each one clear and audible. The hubbub subsided, until Fae heard nothing but that solitary, echoing applause.

"Well well." Black stepped from her platform, clapping slowly as she went. "This *is* exciting." She walked into the ring to stand before Fae. "And here I was, thinking I wouldn't get to fight anyone today." She leaned in, until Fae could feel her breath on her face. Her eyes were ice cold, as if any shred of humanity she'd once had, had long since fled. "So," Black sneered. "Who the fuck are you?"

Anson's presence on her was like a black shroud, blotting out light until the room fell into shadow around her. The lamps seemed to dim, the faces fading into a foggy backdrop.

And the new facets within Fae that had been Aethyr-gifted to face this very evil, shrank away from the darkness.

Leaving her exposed; just a human, raised by elves.

In way over her head.

Her powers dried up on her fingertips, and her confidence evaporated with them, along with any scrap of notion that she knew what she was doing. She had carried the Aethyr into the dark fog, where they couldn't enter, where their foe lay, and now those parts that granted her her power cowered inside when she needed them most.

Frozen in place, she heard a scuffle off to her left. Her eyes flicked towards it.

And her heart fell.

Ty stood at the front of the crowd of red-bands, holding his arms away from his body in a sign of surrender, his hands empty. In front of him stood Laina, looking nervously from side to side with her head held high. Behind them, Wyn and Elas strained against the grip of two red-bands at their sides. Another held Thom's axe at his back, while he stood stoically resigned at Ty's side. Hal and Jesse were nowhere to be seen.

Fae's breath left her in a rush. This would end here with her. One way or another.

She turned back to face Black.

And the earth shook.

50

A SHARD OF A BROKEN GOD

"KAGOS!" Max heard Aiya's bloodcurdling scream just before the ground pitched beneath her feet, throwing her sideways on Immrith's back. She looked up to see Kagos lumbering to his feet in the middle of the bailey.

What are you doing? she yelled at him, ducking a wayward swing of Immrith's empty fist, his war-hammer thankfully in the other hand.

It may surprise you to know, Kagos's lofty voice responded, *that I would much rather be airborne as well.* He turned his giant head to eyeball her across the courtyard. *One of these misbegotten apes has punctured my wing. Which makes flying such tight manoeuvres as required in these circumstances rather impossible, I'm afraid. So here I am.* He punctuated the last with an impressive gout of flame at the nearest group of red-bands that decided to run at him. He'd given up on trying to spare the Survivors; now his fire burned indiscriminately, and at least half the advancing enemy fell back, clothes, hair, and skin aflame.

Behind the curve of his neck, Max saw Aiya slide to the ground beside him. The second the dragonrider hit the ground, she sprinted straight for Max, her long braid streaming out behind her.

Max slid from Immrith's back, dodging beneath the knot of fighters around the centaur to meet her.

The second she reached her, Aiya grabbed Max by the shirt, pulling her away from the violence and out of the battle. She slotted them into the space between a saddlery and the stables, and it smelled of straw and horses and leather polish.

Aiya whirled on Max. "*What* were you thinking?" she yelled angrily, dark eyes blazing.

Max would have taken a step back, but Aiya held her arm in a vice-like grip. "What do you mean?" she sputtered. "Kagos told me to be here!"

"To sit in the corner so he could keep an eye on you! Not to rush into the middle of a battle on the back of a centaur!" Aiya continued yelling somewhat hysterically. "The reason he's grounded is because he's trying to protect *you*!"

"Why? Because I understand his language? So what?"

"Yes, because you hear Draconic!" Aiya gripped both her shoulders now. "Because dragonfire won't touch you! Because you represent a new hope for dragonkind!"

A wall of flame spread across the courtyard, and Aiya's gaze shifted to watch Kagos in the midst of the fight. A tear rolled down her cheek, and she tore her eyes away to stare at Max with burning intensity.

"Dragon eggs only hatch when they hear their mother," she said, her eyes boring into Max's. "But in the absence of the mother, a rider can coax the hatchling forth." She paused. "Riders are rare, Max, and we don't know why they happen. But *you're* a rider, Max. That's why Kagos's fire didn't touch you. It's why you can hear him speak into your mind."

"But..." Max stared, her mind going a hundred miles a minute. "The dragons are dying. Kagos said it himself, they're all old ones left! And... you left me behind before! You're a rider, why can't you do it?"

"I'm already partnered," Aiya said, her lips curling in a bittersweet smile. "You're not." She let out a frustrated sigh and ran her hands over her hair before fixing Max with a look so intent the girl thought she might burst a blood vessel. "Listen, it takes decades, sometimes longer, for a dragon pair to produce a clutch of eggs, and years again before they're ready to hatch. And you're right: only the old ones are left now — there are no more mated pairs left alive, they were all hunted down by poacher scum. But there are dragon eggs in Hearthstone — the last clutch. There's been no one to call them forth all these years, and there are no more riders in Alyla. We'd all given up hope." Aiya straightened, clearing the lump from her throat. "No one thought to look for *human* riders." Just then, a bellowing roar came from Kagos, shaking loose masonry from the walls to either side of them.

Max peered out to see crossbow quarrels peppering his long neck, each with a line held by a red-band below. There must have been about twenty of them, all hauling Kagos's head to the ground.

Max spun back to Aiya, who was watching over her shoulder. "We have to help him!"

Firelight caught on the wetness on Aiya's face as she shook her head. "He's sacrificing himself so I can get *you* out of here alive," she said. "*You* can call the hatchlings. *You* are the only remaining hope for dragonkind. *Our* job, is to leave."

"What?" Max answered incredulously. "No! You came here to get rid of the Survivors! To give Throldon a fresh start!"

"One you won't be a part of."

"To hell with that!" Max turned, and made for Kagos, pinned in the middle of the courtyard.

Aiya caught her easily. Pressing a pressure-point in Max's neck, she waited for the girl to go limp, and hoisted her over her shoulder. She cast one last look over to Kagos, whose liquid black eyes were watching her.

I entrust the future of my race to you, he said.

Aiya nodded, tears streaming down her face. There were no words, nor time enough to navigate the labyrinth of her feelings.

May we fly again, after this life. His voice was gentle in her mind. *Now go!*

Aiya melted back into the shadows and fled, Max's unconscious form slung over her shoulders.

Across the courtyard, Aren watched as Kagos's head crashed to the stone, as the Survivors finally overwhelmed him.

"Kagos is down!" he called to the others.

Immrith spun. "Then we must help him!" Without hesitation, he plunged through the battle towards the figures anchoring Kagos's neck.

"Immrith! Wait!" Stef yelled, his elven eyes catching the glint of arrows released into the fray. "Arrows!"

Aren ducked. Wil ducked. Stef ducked.

An arrow thudded home in Immrith's back halfway into his headlong flight to Kagos's aid. He staggered. Another hammered into his shoulder, throwing his balance even more.

He pitched forward, and crashed to the ground.

"Eah!" Wil swore, fending off attacks on two sides. "Immrith! Get up!" He pushed back one assailant, only to have it replaced with another. "Immrith!" But the centaur did not rise.

"Where's Max?" Aren asked suddenly.

Then he was overpowered, the odds now stacked impossibly against the three scouts. Stef was dragged to the ground moments later, quickly followed by Wil. And they were in no position to help anyone anymore.

You're on your own now, Spiritchild. Kagos's voice came though to Fae as she stood before Throldon's notorious Lady Black.

What? she gasped, looking across at Ty, her eyes going wide.

Immrith is down. I am incapacitated, Kagos summarised. *The elves are taken. I have sent Aiya to take the girl back to Hearthstone. She is important.* The last held a hint of regret, but it was hardened by resolve. *Let us hope you have what is needed to take it from here.*

She didn't.

Fae suddenly felt very alone, standing against an impossible foe.

And she was frozen with fear.

Black stepped closer, so that her body was inches from Fae's. "I said," she repeated, her voice lowered to a dangerous purr. "Who, *the fuck*, are you?" She was standing so close that Fae didn't see the right hook coming until she was sprawled across the floor on her back. Her head spun, flashing shapes floating across her vision as the room seesawed back and forth.

The Survivor boy cleared the ring, and someone else pulled the red-haired girl away, leaving Fae alone in the circle with Lady Black, leader of the Survivors, and host to a shard of a broken god.

Fae staggered to her feet. She couldn't imagine what it was she intended to do, but whatever it was, she knew it would be better accomplished standing. She reached behind for her swords.

Black waggled a finger at her. "Ah ah ah," she sang in a voice that chilled Fae to the core. "No weapons here." She held her arms out to the sides and turned slowly, taking in the whole of the Great Hall and its occupants. "Here, you prove yourself as you are." She spun suddenly, whipping her arms around to strike Fae with such force, she was facing the wrong way before her feet even left the ground.

Fae met the floor with a crack that jarred through her entire body, fuzzing her senses with pain. She lay stunned on the ground, the cool tiles soothing against her pulsating cheek.

Someone hauled on her sword sheath, and she thought for a moment that she would be dragged to her feet, when the straps were cut, and she was dropped back to land face-down on the floor.

"Fae!" she heard Elas yell. "Fae, you've got to get up! Get u— oof!" The muffled thump of flesh striking flesh, and the next voice Fae heard was cold and heartless.

"Yes." Black sneered. "I was expecting a bit more from someone with the audacity to walk into my ring so blithely." She came to stand over Fae's prone form. "Maybe she's just stupid." There was a ripple of laughter from the assembled red-bands. A boot connected with Fae's side, flipping her over to crash onto her back. She scrambled away, and lurched to her feet.

"So, Fae, is it?" Black said, advancing again. "What brings you to my Circle of Strength? Was it to fight Jacob?" She waved towards the young red-band who'd been about to fight. "Because I've got to tell you, you've got a way to go before you could challenge him." A ripple of snide laughter swelled across the crowd. "Or are you here to liberate my prospects?" She glanced significantly at the caged humans. "Tut tut," she said, tick-tocking her finger from side to side. "Those who are worthy learn to be strong and fearless here. I can't allow you to deny us that." She paused. "Those who are not—" she shrugged carelessly "—are no loss."

An ember sparked inside Fae.

"What happens to them?" she asked, her voice rough. "The ones that aren't... 'worthy'?"

"She speaks!" Black roared, throwing her arms up. The Survivors laughed on cue. Black stepped forward. "Well, you see, Fae," she said, with the air of explaining something to a particularly slow child, "if they're not worthy, then they're just dragging the human race down. Bearing weak children. Taking up space. *Depending* on others." She turned, addressing the crowd. "That's one thing my predecessor had right. Being *dependent* on another, is *weakness*." She spat the words out, and the assembled Survivors murmured their approval. Black turned back to Fae. "And we don't do weakness here." She stepped closer. "So if they're not worthy, they're *examples*. Of what survival *isn't*."

"What does that mean?" Fae said through gritted teeth.

Black's smirk spread into a cruel smile. "Shall we show you?" A rumble of assent moved through the crowd. Black heard it, and turned to her audience. "Shall we show her?" she shouted. And a roar of vicious cheers replied. She turned to the bench where her fighters sat waiting. "Jacob," she called, gesturing the boy over. He jumped to obey, rushing to her side. Taking him by the shoulders, Black turned him to Fae. "Jacob, please show Fae here, what we do with the unworthy."

The boy's foggy expression hesitated, then hardened, and he nodded sharply. Fae stared between him and Black, who waved somebody forward from the edge of the circle. Within moments, one of the 'prospects' was shoved into the ring — another boy this time.

Black snapped her fingers, and two red-bands detached from the crowd to yank Fae back to the edge of the ring, holding her fast.

"It seems only fair that we educate our newcomer, don't you agree?" Black called out to the crowd, who bellowed their agreement. She stepped to the edge of the circle, a few paces from Fae, remaining inside the line of the rope. She folded her arms across her chest.

"Begin," she commanded.

Jacob flew at the boy, all tooth and nails and scrawny limbs. With Fae's Aethyrial advantage vanished, her feeble efforts to free herself from the grip of the men to her sides were fruitless. Their hands were like iron manacles about her arms, and she could do nothing except watch.

Jacob latched onto the boy's arm, twisted, and flipped him onto his back in one practiced move. He leapt astride the boy, and rained blow after blow down on him. The boy tried to fight back, to rotate his position, anything, but Jacob had been trained. He was slippery, and nimble, and worked his way around the boy's defences easily. In the end, the boy threw his arms over his head while Jacob beat on his body. Over. And over.

The ruthless cheers of the Survivors faded into the distance, for all that they screamed into Fae's ear. But Jacob's laboured breathing, as he struck the boy curled up on the ground, came to her clear as a bell, amplified above the noise of the crowd. Fae looked closer, beyond the violence, and saw that Jacob wasn't as battle-hardened as Black would have her think. His face was screwed up into an anguished grimace, his cheeks wet with tears.

Black saw it too. She strode into the ring to pull Jacob off the prospect, and threw him bodily across the circle, where he landed in a crumpled heap.

She sneered at his limp form. "Pathetic." She looked over at the bench. "Annabel, Judith, these two need dealing with. Show us how it should be done." Two girls stood at the edge of the ring — one with bright copper hair pulled back in a pony's tail, the other with straight black hair cropped short. Both wore the foggy expressions of the other children, but it looked to Fae like they'd long retreated beyond the fog. Chosen its numbing greyness, rather than the pained confusion of the others. Their eyes were dull, their faces slack. They didn't snarl or cry. They stood with the lazy ease of someone who knew exactly what they had to do, safe in the knowledge that it posed no challenge. They moved like puppets on strings; like they weren't even driving their own motions.

Both boys appeared unconscious as the girls moved towards them. They didn't rise to fight, or scurry away. They were utterly helpless.

The girls parted ways halfway across the ring, each heading to a different boy.

Fae watched in mute horror, fearing what they intended, and yet fervently hoping she was wrong.

But all her fervent hope didn't stop the girls from approaching their victims, reaching down in perfect, careless synchrony, and snapping two boys' necks.

And the crowd roared.

51

PAINFUL ENOUGH TO KILL

Something in Fae snapped.

Her muscles locked up, her body a wild animal waiting to pounce.

"No!" A yell went up, and Hal appeared from the crowd, where he'd been hiding in plain sight. He pushed his way to the front of the crowd and threw himself into the ring, falling to his knees on the ground beside Jacob.

"Who are you?" Black demanded. "What the fuck is going on here?"

Hal ignored her, gently placing his fingers at Jacob's throat to feel for a pulse. He stilled, then let his hand fall away. When he lifted his head, his face was a mask of hatred and pain. Old pain, made fresh, and raw.

"You kill children?" He spoke in lowered tones, his lips pulled back in a feral snarl. "You're no better than the Unity." He rose to his feet, lifting his halbert in a white-knuckled grip, his whole frame shaking with rage. "They murdered children too." His voice was rough with emotions. The same emotions Fae had seen him bury before, now laid bare, like exposed nerves, painful and undeniable.

"The Unity exploited the weak, no matter who they were," Black replied. "I *train* them. Make it so that anyone has a chance to be strong. To survive."

"That's what you call this?" Hal thrust a finger towards the bodies of the two boys.

Black shrugged. "The human race must become strong. Those two could not be strong, so they have no place in it."

Fae thought that was just the sort of broken logic that might come from a broken god, when Hal gave a roar, and rushed at Black.

"Hal, no!" she yelled, but he was deafened and blinded by his pain.

Black grinned. She bent her knees and turned side-on, ready for his attack.

Hal charged forward, his pole-arm levelled at his target, but at the last moment, he spun the axe-head up, bringing the butt around to strike at Black's legs. She leapt it easily, hopping in to rap him on the temple with a closed fist. He dodged, and spun, slicing the blade of his halbert across her middle. She jumped back, throwing herself under his swing to kick at his knees. He stepped out of her range, aiming a kick at her head in return.

The exchange went on, each one a skilled fighter. Hal danced around Black as he had done when Fae first saw him. But Black was clearly no novice herself, dodging and weaving and striking with as much accuracy as the ranger. And she was enjoying it.

Just as Hal was beginning to tire, Black timed a backwards leap poorly, and Hal's axe-head cut a line across her belly. But instead of recoiling in shock, she grabbed the shaft of the pole-arm as it passed, and yanked it from Hal's grip.

With a grin, she spun the weapon deftly, and brought it to bear.

And without a moment's pause, speared Hal straight through the chest.

"No!" Laina's composure broke, and she went to run to the ranger. Ty held her back before the red-bands could make a grab for her.

Hal staggered. He fell back, collapsing to the ground, and lay still. Blood spilled fast from his back, where the halbert had punched clean through.

"Shame," Black said, lifting her jerkin to expose the shallow flesh wound she had allowed Hal to inflict. "He would have made a good commander." She turned to the red-belts on the platform. "I hope you were taking notes."

"That's enough," Fae whispered past gritted teeth. She had nothing to fight with, but she burned with an untrammelled rage. It singed from the inside, flaying away layers of her fear like a fire within. Good people were suffering. Good people were *dying*. And this woman was playing games in their blood. The spectre of Anson was a cloak about her shoulders, but her heart was dark and twisted before the god ever latched onto her.

And that dark rot was spreading beyond the reaches of this city to plague the natural order. Threatening the world at large, and putting question marks over lives that Fae cared about. Hal's blood polished the floor red. Anson's influence would see Arolynos dripping blood too.

The fires of her rage flared, and her fear peeled away and crumbled into ash.

Black turned. "What?"

"That's enough," Fae said again, louder.

"Enough what?" Black said, in a mockery of innocence. She stepped casually over the spreading pool of Hal's blood, and kicked aside Jacob's body. "We have trials to complete. We're not finished here yet."

"ENOUGH!" Fae yelled, and inside, she hauled her Aethyrial aspects mercilessly from the corner in which they cowered. The fire smouldering within blazed into a towering inferno, burning away the shroud Black carried about her shoulders.

In the dark fog of the Throldonian Eah'lara, she shone a beacon of white-hot light, an oasis of energies in a desert of death. And from within the oasis, lines of power shot forth, like arrows from a bow, spearing through the darkness to anchor her to the shimmering nebulae of the Spirit Realm beyond the fog. The threads cast out, with her at their centre, and as each one connected back to the world, she felt a surge of power swell within.

In the Great Hall, her skin burned with it. The red-bands holding her stumbled back, throwing their arms over their faces. The crowd of Survivors fell away, until all that was left was her, and Lady Black.

With her spiritual vision overlaying the living world, Fae saw the pulsing fibres connecting her to her power. And she saw the parasitic entity that marked Anson's grip on Black, saw how deeply it snaked inside, until it had made itself a part of her. It clutched at her past — at something from the forge of her making that haunted her still — to force its way into her very soul.

Immediately, Fae launched her powers at the parasite that corrupted the human race, seeking to rip it from her.

Black shrieked in pain, and threw herself at Fae, but she was wild and unfocused. The trained, skilled fighter of a moment ago dissolved into a desperate flurry of untamed blows.

Fae caught her shoulders, and they wrestled in a chaotic tangle of limbs. The momentum of Black's attack forced them backwards, over the rope outline of the ring.

A moment ago, they might have hit a wall of red-banded spectators. But the Survivors had scattered the instant the light within Fae had unleashed upon Anson's shadowy presence.

That light coalesced above her now; while her arms and legs grappled roughly with Throldon's Black Lady, the powers of the Aethyr built, higher and higher until the pressure made her ears pop. A cloud of energies massed within the light, and a storm brewed into existence beneath the ceilings of the Great Hall. Grey clouds hung heavy and ominous over the centre of the room. Flashes of lightning heralded rumbles of thunder. The atmosphere turned electric, currents sparking at random through the air.

Meanwhile, on the other side of the veil that separated the mortal world from Eah'lara, a part of Fae that might once have belonged to Be'ella Tor worked at unstitching a god from his stranglehold on a human. But the darkness clung to Black like a second skin, and it was all Fae could do to hold her at bay while she worked, the other woman far better trained for combat than she was.

Then she lost her footing, and fumbled her hold on her opponent. Black pressed her advantage, lungeing in with teeth bared. Fae's grasp on Anson slipped as well, and what little progress she'd made, was undone in a heartbeat.

She cried out in dismay.

"Enough!" she said again, planting her feet. She threw a hand up, palm out.

Black flew backwards as if Fae had struck her with the force of a war hammer. She soared through the air, and a line of spiritual energy connecting Fae's palm directly to Black's heart reeled out, caught on something within. Something that had its roots tangled into the Survivor's very foundations.

The line snapped taut, and Black let out a blood-curdling scream as she collapsed to the ground.

Sending her awareness along the thread, Fae felt the snarl at the end, felt it tug at the bars of Black's soul; the cage designed to protect and defend her inner, most vulnerable self, serving only to lock her in with a twisted, corrupt entity bent on achieving ultimate dominion.

I see you. Fae's eyes fixed onto the pool of black smoke wrapped around the mind and soul of Tamra Walker. A single, red eye blinked open within it, and glared balefully back at her.

Tamra. A voice crackled into the hall, echoing hollowly beneath the vaulted ceilings. *We are threatened.*

Across the room, Black stumbled to her feet. Her eyes flashed wildly, her hair escaping in vine-like tendrils around her face. She bent, and pulled a dagger from her boot. Then, letting loose an animal scream of rage, she charged.

Fae yanked on the thread caught deep within Tamra.

It won't work. The voice of Anson's shadow broke as it spoke. *We are one.*

Fae braced for impact as Black barrelled into her, throwing them both to the ground. She had enough presence of mind to lift a knee as they fell, getting her foot onto Black's chest and using her forward momentum to push her straight over her head. Black somersaulted across the floor, landing in a sprawled crouch behind Fae. Fae scrambled to her feet just in time to grab Black's knife-wielding arm before the blade made it to her throat.

They grappled, neither gaining the upper hand. Then, maintaining a grip on Black's wrist, Fae dropped her hand, twisting and bringing her elbow up to smash into the side of Black's face. While Tamra staggered, dazed, Fae gathered up the thread again.

She was nothing without me, Anson's voice echoed loudly through the hall, cutting in and out, only a small part of the original whole. *Just a weak, pathetic victim.* The voice laughed softly. *But we had one thing in common. Strength. We need it. We hunger for it. Yearn for it. Her ache for strength is a near match for mine. An ache painful enough to kill for.* The laugh became maniacal, and in the smoke, Fae saw an ice-white grin emerge, one half wide and toothy, the other half thin and shrivelled. She tugged on the god's hook in Black, but it held fast.

I started moulding her from the moment my former host took me to that house that reeked of shame and despair. The laugh that curled from the smoke was vulgar and mocking. *It took only the barest nudge, for her to use that hunger, for her to become what I needed.* The mockery of a smile smirked in the curls of darkness above. *And when she snapped, I took her, like I took him, and his father before him. The blood on her hands made her mine.*

Before her, Black pushed to her feet again. She shook herself off, and brought her fists up to guard her face. Gone was the feral loss of discipline. When she came at Fae again, she was cold, calculating, and vicious.

Her first strike was a feint at Fae's head, which she fell for, followed by a hard jab to the kidneys. As Fae folded, Black's knee came up to connect with her face, and stars blinked in front of her eyes. Black grabbed her shoulders, pushing her upright to deliver a savage blow to her side ribs.

Something snapped, and Fae immediately felt her chest stutter. She tried to draw breath, but her lungs wouldn't — *couldn't* — obey. Unrelenting, Black launched herself into the air, dropping like a stone to drive her fist into Fae's temple.

Fae spun, and crashed into the floor with a bone-jarring crunch. Agony spiked a white-hot javelin through her shoulder, but that was nothing compared to the feeling of her chest caving in, the stabbing sips she gulped at each breath, pain spearing through her with every gasp. The room tipped on its side.

Concussion. Her mind inventoried her injuries. *Dislocated shoulder, broken rib, punctured lung, probably internal bleeding.* And now Black was advancing again, to make that list the least of her problems. Fae gasped, but the air wouldn't come. An ominous gurgling sound filled her throat instead.

And that's why, Anson's voice crackled, the red glare of his one eye staring down at her. *That's why she will win me the world.*

Fae watched helplessly as Tamra Walker's boots came closer, her vision narrowing with every step, each gasp of bloody air smaller than the last. The pressure building in her chest was making it nearly impossible to breathe. Her heart flagged with the effort of keeping her alive, each laboured beat echoing with the whispers of her past.

"Eah waits for you."

Darkness closed around her, and the stutter in her chest came to a stop.

"She is more than the best of us."

Fae sighed, her eyes fluttered closed.

And all she could think was, *But I wasn't enough when it mattered.*

52

THE FIRE WITHIN

P andemonium had broken out when Fae's powers summoned an elemental storm within the four walls of the Great Hall. Her skin cracked as it had in the monument, yellow light spearing out from a fire within her. The storm cloud roiling above thundered, lightning flashing ominously inside. An impossible wind whipped up around Fae and her opponent, enclosing them in a whirlwind and obscuring them from sight.

Ty darted forward, dropping to his knees beside Hal, still bleeding, all the while keeping one eye on the storm. Survivors streamed past them to the open doors, fleeing from a spectacle they had no hope of understanding.

"Laina!" Ty called to Fae's mother. The other healer raced over.

"Is he still...?" she asked, as Ty pressed the fingers of one hand to Hal's throat, feeling for a pulse while the other palm pressed firmly over his chest wound.

Ty closed his eyes. Focused. *There.* He looked up at Laina, and leant his other hand to the task of holding the wound under pressure. "It's weak, but it's there," he said.

Laina nodded, her expression turning stern. "We need to bind it. And quickly!" She glanced uneasily up at the hurricane blowing mere feet from where they knelt. "We need to move him away from here!" Her eye caught on the cage of prisoners, staring wide-eyed at the storm. "What about them?!" she cried.

"Leave that to me!" Jesse called, hurrying past, having already opened the one containing the successful prospects. "Damn locks are hard to pick! At least now there's no need for subtlety!" She cast a pointed eye at the storm, snatched up an abandoned sword and proceeded to attack the bars of the second cage, hacking chunks of the wood away with surprising strength. Thom was a split-second behind her, while Wyn and Elas helped the injured innocents out of the hall.

"Can we do anything?" Elas called, gathering up one of the smaller children in his arms. The young boy watched the storm, lightning flashes reflecting in wide, brown eyes.

Ty looked back at the result of Fae's powers. "Right now," he said, "we stay out of the way."

A great crack of splintering wood announced the opening of the prospect cage, and the final humans joined in the exodus of the Great Hall.

Ty turned back to Hal's wound, packing it with as much cloth as he had. Laina pulled another roll of bandage from her own pack, and strapped it firmly into place. Careful not to jostle him too much, they pulled Hal away from the maelstrom, and into the gallery beyond the hall.

From the relative safety of the arched doorway, Laina set to work on Hal's wound, Briefly peeling back the wadding, she eyed the gaping hole in his chest anxiously. She pressed it back down, and looked up at Ty, her expression hardening. "What have you got?"

Without hesitation, Ty emptied his pack out onto the floor. He snatched up a bottle of florestem, and passed it to her.

"For cleansing the wound, and your hands," he said. Then he picked up a pouch of healer's helper, a thumb of willowbark, and another bottle of tinctured trickleroot. He added appropriate quantities of each to his water-wrap, and gave it a shake. "The more of this we can get into him, the better," he said, dribbling the liquid onto Hal's lips drop by drop. "It would be better if he could have it in a tea — the heat releases the healing properties better — but this is better than nothing at all."

Laina's gaze flicked across to what he was doing, before returning to her assessment of the wound. "What is it?" she asked. He told her. Her eyes flared at the corners. "Sorry I asked," she said. "Alright then, what does it do?" The only name she'd recognised was willowbark.

"It will promote healing in his tissues, dull the pain, and reduce infection and inflammation." Ty shrugged. "It's all I've got. If we were in Arolynos, I'd suggest any number of additional treatments."

"Well, he'll have to be grateful for what he's got," Laina said, her lips pressed together as her hands finally found where most of the bleeding was coming from. "Pass me that suture," she said. Ty obliged. "The spear passed between his lungs, but all this blood is coming from one of his heart vessels." She guided the needle down along her hand, and began stitching the hole closed. "Idiot," she murmured as she worked.

"You can take it up with him after," Ty said, watching her work.

"I intend to," she said. "He's been carrying around his pain from Bredon all this time without dealing with it — I could see it the minute I finally recognised him. Can't believe it took me so long, but I guess time's changed all of us..." She fell silent, focusing on her work. "We all lost something back then. Not one person came out of Bredon unharmed. All of us lost our homes. A lot lost their lives. Most lost family..." She swallowed thickly, her eyes welling. "He had a wife and two children." She began knotting her sutures, leaving unsaid what had become of them. Her eyes flicked briefly to Hal's unconscious face. "But that doesn't give you an excuse to go running into a fight you had no hope of surviving!"

Ty remained silent as she finished stitching the wound closed. She smeared the exit wound with a balm from a small jar she carried, and used the rest of her bandaging to strap Hal's chest.

Sitting back on her heels, she wiped her forearm across her brow, her hands dark with drying blood. She eyed the pallor of Hal's skin, the shallowness of his breathing.

"If I had all my equipment, and a safe hospit to work from, I'd suggest a blood donation," she said. "But we'll just have to hope his stubbornness pulls him through." She looked over at the storm still raging in the Hall. "I hope she's okay," she whispered.

Ty's eyes followed.

And just then, the storm dropped.

Fae felt her powers wane along with the air in her lungs.

Her chest would not, could not expand, and the pain that tore through her every time she tried was too much.

She gasped one last, meagre breath, and darkness finally enveloped her.

The storm stuttered and died, the last of it falling to the ground as warm mist.

Shame, really, Anson's broken voice mused above her. *Together, you could have been unstoppable. Instead, you'll die here, alone.*

Not alone. Six voices swirled in the wake of her power.

The darkness drew back as if burned, and behind the pink filter of her closed eyelids, a bright light glowed red-hot. It grew, and grew, turning around, and around, swelling with every rotation. Then, all of a sudden, the light speared outwards, like spokes on a wheel, following the connecting lines out to the still-healthy Eah'lara.

Choirs of voices filled Fae's ears like a summons, calling her, beckoning, commanding her presence, for all that she could not obey. Then the lights returned, and they were stronger and brighter than before. They spun together, faster and faster, until the air above her shone brilliant white even through her closed eyes.

Then, a single, blinding shaft of light plummeted, arrowing straight down.

And dived *into* Fae.

Fae's spine arced backwards, snapping into an upward curve, her mouth stretched open in a silent scream. Where the light plunged into the depths of her, it wasn't just light; it was warmth and energy and *life*, and it seared her insides with the power of not just the Aethyr, but of Eah'lara itself. The entire embodiment of spirit life poured into her, stretching her at the seams, until past the point at which she thought she could take no more.

The light filled her up, barely contained within her skin, until even her cells were infused with it.

And then it stopped.

No more light poured from above.

It radiated from *within* her.

Fae opened her eyes.

Tamra stood a few paces away, her arm thrown up to shield her eyes from the near-solar glow flooding from Fae's pores.

The dark, smoky shadow of Anson hovered about Black's shoulders still, poised, unsure of what to expect from her next.

That makes two of us, Fae thought. She was numb from head to toe; the only sensation discernible was the warmth of the Aethyrial light that suffused her. She took a blissfully unencumbered breath.

As she exhaled, dust motes danced above her face, catching the light spilling from her to spin like glitter through the air. She breathed again, drinking air like nectar, savouring the ease with which she accomplished so simple a task. But her work was not yet done. She pushed herself onto her elbows, the motion disturbing yet more dust motes to spin through the air. They drifted from her... and curved towards Anson's shadow. They glowed, like the orbs of the Spirit Realm. They rippled with power, like her skin. And as they connected with the shadow, they burned tiny holes through the smoke.

Tamra flinched. Her shadow recoiled. And still, the motes came.

With every breath, more of the glittering, *shining* dust left Fae's body to join the stream arrowing straight for Anson.

Tamra twitched, then began batting at tiny, invisible irritations as she felt their echo homing in on her parasitic god. She screamed in frustration. And then she screamed in pain.

Anson howled like a wild animal as the motes flew at him in droves, a waterfall in reverse of spiritual energy, pouring from Fae, into him.

Fae watched as Tamra's eyes went wild with agony, her fingers clawing at her arms, her chest, her face.

This is killing her, she realised. Pushing her awareness through the throng of tiny orbs, Fae reached out to the place where Anson was twisted into Tamra's soul. She took hold of him and — with his grip finally loosened by her relentless attack — she ripped him out.

Tamra crumpled to the ground, silent and still.

No! Anson's voice rasped though the onslaught. Smoky limbs unfurled towards his host, looking to bind her once again.

Fae saw his intent, and threw her power at him.

Storms of energy burst from her fingertips in the shape of lightning-fire to burn away his shadowy reach. But Anson had no fixed form, and two more tendrils burst from where the first had been severed. Fae burned those away too, and four more appeared, ducking around her power to pull him closer to his host.

Despite the deluge of energy already pouring off Fae, and the blasts of spiritual fire she struck him with, Anson continued to reach for Tamra's crumpled form, sprouting limbs to worm around Fae's fire, determined to seek refuge within his human shield.

Fae redoubled her efforts, hurling bolts of crackling, white fire at his shadow with both hands, forcing him back, one inch at a time. She forced one foot forward, then the other, pushing him away from Tamra, until finally she stood over the unconscious figure of the Lady Black.

Anson's single eye darted to the exit, pinpointing the small group of people watching in the doorway.

No you don't, Fae snarled inside. With a thought, a whirlwind encased their battle once again, rising from the floor to contain the threat she faced, forcing him to deal with her alone. This god wouldn't get another chance to poison anyone else.

Bellowing a broken protest, Anson launched himself directly at Fae, meaning to suffocate her in his darkness. He couldn't possibly hope to infiltrate her — she was so wholly Aethyrial right now, there wasn't enough human for him to grasp. But he could still drown her out, like a swimmer caught under the waves, his blackness cutting off the light of her powers.

Fae reached inside for the towering inferno that burned so hot and so bright.

In the split-second it took her, Anson was over her, his tendrils snaking around to either side, intent on smothering her entirely.

As the shadow closed in, darkness on all sides, Fae grabbed a spear of the fire within her, and thrust it straight up. Into the fractured god that had wrought so much harm on the world, his own Spirit Mother had sacrificed herself to save it.

Had split herself into a million fragments to infuse the world with her love.

Millions of fragments, that had chosen Fae to save them again.

Now it's my turn. Fae knew what she had to do. She was imbued with her spiritual inheritance for a reason. To become a conduit for power. To be used at the right moment.

And that moment was now.

As her javelin of fire pierced the shadow that swarmed her, she poured *everything* through it. Every mote of spiritual presence she had, every drop of Aethyrial power.

All of it pulsed through her, and into Anson.

For an instant, it seemed as though the god would just push through it, and flatten her with his darkness. But then he stuttered to a stop, hovering above her.

And then a howl of pain unlike any other Fae had ever heard burst forth all around her.

It tore through her eardrums in an instant, and she felt a warm line of blood trickling down the side of her face. She gritted her teeth, and held on.

It shattered the tall, stained-glass windows of the Great Hall, deadly shards flying through the storm to slice at her skin. She closed her eyes, but held on.

It shook the very foundations of the keep, sending the floor beneath her bucking. She planted her feet, and held on.

The sound grew keener, climbing in pitch until it screeched through her body like nails down a chalkboard. And then the shadow began to glow. Power saturated Anson beyond the point he could either absorb or dispel it.

And then two things happened at once.

Fae's power ran out. The spear of firelight that shone from within her to strike at the heart of Anson ran through her fingers like the end of a rope, and disappeared into the thunderous form above her.

She gasped in horror at its absence. Stared at her hands, no longer glowing.

She had nothing left. No power pulsed within her. No glittering motes drifted nearby.

She was empty. Finished.

She looked up at Anson's writhing shadow.

And he exploded.

The lightning-fire of her gifted powers tore at the very fabric of him like a storm ripping through a straw-bale. Pieces of shadow blew apart, evanescing in an instant as her power flared incandescent against the vaulted ceilings above.

The nebulae of Eah'lara burst out into the mortal world, the Great Hall transformed into a supernova in a jar.

53

JUST ONE

Fifty feet away, beneath the arched doors, Ty ducked as debris flew from the storm at the centre of the room, a tsunami of dust and smoke billowing outward from the point where Fae had been, what felt like a mere heartbeat ago.

He threw himself across Hal as the ground bucked again, the ranger still lying prone on the ground between him and Laina, who sat gaping at the chaos inside.

The platform on which Lady Black had been standing with her red-belted Survivors tipped onto its side, and began hurtling across the floor towards them. It smashed into a supporting column and splintered into lethal kindling; slivered daggers flying through the air.

Ty saw the timber break apart, and pulled Laina out of the way before a particularly jagged piece shot past them.

"We should move!" he yelled at her over the din. But no sooner had he uttered the words, than the light-storm in the middle of the Great Hall was yanked back, pulled in by an invisible force. It shrank as fast as it had appeared, as if being sucked through a hole into nowhere. Debris changed direction mid-flight, hurtling back towards the centre of the room, the retreating storm dragging yet more deadly projectiles to fly through the hall.

And then it was gone, hundreds of airborne missiles dropping to the floor with a clatter that rang out across the tiles.

Ty lifted his head slowly, casting his gaze around the room. The platform wasn't the only thing in the hall that had suffered at the storm's wrath: shattered tiles littered the floor, already abused tapestries hung in fresh tatters from the walls, and not a single piece of glass remained intact, the windows now gaping apertures staring out into the night sky.

Ty blinked.

The fog was gone. Out beyond the empty windows, a crystalline sky sparkled with familiar constellations.

"Fae." Laina's whispered word brought Ty back to himself, and his eyes travelled to the centre of the hall. Fae swayed where she stood, Lady Black on the floor at her feet. As he watched, her eyes blinked slowly.

"I've got him." Jesse appeared at Ty's shoulder, and knelt beside Hal, shooting wary glances into the Great Hall. A group of rescued prospects hovered behind her, various expressions of disbelief adorning their features.

With a nod, Ty rose, and made his way across the debris-littered room.

They'd been lucky. If anyone had been left inside, they would have been cut to ribbons by flying shards of glass, tile, and even chips of stone that had been shaken loose by the battle. As it was, they'd managed to clear the Hall; the only ones left inside were Fae, and Black.

Ty caught Fae just before she slumped to the ground. Her arm hung at an unnatural angle, and her breath was a rasping wheeze in his ear. Her eyelids fluttered open, her pupils sliding in and out of focus as she looked up at him.

He smiled at her. "You did it," he said.

Her eyes blinked slowly again, a quirk at the edge of her lips the only sign that she'd heard him. Then, a small frown.

"I—"

A strangled yell punctured the stillness of the room, and Ty spun just in time to see Tamra Walker haul herself up from the floor, dagger in hand, aiming straight for Fae.

He went to block her attack with his free arm, and damn the gash he was sure to receive as a result, when she dropped to the ground like a stone.

Behind her, Laina stood frozen in place, a broken-off piece of boarding from Black's platform held upraised in her hands. She stared at the unconscious woman on the floor, eyes wide with a mix of shock and horror.

"Yes!" Jesse hollered triumphantly from the doorway, making Laina jump so violently, the timber fell from her fingers to clatter loudly against the tiles. "Knew you had it in you!"

Laina dropped to her knees, and pressed her fingers to Black's throat. She sat statue-still for a moment, then let out a long breath.

"Thank the Mother," she said, relief flooding her voice. "She's just unconscious."

"Shame," Jesse said caustically, coming over to stand beside her.

"I'm a healer," Laina replied crossly. "Not a killer."

"Yes yes," Jesse replied, her tone a vocal eye-roll. "You and your daughter both." She cast a glance at Fae, who was barely holding her own weight, leaning fully into Ty. "Speaking of which, we should get her and Hal somewhere safe." She glanced down at the self-titled leader of the Survivors. "What do we do with her?"

"I might have an idea about that," Wyn volunteered from the door.

And that was when Fae finally lost consciousness.

Laina found them a suite of rooms in the south wing of the castle, and swiftly instructed Elas to lift Hal *carefully* onto the bed in one of them.

Ty strode into the adjacent room, and set Fae down on a wide bed, too short for an elf, but plenty big enough for her. Then he immediately set to work assessing her injuries.

Her shoulder, as he'd suspected, was dislocated, but the more pressing concern was the sound of her breathing: gurgling and laboured, as if her lungs were filling up with fluid. Fighting down the panic rising through his own chest, he got to work. Feeling around her ribs, he found the broken ones, low down on her right side.

"Can I help?" Laina's voice asked from the door. "Hal's as stable as he's going to be... I'd like to keep busy."

Without looking up, Ty replied, "Her lung is punctured. I need a straw or a narrow tube of some sort." Reaching down into his pack, he pulled out his healer's kit, and laid it out on the table beside the bed with quick efficiency. Digging out the last of the trickleroot tincture, he made up the cleansing solution in his bowl, and dropped a small, sharp blade into it.

"Hold on Fae," he murmured, as her chest rasped in another breath.

"Here." Laina reappeared, and handed him a thin, rigid, metal tube. It looked just like a drinking straw, but the straws in Arolynos were usually hollow river-reeds, harvested from the river bank.

Whatever it was, it was perfect for now, and Ty wasted no time in dropping the slender tube into the trickleroot solution. He rolled Fae's shirt halfway up her side, and felt for the broken ribs again. They scraped against each other when he pressed into them, but they had sprung back into position since breaking, leaving the lung punctured, her chest now likely filling with blood. Her breaths were coming in shallower and shallower gasps, barely enough to draw air, her lips turning a worrying shade of blue.

Fishing the blade out of the bowl, Ty slotted it into a smooth, wooden handle, and scooped a handful of solution over Fae's side to cleanse the skin. Then, carefully, he made a small cut in her side, a few inches above the broken ribs. Blood welled along the edge of the blade, a drop running down her side to soak red into the sheets beneath her. Ty put the scalpel back into the bowl, and picked up the small metal pipe. He fed the tube into the cut he'd made, angling it sideways so that the wound would seal better when he was finished. When the tube met the resistance of the muscles between her ribs, he pushed firmly, until the tube finally popped into the space where Fae's lung should have been.

Air and blood rushed out of the tube, soaking the sheets, and Fae woke, gasping in a full breath as her lungs finally expanded properly again. She coughed, flinching in pain as the abrupt motion jarred against the tube in her side, and pulled in another breath.

"Fae!" Ty cried out in relief. "Fae, you're alright!" He swallowed the emotions welling in his chest — there was work yet to do. "Fae, I've released the pressure around your lungs but I still need to relocate your arm. I'm going to get you some willowbark to help with the pain." He willed his shaking hands to still as he took hold of the tube in her side. "Now breathe in nice and deep for me." He waited for her to oblige, and slid the tube out of her chest, pressing the wound closed.

"I'll make the willowbark," Laina said, hovering nervously at the foot of the bed. Ty nodded, and heard her bustle around the room behind him, leaving briefly to get a kettle of hot water from somewhere.

The fact that Fae hadn't responded to him yet worried Ty. She gazed blankly at the ceiling, taking slow breaths, wincing occasionally as the movement made the breaks in her ribs grate together.

Watching her face, Ty noticed the tinge of red in her ash-blonde hair, and reached over to brush the strands back. A smear of dried blood marred the pale skin beneath her ear.

He leaned forward, putting his face above her. "Fae," he said, raising his voice above the softer tones he had been using. "Can you hear me?"

Her eyes flickered to his face, slowly, like her thoughts were swimming through tree sap. When her gaze finally met his, he saw that the bright gold around her eyes had disappeared. He looked closer — not gone, faded. What had been a ring of vivid gold was now a subtle amber halo around the edge of her own ocean-green.

She blinked. "Ty," she said, her voice hoarse, as if she'd been screaming. "Why do you sound so far away?"

Burst eardrums, Ty thought, just as Laina came back into the room. "I need something to bind her ribs," he said aloud, his hand still pressed on the wound in her chest. "I used the last of mine on Hal."

"Of course," Laina replied, setting a steaming cup of willowbark tea on the table. "I spotted a cupboard full of bed linen in one of these rooms. We can tear that up for binding." Ty nodded, and she left again.

Fae blinked at the ceiling, as if seeing something beyond his ability to see.

Back in Arolynos, the Aethyr had healed Fae after her vision — why wasn't that happening now? Was it something to do with the change in her eyes?

"I can't feel anything," she mumbled suddenly, confusion in her voice.

Ty stilled. "What do you mean?" he asked.

"I can't..." She lifted a hand from the sheets, and waved it listlessly about, as if trying to encompass everything in a single gesture. Then she tapped the side of her head. "I can't *feel* any of it." Her eyes widened suddenly, and focused on him. "I can't *see* any of it!"

Not able to make any sense of her words, Ty just stroked her hair. "It's alright," he murmured softly. "It'll be alright." Laina came back then, her arms piled high with off-white sheets that had somehow escaped the worst of the destruction around the keep. Together, they bound Fae's chest tightly, holding both the broken ribs, and the small hole in her side, secure. Then, stacking some extra pillows behind her head, Ty helped her to sip down the cooled willowbark tea.

As Fae's eyes fluttered closed again, Ty pressed a kiss to her head. He waited to make sure the tea had taken full effect, watching her breathe. Content with the easy flow of air in and out of her chest, he sat back, and took hold of her dislocated arm.

Slowly, he pulled the limb straight, and rotated it gently but firmly back into its socket. With a resounding *pop*, her shoulder was back in place. He folded a quick sling from the linen Laina handed him, and looped it around Fae's arm and neck to support the joint while the muscles and ligaments healed around it.

"How is she?" Laina asked softly, as he tucked some clean sheets around Fae.

Ty listened to her breathing for a moment, reassuring himself that the rasping, choking sounds had fully abated, before he turned to Fae's mother.

"Physically," he said, "she'll be alright." He glanced back at Fae's still form on the bed. "There doesn't seem to be any more internal bleeding, which I was worried about."

"But...?" Laina prompted.

Ty sighed. "I don't know," he said, answering her first question. His brow furrowed, and a trickle of fear escaped from the box he'd shoved it into. "I don't know."

Wyn and Elas returned a short while later, having taken Black up to the north wing. Samuel had no qualms about incarcerating those who posed a threat to humanity. Tamra Walker was safe in the custody of her own trusty warden. After ensuring she was otherwise unharmed, and enjoying the small irony, Wyn had left Lady Black in the same cell he'd only recently vacated.

"I'll swing by and check on her in an hour," he'd promised Laina, after she expressed concerns about leaving her unattended with a probable concussion. "You didn't hit her *that* hard, and besides, she's not alone. Samuel's there too."

He, Elas, and Thom had gone on to search for Immrith's team, and Jesse went to round up any captive or injured humans for Laina and Ty to check over.

"The sitting room down the hall has space," Laina said. "And if we need more, there are plenty more rooms we can use."

While they waited for the first of the wounded to arrive, Ty checked on Fae again. It had been a few hours since he'd given her the willowbark; the effects should have begun wearing off. But she remained asleep, lying as he'd left her, propped up on the pillows. He looked in on Eah'lara — as much as he saw it — but there was nothing there to see. Just a slow lightening in the fog as the Aethyr moved back into the blackness around Throldon.

"We're here!" Aren called as he and Stef appeared in the living space outside the bedroom.

Turning from Fae's side, Ty pulled the door to her room almost closed, so he could still see her within. Could remind himself that she was alright, that she'd made it. He went over to greet the two scouts. "Are you hurt?" he asked straight away.

Aren spread his arms and performed a full turn for Ty's inspection. Aside from a few bruises, and a nasty split across his eyebrow, he appeared unharmed. "Nope," he said. Then his face fell. "But Immrith..." He trailed off.

"Immrith didn't make it." Stef finished for his brother. They stood in silence while Ty absorbed the news. Immrith had come all the way from the forgotten wilds past the Northern Tundra to join in their quest, and had arguably been one of the only reasons they had made into the keep in the first place. Without him, Mickey's gang might have overwhelmed them before Kagos's timely arrival. And the clash in the bailey could have gone an entirely different way.

"May Eah take his spirit and carry his soul to a better place," Ty said solemnly. He glanced across to Hal's room, where the ranger still fought for his life, Laina sitting at his bedside. "What of Kagos?" he asked.

"Injured," Stef said. "A few arrows pierced his wings and it seems he can't fly." He cleared his throat, and shifted his weight where he stood. "It also seems he either can't or won't change form while he's injured, but we can't ask him directly because we can't find Aiya *or* Max."

"We were hoping Fae..." Aren started, glancing at the sliver of bedroom visible through the door, to where she lay unmoving on the bed.

Ty shook his head. "She still hasn't woken. We can't expect anything of her right now." He allowed himself a quick look over his shoulder at her, before turning back to the brothers. "How goes it out there?" he asked. "Are the remaining Survivors a problem?"

Aren let slip a satisfied smirk before schooling his expression again. "That's the damnedest thing," he said. "We took out a good number of them on the way in, but there were still plenty to cause us trouble. But then..." He exchanged a look with Stef, who just shrugged his shoulders. "I don't know what happened. The sky went stormy — even in the fog — and then all of a sudden it cleared. Completely. And when the clouds parted, it was like a fog lifted from their eyes as well." He shrugged in an exact copy of his brother. "They're wandering around like lost puppies. Some of them are aggressive-confused, but most are just confused."

"Interesting," Ty said when Aren had finished. "As if Anson's presence was affecting them, as well as their leader."

Aren nodded. "That's as much as we could fathom too," he said. "Max did say those who'd been here the longest were the worst affected."

"Alright then," Ty said, drawing himself up. "Let's take this opportunity to see to the wounded. Aren, Stef, coordinate with the others to have two watching the bailey at all times. I want to know if the situation changes. Otherwise, help Jesse find any other captives or injured, and bring them up here. Laina is setting up a ward for them down the hall. If you find Aiya and Max, let me know." A thought came to him. "Did Kagos give any hint of his intentions?"

Stef shook his head. "Like Aren said, we can't communicate with him in his dragon form. But unless he plans to smash a path through the city and walk back to Hearthstone, I imagine he'll be staying in the bailey until he can either fly, or change back to his other form."

Ty nodded thoughtfully. "See if you can get an answer from him, even if it involves scratching pictures in the dirt. I don't know how long dragons take to heal — he could be there a while."

Both brothers gave a curt nod before heading out of the suite on their assigned tasks.

Ty returned to Fae's room, pulling a dusty, moth-eaten chair over to sit before her.

"Come on Fae," he murmured. "Come back to me."

Fae saw the world pass her by in a strange blur.

She was in shock. She recognised the symptoms in herself, even if she couldn't articulate it. She was numb, unable to focus on any one point without her gaze sliding away. It was like she existed within the bellow of a gong after being struck, wavering in and out of awareness, the world an oscillating after-image of itself.

She blinked her eyes open, the motion too slow, her mind too sluggish to operate even her own body.

She'd poured everything she had into Anson. It was a miracle she was even this conscious.

Inside, she was a hollow, echoing, emptiness.

When her Aethyrial guides had joined with her, she'd been full to the brim. Complete, her missing pieces become whole.

Now, she was back to how she was before she left Arolynos.

Just Fae.

With a piece missing.

A small flare glinted in the periphery of her vision. Her eyes drifted haltingly towards the tiny blaze, but there was nothing there.

Fae let her gaze wander. Heavy curtains hung beside the bed. A soft, cushioned chair sat beside her. There was a dresser, a pitcher and basin atop it. Somewhere nearby, booted feet thudded on tiled floors, scuffed across wooden boards, padded over old carpets. There were windows... but the night was dark, and the room was lit only by the expensive oil-lamps glowing from the hall, and the soft, wavering light of a candle by her bed.

Everything was soft here; the mattress beneath her body, the cotton sheets tucked around her.

And she was still.

Alone with her emptiness.

The light of the candle flickered and caught on the surface of something shiny. She looked up, glacially slow, but there were only soft drapes, dusty furniture, and curtains across the windows.

She was alone.

The only one.

No longer one of seven.

Just one.

How long she lay there, with the grey numbness of her emptiness for company, she couldn't tell. After a time, Ty appeared. He dragged the chair over to sit in front of her. She saw his lips move. Heard his voice. Felt the dark grey of his gaze.

She blinked.

Ty's eyes closed.

And a white-hot poker stabbed pain deep into her skull.

54

CHILD OF SPIRITS

"What did you do?" Laina said, rushing in at the short scream that escaped Fae.

Ty stood so fast his chair tipped backwards. "I didn't do anything!" he swore.

"No," Fae gasped out, her injured chest flaring a warning. "Not you." She screwed her eyes shut against the searing pain that tore through her head.

When she opened them again, pinprick fires bobbed in her vision, waxing and waning as they floated across her line of sight.

"Do you see the fires?" she gasped, balancing on the knife-edge of agony.

Ty exchanged a confused glance with Laina, and quickly scanned the room. "What fires, Fae?" he asked gently.

Fae slammed her eyes shut again. She could *feel* them; tiny pinprick hurts, burning a path into her mind as she struggled to sit up, cradling her head in her free hand, bearing it, but only just.

And then, one of the tiny flames ignited, not in pain, but into light within her. It burned away the numbness. Just a fraction. Just enough. So that she could see.

Fae gasped, like a drowning soul coming up for air. Her eyes flew open, and she *saw* for the first time since burning Anson out of existence.

431

The tiny blazes she saw were Aethyrial motes, floating back into Throldon to fill the wasteland left behind by an old god.

She tried peering into Eah'lara, hoping to see the nebulae that must surely be drifting in too. But while the fog had dispersed, this area of the Spirit Realm had yet to play host to its usual scenery. Aethyrial orbs floated about in sparse numbers, lighting the darkness like fireflies in the night, and the only spiritual threads she could see were the ones she'd cast out in her battle against Anson. It would take a long time for this gaping chasm to heal. But even as she watched, an orb winked out of the Spirit Realm, anchoring itself somewhere in the mortal world, and another shimmering thread appeared, arrowing away to connect to its brethren outside of the city.

Fae smiled, tears burning behind her eyes as she watched the midnight serenity of Eah'lara, its tenacious beauty soothing her jagged thoughts.

At least she had this. Even within the void left behind by her vacated powers, at least she could still witness this. She held a hand out to a nearby mote, the kind of piece that would eventually cluster to form a nebula, the kind that had once clung to her like she was a piece of it.

Intending simply to brush her hand against its warmth, she was stunned when the mote sank into her skin, accompanied by a sharp burst of tingling pain. Looking up, she saw other motes nearby were gravitating towards her, drawn like butterflies to nectar, drip-feeding the gaping hole inside of her.

She opened her eyes to Laina and Ty hovering over her, ready to do whatever they could to help.

"It's okay," Fae said, and she realised that it was true. Her pain was dulling — partially; her chest was still home to a piercing pain that stabbed at her every time she drew breath, and her shoulder was weak and aching, but her head was beginning to clear. Her soul was parched, but the Aethyrial motes were slowly, gradually, refilling her starved aura.

She felt her eyelids grow heavy again.

She knew in her heart that she would never get her seven back; their power had always been borrowed. But she was still Fae.

Still a child of the spirits.

55

KEEP THEM SAFE

Ty encouraged Fae to drink some more willowbark with healer's helper before she could drift off to sleep again. Then her eyes fluttered closed, unable to fight her body's urgent need to rest and heal.

And then, the first of the injured humans arrived.

The first group needing help was led in by Jesse, and comprised mostly of freed prospects with injuries related to their trials. Shortly after, Wyn arrived with Thom and a string of children from the library. They weren't hurt for the most part, but many were dazed and confused. Laina found them another suite of rooms to stay in further along the wing.

And then came the men and women wearing red on their arms.

When the first red-band walked into Laina's make-shift ward, the healer stiffened. Ty, working beside her, looked up to see a woman with a thick scar running from her jaw down to her collarbone, short, dark hair hanging tangled around her ears, and eyes as lost and dazed as the children who'd slept on bookshelves. She cradled one arm in the other, red, melted skin showing through burnt-away cloth.

Ty approached the woman, and touched her lightly on the shoulder. "Can I take a look at your arm for you?" he said gently, as if coaxing a lamb from its mother. The woman's eyes swivelled slowly to focus on him, and she nodded mutely. While Ty led her over to a seat, another two red-bands entered. The shorter of the two men supported the other, his one good eye scanning the room, the other swollen shut thanks to a nasty gash over his brow-bone. The taller man leaned on him heavily, his leg black with too much dried blood.

"Some tall feller said we could get help in the keep," the shorter one said. "Is this the place?"

Laina didn't hesitate. "Yes, come in, put him down, find a seat." She bustled about, finding something for the two to sit on, completely in her element. Dragging an armless occasional chair that had never seen such use over to the men, she eyed them both critically. "Although, I should warn you," she said sternly, "if you start causing trouble under my care, you'll see how little of it I have going spare."

"Yes ma'am," the taller one said, dropping onto the proffered seat. "Good as gold, no trouble at all."

It was the same story with all the rest that came; like children who knew they'd done wrong, they came to Laina's ward, meek as kittens, and surrendered themselves to her care.

Hours later, as dawn bathed a skyline once laden with fog, Aren and Stef returned.

"Wil found where the women were being kept," Aren reported with a growl in his tone. "He's working round the castle with Thom and Elas now, making sure there aren't any others locked away that we don't know about."

"And I don't think we have to worry about remonstrations," Stef added. "All the Survivors we've seen are wondering around like puppets with their strings cut. There won't be any uprisings against us today at least."

"Besides—" Aren's lips kicked up into a sudden grin "—any of the few that are nursing violent tendencies have to walk past Kagos first, and he seems to be in a particularly foul mood, what with being grounded and all."

Ty smiled at their update. "Well, it's good to get good news for once," he said. "Have someone in the gatehouse to keep eyes on the situation regardless, but it looks like we can focus our attention on helping these people at last." He paused. "Any sign of Aiya and Max?"

Stef shook his head. "No. But..." He frowned. "Kagos has been growling and grumbling at every little thing since everyone dropped weapons, but when we told him Aiya and Max were missing, he went very quiet." He exchanged a glance with his brother. "I think he knows something."

Aren considered it. "He did seem very keen for Max to go back to Hearthstone. Do you think he's got Aiya hiding her somewhere?"

Stef shrugged. "I don't know. But I wouldn't be surprised."

"Alright," Ty said. "Let's do what we can for these people." He stepped into the hallway, where humans who couldn't fit in the rooms were lying against the walls. "We can unravel Kagos's secrets later." He turned back to the brothers. "You're both field-trained aren't you?" The brothers nodded. "Good. Anyone who isn't in a room, hasn't been seen yet. See what you can do for them." Another nod, and they split up to handle the swarms of humans needing help.

Sunrise was a blaze of glory shining in through the eastern windows, captivating most of those who had been starved of its colours for months on end.

As the sun finally hoisted itself over the horizon to float freely in the sky, Laina sank to the floor beside Hal's bed. The ranger still hadn't woken yet, but his breathing had evened out, and colour was beginning to come back to his cheeks.

"That water Ty gave you is working then," she muttered to him aimlessly as she checked him over. "I'll have to go and apprentice under the elven healers at this rate, they keep showing me up like this."

"Don't you dare." His voice came out a rasp, and made Laina jump. "You belong here."

"Hal!" she gasped.

"Aye," he croaked. "Still here."

Laina reached up to pour him a cup of water from the jug she'd had one of the children run and fill, since they were well enough, and eager to help. She helped Hal sip from the cup, and grabbed some extra pillows for him to lean back against.

"Did we win?" he asked.

"You'd be dead by now if we hadn't," Laina said, plumping the pillows with more vigour than was strictly necessary. "If you weren't injured I'd slap you for being so stupid!" Her hands trembled even as she tried to keep her voice even.

"Seemed justified at the time," he replied, letting his head drop back against the pillows.

"It was foolish, and did nothing but get you half-dead," she said, jamming her hands onto her hips.

"Yes ma'am, won't do it again," Hal said, with a small twitch of his lips.

"Hm," Laina grumbled. "Rest for now. I'll yell at you more later."

"Can't wait," he sighed. Laina turned to leave him in peace, when his hand grabbed her arm with surprising strength. "Meant what I said though," he said, his eyes boring into hers. "You're needed here. Your people need you now more than ever."

Laina patted his hand, and gently placed it back on the bed. "Sleep," she said. "We can talk about it when you wake." Hal's eyes had already fluttered closed by the time she made it to the door.

Casting one last look at the ranger sleeping peacefully, she pulled the door closed, careful not to make a sound.

Still far too wired to rest herself, Laina took herself up to the north wing to check on Tamra Walker. The former leader of the Survivors was awake, and spitting curses and such vile profanities that even Samuel, who had undoubtedly seen and heard much worse, was wincing at the sting in her words. Exchanging an apologetic glance with the warden, Laina concluded that if Lady Black had enough energy to hurl venom like that, she was unlikely to be suffering much from the concussion she'd definitely given her.

Laina retraced her steps down the tower, meaning to return to the south wing. Passing torn tapestries, broken floor tiles, and crumbling plasterwork wherever she went, she couldn't control the twinge of sadness she felt at seeing the castle fall to such a level of disrepair. It had been a magical place when she'd visited as a child. She'd once run through that hallway, chased by her governess. And there, she'd tripped the pastry chef, and almost ruined an entire morning's work in cakes. She'd been soundly scolded for that one. She even remembered trying to sweet-talk her way past the guards at the front gate to let her out to see the soldiers train in the courtyard.

Following her own nostalgia, Laina found herself standing on the front steps, blinking in the bright light of a clear, spring morning.

There were men and women clearing the courtyard without

instruction, as if everyone knew that it was the done thing to clear the ground after a battle. And in the midst of them all, the hulking form of Kagos crouched, watching them all with an intimidating stare that was enough to make some of the workers completely useless.

"Oh stop it," Laina said, approaching the dragon as yet another person tripped in their hurry to get away from the beast. "They'll never get anything done if you keep glaring at them like that." Huge, black eyes swivelled to regard her, and she could have sworn a giant brow lifted in her direction. "I heard from Ty and the others that you're stuck here while you heal," she continued. "Can I take a look?"

Kagos's eyes definitely widened at that. He inclined his enormous head oh-so-slightly, and extended one wing out to the side.

Laina trudged around to inspect the damage. The thick, leathery membranes had been torn in several places, but she could see the skin already showing signs of knitting together. She reached out a hand and ran her fingers long the edge of the tears. Kagos tensed, jerking his wing away just enough.

"Sorry," she said, pulling her hand back. She turned to walk back to his head, and found his face right behind her, having coiled around to watch her work. "If your other wing is the same, I can make you a salve to speed the healing process if you'd like?" A pause, those black eyes watching, as if measuring her. Then another slight dip of his head. "Alright then."

Then, "You know, no one's been able to find Max or Aiya since the battle," she said, watching him. He was playing the part of not being able to communicate in this form very well, but Laina saw a glimmer of something in his eyes. "Seems to me, if they were really in trouble, you'd be tearing this place apart to find them." There — a twitch at the corner of his mouth. Did dragons smile? Laina smiled back. "When you get back to Hearthstone, tell her I said hello, will you?"

Kagos blinked. And Laina laid a hand against his huge, black snout.

"I understand something about sending a child away to keep them safe."

And she turned, and walked back into the keep.

When Laina finally climbed the stairs to the south wing again, everything had calmed into a steady rhythm. She walked the halls, checking in on every room just to make sure. Until she found herself at Fae's door.

Ty was sitting in the chair at her bedside, watching her breathe. The dark circles under his eyes betrayed his need to rest just as much as the other patients. How much had he slept since they arrived in the city?

He looked up when she knocked softly on the door. "How is she?" she whispered.

His eyes flicked back to Fae, and he ran a hand through his sandy hair. "Stable," he said. "But she hasn't woken again."

"She went through a lot," Laina said, coming over to check her daughter's pulse, to listen to her breathe. "She'll wake again when she's ready." Ty nodded, but said nothing, worry showing in the tension in his jaw. "Why don't you take a break?" Laina suggested gently. "Get some rest. I'll sit with her." Ty looked about ready to protest, then looked up at her. And something in her face must have changed his mind, because he blew out a breath, and stood.

"I'll be just out there," he said, gesturing to the sitting area just beyond the bedrooms.

Laina nodded. "I'll come and get you if anything changes." Ty gave her a look, and she remembered he'd likely know if anything changed, with his elven hearing. But then he was closing the door behind him, and Laina was alone, Fae's even breathing her only companion.

She sank into the chair, still warm from Ty's vigil.

At first, she just sat. It was all she could do. Now that she had finally stopped, the bone-crushing terror that had filled her at seeing Fae in Ty's arms, struggling to breathe, took her right back to that burning village.

Frozen in fear.

Her baby girl unconscious in her arms.

Andrew dead on the ground.

And the images — the scars — of that day mixed with what she saw in the present, until, between roiling emotions and exhaustion, she wasn't sure what was real, and what was a dream. Was it the horror that she lived every night? Or the blessing she'd prayed for in the ashes of her home?

So she sat there — for how long, she didn't know — just watching Fae's chest rise and fall. Rise and fall.

And the knot in her heart loosened with every breath.

Finally, the tightness at her throat eased enough that she drew in a deep, shuddering breath of her own.

And Fae's eyes opened.

"Hi," Laina said softly, not wanting to startle her. She leaned forward in her chair.

Fae blinked. "Hi," she said.

The pause stretched out between them. Laina, her breath catching again just at seeing her daughter alive and well — *almost* well — smiled hopefully. Fae smiled back.

"What a day," she said, lifting her eyes to the ceiling.

A laugh escaped Laina, and it was slightly hysterical, but gods, did it feel good to smile.

"Yes," she breathed. "What a day."

Another pause.

"I remember you now," Fae said suddenly.

"Sorry?"

Fae's eyes slid back to her mother. "I remember you." She took a few, careful breaths, and Laina waited for her to continue. "I was so young when I arrived in Arolynos," Fae said, "that I never remembered anything of my past. It's like my mind blocked it out. Like it knew that it would hurt too much to remember. But when you started telling your story—" she reached out, and Laina grasped her hand between hers "—I remembered. You smelled of lavender, and you liked to dance." Laina breathed a hesitant laugh. She hadn't danced in years. "And—" Fae lifted their clasped hands, her thumb brushing over the ring of carved maple that hadn't left Laina's finger in fifteen years. "And I remember this. And Papa's. His was supposed to be smooth but it was always scarred from all the work he did with his hands." She smiled, her fingers tracing the patterns on Laina's ring. Then her smile faltered. "I wish I remembered more of him."

A floodgate opened within Laina. Years of guilt and regret, feelings that she'd buried with her work, broke over her. Her face crumpled, and tears rolled down her cheeks. She pressed her forehead to their clasped hands as grief poured from her. "I'm so sorry," she sobbed.

Fae's eyes went wide. "What? Why?"

"He told me to run with you. To get out of the village. But they blocked the bridge so I turned back. And... and... I saw him throw himself at those raiders. I watched as they beat him to the ground. And I didn't go to him. I *hid*. When he needed me most, I didn't... I couldn't..." And now she would never see his easy smile again. He would never again make her laugh. And her last memory of him would always be of his broken body, left abandoned in the street as it burned.

"I didn't save him," she whispered. And there it was: her dirty, guilty secret finally spilled out.

Fae was quiet as Laina gulped down air in wet sobs. She waited until she regained her composure before she spoke.

"No," Fae said, not bothering to tell her that it wasn't her fault. Laina already knew that. Underneath all the grief and the guilt, she knew she couldn't have done anything. No, she didn't need to hear of what she couldn't have done. But of what she did.

Fae waited for Laina to lift red-rimmed eyes to meet hers, and gave her a sad smile.

"But you saved me."

56

FOUR CORNERS

Over the course of the following week, the castle began to fill again with people who had once worked within its walls, decades before. And without fail, they all looked to Laina for instructions. She was a natural leader, for all that she worked within the scope of a healer. She cared for everyone equally, and took no nonsense from anyone. It wasn't long before people were asking if she was the new Lady of the castle.

"No no," Fae answered for what felt like the hundredth time. "We just came here to help. No one is claiming leadership." But as the days passed, she heard more and more whispers about a new queen.

The reasons for which became clear when she stopped by to visit Hal, her arm still hanging in its sling, her ribs still strapped together. Ty and Laina had both urged her to rest more, but she was going crazy lying in bed all day, and Hal's room was only next door.

"What's all this?" she said, walking into a room full of children that, only a few days before, had worn haunted, empty stares. She laughed when a handful nearest the door jumped up to see who had entered. One of the youngest, a little girl with blonde bunches called Kiara, hopped from foot to foot where she stood by Hal's bedside. "Is it true?" she squealed. "Is Miss Laina going to be the new queen?"

Fae raised an eyebrow at Hal, who had the decency to look at least slightly sheepish.

"I was just telling them stories," he said. "They put the rest together themselves." At Fae's unrelenting stare, he folded. "Please don't tell Miss Laina," he begged. "She's already after my head."

"The way word is going around, it isn't me you have to worry about," Fae said. "How many 'stories' have you been telling?"

"Loads!" One of the boys, a mousy-haired seven-year-old called Theo spoke up. "Mr Hal tells the best ones!"

"That'll be why they're spreading like wildfire then," Fae said. "You've been helping take water and food around to everyone, haven't you?" she addressed the room. A sea of eager nods replied.

"Hal!" Laina's voice echoed angrily through the south wing.

"Quick kids," Hal said, his eyes comically wide, "scram! You don't want to see this!" He accompanied the last with a wink, and leaned back against the headboard as the children emptied the room. He gestured to the vacant chair by the bed. "May as well take a seat," he said to Fae with a shaky smile.

Laina burst in like a whirlwind, chest heaving as if she'd run the length of the castle, and fixed Hal with a glare to cut steel.

"*Why* have you been telling everyone I'm a queen?!" she demanded incredulously.

"Me?" Hal said with exaggerated innocence.

"Don't try that with me, Halbert," she said glacially, "or I'll start telling everyone your real name is Nellie."

"But," Hal stuttered, "it isn't."

"Exactly!" Laina cried, her voice raising in volume and pitch. "Why would you tell people I'm a queen when I'm not, never have been, and never wanted to be?"

"You're next in line," Hal answered simply. "Malcolm knew it. That's why the Unity hunted you so doggedly."

Laina stared at him, eyes hysterically round. "I *was* a nobleman's daughter. I was *never* heir to anything except Bredon. And that was decades ago! What I am, is a travelling healer on the run! I'm not fit to run a kingdom!"

"You did set up and organise a sprawling network of healers, preachers, and craftsmen to help rebuild a crumbling nation under constant attack," Aren said from the door. Pushing himself away from the doorjamb, he walked into the room and dropped onto the foot of the bed.

"Heard some shouting, thought I'd come and check it out." He grabbed an unwanted apple from the bedside table with a delighted "ooh", and turned back to Laina. "He's right though. These people need a leader. And it's not like Throldon's overflowing with candidates."

Laina gaped at him, her mouth opening and closing like a fish out of water. "I don't believe this," she whispered in disbelief. She turned to Fae, a glimmer of desperate hope in her eyes. "Take me away from here!" she pleaded. "Do whatever it was you did when you carried us through the Spirit Realm!"

Fae fought the smile that threatened to curl her lips. Despite Laina's protests, she couldn't think of anyone better suited to bring Arland back from the decades of brutality it had endured.

She shrugged. "I'm sorry," she said regretfully, and not just because she couldn't help Laina. "My powers are gone."

"What?" Laina gasped, the shock momentarily making her forget her outrage.

Fae nodded. She'd been testing her theory all week. "Erasing Anson took all of it." The power the Aethyr gifted her with had burnt out in her battle with Anson, the well as dry as bone. It would refill, that much she knew; the Aethyrial energies still seemed naturally drawn to her. It would be a slow process, would take time, but there was no need of a Spiritchild anymore. "It was borrowed power anyway." Loaned to her by her seven. She would Listen again, still see into Eah'lara, but she doubted there would ever be more than that.

She chuckled inwardly. *Well, I always wanted to be a Whisperer.* "The funny thing is," she said aloud, a sudden realisation dawning on her like sunrise spilling over a darkened landscape, "I still remember everything."

Laina frowned. "What do you mean?"

Fae smiled. And it was with the overwhelming joy of finding out not all was lost.

"I remember all of their memories. Ben. And Bran. Baev'ill. Bravargh. Be'ella Tor. And Bek." She laughed. "I still remember them!"

"What does that mean though?" Aren asked. "If you don't have their power?"

Fae shook her head, reeling with her happy revelation. "I don't know yet. But I know this is a good thing." She turned to Laina. "And I know you *should* be queen."

"What?" Laina spluttered.

"Aren's right," Fae continued. "You *did* organise hundreds of people into rebuilding this country while it was still in chaos. Does that not sound like something Throldon — and Arland — could desperately use right now?"

"Well yes but..." Laina floundered, grasping for the right words to defend herself. "Not from me!" Her voice pleaded with them, and her eyes met Hal's across the room. Her hands dropped to her sides, defeated. "I'm not a queen," she said.

"Aye," Hal said with gentle eyes. "I know, and you never meant to be one. But these people need someone to lead 'em out of the fog. And I can't think of anyone better suited to the job, than one who's walked through it." Laina squirmed uncomfortably at the thought of ruling.

An idea came to Fae then. "You could always form a council?" she suggested.

"Like the Eldra?" Aren asked. At Fae's answering nod, he considered it, his long fingers tapping against his chin. "That could work. Of course, you're still not inundated with candidates."

"They'll be here," Hal said. "They've just been hiding for thirty years."

"Then *they* should do it!" Laina said. "I am a stranger to Throldon! These people deserve someone they know."

"All these people have known lately is darkness," Aren said solemnly. "It's time someone brought in some light."

"The people should choose," Laina said, her last defence. "I won't force another unwanted leader on them, me or otherwise."

Hal's face broke into a grin of overjoyed triumph. "That won't be an issue."

Because what Hal's little story-time listeners had really been doing, while running errands around the keep, was quietly ascertaining whether or not the people wanted a new leader, and if the founder of the Peacekeepers would be welcome in that position.

The overwhelming majority were in agreement.

"Ryan 'Halbert' Johnson," Laina ground out through gritted teeth, "this conversation is far from over."

"Your wish, your Highness," Hal replied, the widest grin splitting his face in half.

"Don't call me that. I am *not* a queen," Laina repeated. "Fine. But *you*

—" she thrust a finger at the ranger "—will sit on this council with me, whether you want to or not. And the first thing I'm doing is finding *nominated* representatives to sit with us."

Hal inclined his head, still smiling. "A fine choice, *Councilwoman Woods*," he said.

"Hmph," Laina grumbled. She turned to Fae, who had moved to stand by the window, looking out over the bailey wall and the city rooftops beyond. "Help me," she said. "Help me do this."

But Fae was watching glittering threads spear into the city from the parts of Eah'lara beyond the once oppressive fog, and knew that her role was far from over. She shook her head regretfully. "I'm sorry," she said. "But there is still more for me to do. The races need to come together. And they won't do that until someone shows them the way."

"Bring them here," Laina said. "The human race was at the centre of the wrong being done in the world. Let Throldon become a symbol of hope for the future." She seemed to think on it, then nodded, her brow a resolute line. "We can form a council of the races too."

Fae nodded. It was a good idea. "Rebuild your city," she said, and laughed when Laina flinched at the possessive term. "I'll bring the rest."

Ty arrived on the heels of her words. "Bring who?" he said.

Fae turned towards him, reached out a hand to weave her fingers with his as he entered the room. "The other races," she said, "need to come to the table. Bek said it before: the segregation of the races is suffocating the Aethyr; it was the platform on which Anson was able to build his control of humanity." She dipped her head. "My powers might be gone, but I can still do this. I can still fix this."

"We can help," Aren said. "You don't need to travel to the four corners on your own." He looked down at his hands, and his fingers twisted together in his lap. "Stef and I were already talking about going to Equi'tox. Someone should take word of Immrith's death to his people."

"I'm going back to Dvargra anyway," Jesse said, coming around the doorjamb and into the quickly crowding room. "So you can scratch that destination off your list."

"How many of you are waiting out there?" Laina said, moving to the door to look up and down the hall.

Jesse shrugged. "Just finished organising food for the patients," she said, "so everyone's busy doing what needs doing. Thought I'd drop in on Hal while it's quiet."

Ty maintained his cool exterior. "I came for Fae, to ask how long she intends to stay, but it seems she's already decided on her next quest."

"I was just being nosy," Aren said, taking a bite of the apple he'd plundered earlier. Laina glowered at them, still grousing about the prospect of making decisions for an entire city.

"Well, I still need to convince the dragons to send someone," Fae said. "Unless Kagos feels like playing the part of ambassador." She turned to look up at Ty. "I'm hoping the presence of elves goes without saying?" she asked.

"Where you go, I go," was the reply, Ty dropping his head to rest against hers.

"What about Arolynos?" she said. "You're an Eldra, you can't just abandon your duties."

"I'd say liaising with the races of the world for the restoration and improvement of the Aethyr is well within the scope of an Eldra of Arolynos," he said, and his lips curled at the edges. "The Whisperers will never let me hear the end of it."

"Seconded," Aren chimed in. "And of all of the Eldra, I'd say Ty and Sheha are probably the best qualified." He began ticking the others off on his fingers. "Hara has to stay in the Village, that's undebatable, Artimus and Fabre don't have the people skills for it, Jax is *way* too old, and Adara is..." He clicked his fingers in the air, searching for the appropriate word to describe the slightly other-worldly Whisperer. "Well, she's not exactly relatable, is she?"

A small laugh escaped Fae's lips. "Well then," she said, "Liaison to the Council of the Races it is then."

"I'll have to return to Arolynos first, of course," Ty said, his smile taking a momentary downturn. "But then..." His hand squeezed hers.

"Then," she replied, a promise.

EPILOGUE

COUNCIL

T he sun shone bright over Throldon, catching on slick metallic roof-panels and glittering from thousands of window-panes.

Fae stood atop the castle bailey wall, her gaze turned south-east, a pleasant autumn breeze coaxing her hair to play across her face.

An arm came around her waist from behind.

"You're thinking again," Ty murmured laughingly in her ear. "I can hear the cogs whirring."

Fae smiled and leant back into his warmth. "Mm," she mumbled. "Occupational hazard." They looked over the spectacular vista together, lost to their own thoughts.

Ty pulled away, and came to stand beside her.

"The Equiann delegation arrived last night," he said.

"I heard," Fae replied, her attention not fully on his words.

Ty noticed her distraction, and knew the cause of it. "They'll be here," he said, gazing at the horizon himself.

"I know," she said.

"Then come inside," Ty said, turning to position himself between her and the view. "You'll hear them when they arrive anyway."

When it looked like she still wouldn't leave the wall, he asked, "Is Max coming?"

Fae shook her head. "No," she said. "She finally partnered with one of the hatchlings. Kagos has confined her to Hearthstone to train them both." She paused, suppressing a grin. "She called it Pig."

"Her dragon?"

Fae nodded.

Ty chuckled deep in his chest. "I bet Kagos loved that."

Fae's grin escaped despite herself. "Aiya gave her a proper name, but I doubt Max will ever use it. That girl is stubborn as a dragon herself."

Fae sighed, tearing her eyes from where they'd been fixed on the sky. "You're right," she said, returning to the matter at hand. "Let's go be ambassadors."

In the months since her battle against a broken god, not much had changed on the surface of things. But Fae knew, from her obsessive glances into Eah'lara, that the little changes were making a big difference.

The dwarves still lived in Dvargra, humans still occupied Arland, elves still inhabited the forests, and the centaurs remained in the freezing far Northern Tundra. But Throldon was rebuilding, adding plans for a thriving university in the southern suburbs, and a campus that sprawled along the banks of the Amedi River, constructed by skilled craftsmen and women of the three central races. The students and teachers that were beginning to tend to its fledgling classes comprised of dwarves, elves and humans alike. And humans, in turn, were welcomed to study in the elven forests, as well as the mountain stronghold of Dvargra.

Equi'tox lay many long leagues to the north, but Fae had heard reports that small groups of young centaurs were beginning to venture south to investigate Arland.

Dragons remained a very private people, but they had agreed to send a delegate to council.

They were the last to arrive — it turned out Kagos still loved to make an entrance.

Despite the continued separation of the races, across the fabric of the world, in the nebulous realm of the Aethyr, the threads that connected all life across the earth hummed a sweet melody that hadn't existed before. It was as if they showed their approval through song.

It made Fae smile just to think of it.

Walking back through the main gates, Fae and Ty crossed the internal courtyard to enter the Great Hall via a pair of sweeping glass doors that had been installed as part of its restoration. Inside, the Council of the

Races delegates gathered, informally mingling before the official proceedings got underway.

Fanrell, Immrith's older brother, stood talking to Sheha, who had taken a teaching position at Throldon's University. Behind the centaur — who shared his brother's near-black hair and burning amber eyes — stood two younger members of his race, looking nervously at the others in the room. Hal was entertaining Stochell to the left of the doors, the dwarven Master Builder apparently describing in detail another of his latest inventions. Lord Graem himself had come as well, and his booming laughter filled the hall as he shared a joke with David, a human who had once been held captive in this very keep.

Fae spotted her mother at the edge of the room, quietly surveying the scene with a practiced eye.

Seeing her daughter approach, Laina straightened without taking her eyes off her guests, and greeted Fae with a nod of her head. "Any sign?" she asked.

Fae shook her head. "Not yet." But she echoed Ty's reassurance nonetheless. "They'll be here."

Laina nodded nervously. "I know, I know," she said, raising one hand to worry at a nail with her teeth.

"Mother," Fae said, gently pulling Laina's hand from her face.

Laina dropped her hands to her sides and shook them out, stretching her fingers to release the tension she held in the joints. "No matter how many times we do this," she said beneath her breath, "I can't help but get nervous." She shot Fae a twitch of a smile. They'd sat down to talk with everyone in the room at one point or another over the past few months; making promises, forging friendships, exchanging news. "But as soon as we're all sitting around that table, it disappears, and it's just like I'm running a hospit again: telling people what to do, helping where I can, delegating to others if they're better suited to the task."

Fae put a hand on her mother's shoulder, and pride beamed through her smile. "You're doing a lot of good here," she said, and gestured to the delegates gathered so far. "And none of them would have any other in your place."

Just as Laina opened her mouth to reply, an earth-sundering roar shook the building.

Fae smiled. "Finally."

"Indeed," Laina said, absently brushing her hands down the front of her skirts, flattening non-existent creases.

Fae gave her a minute. "Ready?" she asked, when Laina eventually stopped fussing and straightened her shoulders.

Her mother nodded, and stepped into the middle of the room.

"Well, as our final guest will shortly — and finally — be joining us—" a ripple of laughter around the room "—shall we take our seats?"

Barely a minute later, Kagos — the only dragon capable of filling the position of delegate from Hearthstone, the others being far too old, or, for the first time in centuries, far too young — strode in with Aiya at his side.

"Kagos, Aiya," Fae said, approaching them while the others moved over to the large, circular table at the centre of the room.

"Spiritchild," Kagos replied, his hands folded into his sleeves. Fae's lips twitched. While she didn't hold the powers of the Aethyr anymore, she supposed his greeting was technically still correct.

"I hope the winds were fair for your journey to us?" she asked.

"They always are," Aiya said, stepping forward to embrace Fae. Kagos maintained his impassive exterior, but Fae knew he was softer than he let on. Being surrounded by hatchlings had revealed him to be a doting guardian to the new young in Hearthstone.

"It's good to see you both," she said when Aiya stepped back. She shot a glance at the table over her shoulder. "Everyone is here, and I know you'll be eager to get back." Hearthstone had become a lot busier since the liberation of Throldon; the discovery that dragonriders were not only found among the elves, but humans and dwarves too, meant that a little-known clutch of dragon eggs had finally hatched, after centuries of waiting. "How is Max getting on? With Pig?" Her lips quirked up at the corners.

"*Hera,*" Aiya corrected, the twinkle in her eye offset by the glower in Kagos's expression, "is doing well, thank you. And Max is running us just as ragged, more so actually, now that the hatchling joins her on every escapade." Fae couldn't suppress the laugh that bubbled past her lips. Max had been a force to be reckoned with even before Aiya had smuggled her away to Hearthstone. Fae could well imagine the sort of antics the former street urchin would be getting up to now.

Schooling her features, Fae stepped back with a smile, and gestured to where the other delegates were taking their seats. "Shall we?"

Aiya nodded gratefully, and moved to follow their example, Kagos sweeping after her.

Ty gave the dragon a brief nod of acknowledgement as he passed, and stepped up to Fae.

"Ready?" he said.

Fae looked over the assembled members of the Council. Centaurs, dwarves, elves, humans, and dragons — all were represented.

And, last but not least, as Fae stepped up to the table, the spirits of the world.

As she took her seat, she shot her mother a smile, which Laina returned.

"Right." Laina stood. Her eyes scanned around the table. "We've had... a difficult few years. We've lived in fear. In fear of what we might do. In fear of what we *have* done." She took a breath. "But it is our capacity to love, in spite of that fear that makes us stronger." Spreading steady hands to take in all assembled, she said, "It is in that vein, that I call this, our first Council of the Races, to order. Welcome all.

"Let's begin."

ACKNOWLEDGMENTS

Fae's story has been nearly ten years in the making, many of those spent between just me and her. But the more people that have been involved in Spiritchild, the better it has become. I owe its final form — and my thanks! — to so many people, without whom it would not be the book it is today.

Firstly, Sara, editor extraordinaire, whose insight and input really can't even be quantified. Your early feedback helped me shape this book into what it needed to be. I cannot thank you enough for your help and support.

To Stu, for urging me to get an editor in the first place. Sound advice, thanks.

To Dannie, critique partner, carbon-copy across the pond, and friend. Thank you for letting me read your work, for reading my work in turn, and for correcting my numerous mispronunciations! Thank you for being the best cheerleader I could ever ask for.

To my beta readers, Ashlin, Tamiyah, and Ghabiba. Thank you for taking the time to do a favour for a stranger. Your perspectives got me back to being excited about my own work again.

To the amazing Lena Yang, for bringing Arland to life and giving my little story a more beautiful face than I could ever have dreamed of.

To Jack, Lotti, Lauren, and Romy, for being some of my first readers of a totally different story, but whose feedback encouraged me to keep going anyway.

To Laura Lam and Elora Burrell for answering my incessant questions about publishing.

To my parents, for being there for me through all my endeavours. There are so many things to thank you for that won't all fit here. Just know that I am so grateful to have you both. Without your loving support, I would not be the person I am today, and this book wouldn't be in your hands.

To my amazing boys. Thank you for helping me write my author bio, and for being so excited that mummy wrote a book.

And lastly to Jonny, for believing in me when I didn't, for pushing me to fulfil my dreams, and for being the first reader of all my work.

Now you can read the next one.